Advance praise for Kelly Gay's electrifying novel

THE BETTER PART OF DARKNESS

"Kelly Gay's sprawling tour of Underground Atlanta puts me in mind of an estrogen-driven *Blade Runner*, with an imaginative otherworldly population . . . and a heroine who doesn't take crap from any of them. Her dark urban setting is so gritty, vivid, and original that it flaunts one of the greatest qualities of good fantasy: utter believability. A fork would stand up straight in world-building of this complexity, yet it's balanced by the simple story of a mother who will risk anything for those she loves. Kelly Gay whisked me into a dangerous world and made me want to stick around. This is the urban fantasy novel I didn't know I was looking for, and I can't wait to spend more time with Charlie Madigan."

—Vicki Pettersson, *New York Times* bestselling author of
The Sign of the Zodiac series

"A solid action-packed book with a kickass heroine. Kelly Gay knows her craft."

—Lilith Saintcrow, author of the Dante Valentine
and Jill Kismet series

"A smart, sexy, and exciting debut. Charlie Madigan is the epitome of the modern kick-butt heroine with a sassy demeanor and a heart of gold."

—Jenna Black, author of the Morgan Kingsley series

This title is also available as an eBook

THE
BETTER
PART OF
DARKNESS

KELLY GAY

POCKET BOOKS
New York London Toronto Sydney

Pocket Books
A Division of Simon & Schuster, Inc.
1230 Avenue of the Americas
New York, NY 10020

Copyright © 2009 by Kelly Gay

First Pocket Books paperback edition December 2009

POCKET and colophon are registered trademarks of Simon & Schuster, Inc.

For information about special discounts for bulk purchases, please contact Simon & Schuster Special Sales at 1-866-506-1949 or business@simonandschuster.com.

The Simon & Schuster Speakers Bureau can bring authors to your live event. For more information or to book an event contact the Simon & Schuster Speakers Bureau at 1-866-248-3049 or visit our website at www.simonspeakers.com.

Designed by Jill Putorti
Cover design by John Vairo Jr.
Cover art by Chris McGrath

Manufactured in the United States of America

10 9 8 7 6 5 4 3 2 1

ISBN 978-1-5011-0193-9
ISBN 978-1-4391-5546-2 (ebook)

For my grandparents:
Herman & Mary Keaton
Alfred & Joan Hogan
Thelma Dear

I

"You told a two-thousand-year-old oracle to *prove it*." Hank kept pace beside me, nursing his bloody nose with a handful of fast-food napkins I'd pulled from the glove box earlier. "I mean, do you ever think before the words spew out of your mouth, Charlie?"

"Yeah, all the time." I jogged up the four brick steps. "If Alessandra didn't have to act like a know-it-all, then I wouldn't have to say things to her."

"She *is* a know-it-all!"

A tired huff escaped me as I opened the front door to Hope Ridge School for Girls and fixed Hank with a deadpan look. "You've been whining ever since we left."

He swept past me, riding high on his martyrdom. "I'm not whining, I'm complaining. About you. And your incredible talent for pissing off people way more powerful than yourself."

I was exhausted from another sleepless night, and Hank's bitching grated on my last nerve. "Well, what do you want me to say, Hank?"

We strode at a fast clip down the empty hallway, passing Emma's homeroom door. Hope Ridge was my daughter's school. I'd been there hundreds of times in the last four years. But never like this.

Granted, the call that went over the wire was for paramedics, not ITF. The only reason we'd come was to make sure everything was okay. Otherwise we'd be over at Thumbs Up having a late breakfast.

"How about I'm sorry," Hank was saying. "Sorry, Hank, for always getting you punched, kicked, cursed out, et cetera, et cetera . . ." He dabbed at his nose a few times. The bleeding had finally stopped. "I don't know why they always hit *me* when you're the one who—"

Two school security guards blocked the restroom door. Hank had the good sense to end the conversation as we approached.

"She's in there," one of them said, holding the door open.

I nodded my thanks, stepped inside, and immediately froze. My lungs deflated on a stunned exhale. "Shit."

Hank let the door close behind us, gave a quick once-over of the victim on the floor, and then studied my shocked face. "What? You know this girl?"

I stared down at the female body curled into a fetal position, one hand under her cheek, as though she'd simply decided to lie down on the ugly green-and-white tiled floor of the girls' bathroom and take a nap.

Numbness and disbelief stole over me. I blinked hard, wanting to erase what I was seeing, wanting to go back to this morning and somehow change the course of events that had led to this.

"Charlie?"

I didn't answer. My voice wouldn't come.

Hank knelt by the right shoulder of the girl, rested one arm casually across his thigh, and stared up at me. Annoyed wrinkles creased the corners of his mouth. Nothing unusual. Hank looked at me like that all the time.

"Hello? Earth to Madigan. What the hell's with you today?"

I did a mental shake to regain my clarity. Didn't help much. I knew what I had to do. Investigate. Gather information. But I couldn't remember how to begin. Nothing had hit so close to home before. Hank's big form made the teenage girl on the floor look so small, so childlike . . . so innocent.

"Wait a second," he said as it dawned on him, "October tenth. Your favorite day of the year. How could I forget? An entire day of you being loopy as hell." He sighed and raised his perfect face to the ceiling. "What did I do to deserve this?"

"Uh, you invaded my world, my city, my life.

How's *that* for starters?" I shot him my trademark smile—cynical and slightly twisted.

Yeah, October tenth was my favorite freaking day of the year. The thirteenth anniversary. The day heaven and hell came out of the closet. Literally.

It wasn't a day one tended to forget.

"Charlie?"

"Yeah," I answered automatically.

I had to regain control of myself. I was good at my job and now it meant more than ever because I knew this girl. I'd practically watched her grow up. I'd just seen her this morning, for God's sake.

"Yeah, I know her. Don't you recognize her?" My voice didn't break, but my heart hurt like a sonofa-bitch. "Amanda Mott. She's"—I swallowed—"*was* Emma's friend and babysitter. Big sister, really . . ."

Hank gave a solemn nod. "Thus the 'shit' comment."

"Thus the 'shit' comment."

"She have any illnesses you know of? Depression? Unstable?"

"No, nothing like that. She's a good kid, Hank."

His troubled sigh echoed in the sterile bathroom. I watched him turn his attention back to Amanda's body, leaning closer—too close.

I knelt down. "Jesus, Hank, are you sniffing her?"

Blue topaz eyes met mine, and he hit me with a full-on grin. Sometimes, when he did that, it stole my breath for a split second. He dragged his fingers through thick, wavy hair the color of sunshine on gold and then frowned. "You don't smell that?"

I leaned closer and sniffed. "Uh, no."

"Figures," he muttered. "You people are so out of touch."

Oh, did I mention? Hank wasn't human.

All part of the policy. Integrate. Work together. Build relationships. Hank and I have been partners for three years now, both assigned to the ITF—Integration Task Force—which has pretty much taken over the policing and monitoring of *all* immigrant beings . . . whether from here or somewhere else.

No one had been happy about being assigned to work with an off-world partner. In fact, there wasn't a law enforcement officer out there who'd been comfortable with the new assignments. But we soon saw the necessity. With the influx of any *alien*, illegal or otherwise, crime rose. Better to have the insider knowledge to deal with it.

Hank was a siren. Particularly useful in police work. Criminals, suspects, witnesses—they all *wanted* to tell the truth just to please him. All he had to do was take off his voice modifier. Developed by Mott Technologies and made of thick iridescent metal with two balls at the ends, similar to a Celtic torc, the voice-mod adjusted Hank's supernaturally alluring voice into something we mere mortals could handle without embarrassing ourselves. And it wasn't just women. Men, kids, babies, animals, you name it. Any living creature was drawn to Hank like he was the village piper. I liked to call him the village idiot, but, hey, that's just me.

Hank's expression became serious, his frown deepening. He reached out and put two fingers on the side of Amanda's neck and then closed his eyes. I waited, knowing not to interrupt. Hank was right, for the most part. Humans *were* more out of touch in the psychic sense, though ITF had begun hiring any psychically-inclined officer they could get their hands on. Off-worlders, however, were blessed with an over-abundance of senses.

"You gotta be kidding me." He removed his fingers and gave me a frank look. "She's not dead."

"What?"

"She's not dead."

Immediately I felt for her pulse. Nothing. "I swear to God, Hank, I'll put a bullet in your belly and send you back to Elysia if you're messing with me." And I'd done it once before, so he knew to take me seriously.

"Jeez, Charlie, give me some credit will you? I wouldn't kid you about this."

Emma loved Amanda like any devoted little sister would. She also adored Hank. And I knew that if this affected her, then Hank wouldn't mess with me on something so personal.

I stared at my partner over Amanda's body for a hard second, then shot to my feet and radioed the paramedics with the news as Hank began walking slowly down the row of stalls, searching each one for clues as to what might've caused Amanda to drop into a death-like sleep on the cold, dirty floor during third period Algebra.

I crouched next to Amanda, wanting so badly to tuck the loose strands of white-blonde hair behind her ear. But I didn't dare. *God, please don't let this be what I think it is.*

As we waited for the paramedics, I used the time to scan her body, searching over the Black Watch plaid skirt, the knee-high white socks, the chunky black Mary Janes, and the white blouse. It was the same uniform Emma had worn to school, the same one she wore every day. Nothing seemed out of place, except for Amanda herself. She looked peaceful, happy even.

The medical examiner entered the bathroom with her hard, shiny black case and equally shiny black bob, which curved under a small oval face, determined red lips, and dark Asian eyes. She'd gotten another new pair of glasses and they framed her eyes perfectly, as did the other twenty-odd pairs she owned. Liz bought designer eyeglasses like some women bought expensive shoes. "Hey, Madigan." She shut the door behind her. "How is it you can afford to send your kid to a swanky place like this?"

I was going to kill Hank. The blabbermouth.

I stood and moved aside. "It's called child support. Automatic draft is a wondrous thing."

"Ah, that would explain it." She set down her case, opened it, and withdrew a small pair of latex gloves, which she put on with a loud snap. Then she knelt next to Amanda to check her pulse and listen to her heartbeat. "Heard over the radio you have a live one here." She sighed, preferring to analyze the dead over the living. "Not exactly my specialty but . . . How old is she?"

"Sixteen," I answered quietly, allowing Liz to be the brilliant medical examiner that she was. Of course it didn't hurt that she was also a kick-ass necromancer. Usually, what the dead couldn't tell us from our investigation, they could tell Liz. But we always tried to solve a case ourselves. It took a massive amount of energy and life force to raise the dead. And if Liz did it for every John Doe who rolled through the door, she would've lost her own life a long time ago. After a long moment, she removed the earpieces to the stethoscope.

"Anything?" I asked.

"Heartbeat is so damn faint and slow you can hardly hear it with the stethoscope. At this rate, she should be going into cardiac arrest. Looks like all the others."

I glanced impatiently at the door. Where the hell were the medics?

Still hopeful, Liz examined Amanda's skull. "There appears to be no external damage to her body at all. Maybe an aneurysm, or . . ." She lifted Amanda's eyelid, and we both gasped even though we'd seen this a dozen times in the last week.

I knelt down. "Damn."

A cloudy white film glazed over Amanda's eye. Goose bumps crept up my arms and legs, a sign of foreboding that left me downright cold. The Pine-Sol scent of the room was starting to give me a head-ache.

"Looks like *ash* has just moved uptown," Liz said on a resigned breath.

Hank dropped to his haunches next to me and took in this new information. A steel curtain slid over his features. Hank *always* showed his emotions. And with the realization of what we were seeing, *ash* making its way from Underground Atlanta into a midtown private school, Hank should've been cursing or hitting something by now. I studied him intently and didn't miss the telltale flex of his jaw before he stood. Yeah, something was definitely up.

"Mom! Mom, what's going on?" Emma's terrified voice echoed from the hallway.

Motherhood and work. Usually I had no trouble keeping the two separated, but this time the lines were seriously blurred. "Damn it." I closed my eyes for a second, hating that they had crossed, hating that they'd even come close. I drew in a deep breath and switched gears from detective to mom. "Hold on a sec," I told Hank and Liz and then walked calmly into the hallway, mentally preparing myself.

Seeing her standing there in her uniform, all tall and thin, approaching twelve way too fast, it suddenly hit me how much Emma had grown in the last year. A rush of sad realization squeezed my chest. Time was racing by where my daughter was concerned. She pressed against the police tape, which had gone up while we were inside, and pushed against the school security officer. He held her back with a hand on her shoulder. My hand went to the service weapon on my hip. An automatic gesture. I didn't intend to use it, but the guy had better get his paws off my kid.

"Hey." I placed my hand on his left shoulder, probably harder than I should have. "I got it."

He hesitated. He might be the big guy here at school, but he knew not to mess with an ITF agent. Our training and selection process had become legendary. Not many people could look a hellhound in the eye and know how to defeat it. We'd been trained to face every being and beast from both worlds, and we all had the scars and nightmares to prove it.

"Ma'am." He nodded, stepping back.

I turned to my daughter, lowering my voice. "What are you doing out of class?" I had to show my confident side, let her know everything would be all right. But my heart pounded. She was highly intuitive and knew me better than anyone. I reached out to smooth the wavy brown bangs behind her ear. She always wore a ponytail to school—couldn't convince her to do anything different.

She did a quick wave with her wooden bathroom pass. "Mom," she began in an I'm-not-a-stupid-kid-I-know-what's-going-on tone, "they told us to stay in class, that something happened with a student, but I saw you and Hank from the window and said I had to *go*." She leaned close, her big brown eyes turning wide and glassy. "Amanda was supposed to be my lab buddy today, but she never showed." Her nostrils flared and tears rose to the surface. "It's not her, is it?"

I opened my mouth to answer at the same moment the paramedics burst through the front door and raced down the hall. Great. I turned back to her. Two lines of tears trailed down her cheeks. Her bottom lip trembled, tugging hard on my protective instincts.

"Oh, God. I knew it!" There was a hint of accusation in her tone, as though I somehow had control over what had happened.

"Oh, baby." I pulled her close, hugging her tight and smoothing back her hair, breathing in the familiar scent of Cherry Blast shampoo. She was too young to know this kind of worry and fear. But Emma was a strong kid. She'd had to fly by the seat of her pants right along with me when I became a mother at nineteen, and she'd handled *that* learning curve like a champ. And she'd been able to get through the divorce with way more strength and understanding than me.

We'd get through this. And I damned sure as hell was going to find out who was flooding the city with *ash*. The optimistic part of me wanted to believe there was another explanation for Amanda's condition, that somehow it was just a medical issue. But I knew it was a silly hope. No medical problems I knew of turned your eyes into something out of *The Exorcist*. How in the hell had it spread so quickly?

"It'll be all right, kiddo." I leaned back and gazed down at her, giving her my most reassuring smile. She was the one innocent, good thing in my world. And

I intended to keep it that way. "Amanda will make it, you'll see. She's not hurt, not bleeding; she's just asleep and we can't figure out why."

I kissed her forehead, pausing there for a moment to breathe in her scent again. No one else could give me that kind of immediate peace. She grounded me, kept me always looking forward and never back. Kept me from lingering too long on all the evil things I'd witnessed over my career and in my past. I straightened and drew in a deep, cleansing breath, then looked her straight in the eye. "But we'll fix this, I promise. Okay?"

Her mouth dropped open. One hand went to her hip. "Okay? That's it? *Okay?* Like I'm eight years old or something?" Her chin lifted a notch, and her eyes glinted in opposition. "It's not okay. I want to see her."

"You know I couldn't let you, even if I wanted to, *which* I don't."

"Well, I'm not leaving," she said, "until I see her." Attitude poured off her in maddening waves that, in any other circumstance, would've riled me. But the challenging stance and the belligerent cock to her head couldn't hide her fear. She was like a wounded puppy—scared to death, too small to defend itself, yet baring its teeth anyway.

I took her shoulders and turned her around to face the way she'd come. "There's not a thing you can do right now. Let me do my job, okay? We'll talk tonight."

Her chin didn't drop, but her tone did. "Fine."

I watched her shuffle down the hall, wanting nothing more than to run to her and give her one more hug, but I couldn't. I had to make good on my promise. She stopped at her classroom door and glanced back at me, the uniform reminding me of the first time she wore it in third grade. So young then. So young now. Even from that distance, I saw her vulnerable look and the deep sigh that escaped her lips.

"She's hurting," Hank observed quietly, coming to stand beside me as Emma went inside her classroom.

"Yeah, I don't need super senses to figure that out." I marched away from him, down the hall in the opposite direction, needing some air before I totally lost it.

Usually on cases, I had no trouble remaining distant and methodical. Don't get close, and you don't lose your objectivity. *And you don't get yourself beaten to death running down a back alley after a pissed-off ghoul before your partner gets there to back you up.* I'd learned my lesson. And I hadn't made a mistake like that again.

I couldn't make one now.

The unmistakable scent of autumn, of changing leaves and cool soil, rode on a leisurely breeze, helping to calm my emotions as I stepped into the courtyard where the kids often ate lunch on nice days like this.

I turned my face to the warm sunlight, letting my eyelids close. The voices on my radio drifted into the background along with the birds in the court-yard and the sound of cars on the side street beyond the high stone walls that surrounded the school grounds.

Just a moment's peace was all I was after, but as my mind drifted all I could think about was the irony. I busted my ass every day to afford the best and safest school for Emma, to pay for everything else myself and use Will's child support solely for her education.

Kindergarten through twelfth grade, Hope Ridge was one of the best private schools in Atlanta. And, despite all that, I couldn't protect her from the harsh realities of life. I knew what it was like to be a victim, and I knew what it was like to love a victim, to feel helpless and lost. Crime happened anywhere and in the safest places. It was inevitable. But, still, part of me had been convinced that if I worked hard enough, somehow my child would be exempt.

The mention of Amanda's name over the radio interrupted my thoughts. They were taking her to Grady Memorial Hospital. All her vital signs were normal except her heartbeat. She didn't appear to be worsening.

Ash had hit the market so fast, just in the last few weeks, that we still didn't know what we were dealing with. Chemically engineered? An airborne agent? An ingested substance from Elysia or Charbydon? There were so many mysterious things brought into the country with the influx of our new *neighbors*. I scrubbed my face with both hands, feeling overwhelmed. Protecting citizens was hard enough, and lately, as we mingled more and more with the off-worlders, it felt as though we were patrolling blind.

At least I had Hank.

And he knew way more than he let on. I turned and headed back into the building, steeling my resolve. He'd spill his alien guts one way or another.

The soles of my black boots echoed in the empty space as I marched down the hall. Ahead, Hank was speaking to the school superintendent and Principal Anton. He pacified their fears. I could see it in their faces, the way they breathed relief and the gratitude they showed as they shook his hand.

Hank turned to me as I approached. I didn't halt my stride, just grabbed his thick bicep and propelled him down the hall with me.

"Whoa, I know you like to manhandle me and all, but this should probably wait until we're alone."

"Shut up, Hank."

I shoved open the front door, stepping out into the bright sunshine only to run into a large group of reporters. Perfect.

"Is it true the victim is Cassius Mott's daughter?"

"Is she like all the others? Is it *ash*?"

"Do you have any leads on what the drug is exactly?"

"Will you bring in a medium to help with the investigation?"

"Hey, aren't you that cop who died a few months back?"

Sometimes, I hated reporters. Especially the ones with memories like elephants.

"C'mon! Back off!" Hank flung out his arms, trying to shield me.

We pushed and elbowed our way to the car parked out front. I slipped behind the wheel and waited for Hank to get in. Once his door was shut, I drove around the corner and down one block where I stopped the car at the curb to question him.

"Okay, spill."

He drew one leg in and propped his arm on the window ledge, obviously in tune with my meaning. "I was going to tell you before the whole Amanda thing . . . I talked to the ER doc from Grady. Some of the tests came back from the first rash of vics. It's definitely an off-world substance. Most likely in powder form since they found some residue in the nostrils and lungs of the two who didn't make it. The effects are almost instantaneous. The few who have woken up from the coma are dying. Once it leaves their system, their bodies begin to shut down." He sighed deeply, shaking his head and staring out the front windshield. "They're doing more tests. So far, no other cities have reported any cases, and security has been increased at all the off-world gates."

"So it started here in Atlanta. It came through our gate."

Figured. Many of the new crimes and problems

stemmed from trafficking in off-world items. Spell-mongers from Elysia and Charbydon had become a big problem, selling all kinds of illegal concoctions and substances. Soul bartering, a gigantic no-no, still occurred in dark alleys and private residences. And none of it would change unless we all suddenly became happy and content with ourselves and our lives. Fat chance of that. Any way to get a leg up, illegal or otherwise, was here to stay.

"We need to figure out where it's coming from. If it's leaking into other schools . . ." My voice broke. "You're a siren," I said, refocusing. "Nothing about this seems familiar, like anything you've come across before?" I was grasping at straws. We'd had an entire off-world team on this for the last week and no one seemed to know anything.

"The condition on the eyes. The guys at the station have considered it, but don't seem to think it's related. Could be a long shot . . ." Hank cleared his throat and I caught a split-second squirm. I turned in the seat, more curious than ever. He spared me a dry glance and then looked straight ahead. "The condition happens naturally when some Elysians get, you know, excited."

"Excited about wha— Oh. Oh! *That* kind of excited. Really?"

"Really. Look," he said, frowning, "it doesn't happen with sirens, but I've seen it with others. It's like an effect of euphoria, happens when they perform certain ritual dances or prayers, or they . . . you know . . ."

"Got it." I held up both hands, putting an immediate halt to any mention of sex. Definitely not something I wanted to discuss with a drop-dead gorgeous siren with all the grace and power of a lion. That was a personal boundary I promised myself long ago I'd never cross. If I did, it would be way too easy to start wanting something I couldn't—and shouldn't—have. Hank was not only my partner, but one of my best friends. Not something I wanted to mess with. "Have you seen this recently?" I asked, wishing I'd rolled down my window for some air.

"I'm never gonna hear the end of this, am I?" He didn't wait for an answer. Instead he said on an irritated breath, "In Underground."

"What place in Underground?" I pressed.

"Helios Alley. The Bath House."

No surprise. Helios Alley catered to off-worlders, Elysians to be exact. Restaurants, clubs, shops, you name it. Two streets over was Solomon Street—Charbydon territory. And the street in between was Mercy Street, a mix of everything—magic shops, psychics, anything supernatural and you'd find it there, legal or not.

If we'd learn anything about *ash*, it'd be in Underground.

My first reaction was to laugh, which I did, but then I saw he wasn't exactly laughing with me. "Are you serious? The Bath House? I didn't take you for a nudist."

His eyes rolled. "It's not a nudist club. It's a public

bath house, like the Romans used to have. Didn't you study history in school?"

"Yeah, and the Romans had all kinds of nasty sex orgies in the baths." I sighed dramatically, shaking my head. "It all starts with a massage . . ."

A spectacular groan came out of Hank's mouth, which expanded his chest and made his white shirt stretch nicely across the broad expanse. Hell, seeing him lounging around naked in some bath would probably be worth the trip downtown. Hank had one of the best bodies I'd ever seen. But then he was a siren—his species had a knack for attraction and seduction.

"I swear, Charlie," he grumbled, turning in the seat to face me with an evil glint in his blue eyes, "if we weren't friends, I'd take off this damned modifier, make you strip naked, and skip all the way down to the station house."

That sobered me up because I knew he had the ability. And because I knew Hank had his limits. "Okay, point taken. So, why The Bath House?"

"Females," he answered without pause. "I'm single. I have a life, unlike *someone* in this car."

"Yeah, well, you can be single without going to extremes. Women throw themselves at you all the time. You don't need to hang out at a nud—er, bath house."

"I do if I'm looking for one of my kind. You think it's easy, getting hit on all the time and not being the tiniest bit interested? The only female sirens in Atlanta are ones who have mates, or work in the private sector, or occasionally hang out at the baths because it reminds them of home."

"Poor you." I put the car in gear. "Try being a single mother, who carries three lethal firearms and can take down a runner at fifty yards. Trust me; it doesn't make a date feel all warm and fuzzy inside."

I pulled into traffic and then made a U-turn at the light to head back to the station. "I have to make babysitting arrangements for tonight." Hank blinked, confused, so I enlightened him with a smile before turning my attention back to the road. "We're going to The Bath House. Looks like you finally got yourself a hot date."

His lips dipped down, leaving a dimple in his left cheek. "Joy," he said, as disgruntled as a teenager being told to clean their room. "Please, please, please, Charlie, don't do anything stupid."

Hank wouldn't care about causing a scene. That's why we made a good team. When it was necessary, neither one of us backed down, no matter what, no matter where. I switched lanes and passed a taxi, a thought suddenly occurring. "What? You like someone there or something?"

He rubbed his hands down his face and muttered, "Oh, Jesus H. Christ."

Hah! A broad grin stretched across my face. "You do!" My laughter filled the car. "You have a crush on someone at The Bath House," I sang. "Hey, doesn't that mean you're shy if you have a crush? Hank's shy!

Oh, my God . . ." I laughed for at least a good half mile. He cursed under his breath and slid down into the seat. Last time I had a date, with an officer from the ninth precinct, Hank had had a major field day. "Payback is a bitch, my friend."

I parked the car in the fire lane off Ellis Street in front of ITF Building One, or as we referred to it: Station One. "It's three right now. I'm gonna head over to the hospital and check on Amanda, make arrangements, and then I'll meet you downtown at eight."

Hank opened the door. "I'll talk to the guys at the lab again about this eye connection. And I'll pick you up at ten." He lifted his hand to stop my argument. "Things don't even start to heat up until then. You'd know that if you weren't celibate." He got out of the car and then leaned back through the window. "Oh, and try to take a beauty nap, and don't look so damned professional if you can help it. Let your hair down, maybe use some of that deep red lipstick you wore on your date with Officer Wandering Eye."

My eyes narrowed, and I opened my mouth, but he flashed me a broad grin, a wink, and then he was gone.

I supposed I deserved that.

2

Underground Atlanta was the hub of off-world activity in the city, an entertainment, shopping, and living district that encompassed six city blocks in the very heart of old Atlanta. In the 1920s city engineers built bridges and viaducts over old, Civil War–era railroad tracks and streets, raising the street level and eventually leaving the ground level almost forgotten until the city revived the area in the late 80s and early 90s. Now it was home to free concerts, restaurants, bars, nightclubs, and specialty shops.

One of those shops belonged to my sister. And, yeah, I could've called her to see if she'd babysit, but since her shop was on Mercy Street, it would give me a chance to talk to one of my informants.

Bryn's place sat in the middle of a long row of shops that lined the left side of the street. There were potted plants out front, a chalkboard sign on the sidewalk advertising sales, and a few wind chimes hung from tall, ornate garden stakes shoved into the planters on either side of the door. I thought she was nuts for having a shop in Underground. But Bryn had some serious smarts when it came to business. She carried items the off-worlders craved, like crafting items, exotic herbs, minerals, rocks, and other trinkets, and she made sure to stock things humans could use as well—anything Wiccan. Books, antiques, charms, clothes . . . But mostly she specialized in herbs, the rarer the better.

I stepped around a three-foot-tall imp carrying a Gucci handbag and approached the back counter. Bryn had her back to me, snipping a few branches from a small potted herb as she spoke to it softly.

"Probably not a smart thing, to turn your back on the customers," I said, looking around at the patrons. The store was packed with plants, items, baskets, and dried herbs hanging from the ceiling, so many corners and dark shelves; you couldn't see a shoplifter at work if you tried.

Bryn turned. "I have a security system."

I frowned at her and leaned on the counter. "A *spell* is not a security system." When would she learn to take care?

She shook her head, looking awfully like Mom when she did that. Her auburn hair had been twisted up into a sloppy arrangement, and her brown eyes held a smile as usual. "Well, I also have Gizmo." She nodded behind me.

I glanced over my shoulder to see a gargoyle, the size of a large cat, perched on top of a tall, dark bookshelf by the door. His head moved with the flow of patrons, watching them closely. "You got a gargoyle? Are you insane?" I held up my hand. "No, wait. Don't answer that." Gargoyles were notorious for misbehaving, like little demon monkeys, always chewing on things, jumping around, making messes. I shook my head. They were also incredibly pricey. "Where'd you get the money for him?"

She leaned over the counter, getting closer and smiling as though she'd pulled off the coup of the century. "I traded a five-pound bag of Elysian sea salt, a box of rare Tibetan incense, and that old petrified toad I had sitting on the counter." She straightened, going on the defensive. "And he's perfectly trained, so wipe that prune-y old look off your face. You're gonna get two wrinkles right between your eyebrows just like Grandma Eunice." She reached out and used the pad of her index finger to vigorously rub the spot on my forehead.

I swatted her away, stepping out of reach. "Will you cut it out? God, you're just like Mom." I felt the frown return and made an attempt to ease my facial muscles. The last thing I wanted was to end up looking like Grandma Eunice, God rest her soul. "Speaking of which, have you heard from Mom and Dad?"

Bryn popped a few M&M's from a small bowl by the register into her mouth and then held up a finger.

From under the counter, she pulled a postcard. "They sent you one, too. Don't you ever check the mail?"

"Occasionally." I took the postcard. One side was a photograph of the Giza plateau in Egypt and the other side had a few scribbled lines about how hot the desert was and how beautiful sailing down the Nile had been. Next stop: Turkey. I slid it back to her. "Any idea when they're coming back?"

She shrugged as I stole a handful of M&M's. "Your guess is as good as mine. Probably another few months, unless they find somewhere else they want to go."

Mom and Dad had saved their entire adult lives for this trip. They'd moved all their furniture into storage and rented me their three-bedroom bungalow in Candler Park, which worked out well since Em and I had already been shacking up in the spare bedroom after the divorce. Plus being in midtown, it was closer to Emma's school and not too far from downtown. *More power to them*, I thought. They deserved to travel the world for as long as they liked. I missed the hell out of them, but it helped that I had Bryn. She reminded me so much of Mom, it was scary.

Bryn was also a gifted earth mage. Even growing up she'd been able to do things—make plants grow and bloom by talking to them or touching them. After the Revelation, what we called the discovery of the new dimensions, she'd begun to take her talent more seriously, and she utilized the new resources to study and learn and cultivate her abilities. Last year, she became the first human member of the Off-World Garden Society and the Atlanta League of Mages.

A high-pitched scream exploded behind me.

Instinct sent my hand to my gun. It was already drawn and pointed in the direction of the scream before my vision landed on the source. My heart pounded as Gizmo flew off his perch and hovered in front of the imp I'd passed earlier.

"Jeez, Charlie, put the gun away, you'll scare my customers." Bryn pushed my gun down and hurried around the counter toward the imp. The hem of her sundress flapped behind her, making me notice her bare feet and trim ankles encased by two sparkling charm anklets.

"Me?" I holstered my weapon, trying not to dwell on how ready I'd been to pull the trigger. "That thing just blew out every eardrum from here to Solomon Street."

I followed Bryn as she navigated the narrow paths in the store. It must be nerves, I decided. Seeing Amanda like that had me on edge. That, and I was about eight months past due for a good night's sleep.

At the entrance, Bryn bent at the waist and held out her hand to the imp. It was female with cocoa-brown skin, large, slanted black eyes, thin lips, freckles, and a shock of orangey-red hair. The imp let out an irritable huff, dug into her Gucci purse, and then slapped a small crystal dragon into Bryn's palm.

Gizmo flew back to the bookcase and folded his gray wings behind his back.

"Nice try, Dix." Bryn gave the imp a triumphant look. "Better luck tomorrow, eh?"

Dix shuffled from the store grumbling, but not before shooting an evil glare at Gizmo.

"You're just going to let her go?"

"Dix is harmless. She comes in every day and tries to take something. Imps like anything glassy and shiny." Bryn set the dragon on the shelf, went back to the counter, and then grabbed the small potted herb. "So what brings you to Hodgepodge?" She plucked a few less-than-stellar leaves without even looking, her attention totally on me.

"I need you to watch Emma tonight. I'm investigating a—"

Her eyes grew round and serious. "The Amanda Mott case, I know. It's all over the news. People are starting to panic, Charlie. It's hitting way too close to home now. Some are saying it's not a drug at all, that it's a virus or epidemic of some kind. They even splashed you and Hank on the screen."

I swore under my breath. God, this day just kept getting better and better. "Damn it. That's just what we need." I scrubbed a hand down my face. "It *is* a narcotic, Bryn, we're sure of that. But other than that . . . hell if I know."

Bryn stared at me quietly for a second. "How are the nightmares?"

I loved my sister, but I really didn't want to talk

about it. Dying on the job and coming back two hours later can really mess your shit up. I shrugged. "Same old, same old. So, can you do it or not?"

"Sure. Why don't you let her spend the night? I can take her to school in the morning before I open the shop."

For a moment I saw worry in her look, but I ignored it. "Thanks."

"It's no biggie." She walked with me to the door. "Just be careful, okay? You still have that charm I gave you?"

I lifted the long chain from around my neck, pulling the flat, circular-cut crystal etched with symbols from my cleavage. It was the size of a silver dollar and always rested warmly against my skin. I waved it at her. "See. Still here."

"Good. Bring Em by around dinnertime."

I gave her a quick nod. "Will do."

Once on the sidewalk, I headed further down Mercy Street. I had one more person to see.

The farther you went down Mercy Street, the darker it seemed to get. Pubs and storefronts spilled into the street, tents and awnings extended selling space, and hawkers lurked in the shadows and called out to passersby. The off-world population was growing so fast, and nowhere was it more evident than here in Underground.

Ask anyone and they can tell you where they were and what they were doing when the news broke. Scientists had discovered (some say "stumbled upon") two parallel planes of existence, which, according to many leaders and believers of the world's major religions, resembled certain aspects of heaven and hell.

They'd been visiting us for thousands of years, using our world as a battleground and neutral zone, interfering in our lives, speaking our languages, doing good works and miracles, and committing horrible crimes. And now we knew the truth. Elysia and Charbydon, and the beings in them, weren't the things of Sunday school lessons and Hallmark figurines.

And the existence of God and an afterlife was as unclear to them as it was to us.

The *friend or foe* debate continued on as usual, but no longer to the point of nuclear war. Eventually, delegations from all sides met, peace treaties were signed, and laws and policies were put into place.

We'd become the promised land for countless off-worlders, many of whom resided in several of our major cities. New York. Miami. Los Angeles. Houston. And the first off-world city, Atlanta.

"Is that the walking dead I see?" a sandpaper voice called from the shadows.

I stopped on the sidewalk as Auggie stepped from the darkness of the old maps-and-bookbinding store. "What are you doing up here?" I'd known him for so long that his slow, raspy voice, grayish-green skin, long, narrow face, and large hooked nose stopped giving me the willies years ago. "The pawnshop finally kick you off their curb?"

He shrugged, his hollowed face pinched in annoyance for a moment. "Something like that."

"Walk with me, Auggie." I turned and ambled down the brick pavement. He fell in step beside me. He was my height; at five-eight that was tall for a goblin. Goblin was what we called his kind here. Every being from Elysia and Charbydon had their own race-names, but their languages were so complicated and difficult to pronounce, we'd given them terms that had been around in our own language for centuries, ones that seemed to fit their appearances and powers. And to their credit, they didn't seem to mind. Hell, most of them, after years of visiting us in secret, already knew how to speak our tongue before they'd been granted official visas, work permits, or permanent citizenship.

Like us, the Elysians and Charbydons had different races and ranks among them—some more powerful than others, some more kind and law-abiding than others, and some more criminal and evil than others. But they all had their weaknesses, weaknesses we, as humans, could (and had to) exploit. And I knew Auggie's weakness all too well.

"I know why you're here," he grated slowly.

Thanks to the media, I thought. "So, what can you tell me?"

His breath came fast, and his mouth parted to reveal a blunt set of yellow teeth. He wrung his slender hands together in anticipation. "What do you have for me?"

Always prepared, I handed him a crisp hundred from my back pocket.

He snatched the bill and held it to his wide nostrils, breathing in deeply. His body shuddered. "Wonderful scent, this one. Is it new?"

"Brand-new. Never been in circulation." That always got him worked up. "So?"

He shoved the beloved bill into his pocket, stopping between two storefronts, edging back into the shadows. "Well, I can tell you this. What you've been seeing over the past week is only the beginning, Charlie Madigan, only the beginning." He gave a nervous laugh.

His black pupils dilated and the dingy yellow surrounding them flashed as he glanced anywhere but at me. "And that's about all I can tell you." He opened his coat, hands shaking, and changed the subject. "You wanna buy a spell? For you, I give you half price." Vials of colored liquids and powders hung from small hooks beneath his coat. "Love, sex, happiness, wealth, I got it all right here, see. How about beauty? I got that, too." He paled. "Oh, I mean, not that you need it. Fuck. No, you don't need it. I just meant . . ." Sweat beaded his thin upper lip and ran down the bony sides of his face.

"I know what you meant," I said, stepping closer to him. "What the hell has got you spooked, Auggie? Whatever it is, you can tell me."

He stepped back, his eyes bulging and the yellow flashing again as they darted around. "No, not this time. No. Sorry. No can do."

I grabbed his wool coat by the collar. The vials clinked against each other like wind chimes in a sudden breeze. "Auggie, two people have died. There are over twenty in the hospital right now." My voice dropped. "I have a sixteen-year-old kid lying comatose on a goddamn bathroom floor. A *kid*. You want that on your conscience? You want to obstruct the law? 'Cause I can promise you you'll be on the next transport back to Charbydon if you don't."

"How about a holding cell?" He gave another nervous laugh. "Charbydon . . . it's too dark there now, not even an inch of moonlight." He gulped. "I can't, Charlie. I can't tell you more."

All I could think about was Emma, the promise I had made, and Amanda, the young girl I'd come to care about. "I swear to God," I forced out between tight lips, "don't make me beat it out of you, Auggie." I wasn't serious in my threat, but the urge was there. Stronger than it had ever been before.

A wave of dizziness rolled over me, followed by a sudden rush of bloodlust, ballooning, pushing against my chest, wanting to escape. I blinked hard, shocked. God, it hurt. I couldn't catch my breath.

Steady, Charlie. It was getting harder and harder to control my emotions lately. Maybe because I hadn't slept through the night since I'd recovered from dying.

I dropped my hold on Auggie's coat, stumbled back, and leaned down, both hands on my knees, trying to regroup and settle myself, trying to breathe.

"You ain't right," Auggie said softly. "You ain't

right at all. You ever think what happened to you may have—"

Fire shot through me. My eyes snapped open, and I grabbed him by the throat and propelled him into the brick wall, lifting him clear off his feet. "Not. Another. Word." My nostrils flared. My voice sounded different. Strength flowed through me—so great that I knew if I wanted, I could snap his neck without effort or shove him clean through the brick wall. Part of me wanted that.

What the hell? No. Calm down.

"Start talking, Auggie, 'cause I don't know . . . how long I can . . . hold out."

He nodded rapidly. I let him slide down the wall until his feet touched the concrete. My hold on his throat lessened, but just enough to allow him to speak. I was shaking hard and confused beyond belief. But getting information was all that mattered right now. I'd figure the rest out later.

"They're calling it *ash*."

"I know that. What else? What is it?"

"It comes from some kind of flower in Charbydon, that's all I know."

"Who's dealing it?"

"Just some guys. Dealers, I guess. They're testing it out, giving it to junkies, other dealers . . . If you overdose, it does the same thing on the eyes, no matter who you are or where you're from."

I squeezed harder. Auggie's eyes bulged. "Who? I need a name, a place."

His body stilled, and his terrified gaze froze over my left shoulder. "Oh, fuck." The color drained from his face, leaving him a washed-out shade of seasick green.

I followed his gaze to see three jinn warriors striding toward us. They were tall, built like linebackers, and wore heavy black sunglasses to shield their sensitive eyes. Their dark gray skin, like soot from a fireplace, was as smooth as polished marble. Their mouths were grim, and they walked with purpose. For thousands of years they held a position of honor in Charbydon as bodyguards to the nobles. Damn.

Auggie began to shake. I released him and took a step back, my hand going to my Nitro-gun.

They stopped in front of us, all of them at least six-four and as menacing as a pack of hungry jackals.

"Hey, fellas," Auggie said in broken falsetto, "just let me finish with the lady here." He turned to me, his desperation almost tangible in the air between us. "What was that you wanted, ma'am? A love spell, right?" The vials rattled from his trembling as he opened the coat. He didn't give me a vial, but slipped a pack of matches into my hand. "There you go."

I met his gaze and it pleaded with me, seeming glassier than before. "Off you go." He gave a nervous chuckle, trying to feign a genial tone for the benefit of the jinn, and then he leaned down and whispered, "Run, Charlie Madigan. *Run.*"

For as long as I'd known Auggie, he'd been selfish and greedy, but always reliable. Mutely, I shook my head at him. No way would I leave him to these guys, especially after he'd just tried to protect me. I shoved the matches in my pocket and turned as the three stepped closer.

"Get lost, *brougá*," the one in the leather jacket spat.

I sneered back, not appreciating being called the equivalent of a disease-infested whore.

Obviously the one in leather was the leader of this three-ring gang. The other two wore parkas. The jinn were severely hot-natured—even in the notorious heat of an Atlanta summer they wore sweatshirts. That was why a Nitro-gun worked so well. It could stun them into submission, freeze their flesh, and stop their blood flow, and eventually the heart, in one Level-5 blast, but that was a shoot-to-kill-only setting, not something an officer would typically use on the street to detain criminals.

"I'm not done with the spellmonger," I told the one who'd spoken. "Why don't you come back later?"

The ringleader made a step toward me. Without thought, I withdrew the gun from the holster under my arm and pointed it straight at his chest; at the same time my other hand held out my badge. A glow built in his violet irises. It meant only one thing.

Attack.

With my thumb, I moved the nitro level up. This jinn was a big one, and I had the distinct feeling he'd fight until his last breath and do his best to take me with him.

"ITF, huh?" A slow, even grin spread across his dark face. He flexed his big, beefy fingers. "I'm going to like breaking you in two. Human bones, they snap like twigs."

Auggie cursed behind me as the situation exploded. One of the jinn was on him in a flash. I got one round off against the jinn directly in front of me before the third struck a massive blow against my chest with the palm of his hand. It lifted me off my feet and sent me flying into the brick wall.

The sudden impact knocked the wind out of me. A bright flash of pain sliced through my skull and back. *Dear God.*

My gun and badge clattered to the sidewalk. I slid down the wall to my feet, crouching down like some animal, one hand on the pavement as a surge of blinding anger, anger so powerful and excruciating, erupted through me, stinging a path all the way to my fingers and toes. It was hot and cold. I couldn't contain it, whatever it was. But it erased the pain, so I welcomed it.

A loud hum vibrated from my core. I straightened as the jinn marched toward me with a leer. Calm settled over me, confidence swelled my chest. I *wanted* to fight, to get down and dirty and give this joker a big ole lesson in southern manners. I had no doubt from Auggie's reaction that they had supplied the *ash*. The same substance that had killed, that had put Amanda, and numerous others, in the hospital.

My gaze darted to my weapon directly between me and the asshole jinn.

He paused. I smiled sarcastically.

The sane part of me screamed. What the hell was I doing? *Dive for the gun!* But the sane Charlie immediately evaporated, overcome by the hum of energy that squelched any opposition. I cocked my head at him. "Come and get it, you alien loser." They hated to be called aliens. And I lived to irritate the hell out of them.

A low growl issued from deep within his chest. He hunched his shoulders and ran at me like a bull after a rodeo clown. At the last second, I sidestepped and stuck my arm out, connecting with the soft tissue of his throat. He gagged and fell back, gasping for air. I didn't give him a second to recover before I jerked him to his feet by the parka collar, but he swung up and hit me in the jaw. Blood surged into my mouth. I grabbed at his head, but, like all jinn males, it was just as smooth and hairless as the rest of him. My fingers found the small, delicate cartilage of his ear, and then the two small metal hoops pierced through the skin. I yanked hard. He screamed.

I kneed him in the gut as the other guy, finished with Auggie, jumped on my back. My knees buckled, and we went down in a free-for-all of hands and feet. One of them fisted my hair, lifted my head, and then slammed my forehead into the pavement.

Pain exploded, radiating over the curve of my head. Tiny rainbow crosses danced in my vision. A wave of nausea clenched my stomach. My strength and confidence wavered. Desperate, I bit the hand closest to me, getting a mouthful of thick, hot blood as black and tasteful as tar. I turned onto my back and kicked as hard as I could.

There was blood in my eyes. I couldn't see. I hurt all over. They were winning, hitting me over and over.

Frustration welled inside me. This wasn't happening. This couldn't happen. Not again!

I tried to tap into the anger of before, into the strange confidence and strength that had overtaken me. *Please come back. Please help me*, I begged, letting my body go slack and opening myself to the strange darkness I knew coiled under the surface even as their fists pounded into my belly and face.

The pain subsided and the familiar hum returned. I breathed a quick sigh of relief, nearly choking on the blood in my mouth, wanting to gag from the metallic spill sliding down my throat and pooling in my tense, empty stomach.

And then I fought back; like an animal, panicked, wild, hearing only my heart pounding through my eardrums and swinging at anything that touched me.

It seemed to go on for hours; a slow-motion dream that wouldn't end.

"Charlie! CHARLENE ELIZABETH MADIGAN, STOP IT RIGHT NOW!"

Rough bands pinned me against the wall. I struggled against them, against the hard, scratchy surface. Tears made a hot trail down my face. The sensation of loss gripped me. Distant sobs echoed in my ears, and I realized with sudden clarity it was me making those horrid gasping sounds.

The wail of sirens filtered through my disorientation along with my sister's voice saying my name over and over again.

I was so tired. Too tired to fight anymore.

Cold water splashed on my face, bringing me sputtering back to reality.

What the hell?

My feet were off the ground, my back pressed flat against the brick wall, held there by thick vines that wrapped around my limbs and torso. The vines had come from a potted plant near the map store.

Bryn stood in front of me, holding an empty bucket and staring up at me with tears and worry.

A crowd had gathered, a group of tourists snapping a few pictures. Others were drawn to the gruesome sight of Auggie's lifeless body surrounded by broken and spilled vials, their liquid framing him in a macabre rainbow of color and blood; and the three jinn bodies, one frozen from the nitro blast and two beaten to death. Blood was everywhere. Mine and theirs. Red and black.

Bryn's chest rose and fell quickly. Her healthy skin had turned ashen. The smile that always lurked in her eyes was gone. "Charlie," she urged again, this time with a catch in her voice.

My mouth was too swollen to talk, but I didn't have to ask. I knew Bryn had done this, had stopped me. I let my head fall back against the brick and pain shot through my skull. Bryn closed her eyes and mumbled. The vines withdrew, setting me gently on my feet. I crumpled to the sidewalk, and she was there, holding me, getting blood all over her pretty yellow sundress. She smoothed the damp hair from my face and talked to me in a soft, soothing voice, rocking me back and forth, her cheek pressed against my temple. The scent of herbs and spices clung to her clothes, skin, and hair. It was a good smell, the kind that eased my confusion.

She was crying, saying she couldn't lose me, not again, and not after Connor.

Our brother. My twin.

A senseless act of violence when we were teens, and he was gone.

He was the reason I went into law enforcement, to protect my family, to keep assholes and killers off the streets of my hometown. Bryn had been fourteen when Connor's car was hijacked with him inside. Two black crafters jacked up on meth had held a gun to his head and made him drive out to Piedmont Park, get out of the car, and beg for his life on his hands and knees. They taped it with a handheld recorder. And then they executed him, took his car, and made it all the way to Vegas, where they bragged to the wrong person about what they'd done.

I'd felt it the moment Connor died. The feeling has never left me.

Bryn's rambling continued, but I didn't hear her words, just the sound of her aching, choked voice. Thinking of Connor cleansed the mud from my brain and hardened my soul. He had made me strong, and I wasn't about to start crumbling now.

I lifted my head and stood with Bryn's help just as police and paramedics arrived.

"Charlie," she whispered. "You're healing."

"What?"

She stared at me oddly. I could barely see her through the swollen skin around my eyes. "The cuts on your face, they're healing."

I touched the split lip, the movement of my arm painful. Everything hurt. *Breathing* hurt. "Are you doing it?" I struggled to ask.

"No, it's not me. It's you."

"It's not me." No, it couldn't have been me. I didn't have powers like Bryn. And I was okay with that. I had my own kind of magic. It was called a Nitro-gun, a 9mm SIG Sauer, and a Hefty (a Taser-like High Frequency Tag capable of disabling or destroying the sound-sensitive Elysians). That was all the conjuring I needed.

Hank raced down the sidewalk, his face contorted with fear. He skidded to a stop beside us, his breath coming out fast and heavy. Hard, dark sapphire orbs replaced the vibrant blue sparkle of his eyes; they had changed as they always did with any kind of heightened emotion. There was only one other time I'd seen him this distraught. Eight months ago. When I was dying. When he hovered over me in the dark alley between Mercy and Solomon Streets, willing me to live, calling for backup over and over again until his voice broke and praying to a God he had never had much faith in, making every promise in the book if only I'd survive.

"Damn it, Charlie. Are you okay? Did the medics check you out? God, you're a mess."

"I'm fine."

He briefly examined the chaos of the scene. His jaw started to twitch. Never a good sign. He propped both hands on his hips, his voice clipped and tight when he spoke. "You did this?"

Feeling stronger, I picked up my firearm slowly, ignoring the pain, and slid it into the holster under my left arm. "I got one round off," I said, not meeting his intense gaze. "The other two, guess I just got lucky." I warned Bryn with my look to be quiet. "They may look strong, but they don't know how to fight dirty." It was lame, I knew, but what else could I say? That a weird surge of strength had possessed me and allowed me to kill two jinn with my bare hands? Yeah, right. Even I didn't believe it. There had to be some other explanation.

Hank dragged his fingers through his hair, looking from the bodies to me and then back again. "You had better hope none of these guys were from the local jinn tribe . . ."

I couldn't entertain the thought of jinn retribution. Not right now. Instead, I walked away, passing the paramedics as they placed the bodies in bags, to the officer on the scene to give him my statement.

About a half hour later, Hank and Bryn walked, or rather stalked, me to my car.

"I can't believe you came down here alone," Hank muttered, finally breaking the silence.

I'd seen it coming. "I come down here *alone* all the time. So do you."

"Yeah, well, you're supposed to wait for your partner. I'd think you'd have learned your lesson by now."

Oh, hell no. He wasn't about to make me feel guilty about this. I grabbed his arm, standing toe-to-toe with him. "I *did* learn my lesson, Hank. I was already down here getting Bryn to babysit. And you and I both talk to Auggie, to get the scoop, whenever we're here. Alone or not. I didn't attack the jinn or go after them. *They* jumped *me*. So get the hell off my back."

Enough of this crap. I left them both standing in the plaza, went to my car, and then peeled away from the curb.

3

My entire body shook like a mini-earthquake as I drove to Station One. Aftershock. I managed to find a parking space in the back, near the dumpster where no one would see my car. Adrenaline still coursed through my veins, making me feel like some kind of junkie who needed a fix.

What did you do, Charlie? The question kept repeating over and over as I rummaged through the glove box for napkins, found a handful, and then began scrubbing the blood from my face, neck, and hands. The better question to ask myself was: *how* did you?

I yanked down the mirror, stunned by the red-and-black blood-streaked face staring back at me. I didn't recognize this person—gaunt, wide-eyed, and scared shitless. Everyone said Bryn and I bore a close resemblance, though my hair was more on the brown side than auburn, but looking in the mirror I saw no resemblance to anyone human at all.

I could be an extra from *Night of the Living Dead*.

The scent of blood, iron, and tar filled the car, and as soon as I noticed, my stomach curdled and a cold sweat broke through my achy skin. Unable to hold it in, I opened the car door and puked on the concrete. Twice.

My lungs couldn't fill fast enough with air and it took several seconds for my breathing to return to normal. Once it did, I grabbed the keys, ignored the shaky legs, and hurried into the back of the brick building, heading up the back stairs to the showers.

I didn't allow myself to think or feel the hollow ache in my stomach, just went straight to my locker, undressed, grabbed my toiletries, and stepped into the shower.

Hot water stung my skin, almost too hot, but it had to be that way. I *needed* to be clean. Bloody water and thick suds pooled like pink cotton candy at my feet, sliding off my hair and skin as I scrubbed and shampooed until, finally, the water ran clear.

It had all gone so wrong. And Auggie. Poor, harmless Auggie was dead, and I should've been dead, too.

Again.

Ever since that night eight months ago, I'd hardly gotten into an altercation of any kind while on the job. Sure, we had runners, ducked a few punches, and exchanged fire a few times, but nothing like this. I had told myself the last time, when I woke in the hospital alive and saw Emma's pale face: I'd never take another chance. Even if it meant letting a crook go.

So why had I *wanted* to fight? I'd purposefully invited an ass-kicking. I could have run, just as Auggie urged me to, yet I hadn't.

Lately, I didn't know who the hell I was anymore.

Screw this. I should just retire to a desk job. It was the right thing to do and the only option if I wanted to raise my child and be a good mom. She needed me to be there for her. She needed that kind of stability in her life. Not someone who might never come back from her shift.

My palms flattened on the shower wall. I let my head fall low between my shoulder blades. My throat closed, and my chest hurt, but it was the right decision. It had to be.

After I stepped out of the shower and dried off, I inspected my naked body in the long mirror. Bryn had been right. Somehow, I'd healed. I closed my eyes tightly and shook the cobwebs from my mind. When I opened them again, nothing had changed. It was almost too much for one day. A sharp laugh escaped me, sounding awfully demented in the quiet of the locker room.

"There has to be some explanation," I whispered, studying my body. My swollen eyes had healed, though dark circles lingered beneath. My split lip was almost gone. A few ugly bruises colored my left rib cage and collarbone, and there was a faint yellow bruise on my jaw. Otherwise, I looked my normal self: tall, lanky, and fit.

My hand rubbed my flat stomach. It still amazed me that I'd grown a child in that small space—and that my boobs had skyrocketed from a 36B to a 40C. Will, my ex, had loved every second of that. The memory made me smile.

We all looked alike: me, Bryn, and Emma. The same big, light-brown irises flecked with gold and copper, the same high cheekbones and determined chins, the same lips—you could pick out a Madigan anywhere by our lips. They were full, more puckered than wide. Well, that's what I thought when I'd watch Emma sleep. We each had a right-sided dimple—except Bryn; she had a matching pair—and straight noses, with just the faintest tilt.

I saw my sister and my daughter in the face that stared back at me, a face that nodded with a single-minded purpose.

I dressed quickly in clean street clothes: jeans, boots, and a deep red V-neck T. Then I hooked my badge onto my belt loop, replaced my shoulder holster and firearms, dried my hair with one of the wall-attached dryers, and then twisted it up with a clip. The tension eased out of me as I regarded my image in the long over-the-sink mirror. Minus the mascara and clear lip gloss I usually wore to work, I looked like the same old Charlie. Hair up. Small diamond studs in my ears. And my T-shirt of choice. The cotton V-neck. I slipped Bryn's charm over my head, finding comfort in the weight and warmth of the disk as it settled between my breasts.

Feeling a little better at seeing the usual me, I shoved my soiled clothes into a bag, making sure to pull out the matches Auggie had slid into my palm before he died, and then made my way down to the evidence room to turn in the gun I'd used on the first jinn to attack me, as well as the bloody clothes. The matches I tucked safely into the back pocket of my jeans.

As I rounded the corner, a couple spilled into the hallway from the chief's office. Crap. I was already pivoting on my heels when a voice called out:

"Charlie! Oh, thank God."

The last thing I needed was to go through the wringer with the Motts, but since they knew me from all the times Amanda had babysat and stayed at the house, I had no choice but to turn around with a fake smile plastered on my face.

Marti, Amanda's mom, rushed toward me. "We just came from the hospital. The doctors can't tell us anything. We heard you were at the school. Please tell us our baby is going to be okay."

Cold and bony, her hands gripped both of mine with a strength that surprised me considering how thin and fragile she appeared in her black slacks, light-weight pink sweater set, and expensive blonde bob. Gently, I removed her manicured claws and used the most calming tone I could muster. "We're doing everything we can to figure out what happened, Marti. And how to fix it."

A snort broke out behind her. "Hanging out at the station doesn't seem like—"

"Cass," Marti warned her husband with a light hand on his arm even as she continued to smile at me.

Cassius Mott was the younger brother of celebrated research scientist Titus Mott. And he was the biggest good-for-nothing I'd ever known. Besides being a first-rate asshole, he squandered his share of the Mott fortune day after day on drugs, fast cars, gambling, partying, and probably a whole slew of other illegal activities. He was tall, dark-haired, and probably good-looking if one could get past the attitude. Which I couldn't.

"Have you found any leads?" Marti asked gently, always softening the crassness of her husband. "No one can tell us anything. If there's a cure, if she'll wake up . . ."

I thought of the matches Auggie gave me. "Nothing solid, but we're doing our best. I wouldn't settle for anything less." Three years ago we'd met at Hope Ridge. She needed help with carpooling, and I needed a babysitter in the afternoons for Em. It had worked out perfectly. "Look, I care about Amanda, too. She's been a great big sister to Emma and a big help to me. I'm going to do everything I can to figure this out."

"I know you will."

Cass rolled his eyes, looking as though he'd rather be anywhere but here, finding out about his kid. Asshole. "I don't know why my brother even bothers with you people. Come on, Marti." He marched away, straightening the collar on his salmon-colored golf shirt, Marti giving me a hopeless look and then trailing in his wake. I wanted to run to her and shake some sense into her, but after three years of subtly placed comments over my kitchen table, I knew she wouldn't listen. Not until she reached a breaking point. If she even had one.

Chief Abernathy stepped into the hallway and followed my gaze to the retreating figures with a hard set to his square jaw. He must've heard the exchange in the hallway, and he hadn't liked it one bit.

A bear of a man, the chief had street-tough senses and a boxer's intimidating face. His hands were as big as oven mitts and solid as a rock, just like the rest of him. "That guy rubs everybody the wrong way," he commented, in a deep voice reminiscent of Barry White.

"Yeah."

"But," he said, "his brother donates a shitload to this department."

"Is that a warning to be nice?" I finally looked at him as the Motts disappeared around the corner.

"It is what it is, Madigan. We make nice with the folks who provide us with state-of-the-art weapons and funding. So, you wanna tell me what happened in Underground?"

"Just defending myself. They seemed to have a grudge against ITF."

He chuckled. "Who doesn't? Listen, the doc is looking for you."

"But—" I had to talk to him about a transfer.

"No buts, Madigan. You've missed the last two psych evaluations. Make sure you stop by her office on the way out." He turned back to his office, but paused and gave me the infamous eye—a piercing black stare no one could take for more than a few seconds. "And I'm not asking."

I inhaled deeply. The last thing I wanted was to be analyzed by some Ph.D. who didn't know the first thing about tracking a crook, facing a ghoul with a bad attitude, or dodging a bullet. Emma would be home from school soon, and I didn't have time for this. Screw the doc.

As I started down the hall, the chief stuck his head out of his office, holding a cell phone a few inches away from his ear. "I mean it, Madigan. Go see her."

Great.

I did a one-eighty and headed back the other way with a sharp glare at the chief, but he'd already shut his office door.

Fine. But I was going to make this as quick as possible.

Doctor Berkowitz, or Doctor Berk, as we called her, peeked over the upper rim of her stylish horn-rimmed glasses as I entered the Loony Room . . . er, office.

"Officer Madigan, please have a seat." She set aside the papers on her desk, folded her delicate hands on the polished surface, and waited for me to comply.

The brown leather chair begged me to sink down into its comfy cushions and lay open all my deepest and darkest fears. I perched on the edge, not falling for tricks. My hands fell limp in my lap, and I had to concentrate damn hard to keep them relaxed and to keep my pulse normal. "No offense, but I don't have a lot of time."

I wasn't trying to be a bitch, really. I actually liked Katherine. Despite her soft appearance, she was as tough as nails. Maybe in another life we would've been friends, but the fact that she wanted to probe my mind and my past kept her eternally at arm's length.

Leaning back in her chair, she studied me for a long moment. I couldn't look her in the eyes, so I chose a spot over her left shoulder. Okay, so I had somewhat of a phobia when it came to therapists. At least I wasn't in denial about it.

"I'll take whatever time you've got, Detective. Now, let's see," she began, rummaging through the files on her desk, pulling mine out to open it.

You should pick up some milk on the way home, I thought.

"Last time you came to see me, you still struggled with exhaustion from the nightmares. How's that been going?"

Ooh, and maybe some chocolate chip cookie dough ice cream. Oh, my God. Good stuff.

"Detective?"

"Oh, um, better. It's been better." God, this was

like being on trial. "Still have them, but they're not as bad or as frequent." *What else are you forgetting? Laundry detergent. Deodorant. Maybe you should get a new kind this time. The Fresh Rain scent is getting old.*

"That's good. And how are you doing with the meditation I recommended?"

"Fine." *Ooh, or maybe that new pear one. Pear Seduction. No, that's not it. Pear . . . something.*

She frowned at me. "Did you try it at all?"

I didn't answer, just gave her an apologetic smile. *Pear Seduction? Jeez. How lame is that? Man, you really need to get laid.*

Katherine removed her glasses and leaned forward. "Listen, Charlie, it's important to take care of yourself here."

Pear Abundance . . .

"You still have a long way to go if you want to totally recover from your death experience. You've suppressed so much of how it made you feel."

Pear Medley . . .

"You need to let it out, embrace your thoughts, the past, and the things you remember about that time."

Pear Showers . . .

"You've come out of this a different person, and change is okay. It's the events in our lives that shape who we are. Don't fight it."

Pear Whispers! Yes! I knew I'd get it.

She paused and leaned back again, rolling her pencil through her fingers. "I think the nightmares are because you're suppressing the memories of being dead, of what you experienced, the feeling you had during this time. You'll have to deal with it sooner or later, or it's going to break you."

"Doctor Berk," I said, tiredly and with a sudden urge for pears. "I really do appreciate what you're trying to do here, but me dying was just that. I died. I was brought back. It's over. End of story. I don't remember anything, and honestly, I don't want to. The only thing that matters is that I woke up, and"—I stood—"I really need to get home and take care of my kid. See you around."

After stopping off at the store, I drove home, put the groceries away, kicked off my shoes and socks, and then waited for Emma on the front porch swing with a cereal bowl full of chocolate chip cookie dough ice cream. After the day I'd had, I deserved a little comfort food. I put Doctor Berk completely out of my mind and started obsessing again about my decision to transfer to a desk job.

I just sat there, slowly swinging and spooning ice cream into my mouth. The cold felt good on the small cuts that remained on the inside of my lip and cheek, and it helped with the stiffness in my mouth and jaw. The cookie dough bits didn't hurt, either.

Truth was, I was nervous. Nervous to tell Emma of the decision I'd made and what she'd think about it.

Part of me felt like I was letting my brother down

and even letting Emma down by giving up my part in keeping our city safe, but another part of me felt sure I was making the right move, and, more importantly, that Emma would appreciate not having to worry about me and all the dangers that came with my job.

A brand-new black-and-tan Ford F-250 pickup slowed as it approached the house. It parked directly across the narrow neighborhood street from my driveway. There were no houses across the street, just a sidewalk and then the green grass of a large baseball field, a walking path, and soccer fields. Sometimes at dawn, when the nightmares would wake me, I'd make some decaf and sit on the porch swing, watching the mist hover above the fields, and try to clear my mind.

I'd never seen this vehicle in the neighborhood before. The ignition shut off and the door popped open. The spoon paused in my mouth, and I stopped the swing with my toe.

It was Will. My ex.

Before I could drum up something sarcastic to think concerning the new truck, old feelings and memories swept through me and made my stomach flip like some lovesick teen. God, he looked good—another spoonful of ice cream made it to my mouth—really, really good.

Will was six-three, athletic, and had a smile that could melt snow. From his working outside, the sun had lightened his brown hair and streaked it golden in places. He kept it short, complementing the faint stubble that grew along a strong jaw, stubborn chin, and surprisingly soft lips.

He must've been out at a job site because there was dirt on his khakis and light blue button-down shirt. The two top buttons were undone, and the sleeves were rolled to just below his elbows. Jesus, I loved when he did that. It was like the cherry on a man-sundae to see his tanned, muscled forearms and his strong hands.

He shut the door and walked up the driveway.

Heart thumping wildly, I darted into the house, ran to the sink, set the bowl down, and then hurried to the front door, opening it before he could knock and trying to not seem out of breath. For a brief second, a flash of surprise went through his stormy gray-blue eyes. The sun had begun its descent over the park, a beam bathing me in a wash of heat.

Will's blunt gaze swept over me as I blocked the doorway, my blood pressure rising. He let his eyes linger on the parts of me he'd always loved, and I wanted to shrink away because my nipples chose that moment to turn as hard as glass beads. *Thanks a lot, ladies.* With an evil eye, I crossed my arms over my chest and stood aside.

"Charlie," he said in a deep Southern drawl, bestowing a wonderful blend of faded cologne and masculine skin on my sense of smell as he passed by.

I padded behind him into the kitchen. "What are you doing here?"

He glanced around the space, checking on things,

making sure everything was in order; that nothing needed to be fixed. Then he turned to me, leaning his hip on the edge of the granite countertop and crossing his arms over his chest. I could almost hear the sounds of a construction site, and it gave me a sudden flash of Will standing in front of a two-by-four frame of a new house with blueprints spread across the hood of his truck.

Now he was a successful builder and architect and had just started his own firm. Just like he'd always dreamed. And he must be doing pretty well if the new truck was any indication. My mistrust came to the surface. Had he earned the truck and the success on his own merits . . . or was he dabbling in black crafting again?

"I can't come by just to check on you?"

I swallowed, trying to temper the loud buzz of awareness gripping me. "You never come by to 'check on me.' " I walked past him to the fridge to get two bottled waters, handing him one and then taking a stance on the other side of the kitchen table. His Adam's apple slid up and down along his throat with every swallow. He had such a nice throat.

Snap out of it, Charlie!

After the day I'd had, I was exhausted, beaten, and at my weakest. And I knew it. Damn Will and his timing. Irritated, I asked, "So, where'd you get the truck?"

His lips thinned, and he let out a tired exhale. "How many times do I have to say it, Charlie? I haven't practiced since that night."

That night was eight months ago when he'd boasted to a Master Crafter that no one could use coercion on him—that he'd become too skilled and strong. The stakes: his marriage oath.

Guess who lost?

She had him naked and in bed in under two minutes.

He came clean the next morning. He'd called it black crafting's version of rape. I called it cheating and lying and a damn good reason to divorce.

"Ever hear of letting go?" He faked a lightbulb moment. "Oh, no, wait. Then you'd actually have to forgive me. God forbid." He tossed his head back and swallowed about half the bottle. "It's not my fault you went and beat the shit out of her. And it's not my fault she tried to have you killed for it." Immediately, the mistake of his words spawned a weighty silence that broke only when he scrubbed a hand down his face and sighed.

Tried? I blinked at him and forced my jaw not to drop. I did go and confront her, but she threw the first punch; I just finished things. And she didn't just *try* to have me killed, she succeeded. The ghoul I'd chased down the back alley in Underground eight months ago had been working for her, and he'd completed his job with all the finesse of a brutal killer. I died that night because, in a roundabout way, of Will's addiction to black crafting. The man I loved. The man I trusted.

I ignored the comment. "So again: What are you doing here?"

He rubbed the inside corners of his eyes and then pinched the bridge of his nose, letting out a loud sigh. My hard outer shell cracked just a little. He seemed beat.

"Look, Charlie . . ." He fidgeted with the water bottle, looking down as though he was nervous.

Will, nervous? I studied him more closely. He opened his mouth, got out one syllable, and then closed it. Instantly, alarm bells sounded in my head.

He cleared his throat. "I heard about the Mott case. Does Emma know?"

There was no doubt in my mind he'd changed the subject. Will had something that he didn't know how to say, and the only thing that could make him this nervous was . . . a disturbing sense of numbness dropped into my gut. "Oh, my God, are you getting remarried?"

Awkward silence filled the room. Will blinked, floundering for a second to make sense of my left-field outburst. Heat stung my cheeks. Great. My shoulders hunched, and all I wanted was to slide underneath the table and disappear. Will had practiced black crafting right under my nose for years because, when it came right down to it, he was insecure. And now here I was waving my insecurities around like a giant Yellow Jackets flag at a Georgia Tech basketball game.

His entire body had stilled. All of his focus zoned straight in on my sudden revelation. "*What* did you just say?"

"Never mind." I rubbed my face.

"Why would you think I'm getting married?"

I peeked at him over the tips of my fingers. "Let's just drop it, okay?"

"Nuh-uh. You don't get off that easy." He pushed off the counter and then pulled out the chair across from me, turning it around to sit and rest his arms across the back. "What made you say that?"

"I don't know." I shrugged. "You just seemed like you had something to say, something that bothered you. I thought . . ."

The bastard had the nerve to grin the smile that could melt snow. In fact, his utter pleasure at my expense lit up his entire face. "Charlie, I'm not engaged. I don't have a girlfriend. I've seen a few women here and there, but nothing serious."

"Great. Wonderful. Good for you," I muttered, rolling my eyes. Conversing with my ex was obviously a bad idea. My emotions were going haywire, and I couldn't seem to think straight. It was perfectly normal to miss him. I mean, we were together for twelve years. Totally normal to miss being close, to miss wanting that kind of connection. "Emma should be home soon."

"Charlie." His voice came out low and serious. I didn't want to look at him, but he waited until I finally lifted my gaze to his. He stared at me from across the table for a long moment, his expression wide open and honest as hell. "I still love you, you know."

The world came to a screeching halt.

I shot up from the table. All the old hurts came rushing back, constricting my chest so that breathing took more effort than it should. "God*dammit*, Will. You can't say things like that."

He stood. "Why not? It's true. I've never stopped, not even when——"

I held up my hand, not wanting to hear or think about the night he'd risked our marriage out of pure male pride and a gigantic helping of stupidity.

"Fine." He grabbed my arm, making me face him. "But I know what I did, Charlie. And one day you'll see beyond all this pain I caused you. And as much as you try to deny it, you know, in my heart, I never wanted to cheat. You know I believed so much in us, in our promise, that I'd pit it against——"

"You never should have! That's the whole point! You don't risk something so important. You don't bet on our vows. And you sure as shit don't lie and hide what you're doing!" I jerked my arm away from him. "Especially when it's wrong. Black crafting is *wrong*, Will, no matter what spin you put on it. And you hid it, lied to me, for years. You knew how I felt about it, that those guys who killed my brother were black crafters. I even *died* because of it! You could have built up the business all on your own. You had it in you. You didn't need to resort to crafting."

"I tried for years! You think it was easy being straight out of high school with a family to support and no college education? I started crafting to help us, to give us an edge. Don't you think I——" He stopped himself, his lips snapping shut and the muscle in his jaw flexing.

His hand closed around my arm again. "I know what I lost, believe me, I do. I know it every second of every goddamn day, and I'm tired of being punished. I'm tired of being without you and Em." He grabbed my other arm. His palms felt so rough and warm on my skin. He took a breath and searched my face. We were so close our stomachs touched. "I made a horrible mistake, but I'm clean now. I've been clean since that night. My addiction ruined everything, I know, and you had every right to divorce that guy. But that's not who I am anymore, Charlie."

His hand cupped my cheek. His plea rang in my head and squeezed my heart. Despite everything, I still had deep feelings for him, and, God, how I missed him. I swallowed, willing myself not to cry, to show weakness.

"Charlie." He touched his forehead to mine, his voice dropping to a heartbroken whisper. "God, I miss you." He let out a shaky breath, touched his nose to mine, and then tilted his head slightly to kiss me.

The hurt vanished with the press of his warm lips against mine, the intimate touch sending a confetti-like explosion to the pit of my stomach. My heart pounded in my ears, my legs weakened. "Will," I whispered against his lips, meaning to regretfully pull away, but the moment I opened my mouth, his tongue brushed my bottom lip. I moaned, parting my lips to allow him in.

Dear God, the man could kiss.

That first touch of tongue on tongue ignited a desperate need to *feel* again just for a moment. His tongue slid against mine, unhurried and confident. He walked me back against the wall, pressing his erection into my hip bone and his thigh between my legs. Need blossomed from that point and sped like lightning throughout my body, making me lose hold on reality. All I wanted was Will. On me. In me. As close to me as he could get. The familiarity of his smell, his touch, his taste. Overwhelmed, I pulled away from him to catch my breath. His hand was on my breast.

"My pants," I blurted out, not caring anymore. Not caring that my voice shook or my hands trembled. It had been so long. And Will knew every button to push, knew just how I liked it. "Get them off."

We had a good ten minutes before the bus arrived. Plenty of time. I managed to get the zipper halfway down before he took over and pulled them over my knees, and then distraction drove his hand straight to my panties. My breath caught with anticipation. His hand cupped me, pressing, making me squirm. "Will." He kissed me again, this time hungry and deep.

Then, suddenly, he was gone and the air rushed between us, cooling my scorched skin. I opened my heavy eyelids and blinked, feeling woozy and unbalanced. He stood back from me, dragging shaky fingers through his hair and letting out a disturbed huff.

"Charlie . . ." He paused, struggling with the words. "Do you still love me?"

My heart continued pounding, and I still felt his hands and mouth everywhere. I shook my head, trying to clear the sex-induced fog from my brain.

When I didn't answer, he stepped back more, looking confused, as though I should have fallen down at his feet and confessed my undying adulation. "No. I don't want you like this," he said, "not like this."

Understanding dawned just before the humiliation took over. Bitter cold swept through me, extinguishing any stubborn flames. "Like what, Will? I'm standing here with my pants down around my ankles and you're just going to walk away because I'm not going to say I love you?" Still trembling, I jerked my pants over my hips, feeling the pressure of tears rise to my eyes. "Go to hell."

4

It took all my effort *not* to slam my fist into Will's face. I stayed against the wall, fingers flexing, trying to regain some control and hurting more than I had in months. I was an idiot.

Will braced his hand on the opposite wall, letting his head fall low, his rugged profile grim. He shook his head and stared at me, so full of regret. Whatever was going on in his head was far more complicated than I'd thought.

I hated that his scent evoked so much history between us. We'd spent our young adulthood together, built a life together. Two nineteen-year-olds facing the world. As a team. It hurt just to look at him. In the last six months, he'd succeeded brilliantly in his career, but was it on his own merits? He claimed to have quit practicing after that night. Friends, family, everyone believed him. And I guess I did, too, or else I'd never allow Emma to spend time with him. I also knew that he never meant for things to get so out of hand, but there was a mountain of emotional obstacles for us to overcome. He wanted too much, too fast.

I had to learn to trust him again. And right now, that seemed impossible.

With a determined gaze, he moved toward me, not stopping until his mouth was on mine. I sucked in a small, surprised gasp, pulling his warm breath inside me without meaning to. He kissed me hard and meaningfully. No tongue, but with so much emotion that tears welled in my eyes. I knew he loved me, and his sorrow and regret tore me in half.

The squeal of bus brakes broke us apart.

Grateful for the reprieve, I sidestepped my ex-husband, straightened my shirt, and redid my hair as Will went to the sink and splashed water onto his face. He was just as shaken as I was.

The entire visit had rattled me to the bone. Emma and I had been doing just fine on our own. We'd settled into a comfortable routine in the last few months, had pushed past the initial hurt of divorce and were moving forward. *Damn him!*

He dried off and then finished the bottle of water as Emma came through the door.

"Daddy!"

Like magic, the dark aura of emotion surrounding him lifted and a wide, genuine grin split his handsome face. For a moment, it was as if they were the only two people in the world.

"Hey, you. How's my girl?" He set her on the counter.

"Fine." Her brown eyes grew larger and more serious. "Amanda is in the hospital." Her confident gaze flicked to me. "But Mom's going to help her."

Tall order, Charlie. I plastered a mom-smile on my face, ignoring the concern that her trust and matter-of-factness stirred in my gut. She believed in me. And there was nothing worse than letting your kid down. Nothing. "Why don't you go wash your hands and put your things in your room?"

She hopped off the counter, the soles of her Mary Janes thudding on the tile floor. "Am I going with Dad tonight?"

Will glanced from Em to me, and I could see he was up for it. I shook my head. "No, Aunt Bryn wants to have a sleepover."

"Why don't I take her now," Will said, "and then I'll drive her over to Bryn's after dinner."

I hesitated, suddenly not wanting to be left alone after the day I'd had. But Emma loved her father so much. I couldn't say no. "All right, but make sure she does her homework."

"I'm taking my DS and my iPod!" Emma yelled, running from the room and pounding up the steps. I followed at a more sedate pace, picking up the backpack she'd let fall on the kitchen floor. Will stopped me with a hand on my arm. "You sure it's okay?"

"Yeah, it's fine." But I didn't *feel* fine; I felt torn apart and downright sluggish as I followed my daughter up the stairs.

I packed Em's clothes while she washed up. When she came into her bedroom, I patted the bed. "Hey, kid, I want to ask you something."

The mattress dipped with her weight. Then she noticed the backpack and frowned. *"Mom."* I sighed as she unzipped the bag and pulled out all of the clothes I'd just packed. "I can pack myself. And I hate these underwear *and* these socks." She went to her dresser and rooted through drawers, shoving clothing into her backpack without folding. "So, what's going on?" she asked over her shoulder, turning her attention to the small stack of DS games on her desk.

Emma and I had a pact. We always consulted each other before any major decisions were made. It was my way of making sure she felt included. "So . . . how would you feel if I took a desk job at the station instead of working out in the city?"

She turned, eyeballing me like I'd sprouted a shiitake mushroom on the tip of my nose. Then she walked over and placed her soft palm on my cheeks and forehead, testing for signs of illness.

"Ha, ha. Very funny."

She stepped back and put a hand on her hip. "Okay," she said slowly, "and *why* would you want to quit your job?"

I returned her attitude-ridden look. It wasn't like I was saying I wanted to move to Antarctica. "Because it would be safer that way, and I don't want you to worry about me."

"Mom. If you do that, who's gonna help Amanda?"

I blinked. My mouth opened but nothing came out. I'd promised to help Amanda, and I'd also promised myself I'd be a better mom and take a safer job. Two things that couldn't exactly be accomplished at once. I rubbed my hands down my face and let out a deep breath.

"You can't quit now. Amanda needs you." Em straightened, bent one knee, and cocked her hip, giving me her best superhero pose—hands on hips, chin lifted, and eyes looking off into the distance. "Atlanta *needs* you. The very world itself might, one day, *need* you."

Despite myself, I laughed. She giggled, blew a wild strand of hair from her eye, and then zipped the bag. When she turned to me, slinging the bag over her shoulder, she shrugged, pleased with her summation and logic. "Plus, Hank would never forgive you if you quit." She waited by the door.

I stood, thrown by her reaction. I'd underestimated her, which was an easy thing to do when you didn't want your kid to grow up. "Maybe after Amanda's case then," I said, more to myself.

"Mom"—she snapped the air a few times, feigning a teenager look and tone—"snap out of it."

"Yeah, I'm coming," I muttered, following her bobbing form and swinging ponytail down the stairs, and wondering why her reaction hurt. *Because she's growing up*. What did I expect, her to jump in my arms and cry grateful tears?

I padded barefoot through the kitchen, down the porch steps, and over the front yard, hurrying to catch up with her before she made it across the street. At the edge of the grass, I caught her around the waist. She squealed in fake protest as I laid several kisses on her cheek and neck. She might pretend to be too old for hugs and kisses, but she loved them just as much as I loved giving them. "Have fun," I said close to her ear and then let her go. Laughing, she hurried around to the passenger side door.

Will slid into the truck and shut the door, leaning out of the open window. "We'll talk later."

I really wanted to respond with a "whatever," but I nodded, reluctant to admit the feelings I still had for him.

His only intentional crime had been hiding his addiction to black crafting. All the other stuff had been out his control at that point. The real Will never would have made that bet, or cheated on me. And I knew he wasn't crafting these days. Just like drug abuse or alcoholism, once one knew the symptoms and signs, it was easy to spot a black crafting addict. It left a weak scent of soot on them, like charred pieces left for years in an old, damp fireplace, and it left a trace of smut, of darkness, on a person. It surrounded them like an aura, but it was so faint it was hard to detect if you weren't looking for it.

I stepped onto the front lawn, watching them drive

down the street until the truck disappeared around the corner. Exhaustion fell over me like a heavy down comforter. It was only late afternoon and already my body wanted to shut down. It had been one hell of a day so far. Maybe with Em gone, I could actually get in a good nap before heading back to Underground later with Hank.

I made my way back inside the house and up the stairs.

In my bedroom, I stripped off my clothes and could smell Will everywhere, all over me. It felt good, which surprised me. I thought I'd feel something more along the lines of sadness and grief for what we'd lost, but I only felt comforted by the remnants of his presence.

Leaving on my underwear, I slipped under the covers, pulling them all around me, and snuggled down deep in the cool sheets.

Yeah, this was definitely what I needed.

The hospital morgue.

Two women were there. One on the cold, narrow table. And the other, a thought or conscience without form, hovering above, looking down at the sight with confusion and mild curiosity. That figure on the table was revolting. Gray, bruised, and beaten. Skull cracked open. Dead.

She, the one above, tried to remember by what. Was it a baseball bat? A crowbar? An iron staff?

The woman on the table was naked, covered to her arm-pits with a white sheet. She was a complete mess, but she hadn't always been that way . . . She'd been pretty once. Had liked the shape of her breasts and her long legs. Liked the way her wavy mahogany hair brushed her lower back when she was naked. She liked the dimple when she smiled and the pouty lips that always drew men's eyes. She'd been happy once.

Something tugged hard on the consciousness floating above the body, pulling her toward the ceiling. A light was there. But it was far, far away and before it swam shadows, darting in and out of the murkiness. She wondered if she could dodge the shadows without trial and pass into that soft, beckoning light.

No, no, she couldn't go. Not yet.

She couldn't remember why, but knew there was a reason, a monumental reason, why she couldn't go.

Still, the light tugged.

Others came into the room. She could see their shapes but not their features; only the body on the table remained vivid and clear to her. They spoke, and it sounded as though the voices were underwater. She pulled away from the ceiling to hover closer.

"Can she be saved? She's been gone for some time," the tall figure said. He wore black. Perhaps it was hair, but it could've been a hood. She couldn't tell. His voice, though muffled, was deep and powerful.

He was somebody. *Somehow she knew this.*

"If she can't, then this won't hurt her," the other said. He was swathed in white. Perhaps it was a lab coat or a cloak, but

he had no hood. His hair was brown, and he was tall, just not as tall as the other. "But if she can," he said, "then all our work will be worth it."

He pulled the white sheet to her waist, revealing her breasts, her startling injuries, and the bruises on her chest where they'd performed CPR. He turned her wrist, revealing the soft part of her arm. Then he stuck a needle into her vein.

The dark one smoothed her hair from her forehead, hair that was matted with blood. He whispered to her.

The light from behind pulled stronger. The shadows dipped and flew closer, crying out in screeching misery, though the volume was dulled by an unseen barrier.

The dark one looked up at the ceiling abruptly as though he sensed something there, but after a moment he turned his attention back to the woman.

The consciousness was caught suddenly in a tug of war; the light pulling her upward and the dead woman on the table pulling her down. Panicked, she fought against both.

"Now, we wait," the white one said.

Amid the panic, she still knew she had to go back, had that reason, that thing just on the edge of her memory. And she was afraid of the shadows, afraid they'd get her before she could make it to the light. So she dove toward the body, away from the screams and cries of the shadows and away from the peace of the light.

And before she lost the sense of being separated, she realized as she melded with her body, that she'd just dove straight into hell.

She screamed inside.

Fire. Dear God, she was on fire!

The rush was so loud and hot, her eardrums felt as though they bled lava. And then the images started, bursting through her damaged, swollen mind. So much pain. Everywhere. She wanted to die, and she would have if she hadn't already. Death. Murder. Sex. Blood, so much blood. Dark figures. Torture. Pain. And power. Dark power. It hurt. Hurt because there was light, too, and it battled inside her, tearing her apart, fighting for domination. Good things. Good deeds. Love. Growth. Seeds sprouting through green grass, unfurling and growing into sturdy, ancient trees. Crows cawing endlessly. The drip of water. It was too much, too many images, too quickly. She screamed again.

And then she was outside in a circular meadow, naked under a full moon. Surrounded. On her knees. And the man in black and the man in white took turns slicing away small pieces of her flesh, like children who dole out portions.

This piece is mine, that piece is yours. One for me, one for you.

I shot up into a sitting position on the bed, my heart thumping hard and fast against my rib cage. My fists clenched the sheet, and my eyes were wide open, but unfocused. My lungs burned as adrenaline pumped through my system, tasting like dry iron on my tongue.

Breathe, Charlie. No big deal. Just breathe.

Repeating the mantra over and over, I felt the

adrenaline finally slow, allowing me to draw in long drafts of air until my lungs didn't hurt so much.

Chills erupted all over my skin, the nightmare of my death leaving me feeling cold and clammy. Like a corpse. I might have claimed to be used to it by now, but, honestly, every time I woke, it felt like the first time. The only difference: each time left me more exhausted and weak.

Relaxing my death grip on the sheet, I scrubbed both hands down my face to stir the blood flow and then rubbed my cold arms for warmth.

Concentrating on getting warm instead of being picked apart by good and evil allowed my blood pressure to return to some semblance of normalcy.

Then I closed my eyes, regulated my breathing as Doctor Berk had instructed, and pulled my feet inward until I sat cross-legged on the bed. My wrists rested on my knees. Mostly, I did this to calm down and push back all those images bouncing around my mind.

When I woke, especially the last few months, the sensation, something akin to strength or power, vibrated through my veins, making me feel as though my whole body hummed just a little. So I banked it, used the meditation to push all that good and evil shit aside and pull up my humanity. Me. Charlie Madigan. *That* was who I was. Not some weirdo walking dead person whose insides raged every damn night with images of darkness and light.

Once I had my mind under control, I glanced

around my bedroom, drawn to the only light in the dark room. My alarm clock.

"Damn it!"

I had just enough time to get dressed and meet Hank for our trip to Underground.

Ten minutes later I stood in front of the full-length mirror and sighed. Well, this would have to do. My hair was down and messy from the nap, but finger-combing had gotten out the worst of the tangles. I had on the jeans and red V-neck T from earlier. I added faded brown cowgirl boots Bryn had given to me for my birthday last year and put a pair of gold hoops in my earlobes.

Full-blown makeup had never been my thing, so I washed my face, put on some lotion, let it dry, and then dusted my face with powder, added a little brown eyeliner, went heavy on the black mascara, and then applied some lipstick that matched my shirt. It made my lips look insanely obvious, like an overripe plum. I looked as though I was on the prowl for sex—not exactly what I had pictured wearing to The Bath House. But, the hell with it, maybe I'd get lucky. My reflection frowned back at me. Or not.

Downstairs, I pulled my old suede jacket from the closet, the faint scent of leather making me breathe in a little deeper. It was tailored to look like a short blazer, but it would hide my firearms, and it was light enough to keep me from overheating. Functional and stylish.

Headlights from Hank's car flashed across the front window. I hit the inside light switch to off, turned the porch light on, grabbed my keys off the foyer table, and then slid my weapons into their holsters. I answered the door with one hand and tugged my hair from underneath the jacket with the other.

Hank's large form hovered in the doorway, the serious expression on his handsome face going all cocky. "Hey, is Charlie here?"

I shook my hair out. "Ha, ha. You're not funny." I was becoming more and more convinced my daughter was getting her sense of humor from Hank.

A slow smile lit his face as he looked me up and down. "This may be the first time you've ever taken my advice. You look . . ." He paused, trying to find the right words.

"Like I just got out of bed?" I pulled the door closed, locked it, and then ushered him off the porch and down the driveway.

"No . . . I like it. It's a good look on you."

"It's not a *look*. I just woke up. But I did do the lipstick for you, so we're even about the whole oracle thing."

He grabbed his chest and grinned at me over the hood of his shiny black Mercedes coupe. The street lamp highlighted the sparkle in his blue topaz eyes. "For me? You're the best, Charlie."

"Yeah, yeah," I said dryly, opening the door and sliding into the supple leather passenger seat.

My spirits lifted, and the memory of my nightmare quietly slipped into the far recesses of my mind. Thank God for Hank. Thank God I hadn't been partnered with a stiff. If there was anyone, besides Emma, who could change my mood for the better, it was Hank.

As soon as he backed out of the driveway and slid the gear into drive, I held out the matches. He grabbed them, holding them in front of the steering wheel so he could watch the road and take a look at the graphics. "Where'd you get these? Because I know you've never been there. Veritas is a members-only club. Most people who go to The Bath House, even regulars, don't know it exists."

"Exactly why we should crash the party."

He winced. "No crashing. Subtle investigation. Come on, say it with me . . . *Subtle investigaaa*— Eh, forget it. Lost cause, I know." He tossed the matches back to me. "How'd you get them?"

"Auggie. He gave them to me right before he died. Those guys that attacked us, they had to be the ones supplying the *ash*. Auggie was seriously spooked. I'd never seen him like that before. He said the drug is made from a Charbydon flower."

He grabbed his cell and began texting.

I stiffened and grabbed the dashboard as his fingers flew over the smooth black keyboard. "I hate when you drive and do that."

He smiled without looking at me. "I know." He finished and then tossed the cell back into the empty cup holder. His speed verged on texting genius. "Research should be able to put together some possibilities. That might narrow things down a bit, give us some idea of where it's grown, who could be making it."

"My money is on the jinn."

"Could be. Or could be they're just the movers, not the source."

Hank took a left onto Courtland as I glanced at the digital clock in the console. The Bath House was one street over from Bryn's apartment above her shop on Mercy Street. But it was past ten now, and Emma would already be asleep. Still, I made sure my cell phone was loud enough to hear in case Bryn called and then I refastened it back on my belt.

"Oh, yeah, I stopped by the hospital," Hank said on an afterthought, "to check on Amanda."

"You did?" I gave his shoulder a good squeeze.

He shrugged, and I knew the ego was coming. "I know, I know. I'm just a well-rounded, sensitive guy." He flicked on the right blinker to turn. "She's still in a coma, but stable. Just like the others."

I, on the other hand, felt horrible for not stopping by the hospital. I'd had every intention, but then there'd been Doctor Berk, stopping by the store, and then making it home in time to get Em off the bus. And, of course, Will had showed up.

"It's not like there's anything you can do for her, Charlie. She wouldn't even know you're there. And besides, from what we're hearing about the ones who have woken up, it's like being in a constant state of bliss."

"Yeah, and now those same people are in a living hell. They can't function, they're dying. It's more than withdrawal." I stared at the glittering city lights, frustrated that we couldn't help those people, that answers weren't coming fast enough.

We rode the remainder of the way in silence, and I let my thoughts and gaze drift to the pulsating city, to the people and beings on the sidewalks and crosswalks, in cars and using the buses, entering and exiting shops and offices.

Atlanta was diverse before the Revelation, but now it was like a living, breathing Jackson Pollock painting; so many shades, so many vibrant colors all jumbled together on an ever-shrinking city canvas. Humans of every kind. Elysians of every race. Charbydons of every ilk. All on display right here beneath the hazy glow of city lights reflected against the night sky. It made me think of a huge cauldron, a witch's brew where all of us, every ingredient, affected the next. And it boiled and bubbled, always moving, always growing, always needing to be fed and tended.

There was no denying that I thrived here; loved it here. I was meant to traverse this landscape and interact with its occupants. I was like one of those witches; playing her role, tending to the cauldron, to see that it didn't grow cold or boil over.

And if we didn't find a way to stop *ash* from spreading we might as well jump right into the pot and call it quits.

My stomach growled loudly in the quiet containment of the coupe.

"Let me guess, you didn't eat dinner again," Hank said, throwing me a quick parental glance.

A compliant shrug was all I gave for an answer, choosing to return my attention to the view, wondering if retiring to a desk job was really the right thing to do. Hell, the chief would have a fit. Telling him was going to be just as hard as sitting on Doctor Berk's plush chair. I chewed the inside of my cheek, but none of the scenarios flitting through my mind were going to help me with the chief.

Hank found a parking spot near Underground and soon we made our way to Helios Alley.

Underground at night was a hell of a lot different than during the day. Restaurants and nightclubs opened their doors. People spilled into the streets, barhopping or chatting, or just hanging out on the outdoor seating or around open fires burning in city-approved containment barrels. It had become like Bourbon Street in New Orleans. No cars allowed, just locals, tourists, and drunks everywhere. And music. Nearly every place you passed was different. Techno. Country. R&B. Alt-rock. And nestled in between were tourist traps, restaurants, antique stores, and magic shops.

Hank and I walked side by side, scanning the revelers and avoiding the drunks and irritating people who darted in front of us like they had the right-of-way. I hated being around drunks, unless, of course, I was one of them, which happened rarely in my hectic life.

A dark-haired woman in a bridal veil bumped into my left shoulder, spilling her drink over the rim of a red plastic cup. I stepped out of the way before it drenched me. She didn't even notice, just continued with her friends to other side of the street and another bar.

"You look nice, by the way," I told Hank as we moved closer to the sidewalk. "Whoever she is, she'll like it."

I wasn't just being polite. Hank looked like a Calvin Klein ad come to life. His blond hair was swept back, but just enough to look naturally windblown. He wore a soft, white linen shirt with the top two buttons undone and khakis. He appeared as though he'd just stepped off some exclusive beach in Tahiti.

"Tonight's not exactly singles night." He increased his stride and slipped by a slow couple walking hand in hand. "We've got work to do."

"Don't sound so disappointed. This is perfect. If she does notice you and you're forced to ignore her, it'll just make her want you more."

He rolled his eyes, a smile tugging the corner of his mouth. "Your logic needs a serious overhaul. You doing okay?"

"Yeah, I'm fine. Why?"

He shrugged, shoving his hands into his pockets. He had such an easy, confident swagger. "Well, seeing as you've had the day from hell . . . You sure you're up for this? I mean, I don't want you poofing out on me in the middle of things."

"It's pooping." His eyes went wide. Okay, that didn't sound right. "The phrase, it's called pooping out, not—" The corner of his mouth started twitching, and his eyes glistened. I smacked his arm. "Damn it, Hank!" His laugh filled the space around us, rich and warm and slightly contagious. But I refused to even grant him a smile.

"I can't believe you fell for that one," he said between bursts of laughter.

"You're so juvenile."

"And your point?"

I shook my head. "Exactly."

He ignored my summation and said in a singsong voice, "I got you to say poo—"

"Hank!" God. What was it with him tonight? "Don't you have better things to do than to make me say immature words?"

His chin cocked thoughtfully and then, "Not at the moment, no."

"Well, knock it off. And for the record, I won't be *pooping out* on you tonight or any other night for that matter." Please. I could deal with plenty. If only he knew.

The revelers thinned out as we approached an area where there were more stores than bars. Mostly upscale boutiques, hair salons, and spas. A few spas had eateries with outdoor seating and table umbrellas lined with white Christmas lights. There was still activity here, but it was definitely more subdued.

Potted palms framed the tall, recessed double doors of The Bath House. Dark and polished, the wooden doors' rectangular panels had been carved to depict sea creatures, both mythological and real, some in extremely suggestive positions. Hank pulled his wallet from his back pocket and then slipped a membership card into the slot built in near the door. Once the machine read his card, the door popped open.

I resisted the urge to comment about his membership card. But only for a second. "So, how often exactly do you frequent the House of Bath?"

Following him into the foyer, I linked my hands behind my back and let out a low whistle. The foyer rose two stories and housed tall palm trees and exotic blooming vines. Small parrots and songbirds flitted about in the green canopy above us. The floor was made of thousands of small mosaic tiles, which glittered in the light. Large candelabras burned four to a side.

"I try to make it at least once a week. And don't give me that look, Charlie. This reminds us of home. It's part of our culture. We love the baths. And we're not ashamed of our bodies either."

I held up my hands. "What? I didn't say anything."

"You don't have to," he grumbled. "If you went to my world, you'd understand."

"Yeah, but hardly anyone is permitted. Seems grossly unfair, don't you think?"

This was an old argument between us. And millions of other people. Seemed it was all fine and dandy for the beings of Elysia and Charbydon to make our world home, but when the tables were turned, the Elysian government permitted only a small number of humans to visit their world each year. No permanent citizenship, no work visas. Just visit. They lived in a pristine environment and didn't want it contaminated with tourists and disease. Total insult if you ask me.

And no one, unless they were seriously screwed in the head, wanted to go to Charbydon. But Earth, America in particular, had once again become the land of opportunity.

"Welcome to The Bath House," a female nymph said as we approached a white marble countertop. "I see you've brought a guest this evening, Mister Williams." She placed two towels and two white gowns on the counter. "Enjoy your visit."

Upon becoming a legal citizen, Hank had adopted his first and last name after the country singer. Apparently, he had a serious soft spot for the musician.

I followed his lead, taking the gown and towel. He leaned close to me as we walked past the counter. "You can put the gown on in the locker room."

"Whoa." I stopped and waited for him to turn

around. "You didn't say anything about wearing something this flimsy."

A few Elysians padded past us, barefoot and naked, or dressed in white gowns and sarongs. Hank edged closer to a grouping of potted plants, his voice tight. "It's either that or nothing at all. Your choice."

I lifted an eyebrow, standing toe-to-toe with all six foot four inches of him. "Forget it. I'm not changing."

My pulse raced. I was *way* too hard up to be in a place like this with naked bodies and perfect males everywhere I turned. If Will, damn him, hadn't pushed me away, I wouldn't be having such a hormonal time. "And another thing, where the hell am I supposed to put my weapons?"

An annoyed huff escaped Hank's lips, and he pulled me into the shadows of a palm tree. "Look, no one's gonna talk to you if you're dressed like that. You'll stick out like a sore finger."

"Thumb."

"What?"

"Thumb. You'll stick out like a sore thumb."

He rolled his eyes, clearly at the end of his rope. "Whatever. Just go in and change. Nothing's going to go wrong in here."

I gave him my "yeah, right" look. I mean, this was Hank and Charlie, known to get into trouble in the weirdest places. But he did have a point. I would look completely out of place. We had nothing to go on but a pack of matches, and we'd have to blend in and strike up conversations where we could.

"Fine," I ground out, leaving Hank where he stood and heading to the female locker room.

A nymph attendant stood inside next to a long countertop complete with just about anything one would need to "spruce up." Just like ghouls were cousins of goblins, and imps were cousins of the fae, nymphs were close cousins of sirens. But their skin was naturally tanner than sirens', their hair usually darker. They were the only race able to shape-shift without the aid of a spell or charm, and they had an intimate, sometimes fanatical, relationship with nature.

The attendant wore her black hair in a bun with ringlets around her face and a gold headband atop her head. A gown of linen draped over her shoulders, similar to the gowns depicted on statues of ancient Greek goddesses. All of the attendants I'd glimpsed so far wore the same headband, hairstyle, and gown.

I gave her a tight smile and headed for a stall. Once the curtain was jerked shut, I shook out the gown, immediately struck by another surge of denial. In the water, the soft white linen would be see-through. The straps were gathered at the top, there was a high waist, and then the soft material fell to mid-thigh. I guessed you were supposed to go commando underneath, but hell if I'd go there.

I left on my bra and panties (thank God they were white), pulled the gown over my head, and then carried all my clothes, firearms tucked under my jacket, to the attendant to ask for a locker and a key.

There was no key. Instead, she wrote down my

name, assigned me a locker number, and would unlock it when I returned. Apparently, there was no place to *put* a key. Figured.

On my way out, I caught a glimpse of myself in the mirror and nearly tripped. I backed up to get a better look. Hank had been right. I sure as hell fit in now. The only difference between me and the attendants was the quality of the gown and my hair, which hung long and loose down my back.

Who knew I could pull off Greek goddess so well?

5

Hank waited outside the locker room in an above-the-knee white sarong, his arms folded across his bare chest and his toe tapping on the mosaic tile.

Holy Mary, Mother of God. An appreciative breath whistled through my lips.

All two hundred pounds of him glowed with tanned skin pulled taut over fantastic shoulders, cut abs, and gorgeous legs and feet. Yeah, I'd been right for once. Seeing Hank half-naked had been worth the trip.

I was grinning like an idiot and couldn't hide it. One of Hank's perfectly arched eyebrows lifted slowly and knowingly at my blatant perusal. Then his lips twitched, and his eyes sparkled as he flipped the tables and ogled my outfit. That made me find my voice. "Is that a loincloth?"

The burgeoning grin on his lips froze. "It's not a loincloth."

"It looks *exactly* like a loincloth."

His expression turned sour as I cocked my head and gave him a smart look. Satisfied I'd gotten the last word, I strode off toward the main bath.

"You left your underwear on?" His exasperated voice came from behind me.

I stopped, stuck my hip out, and looked over my shoulder, trying to see my rear. "What? You can see them?"

"God, get me through this," he muttered on a long exhale, grabbing my arm and steering me forward. I was pretty good at leaving him speechless. He didn't say another word about my undies.

The wide corridor opened into the enormous main bath. Swimming pool, really. Columns held up a mural ceiling and ringed the rectangular room. In places, steam trickled like smoke from the surface of the pool. Beautiful beings swam in the water, lounged on the bath steps, or gathered around low tables, lying on their sides atop pillows and eating finger foods.

"So this is how you guys do it in Elysia."

Hank shrugged. "For the most part. C'mon, let's mingle."

"And get close to Veritas."

A tall nude male, a *very fine* tall nude male with an exquisite form and dark skin so wet and gleaming it looked almost black in the soft candlelight, padded by and gave me a quick once-over and then a smile. A light, fluttery sensation bloomed in my belly. I returned his greeting halfheartedly, waiting until he passed to let out a whoosh of air. Dear God. Everything inside of me screamed to turn around and go home. This could not end well.

Suddenly, I noticed every bit of seduction in the room. The nymphs giving massages. The couple in the pool running their hands all over each other's wet bodies. The blatant nakedness. The open stares of admiration and interest. How could this not turn into one gigantic orgy?

It was too hot in the baths. Too damn hot to even catch my breath and slow my heart rate. A low laugh issued beside me. "Shut up, Hank."

"Only humans seem to equate nakedness with sex. Like there can be no other outcome," Hank said. Was I that transparent? "Or is it that you're such a prude that all this skin is what has you red-faced and panting?" He jumped away before I could swat him.

Maybe I *had* become a prude. Lack of sex could do that to a girl. Which didn't explain how one minute, I'm sucking face and begging for it with my ex-husband, and the next I'm so damned flustered and embarrassed at seeing naked bodies at The Bath House. Perhaps I was teetering between eternal prude-dom and desperate sex seeker.

Yeah, and you're the Queen of Denial, Charlie. There was no doubt in my mind if I wanted to find a partner tonight, I could. But I wouldn't. Despite its reputation of being addictive, the idea of sex with an offworlder freaked me out a little. Okay, a lot. And this place was full of them. I was probably the only human here.

Like all Elysians of status, Hank strolled toward the pool as though he owned it while I stood in perfect idiot stance watching him. Splitting up was the best and fastest way to find information, but part of me wished he'd stuck to my side like glue.

Chin up, I encouraged myself, taking a deep breath and stepping into a room designed to be an overdose for the senses.

Deep red brocade curtains hung between columns and were held back with gold rope ties. They framed the massive space and separated the lounging areas from the main pool along with the help of strategically placed ferns. Tall urn-style fountains at each corner sent cascades of water into the pool. The rhythmic cadence mixed beautifully with piped-in music, which sounded suspiciously like Enya. Trays of candles and herbs floated on the surface of the water. I couldn't detect the scent of chlorine at all.

The heavy air made my skin dewy and my movements slow. Hank was already waist deep in the water talking to a group of males, so I headed to a long marble table and sat diagonally from two females and a male. A server immediately brought me wine, water, and a tray of fruits. Grateful, I downed half the water, welcoming the cool relief.

The females were divinities, commonly referred to as Adonai. They liked to think of themselves as gods or, at the very least, *angels*, but they were simply the ruling elite of Elysia who just happened to have bodies like six-foot-tall Norwegian supermodels, and egos the size of Mount Everest. And these two were no different.

"When did they start allowing *humans* in here?" one of the females asked the other, but loud enough for me to hear, which was her intent.

I gave her a syrupy smile, when what I really wanted to do was reach over the table and smack the living crap out of her. "Oh, I don't know," I answered, letting my aggravation show, "maybe since we *live* here and this is *our* planet." I feigned a lightbulb moment. "Hey, I have an idea. If you don't like humans, go the hell back home."

I hated when the high ranks made the *choice* to move here and then did nothing but complain about Atlanta and humans.

The Adonai sniffed and left the table. *Bitches.*

"You're human," the male said, shifting to face me, one elbow propped on the table.

I turned my attention to him. "You're a warlock." Well, nymph by race, but warlock by trade.

Warlocks, the warrior sect of mages, were tougher, harder, and stricter than any other Elysian class. And when they weren't wearing any clothes, like this one, identifying them was a no-brainer. He had the physique of a fighter and bore the mark of the warlock tattooed around his wrist—a black dragon swallowing its tail.

He lifted his water glass to give me a mock toast, emerald green eyes flashing beneath slashes of black eyebrows. The guy was dangerous looking, with thick bone structure and ebony hair that fell just below his jaw, making me think of green meadows and Celtic barbarians. For a moment, I thought I saw a green light illuminated around him, but that could've been the heat getting to me.

The warlock, grinning now, moved around the table and sat down next to me.

I held my breath. *Don't look down, Madigan. Don't. Look. Down.*

When a hot naked male sits next to you, the law of the universe dictates one's eyes must turn south. It's the nature of things. But I held out, easing my death grip from the water glass and focusing solely on his face. He had a very calm, knowing look about him, and his dark hair and the tattoos on his arms made him appear capable of handling any situation. It made me wonder what guise he took when not in his natural nymph form. Something sleek, dark, and predatory, no doubt.

"First time?"

I glanced around the room, wishing my cheeks weren't burning. "Is it that obvious?"

A low laugh escaped him, and he leaned in with a conspiratorial wink. "The brassiere straps kind of give you away."

My lips formed a silent *O*. I shoved the straps back under the gown, feeling like I was in high school all over again, complete with the Barbie twins from hell and the humiliation of making an ass out of myself in front of a gorgeous guy. I finished off the water just for something to do. An awkward silence descended. I gave him a tight smile and then drummed my fingers on the table. He appeared far more comfortable than I did.

"What's your name?" He picked a grape from the tray and placed it into his mouth.

The tongue curling over the grape and the lips that closed briefly around his finger made me forget the question. "Hmm?"

He laughed. "Your name? I'm assuming you have one."

"Charlie. It's Charlie." I wondered if Hank was having better luck than me.

He held out his hand. "Aaron."

On impulse, I slipped my hand into his. Immediately, a zing shot up my arm and sent my body humming, as though a switch had been turned on, making me feel more alive, more in tune somehow. A gasp flew through my lips, and I jerked my hand away, rubbing the tingling skin.

Aaron cocked his head, staring at me strangely. "Not a mage," he said thoughtfully, trying to figure me out.

"No off-world anything," I corrected, trying to shake off the weird sensation.

His brow furrowed, his demeanor changing from naked warlock to naked scholar. "No . . . there's something. Are you in training?"

"Me. In training." I gave a short laugh. "Yeah, the day Charbydon starts sprouting daisies is the day I'll start crafting." I held up my hands in a gesture of innocence. "No superpowers in this body."

"You look familiar, too."

Then it hit me, and I blurted out before I could stop myself, "You must know my sister, Bryn. She's a member of your league."

Damn, damn, damn!

God! *Idiot, Charlie!* I wanted to smack myself in the forehead, but instead I pinched the bridge of my nose, wanting to forget the whole thing, wanting to forget the entire day, in fact. I grabbed the wineglass and downed half. I'd just blown my cover.

"Ah. That's it. I do know her," Aaron was saying. I glanced over and saw his expression change briefly to chagrin before returning to its calm, slightly amused state. I raised my eyebrow in question. "Alas, she has no desire for the likes of me."

"Poor you," I said, fiddling with the wineglass, "I'm sure somehow you'll cope."

He shrugged, unable to argue with my prophetic words. "So, you're the detective."

The total imbecile, you mean. I never should've blurted out Bryn's name. Just put me in a room with a gorgeous naked man and I lose every ounce of training I ever had.

Aaron's gaze turned soft. He leaned in. "Your secret is safe with me."

Right. This wasn't a game. And if it was, I'd just lost big time.

"Really, Charlie," he said.

Not that I truly believed him, but what else could I do but make the best of it? I faced him square-on. "Then you won't mind answering a few questions."

He sat back in the chair, stretched his legs out, and tucked his hands behind his head, displaying his nakedness in all its glory. "Shoot."

Oh, boy. "Will you *please* sit up? How can I question you like that?" Amusement brightened his eyes, but he complied. I continued before I could think about the pose he'd just given me. "Who would you talk to if you wanted to get into Veritas?"

"Veritas?"

I lowered my voice. "I already know it exists, so you can cut the act. I want to know where they meet and when."

Aaron finished off his water and waved a nymph over to refill the glass. Then he plucked a peach from the fruit basket and took a healthy bite. "I know *of* it, nothing more."

"And what do you know about *ash*?"

"Is that what they're calling it?"

"Yeah. You know anything about it?"

"Not a thing. I heard on the news it might be a virus of some kind."

A groan escaped before I could help it. "No. It's not a damned virus. It's a narcotic, a drug." I was getting tired of the media spin and the panic it was causing. Talk about responsible journalism. "Look, I know the drill in places like this. Spend enough money, and The Bath House will cater to anything and everything in its back rooms. Sex, drugs, you name it. Who would I see if I wanted to get a fix?"

"Maybe that's true for some patrons," he said

slowly. "Not for me. Some of us do just come here to unwind." He stared hard and unblinking at me until I acknowledged his statement. I dipped my head. "What goes on in the back rooms, I wouldn't know. Neither would most you see here."

"Fine. Good for you. But if you *were* into something like that, who would you talk to?"

"Zara, maybe. She's head concierge here. Probably knows how to get whatever a client wants."

I caught sight of Hank coming out of the water. He motioned to me. I turned to Aaron and stood. Showtime. "Thanks for the info." He bent forward and went to stand, but I raised my hand. "No! You're fine. Really. Please, don't get up." *Please, don't get up.*

He eased back down, grinning. "Say hello to your sister for me."

I shot him an eye roll and then hurried toward Hank. Whatever. I wasn't a love messenger for my sister, and I sure as hell wouldn't tell her Aaron said hi. She didn't need someone like him in her life. He was a player even if he did deny it.

I made my way to my partner's glistening wet body and equally wet see-through sarong. Great. A woman needed blinders if she wanted to function like a normal human being in this place.

"Anything?" I asked, trying to be all business and not look where I shouldn't.

"Zara."

"That's what I got, too."

Together we went farther into The Bath House, our

bare footsteps silent on the warm tiles. We passed room after room filled with luxury and decadence. Massage rooms, small baths, lounging areas, and banquettes. The scents of massage oils and food hung heavy in the air, and the distinct sounds of pleasure kept my face burning. Reluctant, yet curious at the same time, I scanned the rooms for suspicious activity, but all I saw were males and females flirting, talking, making out, and doing other things that I let my gaze skip over.

"There she is," Hank said as we came upon another counter hidden among palms, plants, and statues.

A siren looked up from a computer monitor. When she saw us, her face turned red. Good. At least I wasn't the only one now. "Hank." Her deeply sensual voice quivered slightly. In a nervous gesture, she swept her straight strawberry blonde hair behind one ear. "It's been a while. How are you?"

Immediately, Hank covered his discomfort with a stern set to his jaw. Oh, perfect. *This* was his crush?

He cleared his throat. "My friend and I were looking for something a little more fun than the usual. You have any ideas?"

Zara stared at Hank like he'd just stolen her tricycle, and then the look was gone, replaced by a jaded hardness only another female could detect, the disappointment on her flawless face as clear as day. This was like watching the National Geographic Channel. The first blundering meeting of siren mates.

"We don't offer anything other than what's on the services list," she said tightly.

He leaned forward with a cheesy, condescending smirk. "We all know that's not true, so—"

I smacked Hank's bare arm and nudged him over with my hip. "Zara." I had to step in before Hank made a complete fool of himself. Couldn't he see she liked him, too? "We're ITF. And we need you to help us out before we have to close up shop and get the entire department down here with a search warrant."

Shock widened her eyes. Her gaze darted from me to Hank, who stared at me, mouth hung open.

I shrugged. "What?"

"You're ITF?" She wasn't looking at me, but Hank.

"Way to go, Madigan," he grumbled before turning to her and admitting to the truth of my words.

"You can thank me later," I quipped under my breath, stepping closer to the counter. "Zara, we need your help. Specifically, we need to know if any new drug has passed through here, who brought it, and from where. We also have to get into Veritas."

Her perfect skin turned a shade paler. "I'd lose my job if I let anyone into Veritas."

"You'll probably lose it if you don't cooperate, we're forced to close this place down, and your boss loses thousands in revenue."

Hank scrubbed his hands down his face. "No one will know you let us in. We'll keep it confidential. Lie if we have to." He bumped me. "Right, Charlie?"

"Absolutely."

She chewed on her bottom lip for a moment and

then stood suddenly. With a grim set to her jaw, she flipped her long hair behind squared shoulders and turned off the computer monitor. "I never liked Veritas anyway. Follow me."

The statuesque siren was only a few inches shy of six feet, way taller than I would've guessed. That annoyed me. Then I became annoyed at my annoyance. Why did I care how tall she was, or that she had the backside of a warrior goddess, or that her hair was gorgeous? I bet she ironed it. I bet it wasn't naturally that glossy and straight.

I shook away the mental pettiness and tried to focus on the job at hand. Zara had nothing to do with me or the investigation. So far she seemed cooperative and smart. Not a bad choice in mates. Jealousy was something I rarely experienced and it wasn't something I intended to feel for Hank's future romance.

Zara led us to the rear of The Bath House and then up a flight of winding stairs hidden by vines and palms. The air became wetter and thicker as we ascended, making the scent of greenery stronger and my bare feet stick to the hardwood stairs with each step. The palms rustled and wings flapped as the birds sought heavier cover as we approached the landing.

Once there, Zara entered a key code to open a dark wooden door. I knew the minute the air hissed out that trouble had finally found us.

"To get out you hit the same code. One. Five. Seven. Seven."

I nodded my thanks while recording the code into

memory, then made nice and stepped into the dimly lit hallway, allowing them a moment alone.

Immediately, I was hit with the shock of air-conditioned air. Goose bumps sprouted on my bare arms and thighs. Wishing Hank would hurry, I rubbed the bumps and scanned the hall. Dark hardwood floors. Nice Oriental runner. Wrought iron sconces, which provided light on both sides of the hallway.

More than anything I wished I had my firearms. We trained twice a week in hand-to-hand combat to condition our physical strength, learn new moves, and constantly remind ourselves that sometimes we'd have to rely on brute force, but God I felt vulnerable without them.

This was just nosing around, though. It wasn't like we were there to arrest anyone.

After a brief conversation, Hank joined me, letting the door close quietly behind us. The hair on the back of my neck stood as we progressed in barefoot silence down the elegant hallway, passing an antique gilded mirror hung over a hall table, oil paintings of fowl and hunting dogs, and tall Asian vases. The feeling of premonition was so great in me that I had to force myself to walk forward. My vision wavered a few times, making me blink hard and shake the cobwebs away.

"Zara said the club is not in session tonight," Hank told me in a low voice. "Most members only come on meeting nights."

"Most. Means we need to stay alert. Play innocent

if anyone finds us. Say we found the staircase and were just pressing numbers and the door opened." The strength in my legs continued to weaken. A small tremble began in my hands. I shook them, annoyed by the sudden onslaught.

"Sounds good to me. What's wrong with your hand?"

"Nothing." I opened and closed my fists. "Just pins and needles." I was so cold.

We inched down the hallway, checking each door. The rooms held leather couches and chairs. A cigar room. Billiards. A small bath. A few bedrooms. Finally, we heard voices coming from one of the rooms at the end of the hall.

I lifted my hand to stop Hank, tiptoed to the door, and then pressed my ear to the cold, smooth wood. My legs were so weak now, I had to kneel down. Hank didn't listen. I felt his presence above me and looked up to see him lean over me and put his ear on the door. I gave him a sharp look, but he wasn't paying attention. If I turned my head, my nose would be inches from his crotch.

I jabbed him in the thigh, and he glanced down at me with an irritated expression. *Move over*, I mouthed, jerking my thumb to the left. His eyes lit with laughter as he realized my position—on my knees in front of his sarong-encased manhood. I wasn't laughing. He mouthed back, *Sorry*.

Voices came from beyond the door.

"It's all over the news."

"Why contain it? I say we use it to our advantage. It's perfect timing."

"It could backfire, make us look like opportunists."

Three voices. One vaguely familiar. I closed my eyes, thinking it would somehow allow me to hear better, but all I saw were flashes of my dream. Those terrible images. I gasped and lost my balance, catching myself with both hands on the soft carpet.

"What? What it is?" Hank whispered.

"Nothing." I shook it off, reaching for my weapon. It wasn't there. Shit. "We need to get into that room."

"We don't have backup. Or weapons."

I pushed to my feet and stepped back, biting my lip. We could break the door down, but that would tip off whoever was inside that we were the law. We could wait for them to come out, but that could take hours and there might be another exit from the room.

I turned to Hank. "Put your arms around me."

He blinked. "What?"

"Our plan. We embrace, *fall* into the door. It bursts open. We get a good look at them and then act like we were just looking for a place to . . ."

"Get it on." His face split into a blinding, deep-dimpled grin. "I like the way you think, Madigan."

"Focus, Hank."

We backed away from the door. All business, I wrapped my arms lightly around him, hesitant to touch his smooth, bare skin. My hands settled against his warm back, and I tried not to dwell on the hard muscle under my palms. Hank took my cue, but in his usual all-consuming way. He enveloped me, holding me tightly, one big hand between my shoulder blades and the other splayed way too low on my back. He really didn't need to press so hard or make sure my hips were that snug against him. I had a feeling if I looked up, it'd be to see him grinning like a damn fool and enjoying this immensely. And the last thing I wanted was to make eye contact lest he see how truly uncomfortable this position had become.

I tried to ignore the scent of his skin mixed with faint traces of the herby stuff that perfumed the baths. And just for a moment, the urge was there to snuggle into him and enjoy the protection and the instant warmth that vanquished the cold.

"Let my shoulder hit the door," he said, practically lifting me off my feet. "Ready?"

Tensing, I nodded without looking at him.

We rushed the door, twisting before impact so that his shoulder hit the wood, and rammed the door hard enough to fly through.

The breath whooshed out of me as my back connected with hardwood floor and Hank landed on my stomach and chest. So much for chivalry. I'd taken the brunt of the fall, cushioning his landing. He lay sprawled halfway on top of me, our legs intertwined and my gown riding high on my hips. His body shook, and I realized he was laughing, his face buried in my hair and against my neck. I wasn't sure if it was for real or for the benefit of the room's occupants.

Recovering my breath, I decided to follow his lead, laughed, and then brushed the hair from my face to see two startled males standing in front of a large desk, staring down at us with a mix of outrage and shock.

"Who the hell are you? Who let you in here?" A thin, dark-haired male stared down at us, his narrow face pinched and red and very familiar

Hank untangled himself from me and helped me stand. My hand was in his when I recognized the accent of the male who'd spoken and immediately realized why he looked so familiar. Otorius, Representative of the Charbydon Political Party here in Atlanta. What the hell was a Charbydon noble doing in a strictly Elysian place of business? And it wasn't every day you came across a noble—there were so few of them. The significance didn't escape me as I feigned an embarrassed smile while rearranging my gown.

"Sorry, fellas," Hank said, wrapping an arm around my waist and squeezing. "Just, you know, looking for a quiet spot with my lady."

I stifled a groan. He was enjoying this charade way too much.

I turned my attention to the other one in the room and guessed from the cut of his suit and the confidence in his bearing that he was also a noble. In ancient times, we called them gods. They preferred the term Overlords, but I refused to call them that, arrogant bastards. They had the same enormous ego of the Adonai, making me wonder if the "First Ones" myth was true, if somewhere deep in the off-worlders' ancient history the Elysian Adonai and the Charbydon nobles came from the same stock. Say that now, to either side, and you'd get your heart served to you on a silver platter.

The unidentified noble was leaning his hip on the desk, hands shoved into the pockets of black slacks, regarding me with open interest.

Calmly, I met his stare. A slight grin played on his mouth. Easy, absolute confidence surrounded him, and there was a sultry charisma that clung to him. Jet-black hair framed a face with hard angles, and eyebrows that reminded me of a crow's wings in flight. He cocked one of those eyebrows at me, and I tried not to notice that my stomach did a gentle, surprising pull. Immediately, I suspected an allure charm.

"How did you get through the main entrance?" Otorius asked.

I played the submissive woman and let Hank explain the scenario we'd concocted. We were met with some serious suspicion. But Hank just cocked a grin and said, "Guess we got lucky, right, babe?"

"Right."

Then the chair behind the desk turned around.

My heart stopped.

If Hank's arm hadn't been around me, I would've fallen.

The being who sat behind it came from my worst nightmare. The one I'd had every night since my death.

It was the dark one in the field who'd picked the flesh from my bones. He was here. And he was real.

Fear clawed at my mind, and my mouth went bone dry. I couldn't swallow, couldn't catch my breath. Every hair on my arms and legs stood straight.

My heart started again, hammering way too fast. I couldn't believe what I was seeing, so I blinked hard, trying to clear my vision, knowing I couldn't be looking at the same male who'd invaded my dreams. But somehow it was. I might not have seen his face clearly in my nightmare, but I *knew* it was him. Somehow I knew.

His stare was on me from the moment he turned around and his eyes pierced me with horror, with every childhood dread and image of evil, all wrapped up in a face that spoke of calm, efficient brutality. A diabolical face.

I swayed. My fingernails dug into Hank's arm. From the corner of my eye I saw him glance down questioningly.

"Who are you?" I choked out, trying desperately to hold on to reality and not give in to the weakness in my knees and the roll of my stomach.

His lips split slowly into a smile that didn't move to his flat black eyes. "Come now, Charlie. You don't remember?"

That smile cut a swath of terror straight to my soul. I had the distinct sense that I was falling as blackness claimed my vision.

6

"Charlie?" My partner's voice filtered through the haze, sounding like the distant echo of a bank teller at a drive-through window. But that couldn't be right, because I felt his warm hand around my upper arm.

Sludge filled my mind.

"Damn it, wake up," Hank ground out, shaking me a little.

"Does she need a doctor?" another voice asked. Had to be the cute one.

In The Bath House. Upstairs. Veritas. Oh, God! I was still here with them! I sat up, gasping.

Hank knelt back, his face scrunched with concern. "You all right?"

I swallowed the giant-sized lump in my throat and nodded, standing with his help and then straightening my gown with trembling hands.

The monster still sat behind the desk, eyeing me with avid speculation. He was middle-aged and aging gracefully, which, for a Charbydon noble, should put him somewhere around four or five *thousand* years old. His white hair was swept back from his face. The widow's peak over his forehead made him look sinister and accentuated his patrician nose, causing it to appear more hooked than it really was. The white of his dress shirt set off dark olive skin, and with slanted black eyes and a cruel mouth, he looked like malice in a stylish gray suit.

I knew this being, but I didn't *know* him. And I began to wonder if some of my dream stemmed from my time in the hospital. How did he know my name? Did he visit me in the hospital? I just couldn't remember.

I backed from the room, grabbing Hank's arm and mumbling something about how we should get back. My smile was tight, but I kept my shoulders back and my chin up. Being weak in a room full of men wasn't my idea of a good time. And right now I was seriously vulnerable and confused.

The good-looking noble slid a questioning glance to the monster behind the desk. But he shook his head slightly. They were letting us go.

Hank supported most of my weight as we backed out of the room and into the hallway. As soon as we were out of earshot, he asked, "Charlie, what happened?"

"Out of here," I gasped. "Let's just get out of here."

I stumbled down the hall, gaining speed and

strength. By the time we made it to the locked door, I was breathing hard, but feeling a whole lot better by putting some distance between me and my nightmare.

Hank punched in the key code and we hurried down the winding stairs. He hadn't let go of my hand, afraid I'd fall, or worse, faint again. But I leaned on him less and less. Once we hit the mosaic tile on the first floor, he dropped my hand, and we continued to the locker room at a fast walk.

"You recognize the other two?" I asked, knowing he knew Otorius's face as well as I did.

"No." He gave me an odd glance. "But the one behind the desk . . . Seemed like you knew him. He sure as hell knew you."

"Yeah. I don't know. The ITF database might help with identifying them."

We broke apart, Hank heading to the left and me veering to the right. Once I was in the locker room, I retrieved the key from the nymph and then took my things into an empty stall. The gown came off quickly and fell in a heap in the corner of the stall. The urge to get out of there was so fierce; my hands still shook as I jerked on my clothes and slipped my arms through my weapon harness. Only then did a relieved sigh break the silence and calm my nerves. Never had I felt so grateful and more relaxed than when I slid my firearms into their holsters.

Now, I was prepared. Now, I had leverage. *This* was my magic.

Hank waited for me by the door. Together, we left

The Bath House and headed up Helios Alley toward the parking lot, neither one of us speaking.

The nightlife had peaked. It was way beyond the witching hour and groups of inebriated pub crawlers blocked our way. We veered around a few Georgia Tech students making their way across the street. All I wanted was to get as far away from Veritas and the man behind the desk as I could. If it wasn't for Hank next to me, I would have run.

We snaked around a Wiccan couple holding hands and finally found ourselves free from the throng of people. A street lamp buzzed on and off. The next one had completely died out. The heels of my boots clicked loudly on the asphalt as we drew away from the revelers and the sounds of music spilling from the pubs and dance clubs. The sudden passing from the loud and boisterous to the dim, eerie quiet sent a shiver along my spine and gave me that creepy sensation of someone lurking behind me. *You're freaking yourself out*, I thought, glancing over my shoulder, but there was no one there.

"That guy, the older one," Hank said, breaking the quiet. "You *sure* you've never met him?"

"I don't think so. I guess I could have at some point . . ." I shook my head, feeling bad and embarrassed since lately it seemed like Hank was always pulling me out of sticky situations. I was stronger than this. "I'm sorry for breaking down on you like that." I wanted to say more, to try and explain, but what could I say? I didn't even know myself. "It doesn't make sense. Charbydon nobles in Elysian territory. That alone is a major red flag. If Veritas is some exclusive club where nobles and Elysians meet, it can't be for bake sales and charity events. They're up to something."

Hank dug out his car keys as we approached the car. "Charlie, I want you to be extra careful. This investigation, everything today, nothing is making sense."

"Yeah, I know."

Hank's profile was seriously grim. He knew something wasn't quite right. And I trusted his instincts. Hell, many times I'd banked my life on his intuition. But this time I felt the same. It was like a huge satellite sat atop my head, blaring the signals—warning, dread, suspicion . . . They were drowning me, but at the same time pushing me to figure it all out.

At the car, he beeped the alarm system off. "You sure you're okay? 'Cause you look like a ghost."

"Gee, thanks." I opened the door.

"You can confide in me, you know," he said over the roof of the car, his deep tone going deeper. "I'm not human. I might understand a hell of a lot better than Berkowitz."

Yes, his super senses had saved my butt a gazillion times, but they could also be a *pain* in my butt. Like now, when I didn't want to talk about it. I let out a big sigh and rested my elbows on the roof. "Hank, please don't read into me. I know, all right? I know something's off with me. But there's no point in talking about it when I haven't even figured out what the hell's wrong."

He bit back his reply, jaw flexing, and stared off into the dark parking deck. "One of these days, Charlie, you'll need to rely on somebody. Somebody who could have answers. Look, if you don't want to talk to me, then talk to Bryn or Doctor Berk. Someone. You *healed* yourself today." He paused to let that statement sink in. "And now you're passing out. What's next, morphing into a werewolf and howling at the full moon?"

I slid into the passenger seat and waited for Hank to get in. His words echoed in my mind. What *was* next? If only I knew.

He started the car and then glanced over at me with a warning. "I'm serious, Charlie. Talk to someone, go to see a doctor. 'Cause if you don't I'll make you."

My gaze snapped to the thick voice-mod around his neck. He could make me do whatever he wanted, and the jerk was holding it over my head. "You wouldn't."

"Try me. I happen to value my life, and the next time we're in the thick of things, I don't want my partner wigging out. If you don't think you owe it to yourself, then think of the rest of us." With that, he hit the radio, obviously done talking to me, and pulled out of the parking space.

Guess he told me.

Hank Williams Jr. blared from the custom speakers as we drove down Alabama Street. The down-to-earth, whiskey-rich voice soothed some of the physical symptoms of the stress and anxiety that plagued me, but my mind remained on overdrive. All I could think about was the noble's face, the familiar voice, and the surge of fear and realization that momentarily froze me solid. For eight months I'd dreamt of that shadowy figure. To find out he was a real, living being . . . I was in way over my head.

Something had happened to me the night I died. Something I didn't want to remember or acknowledge. Until now.

Hank remained silent, allowing me my thoughts and no doubt drifting into his own. Worry, stress, and frustration poured off him in waves. I rolled the window down, the car becoming stuffy and overheated with his emotions. He wanted so badly to have me confide in him. Hell, I wished I knew what to tell him.

After we parked and headed inside the station, we took the stairs to the second floor where it opened into a loft-style space with desks for the detectives in the center of the room and enclosed offices for the higher-ups along the perimeter. The first floor we used for booking and containment.

Hank and I shared a large desk. Our flat-screen monitors backed into one another, making a nice barrier and giving us some private space in which to work. We had to lean sideways and crane our heads over the mounds of files on either side of the monitors in order to make eye contact.

Tonight, we both settled into serious work mode,

Hank writing a report and then in his notebook, jotting down conversations and his own gut feelings about the encounter, while I logged on to the ITF database of known felons, suspects, and immigrants, looking for a match. I sipped on the hot coffee I'd made in the break room before we sat down, sighing at the comforting taste of coffee bean, half-and-half, and Splenda. I didn't like it overly sweet, but just sweet enough to cut the harsh nicotine taste of straight black. Most of the detectives and officers drank it black whether they liked it that way or not. But then, I'd never been a conformist, and they still made fun of me. Oh, well. Black tasted like tar and made my tongue fuzzy.

I'd had a sneaking suspicion I wouldn't find the two Charbydon nobles under felons or suspects, so I did a search on legally registered nobles aged five hundred years plus, male, living in Atlanta.

Bingo.

"Found you, you bastard," I muttered, refusing to be fearful of a JPEG.

"Which one?" Hank came around the desk to hover over my shoulder. He let out a low whistle. "Damn." He plowed his fingers through his hair and then rested his hand on the back of my chair. "Can you say roadblock?"

We were looking at one of the most influential Charbydons on the planet. I let out a heavy sigh. It would make our investigation a heck of a lot harder. But at least now we had a name. Mynogan, High Elder of the House of Abaddon. I tapped my pencil against my chin. Mynogan. The monster finally had a name.

"So," I began, thinking out loud more than anything, "what were three nobles doing in Veritas?"

Hank returned to his side of the desk. "Well they sure as hell weren't knitting booties for needy babies."

I decided to start with Otorius and did a Google search on the Charbydon Political Party in Atlanta. In the last year, the party had tried to move away from the stereotypical unlawfulness that had at first characterized most of the Charbydons. While they wanted entry into our world along with the Elysians, they had a difficult time conforming to the rules put in place to guard us and them, and they really had a difficult time coming to accept peace with the Elysians. They still didn't follow all of the Federation's policies. But, lately, many of the nobles had been trying to rectify this, and they'd started by forming their own political party, getting the message out that they wanted to be part of a law-abiding society and to contribute as law-abiding residents.

"Says here, there's a political rally tomorrow morning at Centennial Olympic Park." I clicked through a few more pages, looking for any information on the other noble. But there was nothing. Easing back in my chair, I let out a tired sigh. "We'll need to get a member list of everyone in Veritas. Auggie's death and the *ash* point straight to that place. He wouldn't have given me those matches otherwise. If the CPP isn't involved, then someone on the roster is, or at least knows something."

"I'll talk to Zara, see if she can dig up the names."

On a hunch, I pulled the names of the jinn who'd attacked me in Underground. There wasn't much in their file, but the employment listing confirmed my suspicion. At one time or another, two of the three jinn had worked as bodyguards to members of the CPP. I printed out the records and handed them to Hank over the monitor. "Take a look at this."

Hank scanned the records. "None of them were working for the CPP when they attacked you, though," he said, echoing my own thoughts.

If we took this to the chief now, he'd say the same thing. It didn't prove anything. But to me it was like a big neon sign. The CPP wasn't as law-abiding as it pretended to be.

Hank's gaze met mine. "Says two of them were members of the local tribe."

I nodded, knowing my look was as somber as his, but then I offered him a small smile and a shrug. Nothing I could do about that now.

We both knew it was only a matter of time before Grigori Tennin, the jinn boss, leader of the Atlanta tribe, issued a summons. A debt would have to be paid. And if I couldn't afford the monetary value attributed to those two jinn, to reimburse the tribe for their loss, I'd be required to pay a blood debt.

I stood, stretching my arms over my head and yawning, too tired to think of jinn retribution. "Let's go home. Tomorrow's going to be a long day."

And, before my head hit the pillow tonight, I had decided to pay a little visit to the doctor who'd saved my life.

After Hank dropped me off at the house, I paused briefly on the porch steps, waiting until the taillights of his Mercedes disappeared around the corner before getting into my old Chevy Tahoe. Mott Technologies owned a massive research facility just off I-85 outside of Atlanta. It was way late, but common knowledge said Titus Mott kept late hours working in his lab.

The guy was Albert Einstein smart, and he was something of a celebrity here in Atlanta and beyond. Many thought he'd hightail it to DC once he and his team discovered the other dimensions, but he'd elected to stay and, with massive government funding, he'd built a research empire. I was also privy to some juicy family gossip, courtesy of Marti when she'd sit at my kitchen table and chat on days when she dropped Amanda off to babysit Emma.

After thirty-five minutes behind the wheel, my headlights illuminated the large gatehouse and landscaped grounds of Mott Technologies' headquarters. Two guards stepped out of the gatehouse as I came to a stop in front of the yellow-and-black barrier. One of the guards walked around the back of the SUV and shined his flashlight into the backseat and then into the passenger side window as the other one approached my side and shined his light rudely in my face. Jerk.

"The facility is closed, ma'am," he said. Lucky I didn't snag said flashlight and clock him over the head with it.

"Yeah, unfortunately crime doesn't take the night off, fellas." I propped my elbow on the window ledge and showed him my badge. "I need to speak with Doctor Mott."

The guy's expression didn't waver, my badge having little effect on him. He was probably Atlanta PD or ex-military moonlighting for a few extra bucks. "Sorry, no visitors."

Tucking my hair behind my ear, I leaned closer, too tired to deal with this crap right now. "Number one, I'm not a visitor, and number two, just tell him I'm here. He'll want to see me."

Lines wrinkled his forehead, but he took my ID and told me to wait—like I was going anywhere with the other guard at my passenger window holding a semi-automatic and a gate in front of me.

Fingers tapping the steering wheel, I waited as the guard went into the small gatehouse and picked up the phone. Finally, the gate began to lift, and he waved me through as I snagged my ID from his outstretched hand. "Just drive on to the visitor entrance. Someone will meet you there."

Honestly, I hadn't really expected to get in, and I wasn't even sure Mott remembered me. The last time I'd seen him was a chance encounter at the station when he'd unveiled the new and improved Nitro-gun to the chief. Mott had remembered me then. He'd even asked how I was getting along after my ordeal.

By chance, he'd been at the hospital the night they brought me in. And when the emergency room doctor pronounced me dead, Mott had stepped in, claiming a person could be brought back to life much longer after having been dead than traditionally thought. He'd worked on me until he proved himself right, after all the others had left him alone in that dim, sterile room, thinking it was a lost cause.

The dead cop and the wacky doctor. Imagine their surprise when my heart started beating again.

Thinking of Titus Mott made my blood pressure rise as I drove down the long, winding blacktop road framed by mature live oaks. The guy had saved my life. And we'd never spoken about what had happened in that room.

Mist had settled on the park-like grounds, and to my left, the moonlight reflected off the surface of a small lake. I'd left the window down to allow the crisp night air inside. The tangy smell of grass and leaves came with it. Bullfrogs echoed over the soft hum of the engine and the press of the tires on asphalt. It was beautiful out here; the kind of night that made me want to run, to leave all my troubles behind, race through the mist, and become part of the beauty all around me.

The road forked, drawing my attention back to the drive. I followed the visitor sign to the large, glass front entrance and parked in the reserved space closest to the main entrance. I hit the lights and turned off the ignition, the empty, dimly lit lot giving me the willies. *Deep breath, Charlie.*

The night air was cooler here in the woods surrounding the facility, refreshing and clean. I drew it inside of me in long inhalations, letting it calm me before moving to the door.

A circular reception desk and small lamp, still turned on, were visible through the glass front. There was no one waiting, and the door was locked. I stepped back, feeling like a moron. The security cameras caught my eye, and I turned in their direction, motioning toward the door. The bastards knew I was there. I resisted the urge to flip them the bird.

Keys finally jingled in the door. A short young man in a white lab coat slipped every key on the ring into the lock before finally getting the right one. Successful, he gave me a quick victory smile and shoved his glasses back up to the bridge of his nose.

"Sorry about that, Detective," he mumbled as I entered the sterile lobby. He fell in step beside me, directing me across the polished wood floor to the executive elevator. "Doctor Mott is in his lab, but"—he slid a card key into the elevator slot—"he's looking forward to speaking with you."

Relief surged through me as I stepped into the elevator. "I wasn't sure he'd remember me," I confessed.

"Oh, no worries there. He never forgets a face or a name. Genius and all . . ." He pressed the sixth button.

Instinctively, I braced for the lift, but gasped as the elevator went down instead.

"Should've warned you about that. All the labs are underground." He stuck out his hand. "I'm Andy Myers, Doctor Mott's assistant. Well, one of them. He has a herd of us."

I shook his hand. "Nice to meet you."

We faced the doors, waiting in that polite yet awkward silence. I caught Andy staring intermittently at me and each time our eyes met, he smiled quickly and then looked away. It didn't make an ounce of sense, but I had the feeling he was particularly excited to see me, like a kid with a juicy secret just itching to tell all his friends. His reaction made me more self-conscious than I already was.

Get over it, Charlie. Nothing to be nervous about.

I squared my shoulders and focused on the steel door in front of me, using the moment to tuck my hair behind my ears, scolding myself for not remembering to grab a clip before I'd left for The Bath House earlier. I rarely wore it down for work and was so used to having it up and out of my line of sight that when it was down, it became one of those incredibly irritating distractions. I should cut it all off; I just never could bring myself to actually do it.

The elevator came to a stop, gravity pulling me and my queasy stomach down for a fraction of a second before the doors slid open to reveal a long, white-tiled hallway. As soon as the opening was large enough, I darted between the doors. Being underground, being *here*, about to speak to Mott . . . I'd avoided this for so long. And now the walls closed in on me.

Andy joined me a second later. "This way," he said, walking ahead of me.

I fell in step behind him, struck by the complete stillness and hush, like we had stepped into a vacuum of space. A faint chemical scent, similar to rubbing alcohol, hung in the air. Lab doors were evenly spaced, all with keypads and no windows. It suddenly seemed more like Fort Knox than a lab.

"Here we are." Andy slid his key card into the slot attached to a door.

It was now or never. And I'd come too far to back out now. With a deep breath, I entered the lab as Andy clicked the door closed behind me.

He was here somewhere, lost in the cavernous space of stainless steel, lab tables, cabinets, and beakers. One corner of the lab looked like a hospital room, complete with a wall of one-way viewing glass. But what stunned me into stillness was the god-like being lying on the hospital bed secured in a series of straps. He was male, a red-haired throwback to the time of Viking warriors. A being so perfect he could be none other than Adonai, an Elysian divinity. He wore a white T-shirt and blue-and-white-striped pajama pants. His feet were bare. IVs stuck into the veins in his arm and the top of his right hand. Equipment monitored his breathing and brain patterns.

What the hell was this?

Abruptly, the Adonai turned his head and opened his eyes, staring directly at me. My heart stopped. His gaze bored into mine like twin heat-seeking missiles fueled by intense blue flame. An arched brow cocked. "Like what you see?" he asked in a husky voice ripped with contained rage.

A bang made me jump. *Jesus!* The metallic echo sent a shot of adrenaline through my nerves as someone ground out, "Mother—"

"Ahem!" Andy cleared his throat.

Shuffling. Another bang.

Titus Mott poked his head from behind one of the lab tables opposite the mock hospital room, slapped his hands on the table, and pushed to his feet. He grimaced as he rubbed a spot on the back of his head, messing his thick brown hair so that some of it stood up straight. It made him look like he'd just gotten out of bed.

"She's here, Doctor," Andy said.

"What?"

Andy motioned to me. "Detective Madigan."

And just like that, I suddenly became the kid introduced to class mid-year. Standing in front of twenty faces and praying to be accepted and liked.

Mott adjusted his glasses. The frames were made of light wire and gave him an edgy, hip look. He was young for what he'd accomplished so far in his life. An interview he'd done with *Forbes* magazine said he was forty-eight. There was just the faintest hint of graying at his left temple. He hadn't shaved in at least a day, maybe two.

He adjusted his lab coat, slipped something in his pocket, and then approached me with his hand outstretched. "It's good to see you, Detective. Really good." He shook my hand warmly, his smile genuine.

This was going a long way toward relieving my anxiety. Now if the Adonai would stop his creepy ogling, I'd actually feel somewhat normal. "I'm glad you still remember me."

He motioned to Andy. "You can go, Andy. Thank you." Andy nodded and quietly left the room. "How about we go into my office?"

With a quick glance at the Adonai, I followed Mott. I wanted to like the man who had saved my life, but the lab rat on the table was making it really difficult.

Mott's office wasn't the room behind the glass, but a far corner with a small rug, well-worn couch, and leather chair. An old, scratched-up coffee table sat in the center of the rug. "This is my home away from home," he said, sitting on the couch with a sigh as the cushion gave in to his weight. "Please sit. You want coffee, tea, bottled water, soda?"

"No, thanks." I sat on the leather chair and waited for him to lean over the arm of the couch, open the small fridge, and grab a can of soda for himself. Granted, the reason for coming was to talk about me, but I found myself asking, "Who's the Adonai on the table?"

Mott popped the tab and the can hissed. "His name is Llyran."

"And is Llyran volunteering to be your lab rat?" Nosy question, but I had to ask. Something felt very wrong about the situation.

"Llyran is a Level Ten felon, Detective. It was either this or execution under Federation Law. He chose this."

His words stunned me into silence. A Level Ten felon was as bad as they came. Serial killer. Beyond help, beyond reformation, and unable to live a life sentence among others because he'd kill whoever came close enough. *Stunned* didn't even begin to cover it. Looks were deceiving, and I was the first person who should know that.

Our ancestors may have thought Elysia was heaven, but in reality it didn't come close to our pristine ideals and beliefs. It was a world just as diverse as our own. And just like Earth and Charbydon, Elysia had its good and its evil, and all the gray matter in between. But, damn, it was hard to get past the looks sometimes. It was easier to believe a goblin like Auggie was evil than an angelic-looking being like Llyran.

7

"What are you using him for?" I still didn't like the fact that the man I'd held in such high regard was using another living being for science.

"Well," Titus said, leaning forward, eager to talk shop. "As you know, the nobility from both dimensions are the most powerful, the hardest to defeat. The Nitro-guns and Hefties I created for law enforcement do nothing but stun them for a moment, even on high settings. With Llyran, I'm searching for a way to neutralize his power. In essence, to make him like us long enough, I'm hoping, to catch and detain. The hard part is identifying the genes that give him his power and then creating a viable weapon capable of attacking or subduing those genes. So far we've been successful at large force field containment, which is how Llyran was caught, but out in the field, as you know, a serviceable, easy-to-use weapon will make all the difference."

I was suitably impressed. Without Titus Mott and his inventions, we'd never have a fighting chance. Of course, if it hadn't been for his meddling and eventual discovery of Elysia and Charbydon, the off-worlders never would've come out of the woodwork and into mainstream society. At least he was trying to make up for it now.

"Sounds like you have your work cut out for you," I finally said.

He dipped his head in agreement and then took a long drink of his soda. "So what brings you to my lab, Detective?"

Here it comes.

I drew in a deep breath. "Actually—" *Just breathe. It's no big deal.* "I was hoping you could tell me about that night." Goose bumps lifted the hairs on my arms. "The night I died."

Thank God. I'd gotten the words out. The small of my back grew hot. I resisted the urge to rub my arms and instead focused on Mott. I was a detective, after all. Part of my job was to study body language, and it was hell of a lot easier to focus on him and forget about my own haywire reactions.

His elbows settled on his knees, which touched the edge of the coffee table. He tapped two fingers on the table. "Wow."

I bristled. "Wow, what?"

After a thoughtful pause, he said, "After all these months, I didn't think . . . just a surprise, that's all."

He scratched his stubble, studying me with candid, scientific thoroughness. "Well, you're looking none the worse for wear."

"Thanks." *I think.* I studied him, too, intrigued by the contrasts. Maturity and purpose burned in his eyes, but the rest of him appeared casual and slightly offbeat. He bit his cheek, thinking.

"How about you tell me if there's something specific you'd like to know. Oh, hold on; let me turn on my recorder." He jumped up, brought back a small voice recorder, and placed it on the coffee table.

"Um, I—"

He settled into the cushions, his entire face illuminated with anticipation. I could easily picture him rubbing his hands together in mad scientist glee. "Among other things, I've been researching out-of-body experiences, dying, and resurrection. You don't mind, do you?"

Yeah, I did, but he seemed so excited about hearing what I had to say. "No, it's fine."

"Terrific." He pushed the record button. "Ready when you are."

The nerves returned thanks to that little black box on the table. Mott wasn't what I'd expected, and the Adonai across the room was still staring. I tried to ignore it and get over my fear of talking about that night, but it was harder than I thought.

Maybe I should have taken that drink after all. My mouth had gone bone dry. *Oh, for God's sake, Charlie, just do it. Deep breath a-a-a-nd go . . .*

"I've been having nightmares ever since you brought me back," I forced out in one breath. "I thought it was just a dream, but I'm beginning to wonder whether some of it actually happened that night, after I died."

"Like a repressed memory."

"Right. Do you remember anyone else being in the room with you when you were there?"

"You think someone else was there?"

"You tell me."

He sat back and shrugged. "There were lots of people. In and out. Doctors, nurses. Your partner. I couldn't possibly remember them all."

"But you were left alone with me, when they all gave up. It was just you. You kept trying." He nodded. "And no one came in then, during that time?"

"Charlie." He shifted to look at me squarely, his knee bumping into mine. "Often those who experience near-death see people—loved ones, beings they describe as angels or even God. Is that what you saw?"

"No, it was more like the devil," I muttered, frustrated. "Sorry." I rubbed my face with both hands and let out a tired exhale. "I'm not sure what's real and what's not anymore. I thought I saw someone earlier tonight who looked like the man in my dream. I don't know. Maybe it was just a close resemblance, or maybe I'd seen him before the near-death."

Mott's hand on my knee brought the direction of my thoughts back to him. "Trauma leaves all manner of scars, some unseen." He lifted his comforting hand, leaving a cold spot where warmth had just been. Inventor's hands; stained with ink and covered in cuts, scratches, and calluses, both old and new. "How have you been feeling physically since then?"

"Exhausted. I wake and feel like I've been up all night working."

"Anything else?" he asked in a tone that tried too hard to be casual.

I straightened in the chair. "Why?"

"Often, in the cases I've studied so far, residual effects can linger on a person. Psychic energy. An awakening of sorts. Your brush with death, assuming you had a near-death experience—which by all accounts you seem to be saying you had—could've caused you to come back with a new awareness, added intuition, a stronger sixth sense . . . things like that."

Made sense, I guess. Who was I to say it wasn't possible? Hell, obviously, I'd come back with *something*. Something akin to a war inside me. Something that gave me the strength to kill one minute and the ability to heal the next.

"Are you experiencing a greater psychic awareness?"

Did he mean was I more intuitive, could I sense people's emotions more easily than before? "Yes. But there are other things. I'm stronger. I heal faster than normal." I thought of the green flash I saw briefly around Aaron in The Bath House. "I think I'm starting to see auras or flashes of color around people . . . I know. I've lost my mind, right?"

"No, no, you haven't. Who's to say what happens

during this sort of experience? We still don't know. How's your health?"

"Fine. I haven't been sick in a long time. Just tired." He couldn't help me. My hope deflated. He didn't know any more about near-death than I did. "Are you sure no one else came into the room?"

Mott shook his head and gave me a sorry half-smile. I felt more frustrated than ever. I stood, eager to get out of the lab. The Adonai on the table hadn't stopped staring the entire time, that small, cruel smile still playing on his lips. When I rose, I turned my back to him and focused on Mott. "Thanks for seeing me, Doctor Mott."

"Please, just Titus," he said, standing. "My parents were both historians. Had a thing for Latin names."

I smiled.

He motioned me from his living room. "I enjoyed seeing you again, Detective. I'm sorry I couldn't be of more help. But I'd like for you to come by for a thorough examination. We may yet find a reason for your symptoms. Please schedule it with Andy on your way out."

I nodded and had to turn toward Llyran to step around the chair. Briefly, our eyes connected. His grin widened, but I looked away, not wanting to give him the satisfaction. The guy was a serial killer and deserved whatever the hell Mott was doing to him. "Don't be a stranger, Charlie Madigan," he called, enjoying whatever mind game he was playing. Probably got off on it, the sicko.

★   ★   ★

My eyelids grew heavy on the drive home. It was past 2 A.M. The road stretched out before me, monotonous and empty save for a few stragglers like myself. Lulled by the quiet hum of the car, my emotions reared to the surface. Defeat pricked my ego and spread sour, like heartburn, through my chest.

I was changing inside, and I needed help. I just didn't know where to turn.

Hank and Bryn had repeatedly offered, but I couldn't bring myself to draw them into whatever was going on with me. I didn't want them to see me as any different than the way I used to be before I died. Me. Charlie Madigan. Detective. Human. Mother. Now it seemed I barely resembled myself.

No, I couldn't go to them; somebody in my life had to see me normally. I needed that kind of stability. My fingers flexed on the steering wheel, and I had to consciously stop myself from squeezing so tight. I should've made an appointment with Andy on the way out of the lab, but it hadn't felt right. I kept thinking of Llyran—I didn't want to be Titus Mott's latest lab rat.

In my line of work I was privy to all manner of supernatural beings and experts. Maybe I could find someone neutral, someone who could be objective, someone powerful and knowledgeable enough to know exactly what my problem was. A few names floated around in my head as I hit the blinker to turn onto my street. Unfortunately, I'd pissed off most of them enough times that they'd probably shut the door in my face.

A group of people blocked the street up ahead directly in front of my house. There were bright lights, a camera van, and people with signs. Immediately I hit the lights and pulled the Tahoe to the curb. A couple of my neighbors were walking to or from the scene. A few patrol cars blocked the street and officers were trying to keep order. This couldn't be good. I turned up my scanner and listened.

Someone had thrown a brick through my window.

The police had been called. Then the media.

Now the jinn, with CPP support, were picketing my house.

This was total bullshit. I got out of the car, tugged on my jacket, flipped the collar, and walked casually toward my house, somewhat hidden by the darkness and the row of cars parked along the street across from the house. With every step my anger grew. I loved our little bungalow, and those assholes were trampling all over the lawn, in the flower beds, and some soon-to-be-hurting jerk-off had broken my front window. I stopped behind a parked car, careful not to draw attention from the two jinn stationed near the house. They were looking, hoping I'd show up, hoping, I realized, to issue a summons from Grigori Tennin. Great. Couldn't they have waited until morning, at least?

A line of officers pushed some of the more irate

picketers off my lawn and onto the sidewalk. They were mostly jinn elders and females, goblins, imps, and human sympathizers.

A CPP representative was giving an interview in front of my house. Otorius. The reporter was a human from Channel Two News.

"This kind of police brutality cannot be tolerated. We have rights. We are legal citizens. This incident was nothing but discrimination. Detective Madigan killed three members of our society. She *beat* two of them to death. The CPP is demanding she be held in custody until an internal investigation is complete."

I slinked back into the shadows, wanting nothing more than to wring Otorius's neck. This reeked of political agenda. The nobles saw an opportunity and they'd jumped. Damned if I'd be a scapegoat, and I certainly hadn't done anything wrong.

As I went to head back to the car, a strong hand gripped my arm and pulled me into the shadows of a live oak. "Goddammit, Madigan, have you lost your fucking mind coming here?"

A sigh of relief tore through me. I released my hand from the gun under my jacket, and swallowed down my shock. "Chief."

"If they see you here, it's going to be a bloodbath for one."

My eyes adjusted to the darkness. He was dressed in street clothes and a black leather jacket, his hands shoved into the pockets, looking for all the world like a retired heavyweight world champ you would *not* want to mess with. One who was presently glaring at me with a full-blown frown set in his wide face. I knew him well enough, though, to know the glare really meant worry.

He pulled me farther under the canopy of oak limbs and Spanish moss, his dark eyes darting to the crowd and then back to me. "I'm getting pressure to bring you in, Charlie. The head of the CPP has been calling my cell for the last two hours."

"I don't understand. How—"

"Someone had a video phone in Underground. Your little smackdown with the jinn is all over the news."

I leaned forward, trying to keep my voice down. "They attacked *me*. One of them killed Auggie."

"I know, but the footage. It's brutal, Charlie. It's all over the Internet, too. And it doesn't show them attacking you."

My cheeks went hot. Indignation swelled my chest. "No. Of course it doesn't. They're setting me up."

"Listen," he said, pausing as his cell phone vibrated in his pocket. He glanced at the display. "I can buy you a couple of days; try to find some witnesses who can prove the jinn attacked first. But you gotta lay low until this thing is resolved. The CPP will drag this out until the very end."

"Yeah, and in the meantime they're going to paint their entire race as victims of prejudice and abuse."

"This is all just politics. Give it a few days and they'll find something else to keep them in the spotlight."

My fists clenched hard. That this was happening to me . . . Me! I shook my head, staring across the baseball field. I wasn't a bad officer. I'd never taken a bribe, looked the other way, or committed unwarranted abuse against any criminal or suspect in my custody.

"Watch your back, Charlie. Grigori Tennin will issue a summons. Two of the jinn you killed were local tribesmen."

"I know. So much for their whole law-abiding citizen routine."

"Yeah, and if you can't pay their death price, poof. No body. No evidence. No crime. That's how they work, and the last thing I want is to find out you've gone missing 'cause we both know you don't have the cash or the clout to pay off a blood debt like this."

"Gee, thanks."

If a tribe member was injured or killed and the offender couldn't reimburse the tribe with what Grigori Tennin decided was a fair trade or price, a blood debt was issued. So far, the ITF had been unable to find any evidence of foul play other than word on the street and missing persons reports. We did the best we could, but it was impossible to pin a crime on anyone when there was no evidence, despite the fact that we all knew the jinn still kept to their warlike ways, and each tribe was territorial and unforgiving.

Atlanta's jinn population answered to Grigori Tennin, and it had been that way since the tribe was established here. Most big cities had several tribes, but Atlanta had one. One that was absolute. No jinn made Atlanta home without Tennin's approval.

Like I didn't have enough to deal with already. Now I had to worry about being pulled off the street in order to answer to Grigori, not to mention retribution from the rogues, vigilantes, and sympathizers out there, no doubt whipped into a frenzy after all the media attention.

The chief's big hand squeezed my shoulder. "I know," he said quietly. "Like I said, lay low. Stay away from the house and let me handle the CPP. You did nothing wrong, Charlie. I know that. The department knows that." He grabbed my hand and curled my fingers over a set of car keys. "Go to my house and take my nephew's car. It's the red one. He's doing a semester in South Africa right now. You leave your car. I'll drive it to the station tomorrow. Make sure no one follows you. And for God's sake, stay away from the hospital and Amanda Mott. And you might as well stay away from Hank, too. Tennin will probably have someone on him."

I nodded, squeezing the keys until they bit into my palm. My voice caught. "Thanks, Chief."

"Just don't attract any angry jinn and that'll be thanks enough."

He hunched his wide shoulders and walked down the sidewalk away from my house and away from the direction of my car. I headed the other way, making sure to keep my steps slow and unhurried. My heart pounded. All I could think was that someone had seen me, and was following. I had to get to the car and get to Bryn's as soon as possible.

In the chief's driveway, I slipped inside the sporty red Mustang GT, turned the ignition, leaving the lights off, and backed out into the street, hoping I hadn't woken his wife, Anne-Marie. I shoved the car in gear and headed for Underground.

The parking on Alabama Street had thinned out, allowing me to find a spot near the entrance to Underground. The bars and clubs closed at 4 A.M. If my luck held, the only people passing by would be inebriated stragglers and tired waitstaff. Too tired or drunk to notice me or care.

Hopefully, no one would think to look for me here, a few stores up from the scene of the crime. Bad thing was I'd probably be more recognized down here by the off-worlders than in the 'burbs. But I didn't know where else to go. It was late. I couldn't think straight and had to find a safe place to rest and regroup.

And I desperately needed to see Emma. Just to kiss her while she slept, tuck the covers more securely around her, and watch her for a few minutes. She could center me. Just looking at her reminded me of my priorities, my strength, my purpose.

Underground at this time of night was eerily quiet—a time when your footsteps echoed louder than normal and shadows grew at every turn. I walked at a fast clip across the dimly lit promenade and then down Mercy Street. A few waitresses passed by, but they were in too much of a hurry to get home to notice me. There was a police officer, waiting for the manager to lock the pub across the street and take his money to the bank. Another group headed down my side of the street, but I'd already come to Bryn's door, next to the shop, and was able to turn my back to them as I pressed the buzzer.

I had to press four times before she finally answered. She never answered before that because jerks and drunks were known to walk by and randomly press buzzers.

"Who is it?" she asked in sleepy stereo.

"It's Charlie." I glanced over my shoulder, making sure no one watched. The door buzzed. I turned the knob and pushed.

Bryn's entrance was just a stairwell to a second-floor landing and another door, which led into her apartment over the shop. The door opened before I reached the landing. Bryn stood in the doorway, hands shoved into a cotton waffle-weave robe. Sleep had tangled her loose hair and swollen the delicate skin around her eyes, making her look young and vulnerable. Like my kid sister.

"What's wrong?" She moved aside to let me in.

A small lamp in the living room was on. It was quiet here, too. The shades were drawn, but warmth still surrounded this place, like always. I slid off my jacket and began removing my firearms, setting them on the table in the foyer. Bryn moved into the adjoining kitchen and began making a pot of decaf, yawning as she filled the carafe with water.

I slid onto one of the kitchen counter stools. "How's Em?"

"Good. She did her homework with Will and then we went to visit Amanda at the hospital. I hope that was okay. I know you don't want Em to worry, but I think it made her feel better to go." I gave a nod of agreement, wishing I could've gone too. "We ate dinner, Em took a shower. Everything's fine. *She's* fine." Bryn hit the brew button and then turned toward me. "You on the other hand . . . What happened?"

I let my arms slide over the cool surface of the countertop, wanting nothing more than to lay my head down and drift off to sleep. "The CPP is calling for my arrest after what happened this morning. They're picketing my house. I can't go home right now." I didn't mention the jinn debt. Bryn knew the score. I let my head fall onto my arm. "I just want this all to be over with."

Thankfully, she didn't mention the debt. Instead she went to the fridge and pulled out some cheddar cheese and jalapenos, and then a bag of tortilla chips from the pantry. Comfort food. She spread the chips on a plate. "Do you think Emma is safe? Should she go to school tomorrow?" She sprinkled a generous portion of cheese onto the chips and then added the sliced jalapenos.

"Yeah, security is tight at the school. But I'll have

an officer go over in the morning to keep an eye out. You want an escort?"

She lifted her chin and fixed me with a frank look. "I know it's hard to fathom, but I can take care of us." At that, she put the plate into the microwave. Once it was melting the cheese, she turned back to the fridge and got out salsa and sour cream. Her face was stern as she grabbed two small bowls.

"What about you, Charlie? What about earlier? You killed three jinn and then healed yourself. How long do you think you can keep ignoring what's going on?" She stood in front of the counter, both hands braced in front of her.

I raised my head and straightened my spine. I was too tired to deal with this right now. "Bryn—"

"No, don't," she said. "Don't 'Bryn' me, okay? You almost died today. *Again*. I'm sick of you being like this, Charlie! I'm your sister. And I'm sure as hell not stupid enough to believe whatever excuse you're about to throw at me. What? You can handle it? You can figure it out . . . alone?" Her voice rose, but tempered enough not to wake Emma. The microwave beeped, but she ignored it. "Stop being an idiot. Stop acting like you have no one, that no one is good enough or has the ability to help you. Get off your goddamn high horse, for once."

The microwave beeped again. I stared wide-eyed, stunned by her outburst.

High horse?

My ego wasn't that big to think no one could help

me. Was it? Was that what she really thought? Was that what everyone else thought, too?

The plate of nachos slid onto the counter with a slight rattle. Bryn's cheeks were mottled pink as she grabbed one, shoved it into the sour cream and then into her mouth. She even chewed angry. "Have some before they get cold," she mumbled, leaning into the corner of the counter and taking another one.

Automatically, I did. The first bite of melted cheese, salty nacho, and hot pepper made me realize that I hadn't eaten since breakfast. My stomach let out an eager growl.

"Connor had gifted blood, too," she said, eyes narrowing. "You always denied it, but he did. Just like you deny yours."

The mention of our brother closed my throat and brought a sting of tears to my eyes. Bryn handed me a bottled water from the fridge. The cold liquid soothed my throat and helped temper my emotions. "Can we not talk about him?"

She sighed. "You never want to talk about anything."

"That's not true."

"Uh, yeah it is. You've never talked about him; you do know that, right? You keep it all to yourself." She blinked back sudden tears. Her lips trembled. "I loved him, too. Don't you think I deserve to know what he felt, what he said to you the day he died?" She rolled her eyes to the ceiling and threw her hands in the air. "You know something, Charlie? You do whatever you want, and you never think about anyone but yourself. It'd be too hard for *you* to talk, too hard for *you* to ask for help . . . Does it ever occur to you that the rest of us feel left out, not a part of your little one-woman club?" She paced in front of the counter, gave one last huff, shot me a glare, and then said, "Forget it. I'm going to bed."

What the hell?

Her door shut softly, and I stared at it for a long time, a chip in my hand, paused in midair. Bryn never went off like that. And more startling were her words—words that hit my very heart and made it face truths I didn't want it to. *I* wasn't selfish. How could she say that? But even as I convinced myself of my innocence, I knew she was right. I'd always told myself that I kept things locked away because it would only hurt her. Better she didn't know. Better she didn't get involved in my current state. Better for whom? Who was I to decide that for her?

God, you're a dumbass sometimes.

The last ones in the world I'd ever hurt were my family. But I had. I'd hurt my sister without even realizing it.

I ate another chip, wondering why I felt like I had to carry all my burdens alone. That question rolled around my mind as I finished the nachos and then cleaned up. We hadn't touched the coffee. Typical.

I sat on the couch and removed my shoes, sitting back for a moment to wiggle my toes and let my muscles finally relax. My mind, however, was filled with self-loathing and analyzing. Hell, maybe I deserved to carry my burdens alone. Maybe it was my penance.

I should have listened to my brother's voice in my head the day he died.

He cried out to me, and I didn't listen.

Connor and I were more than your average twins. Bryn was right, he had gifted blood, but then so did I when it came to Connor. From our earliest memories, Connor and I could hear each other's thoughts. As children it was fun. But, as teenagers, we routinely blocked each other out. I mean, who wants to hear lusty teenage boy thoughts or share your secret crush? We'd gotten good at blocking. And I'd gotten good at denying we were special. As a teenager all I wanted was to fit in, not stand out. Especially in a bad way. I'd seen how people had treated my clairvoyant grandmother before the Revelation. Called her a kook, a liar, a weirdo . . . So when Connor called to me, I'd blocked him out as usual. I didn't know he was about to die, that he was trying to ask for my help to save him.

He died because I didn't listen.

Tears pooled in the corners of my eyes. I swiped them away, feeling the familiar anguish of Connor's death return. With a heavy heart, I stood and forced the grief back into the far recesses of my mind, telling myself that I'd had enough for one day.

Emma's room was dark, save for the street light outside making the blinds glow like a night-light. It hurt even more to see her sleeping there, curled up, the covers tucked underneath her chin, which jutted out straight and proud, her lips squashed together and her cheek bunched against her pillow. I loved her so much. I didn't want to hurt her or eventually tune her out like I'd done with Bryn.

I removed my jeans and undid my bra, pulling it out through the sleeve in my shirt, and then slid onto the full-size bed, curling next to her. Instinctively, she snuggled into me, grabbed my arm, and pulled it around her to hold on to it like one of her stuffed animals she slept with at home. My body relaxed. The smell of her hair lingered on the pillows and sheets and low in the air above the bed, and the scent of her skin was still reminiscent of the powdery baby smell of newborns.

My eyelids drifted closed. My breathing slowed. Just a little bit of sleep. Until morning.

8

Bryn talking softly and nudging Emma from sleep woke me before it woke my daughter; she was like her father in that way. Both could sleep like the dead. I didn't move at first, just opened my eyes to see my sister's apologetic grimace. Apparently she'd been trying to let me sleep.

Em snuggled deeper into the mattress and closer into the curve of my body. Then she stilled, realizing I was there. "Mom?"

Her groggy voice pulled a soft smile from my lips, and I propped up on my elbow to kiss her cheek. "Morning, doodlebug."

"Not . . . going . . . to school . . . today." Deep groans of protest went through her as she flipped onto her stomach and buried her face into the pillow. "What are you doing here?"

I rolled onto my back and lifted my hands above my head to stretch. "Yes, you *are* going to school. And I had to sleep here last night because a water pipe burst in the house."

Bryn met my gaze and I shrugged. It was the best I could come up with.

Emma's head immediately lifted. I could barely see her profile through the massive poof of her tangled, wavy hair. "What about Spooky?"

"I'm sure she's fine." Damn. I'd totally forgotten about the cat. Great. If Spooky had gotten out, or worse, gotten hurt by the broken glass or the brick flying through the window, I'd have a devastated kid on my hands.

"C'mon, kiddo, you need to get dressed," Bryn said. "Breakfast is almost ready. I'll go and get Spooky after I drop you off at school."

Saved by my sister. I sat up as Emma shuffled off to use the bathroom and spoke before I could analyze myself out of it. "Bryn . . ." She stopped at the door and turned. "What you said last night. . . . You were right."

She frowned for a second as though she hadn't expected that and then gave me a small smile that didn't reach her eyes. I stared at the closed door, knowing she wasn't about to give in until I confessed everything. She'd had enough. And I couldn't blame her. Made me feel like shit, but I did understand.

In the adjoining bathroom, I brushed my teeth with the spare Bryn kept for me, and then turned on the shower as Emma wiped her face on a hand towel. When I straightened, she was standing by the shower staring thoughtfully at me, her face and lips still puffy from sleep. Her wild hair made her shoulders seem smaller and her bare legs look skinner than they already were. She resembled a little cavewoman standing there, arms hanging limp and tired at her sides. My kid was *not* a morning person.

Her eyes narrowed into a calculating expression so obvious that I had to bite the inside of my cheek to hide my smile. Her voice was still soft and sleepy when she spoke. "Daddy still loves you, you know?"

I released my teeth from my cheek, unsure of what to say, and sat on the toilet lid to give myself some time to form a response.

"And he misses us."

If she hadn't looked so calm and calculating, I would have pulled her into a hug. But this wasn't a raw emotional moment. This was Matchmaking 101.

"Em," I began, and then changed my tactic from what I was about to do, which was pretty much pat my daughter on the head and not address the real issue. No, I didn't want to brush her off, nor did I want to play make-believe. She shoved her wild hair behind both ears. "Here, gimme your brush and I'll fix it." I waited for her to turn around and then dealt with the tangles. "Did he tell you to tell me all this?"

"No. But he's sad and just misses us. I think you should give him a break, Mom."

"Mmm," I responded, not really knowing what to say. "All done." I set the brush on the counter. The bathroom had begun to steam, so I flicked on the exhaust fan. "Go get your breakfast. We'll talk about Dad later. Hey, maybe we'll go to Varsity and get some hot dogs for dinner, okay?" She gave an impatient nod, my attempt at distracting her obviously failing miserably.

"You'll think about it then?"

"Yeah, I'll think about it."

She turned and hugged me with surprising strength, nearly choking me. "Love you."

"Love you, too, kid."

I remained on the toilet lid for a few more seconds, staring at the closed door and wondering how in the hell was I *not* going to disappoint her.

It was a mistake to jump back into things with Will right now, but would she understand that? She was bright, thoughtful, and so open with her feelings. The last thing I wanted was to destroy her optimism and make her a jaded little version of me.

Sighing and wishing I had a magical parenting manual with all the right answers, I stripped down and moved my stiff body into the shower, turning the knob to cool.

The weakness that came with sleep clung valiantly to me even under the cool spray of the shower, but soon my mind woke up and my movements became quicker as I lathered my skin with soap.

My body still felt the same, still looked the same, but inside I was different, changing, able to do things that no human should be able to do. Bryn's words from the night before haunted me. I'd done some remarkable and horrible things, but I wasn't facing them. I was forging ahead with the investigation and telling myself I'd deal with it later. Only, I knew myself well enough to know later would never come. Not if I could help it.

How had I become so good at avoidance?

It was the same with my past, avoiding thoughts of Connor and the guilt that plagued me. And it was the same with Will.

The pipes whined as I turned off the shower and then stepped from the tub. Any thoughts of Connor and Will were pushed aside. I had too much to deal with today, and I couldn't get distracted. That could, quite possibly, get me killed.

After the shower, I crossed the apartment in a towel and my bare feet, speaking quickly to Bryn as she and Emma ate at the counter. "Just need to borrow some clothes."

I heard Bryn say to Emma as I entered my sister's bedroom, "Don't have to worry about your mom borrowing anything nice. She always picks the most *boring* things I own."

Emma giggled.

"I heard that!" I called over my shoulder as I scanned her closet. Sorry, Bryn, but today happened to be the day I actually needed something nice. And her tapered black knee-high skirt and matching black sweater tank with cardigan would do nicely. I even snagged a pair of reasonable pumps.

When I exited the room, Bryn choked on her

orange juice. "Did someone die and I don't know about it?"

Emma came out of the spare bedroom with her backpack. She stopped mid-stride and eyeballed me from toe to head. Then she turned to my sister. "That's a little better than boring, right, Aunt Bryn?"

Bryn handed Emma her lunch bag. "Well, since they *are* my clothes, I'll say yes. It's a start."

"Thanks a lot," I told them both and then focused on my sister. "Do you have a glamour spell lying around? I don't want anyone to recognize me. Something small should do, change of hair color, that sort of thing."

"Sure. A batch just came in at the shop. Hold on a sec and I'll get you one."

The CPP political rally had decided to use the momentum of my case to garner more media attention. Not exactly what I needed if I was to avoid the jinn and sneak into the rally and try to confront Otorius and Mynogan. Finding the source of the *ash* was priority number one, and the only lead I had was the CPP.

After I parked the Mustang, I opened the foil package Bryn had given me and placed the small, paperthin blue wafer onto my tongue. It dissolved instantly, making my eyes burn for a few seconds as an energetic tingle swept through my limbs to my fingertips and toes. Some of the residue hit the back of my throat, making me gag on a taste similar to Nyquil mixed with oregano.

As the party trick worked its magic, I gathered Bryn's big black purse, with my firearms inside, checked the side mirror, and then walked my new blonde-headed, green-eyed self across the parking lot, heels clicking against concrete with quick, no-nonsense steps. For forty-nine bucks you, too, could change your look for an hour or two. Small price to pay for some. Thank God, glamour spells were short-lived, or law enforcement would have one hell of a problem identifying suspects and criminals.

My heart kept a steady beat against my rib cage as I moved toward the large crowd that had gathered in the outdoor venue of Centennial Plaza. A line of limos was parked nearby. The crowd was a mix of humans, jinn, goblins, imps, fae, and the occasional being from Elysia. Reporters from CNN, WSB-TV, 11ALIVE, FOX 5, and every other major news station in Atlanta were there. Maybe I should've brought along a pad and pen. Television cameras were set on either side of the stage as well as individual handhelds carried around by TV crews.

The black outfit soaked up the late morning sun. By the time I weaved my way through the crowd to get a front-row view of the stage, sweat beaded my brow and lower back.

The first speaker stepped onto the stage. The crowd jostled me forward. Otorius. For thirty min-utes, I listened to him spout filth about the department and me in particular. It took everything I had not to vault onto the stage and arrest him simply for being an asshole.

The crowd added to the heat in the plaza, making me remove the cardigan and drape it over my arm. Maybe black wasn't the best choice. I wasn't Charbydon like many of those around me, in their jackets and coats. It made me hot just looking at them.

My sense of smell was unusually strong today. The races of Charbydon and Elysia had very distinct aromas, but they were normally only detectable up close and very personal. I guessed it was the crowd and the heat, but the unmistakable odor of tar covered me in a fine film.

The droning on and on of one distinguished member after another added layers of agitation and impatience. Several times I spied jinn bodyguards scanning the crowd in their jackets and dark glasses, hands behind their backs. But, so far, thanks to Bryn, not one had given me a second glance.

And then I noticed Cassius Mott standing on the edge of the stage, behind the blue curtain, talking to Otorius like they were old friends. His blasé attitude and cheesy grins made my blood boil. His kid was in the hospital and here he was hobnobbing with the CPP of all people? After years in law enforcement, it wasn't that difficult to identify a drug user. And Cass had money and access and years of possession charges swept under the rug thanks to his brother's close association with the ITF. But the fact that he was here, now, was a major red flag. The guy didn't meddle in politics. I doubted he even knew the name of our governor.

More importantly, Cass had the resources to manufacture and/or distribute a new drug. Another suspect added to my mental list.

Finally Mynogan stepped onto the temporary stage, drawing my gaze away from Cass. The crowd cheered and surged forward, pinning me against the barrier around the stage and only a few feet away from a jinn bodyguard. I gave him a geeky smile, shoved the sunglasses back up my nose with my middle finger, and assumed a rather pinched, proper look, keeping my lips thin and cheeks sucked in as I pretended to be engrossed in the speaker.

"Welcome, citizens of Atlanta!" More cheers. "Thank you for coming today. And thank you for coming together, for bringing a sense of community to all races and beliefs. We are all one, and our voice is one . . ."

Blah, blah, blah . . . Yeah, right. Charbydon nobles were as stuck-up and prejudiced as the Adonai. What the hell was he up to? He obviously supported the CPP, was no doubt a registered member by now. He spoke like a politician, looked like a politician, had the resources of a politician . . .

Oh, hell.

The setup was all right there, right in front of my face. He was going to run for office. Just what this city needed—another pompous ass with his own agenda.

As I listened to him speak, hundreds of spidery footsteps crept up my spine. This guy was connected to me in a way that was tearing me apart from the inside out, and damned if I could figure out why. I analyzed him, noting his sharp black suit, his haughty carriage and mannerisms, yet nothing gave me answers. He'd gone without a coat, which I thought was strange, but perhaps nobles were more tolerant of the "cold" of the southern fall season. All I could get from him were super-bad vibes and a queasy stomach.

Images of my nightmare flashed again; him smoothing back the blood-soaked hair from my white face.

I slowed my pulse and regulated my breathing. Several minutes passed.

Over and over, I reminded myself that he had no power over me, unless I allowed it. But I couldn't seem to deliberately control the images and the turmoil inside my head the way I wanted. The only thing I could do was cover them with something else. So I changed my focus, remembering the conversation I'd had with Titus Mott. I felt like an idiot, but what the hell? If I truly had psychic abilities, then this was the perfect place for a test drive.

I tried to sense the different energies around me, carefully reaching out, attempting to separate and pinpoint individual signatures. The dark sunglasses allowed me to study my neighbors openly.

Nothing happened.

I was too distracted, noticing every detail of each person I examined and making up wild backgrounds and MOs for them. Definitely not working. So, I tried closing my eyes and releasing the tension of Mynogan's presence.

Focus.

I opened my mind and envisioned a cool, calming breeze to carry away all the negativity.

Yes, that feels so much better.

Immediately, a friendly energy pricked my consciousness, an aura in my mind that was green and confident in its power. Instinct kicked in and straightaway I thought: *mage.* I peeked and found the owner of that aura, a human, in the crowd and saw with open eyes the vibrant colors of green surrounding her. An energetic high swept through me. The next one was jinn. Red. Hot. Filled with irritation and ego. I scanned more of the crowd: another jinn, a goblin, and a Charbydon noble whose aura was a deep, dark purple, full of intelligence, cunning, and a good-sized helping of self-worth.

Mott had been right. But somehow I'd known. I'd known all along. The super strength and the ability to heal had been a big shock, but this ability, to sense the auras of others in my mind and then to visualize them—I realized I'd had it for a while, just never allowed it to blossom, never intentionally tried to use it. I had always just called it instinct.

My gaze drifted back to Mynogan. Goose bumps sprouted on my arms and thighs. His aura I didn't need or want to see. I had a good idea it was blacker and hotter than newly poured asphalt.

He neared the end of his speech, so I backed away

slowly, slipping in between bodies, bumping shoulders and murmuring apologies as I went. My senses were on overdrive. Body odors. Brief flashes of auras. They compounded, building onto one another until I felt as though I was suffocating under a mound of off-world bodies.

Lungs straining, I managed to break free of the crowd near the curb.

Dear God! I leaned forward, gasping. But just for a moment. My glamour time was almost up, and I couldn't afford to attract attention.

I wasn't sure what my plan was exactly, only that I needed to get to Mynogan. And I'd figured my opportunity would present itself at some point. When it did, I only had a few seconds to make up my mind. The speech ended with a roar.

The bodyguards simultaneously turned their attention to the stage, but that would only last for a second. Without time to think, I sprinted around the limo sandwiched between two black SUVs, opened the passenger door, and slid inside, ducking down into the seat and hoping to hell no one had seen or heard me. The driver was standing outside on the other side, clapping.

Quickly, I pulled my Nitro-gun from the bag and shoved it into the back waistline of the skirt. I prayed this was Mynogan's limo and he wouldn't do something unexpected, like get into one of the SUVs.

I scooted to the far edge of the seat, made my posture straight and my expression blank. Whatever happened, I couldn't lose my cool. Nobles respected control above all else.

The door opened to a throng of legs and reporters' shouts. I held my breath. The first to get in was the third unidentified Charbydon noble from Veritas. His face I remembered well; the classic features, the high cheekbones, and the sardonic mouth. A lock of sable hair fell into his eyes as he dipped his body into the cab of the limo. Eyes I thought were black were, in fact, the darkest midnight blue shot with silver flecks, like stars in a clear night sky. They widened in shock at finding me crouched against the door. But the shock was quickly replaced by a droll smile that cut slits into each side of his cheeks. Mirth and a brief flash of disbelief danced in his eyes as he sat down next to me, a puff of sage and cedar reaching my nose.

I found my breath again, but it was almost sucked permanently from my lungs when Mynogan entered right behind him.

He settled into his seat across from me and the other noble. I braced myself. The only thing that made me feel better was the cold press of my weapon at my back. As his eyes turned to me, no surprise or emotion flitted across his haughty face.

The door shut, the sound echoing finality through my body. My hand itched to pull my gun, just to put a barrier between us.

"All set, sir?" the driver asked, getting into the car.

"Yes, Gavin, thank you," Mynogan answered in an even tone, his black gaze never leaving mine.

The car pulled away from the curb, and a thread of panic wove its way into my psyche. Claustrophobia closed in on me. I was in a tiny car with my worst nightmare.

"Your glamour is fading, Detective Madigan," he said evenly, adjusting the cuffs on his expensive wool jacket. "I'm sure you realize the entire city is looking for you."

My teeth clenched as his words struck anger in me. Much better than fear. I grabbed on to it like a lifeline. "If it wasn't for the CPP . . ."

The male next to me angled in his seat to watch me, his body deceptively relaxed. I ignored him, sensing he was more curious than threatening at the moment. *One predator at a time*, I told myself, redirecting my attention back to Mynogan. "I know this little charade of good citizenship is nothing but a smoke screen."

Mynogan's lips lifted into what was supposed to be a smile, but it was more like a sick grimace. "Is that so?" He tugged his dress shirt cuffs out from under the suit jacket until the proper amount was shown to his satisfaction. "Do you know, Charlene—"

"It's Charlie."

His black stare lifted to mine for a second. "Do you know, Charlene, the kind of power the noble class holds?"

Which translated into: *how stupid are you to get into a limo with two of them?* I bided my time, though, before I had to pull my gun. "Of course I know. You're the nobility of Charbydon. By right of bloodline, the nobles control the government, economy, and entire structure of your world. I know very well the power you hold."

"We're an oligarchy, Detective," the other one said in a deep, mellow tone that sounded way more sensual than it should. "Ruled by two kings, two different royal bloodlines, and overseen by a council of elders."

"Carreg is Lord Lieutenant of the House of Astarot," Mynogan introduced the male next to me. "And I am High Elder of the House of Abaddon."

"I know the history," I said, hiding my surprise at finding them to be actual royals—only royalty served in such high positions in their government. The Astarots and Abaddons kept mostly to their own world, only sending delegates and lesser nobles like Otorius to ours. "Since when do the two Houses agree?" I asked, knowing full well the two ruling families in Charbydon weren't known for working together. They'd managed their world for eons, but were always, according to scholars, at odds. Kind of like Republicans and Democrats.

They exchanged looks, and I detected a brief moment of tension. "We do agree on the continued prosperity of our people," Carreg said slowly. "Cultivating a better relationship with your world will help us in that endeavor."

I started to ask him what he meant, but Mynogan interrupted.

"But do you know the power inside us? The abilities we have, Charlene?"

My nostrils flared. Oh, this guy was pushing it. "The name is Charlie, and unless you want me to start calling you *Mynie* then I'd suggest you use it."

Carreg covered his laugh with a soft cough as Mynogan leaned forward and pierced me with the blackest, most brutal stare. A streak of fear shot through my system, but his refusal to use my official title or my preferred name pissed me off. *Eye for an eye, buddy.*

Pink tinged his perfect olive skin. "I could end your insignificant little life with a thought, Detective." His voice dripped with menace and disgust. "You possess the life span of an insect and hold just as much power. You have no idea the influence we wield."

"Yeah, like walking all over those who are weaker and poorer? You're no better than a schoolyard bully. Some power. You have no intention of bringing the races together, do you?"

Instantly, the limo filled with Mynogan's rage. The whites of his eyes bled to blackness. An oppressive hum of strength and energy engulfed me in the smut of his being and past deeds.

Carreg cleared his throat gently, the sound diffusing some of Mynogan's anger. "You have more courage than I thought, Detective." He cocked his head. "Or is it stupidity?"

"Stupidity," I answered, surprising him. "Of the purest kind. Which makes me unpredictable, wouldn't you say?"

"You mock something you know nothing of," Mynogan said. "I should take your blood right now."

I frowned at the odd statement. "What's that supposed to mean?" Was this the Abaddon way of threatening one's life? Sounded suspiciously vampiric to me, which, as far as I knew, was nothing but pure myth.

A thin grin twisted Mynogan's face, and he lifted a severe white eyebrow. "For all your knowledge, you know very little of my kind."

"Then, by all means, enlighten me." We stopped at another light. From our location, I guessed we were headed back to CPP headquarters, which meant I had to get out of the car soon.

"Better yet," Mynogan said, leaning so close that I was forced to lean back into the seat. "Why don't I just start by picking the flesh from your bones?"

One piece for me. One piece for you.

The breath whooshed from me, and my heart skidded to a painful stop. I pressed myself against the door, flailing for my gun. Air filled my lungs as my fingers closed around the handle. I drew it on him, hand shaking as the whine of the charging weapon filled the silence. "Get away from me." He sat back, happy to have completely unwound me. "You too." I waved the gun at Carreg. "Get over there, next to him."

My gaze flicked to the street. We had stopped at a traffic light, but it was a bad time to bail. The bodyguards could easily follow on foot. "Who are you? How the hell do you know me?"

Mynogan shrugged. "I can be your worst nightmare, Charlene, or I can show you the path to immense power."

I tightened my hold on Bryn's bag and opened the door as the limo started through the intersection. "I'd rather suck face with an imp." And with that, I ducked out of the limo before it cleared the intersection.

Bad plan, Charlie, I thought as I went down hard, tripping in the damn heels and rolling four times, bruising and scraping every part of my body and every bone that poked out and hit the pavement. Once my momentum slowed, I pushed to my feet to the squeal of brakes, horns honking, and the astonished look of the driver behind the limo, and then darted to the sidewalk and around a corner. Adrenaline made me move fast and helped ease the pain, but as soon as I realized no one followed, my steps slowed and my body began to throb and sting from the road burn.

My cell phone rang from inside the bag. I stopped on the sidewalk, fished it out, and flipped it open with one hand.

"Charlie, where the hell are you?"

"I'm fine, Hank." *I just rolled out of a moving car in high heels.* "How are you?" The farther I walked, the more my left ankle hurt. Sharp lines of pain zinged up my leg with every step. I reached down and took off the black pumps, proceeding barefoot.

"Please tell me you're laying low."

"Um . . ."

I held the phone away from my ear as Hank yelled. "Damn it! I knew it! I knew you couldn't stay out of trouble for one day. *One day*, Charlie!" He let out a loud, disappointed huff, making me roll my eyes. "Where are you right now?"

I glanced at the stop sign as I crossed the street. "I'm at the corner of Walton and Forsyth."

"Stay there. I don't care what the chief says, I'm picking you up. Go to the Subshop Deli at Broad Street. I'll meet you there. Someone ransacked your house and broke into the school early this morning."

At the mention of school, I froze, nearly causing a collision with the person walking behind me. "Oh, God, Emma went to school this morning." I started running, the bag slapping against my hip and my ankle forgotten in the sudden panic.

"Calm down. It was before any students got there. Classes have been canceled. Em's at Bryn's and Will is on his way to get her. Oh, and Bryn made me go by and pick up Spooky. Who was, oddly enough, spooked by the break-in." Hank chuckled at himself.

The damn cat could take care of herself. My thoughts were on Em. "Why the hell didn't anyone tell me?!" I shouted into the phone.

"Look at your phone, smart-ass. We've been calling all morning."

The sound of the rally must've drowned out the ring tone. And if it had rung in the limo, I had been too distracted to even notice.

"Fine, just hurry," I said, approaching the deli.

9

The bell chimed over the door as I entered, braced a hand against the glass to slip the pumps back on, and then limped inside where I slid gratefully into an empty booth.

God, I hurt!

It took a minute to regain my composure and take stock. My elbow ached, and the scratches and road-rub along my shoulder, hip, and thigh burned, but not nearly as bad as my ankle, which was growing hotter and achier by the second. Pulling in my leg, I saw the skin was swelling, but not enough to indicate I'd sprained it.

"Hey, miss, you got to order to take up a booth!"

Yeah, yeah.

Quickly, I smoothed my hair and straightened my shirt before standing. Every muscle protested as

I searched the bag for my wallet, pulling out three bucks and some change. At least the counter wasn't too far away. Wincing, I shuffled forward in the torturous black pumps and ordered a large sweet tea and a chocolate chip cookie.

The clerk lifted an eyebrow at my appearance. "You all right?"

With a wry half-smile, I handed him the three bucks. "Yeah. You'd be amazed what a clearance sale at the Apple Store does to some people."

He froze. "There's a clearance sale at the Apple Store?"

"Yeah. Ends today though."

"Dude. Really?"

I nodded. "Yeah. Sorry."

The door jingled. The clerk looked beyond me and gave a nod to the new person. No, I corrected, smelling the distinct scent of tar. Not a person. A jinn. Shit.

My blood pressure rose, and I mentally begged the clerk to hurry the hell up.

The jinn, I noted via a quick sideways glance, was typically large, his bulky form heightened by a Georgia Tech hoodie. He didn't pay me any mind as he stood at my right side, his attention firmly on the overhead menu.

"Hey, Len, how's it going?" the clerk asked as he poured my tea. "Heard about those guys who were killed yesterday in Underground. That's wrong, man, just wrong."

Len turned his head slightly, casting an aloof look at the clerk, the muscle in his dark gray jaw flexing.

The clerk slid my tea across the counter and pulled the cookie from the bin with a napkin. His eyes lit excitedly as he leaned forward toward Len, his voice low when he spoke. "Tennin must be calling for blood, eh?"

I grabbed the tea and cookie, pivoting just as Len turned fully toward the clerk. He hadn't seen my face. But I didn't miss his deep resonating voice as I walked back to the booth. "If she can't pay, it will be in blood, yes."

Poised and alert for an attack, I slid into the booth facing the jinn so I could watch his every move.

If I disappeared, it'd be all-out war against the jinn. But then Tennin didn't really have a choice. Death prices and blood debts had been a way of life for the jinn for thousands of years. If Tennin looked the other way now, it'd be seen as weakness, and he hadn't retained his position as jinn boss for this long by being weak. In fact, it was well known the guy bordered on psychotic.

As the clerk made Len's order, I studied the broad back of the bald-headed warrior, noting his thick gunmetal neck and the beefy hands that flexed and un-flexed at his sides. They lived at the ready, always on alert, always ready to fight.

Memories of the three I'd killed came back to me. The thick black blood they'd bled; the smell of it like liquid tar and iron. I didn't know how in the hell I'd managed to kill three of them, let alone how I was going to thwart a whole damn tribe.

As the jinn paid and approached my booth with a to-go bag, I lowered my head and broke the cookie in half, trying to temper my adrenaline so he wouldn't smell it. I fought a two-second battle with myself. Should I glance at him as he passed? Would that be the normal thing to do, or should I ignore him?

With no time to think, I opened my mouth and shoved in half the cookie. Dim violet eyes met mine as he walked by my table.

I froze.

One dark eyebrow dipped a fraction. At my appearance? At the fact that I smiled at him with a mouth full of cookie? Or that he recognized me as the prey he was charged with bringing in?

It seemed like slow motion had kicked in as we locked gazes, but it was over in the two seconds that it happened. I didn't let out my breath until the bell over the door stopped jingling.

I washed the lump of dry cookie down with the tea, taking a moment to decompress after my near brush with the jinn and get back on track.

Mynogan's last words slowly crept in my head.

He'd tried to lure me with the promise of power. But why? I released a deep sigh, propped my chin in my hand, and gazed out the window. I was no closer to finding out how he knew me or why he existed in my dreams. And, for all my bumps and bruises, I'd gotten no information, not a single clue on the *ash*.

But one thing I did know: after seeing Cassius Mott at the rally, connecting the dots was pretty simple. Amanda was Cass's daughter. Cass was a known drug user. And a new drug was going around. Thanks to his brother, Titus, Cass had a small fortune and access to numerous labs. He *had* to be involved with *ash* in some way, and somehow Amanda had gotten hold of it. My house and the school had been broken into. And the only relation there was Amanda, which meant someone, possibly Cass, was looking for something.

But what? My fingers tapped on the table.

Goose bumps pricked my skin. I sat straighter. They'd been looking for something they hadn't found at school, so they'd gone to my place.

My pulse leapt. What was the one thing a kid kept on her most of the time, the one thing she kept her belongings in besides her locker? Her backpack. Bingo. And I knew exactly where that was. In the backseat of my Tahoe. When I dropped her and Em off at school the previous morning, she'd been so unusually hyper and distracted about her new Betsey Johnson handbag that it was no wonder she'd forgotten to grab her worn-out old backpack. And probably by the time Amanda realized it, she was already on her way to bliss city. The drug could've been coursing through her system from the moment she got into my car, and with Amanda in a coma there was no way to know for sure.

The backpack had to be it.

I got a refill on the sweet tea and then sat back down, waiting for Hank. Will was probably having a fit by now, wondering what the hell was going on with the break-ins at the house and school. I dialed his cell and then hung up before the call went through. I couldn't explain everything to him now. He had to have seen the news, heard all the details from Hank. Bryn would probably fill him in, too, when he arrived to pick up Em.

Instead, I called Bryn at Hodgepodge and spoke briefly to her and then Emma, just to make sure Emma was okay. She couldn't have sounded more normal or more excited that school had been cancelled and she got to spend the day with her dad. Ah, the joys of being a kid.

A horn honked outside. I turned in the booth to see Hank's sleek Mercedes dart into an empty spot at the curb. Grabbing Bryn's bag, I scooted from the booth with my tea, chucked the cookie wrapper, and then hobbled to the car.

All I wanted was to sink into the soft leather seat and close my eyes.

"Whoa," Hank said as I plopped awkwardly into the seat, shoved the Styrofoam cup into the cup holder, and shut the door, "what the hell happened to you?"

I yanked down the visor mirror. Half of my twist was out, my hair long and tangled on one side and up on the other. A few scratches marred my left cheek and jaw, and my mascara was smudged. Bloody skin peeked from a large tear in the left shoulder of Bryn's sweater. "Long story."

He turned down the radio. "Aren't they always?"

After I filled him in on the political rally and subsequent limo ride from hell, Hank took a good five minutes to yell at me. Again. I was really getting sick of his holier-than-thou attitude. We were cops. What did he expect? But I cut him some slack and didn't argue back. He'd been torn in half when I'd died, and his sudden protectiveness stemmed from never wanting to go through that again. I couldn't blame him.

"So you think Cassius Mott has something to do with this?"

"Don't you? It fits. And I have a hunch Mott Tech isn't far behind. Haven't figured out how Mynogan and the jinn fit yet, but they do. I know they do."

"Well, while you were rolling out of limos, I finally got an ID on the third jinn that attacked you and Auggie," he said. "Guess who was signing his paycheck?"

I knew the answer to that.

"Yeah. The CPP," Hank said.

"So Mott and the CPP could be partners, manufacturing the *ash*, and they're using the jinn to distribute it. It'd be a good way to fund their campaign. And maybe Cass wants his own money, to get out from under Titus."

"Eh, too weak. The jinn could've attacked you on their own, Charlie. It might have had nothing to do with the CPP. Plus the only evidence we've got is Auggie pointing the finger at Veritas, and Mynogan happened to be there when we went to take a look. And why would the CPP need to create a drug trade to fund their campaign when they have some of the richest nobles in the universe as members? The jinn or Cass could be solely responsible for this whole operation."

"Thank you, counselor." My cell phone rang again. I didn't recognize the number. "Madigan," I answered.

"Detective." Titus Mott's voice breathed relief into the phone. I held the mouthpiece and leaned over to whisper his name to Hank. "I was hoping you'd have time to come back to the lab."

"For the physical?"

A long pause followed, and my skin tingled.

"I've remembered more details about your death . . . details I think you need to know. Will you come?"

Goose bumps spread like waves down my arms and legs. I swallowed. "Sure. When?"

"This evening, tonight . . . I'll be here until morning. Come anytime."

"All right," I said, trying to sound casual even as warning bells were going off in my head. "This evening then."

Mott mumbled a quick good-bye. I closed the phone and turned to Hank. "He's scared. Spooked, like Auggie was."

"I'm coming with you," Hank said before I could argue. "If Cass is working with the CPP and they are responsible for the *ash*, Titus could be, too . . . I mean, they *are* brothers. It might be a setup, Charlie. If they are involved, they already know you're on to them, especially after your little limo ride. You're not going alone. We'll go in, I'll take off the voice-mod, and we'll get to the bottom of this."

I turned in the seat. "Yeah, and you know it's against the law to do that. We'd need an interrogation warrant for you to use your voice. Civil rights, remember? You go in there and question the head of the CPP and the best-known scientist since Einstein, and we'll have the biggest lawsuit on our hands the department has ever seen."

Sirens couldn't just go around making people follow commands or talk against their will. It had taken years of legislature to create laws and restrictions to protect everyone from the individual powers of the off-worlders. And law enforcement, especially, had to be careful. Use a siren's power before you had an interrogation warrant securely in hand, and it'd make everything a suspect said, criminal or not, inadmissible in court.

"Since when did you go all procedural?" Hank glanced in his rearview mirror before switching lanes.

"Since nailing the people who put Amanda in the hospital and made me enemy number one is a promise I made to my kid and myself. I'm not going to screw it up. If they're responsible, they won't walk free on a technicality."

"Unless we take a mage with us. I'll make them talk, and he'll make them forget we were ever there."

"If only," I said, knowing neither one of us would go that far.

We both had suggested going off the book a time or two, and, yeah, we'd taken a lot of leeway with police procedure, but never anything that would let a suspect off the hook.

"Since we're on the subject of you," he said carefully, "I heard you're thinking about giving Will another chance."

Immediately I realized where he'd gotten his information. Emma.

This morning in the bathroom I told her I'd think about it. Now my mistake was glaringly obvious. I'd given her hope without meaning to, without considering my words and how she'd take them.

The air in the Mercedes turned tense. I swiped the tea and took a long drink.

"Is it true then?"

"I don't know. Will's been clean ever since that night. He's done the twelve-step program for black crafting addiction and still attends meetings. He's even sponsoring a new member. Who knows . . . maybe in the future . . ." I fiddled with the straw in my tea. Why did I feel like a kid suddenly in trouble, like I had to explain myself? "Everyone is guilty of bad judgment once in—"

"*Bad judgment?* I think it was a little more than bad judgment, Charlie! Wagering your marriage, black crafting, basically leading a whole other life in secret . . . Every time he lied about where he was going and what he was doing, it was premeditated. You almost died because of him. Doesn't that matter to you?"

"Of course it does; why the hell do you think I divorced him? Jesus, Hank. Will went through a decade of black crafting addiction. That's what addiction does, it ruins lives, takes lives, destroys everything . . ." Old memories grabbed hold of my heart and the never-ending reservoir of hurt closed my throat. Hank didn't have a clue what it was like to have your entire world pulled out from under you, to grieve for the loss of the fucking fairy tale you *thought* you had. Fuck Hank. He didn't know what it was like to love someone the way I had loved Will. How hard it was, even now, to stop caring completely. Twelve years of loving someone just doesn't go away overnight, divorce or not.

Something stirred inside me, snaking beneath my skin, wanting release, wanting a fight. I swallowed it back down. "Just back off, okay? I know how you feel about it, but . . ." *It's none of your business.*

Sometimes words didn't need to be said aloud to be understood. I could feel him look over at me in shock.

"It *is* my goddamn business, Charlie, whether you like it or not."

Fine. I turned in my seat. I knew where this was heading but I couldn't stop myself. "Then why the hell didn't you say anything? You're a siren. You can sense shit like that. All that time you had to have known, and you're going to sit here and lecture me? *When you knew?*"

So there it was. Finally out in the open. Hank, being an off-worlder, was way more in tune to sensing auras and the taint caused by black crafting. There was no way he had missed sensing it on Will back then. Yet he'd said nothing at the time. Had he told me, maybe that night never would have happened.

"It wasn't my place." He kept his eyes focused on the road.

"So first, it's not your business. And now it is. Which is it, Hank? Because you can't have it both ways."

He held up his hands for a second as though he was about to make a point, but then put them back on the steering wheel. He stared ahead for a long moment, and I knew he was trying his hardest to calm down. We were both treading on the edge of an explosive situation if one of us lost it.

A thought occurred to me. "Let me ask you this then: have you sensed it on him since that night?" I certainly hadn't, and I'd gotten pretty good at detecting the fine, smoky odor since learning of Will's addiction.

"No."

"Well, gee, don't sound so happy about it," I snapped. I returned to my proper sitting position and folded my arms over my chest. "You could give me a little credit, you know. And Will, too. He's been clean for eight months, going to therapy once a week, and he's a good father. So lay off him."

My hypocrisy was not lost on me. Hank was right and he'd said everything that I'd pretty much said to Will earlier. Yet here I was taking up for Will. I knew Will was clean, and I knew it was his addiction that had caused all the trouble in our marriage. But it didn't erase the hurt and the deep sense of betrayal I still felt.

Hank didn't respond, and I let the subject drop.

Talking about Will gave me a rush of nervous energy. Usually a long run or a good workout put me back to rights, but there wasn't exactly time for that. And I hated being on the outs with my partner. So, in typical fashion, I changed the subject to redirect my energy toward something I could better control. "So what do you know about the two Houses of Charbydon? Astarot and Abaddon."

Hank took the ramp to the highway, which wasn't the fastest way to get back to the station.

Focusing on work, on the investigation, was where we needed to put our concentration, not on bickering about the past. He seemed to agree, because his shoulders relaxed a little and his grip loosened on the steering wheel. "Not much. They've been at war for centuries. Mostly political, but they've gone to the battlefield many times over the years. The Astarots blame the Abaddons for causing their moon to fade, among other things."

"How do you cause a moon to fade?"

"Not sure—pollution? Someone messing with the alignment, who knows? Their moon is like the sun is to our planet. It's different than the moon here, stronger, brighter, bigger . . . And now it's dying."

"That's what Auggie meant." I chewed on the straw for a few seconds, and then put the cup back down. "He didn't want to go back home. He said it was dark, too dark, that no light shined."

"Moonlight. The days in Charbydon are said to be blacker than black, a time of rest, but the nights are bright and active."

I remembered Carreg's odd words in the limo, and now I realized what he'd meant. "Both Houses are working together to find a solution. That's what Carreg was referring to in the limo."

Hank cast me a knowing glance. "And who best to help them figure it out? Who is the best and brightest scientist this side of the Atlantic?"

"Titus Mott," we said in unison.

"So Mott Tech is helping them revive their moon. Could be totally unrelated."

I shook my head. "We're missing something. We're missing huge pieces. Don't you feel it? Mynogan. The jinn. The Motts. *Ash.* *My* connection to Mynogan. Hell, even the dying moon. I don't know . . . My gut says it's all related somehow. Yet none of it seems to fit."

"Well, that's what we're here for, kiddo," Hank said, pulling into a parking spot near the station. "To figure it out. Maybe one of the pieces we're missing is in Amanda's backpack."

"Let's hope."

As soon as we stopped, I slid onto the floorboard of the car, knowing the jinn had to be watching the station and the last thing I needed was to be hauled in front of Grigori Tennin. He'd have to wait. Hank set the alarm and then went inside. All he had to do was retrieve Amanda's backpack from the backseat of my vehicle parked in the lot out back. No one would think anything of it. Sounded simple enough, but with everything that had been going wrong, I had my doubts.

A few minutes later he was back, tossing the backpack into the passenger seat above my head. As soon as he pulled away from the station, I got into the seat and searched the pink-and-black REI backpack.

Notebook. Makeup case. Geology textbook. Glitter pens. Crumpled paper and wrappers.

"Nothing."

I checked all the front pockets. Empty. Hank parked the car in an open spot near Dewey's Pub. "Here," he said, grabbing the pack. He pulled out the books and leafed through them.

I fished around in the trash, hoping for a clue. The first thing I uncrumpled was a piece of notebook paper with a boy's name written all over it. A gum wrapper . . . and then a pill wrapper.

"What's this?" I asked more to myself than Hank. It was one of those individual packets with an indentation that held medicine or gum. "This is like those old square gum packs, like Chiclets."

"Chic what?"

"Before your time," I said, examining the packet. The strange thing was there was no brand name written on either side of the paper. I sniffed the inside, surprised to detect a honeysuckle-like scent. There was a perforation line along one edge, as though it had been separated from a bigger pack. No markings or words anywhere.

"This looks just like the other one we found on that vic near Solomon Street." I passed the wrapper to Hank.

He studied it and then sniffed the inside, his forehead wrinkled in concentration. "Sweet," he muttered. "Smells like the other one, too. We should get this to the lab. They've been dying for another sample." He let his head fall back against the headrest, completely still, and his eyes closed for a long time. Frowning, he passed it back to me, the blue in his irises turning darker with his frustration. He scrubbed his hands down his face and sighed. "It's the smell, though. I swear I've come across this scent before."

"Sucks getting old, doesn't it?"

"Speak for yourself." He glanced over his shoulder to pull into traffic. "Sirens don't age."

"True. You don't age on the outside, but the mind is another ballpark. Give it a few hundred years more and you'll be like Doctor Dolittle, attracting all the little birds and creatures of the land." I wiggled my fingers in the air as though they were little birds, flying toward Hank.

"You're insane," he said under his breath.

"And talking to yourself is one of the first signs."

We stopped at a red light, and he turned to me. "Charlie . . . I want to apologize for what I said. I—" He stopped me when I went to speak. "Let me finish. I should have said something back then, found some way to tell you. We were still getting to know each other, and I guess, after a while, I convinced myself you knew. So I just ignored it. And you're right, it's none of my business now. But watching you die . . ." A trace of anguish crossed his face, making his eyes dim. The light turned green, and he quickly faced the windshield. "Anyway, for what it's worth I am sorry."

A wave of emotion lodged in my throat, and I could only nod as we drove through the intersection. I tucked the wrapper into Bryn's large pocketbook. "Well, maybe we can lift a print from this." Most likely not. We'd only get partial prints, if anything. And Amanda's would be the most prevalent.

"Maybe," he echoed.

After a long moment, he said, "I ran into the chief inside. He's putting an undercover officer on Bryn's place, just in case the Charbydon idea of street justice gets out of hand. It's not hard to track you to her or to Emma."

I hated bringing my family into this! I hated that someone was going to great lengths to use me as a scapegoat. And I had a pretty good idea who was behind it. The bastard's black aura would never spread to my family. I'd die before I let Mynogan infect them the way he had infected me. And I sure as hell would take him down with me, if it came to that.

I caught Hank looking in the rearview mirror again. He'd taken the most roundabout way to the station, and now we were headed back toward the interstate when we were just there minutes ago.

"We're being tailed," he said softly.

My stomach flipped as I caught sight of a dark blue SUV in the passenger side mirror. "Mmm. Probably Len from the deli."

"Who?"

"A jinn at the Subshop Deli. How long has he been following us?"

"Since the station for sure."

I turned in the seat to stare directly at the car behind us. "You know we're going to have to talk to Grigori Tennin. Get the jinn off our backs for a while."

A snort issued from Hank's mouth. "Yeah, good luck with that." Then he glanced over and saw I wasn't laughing. "Charlie—"

"What? It's not *your* ass being hunted. And the way I see it, I don't really have a choice. They're all trying to find me and bring me into the summons anyway. No, I need to fix this now, under my terms."

"You mean *we*," Hank corrected. "We need to fix this." He glanced in the rearview mirror, his profile going hard and grim. "Time to walk the line, kiddo. You thinking what I'm thinking?"

Anticipation fired my blood, and, despite my better judgment, I was still itching for that fight. "Absolutely."

Hank navigated the car away from the interstate and down a small side street lined with warehouses that eventually dipped under the highway overpass. It was the perfect place for a trap. I turned in the seat, withdrew my Nitro-gun, and set the weapon to a hard freeze.

Once we cleared the overpass, the Mercedes accelerated fast, drawing away from the SUV. But no sooner than Hank had gunned it, he slammed on the brakes and did a one-eighty, turning to face the SUV, which braked hard, skidding head-on, straight toward us.

We were out of the car, weapons drawn just before the SUV's locked-up tires came to a smoking halt inches from Hank's fender. Before the driver had a chance to reverse, I ran to the window, aimed the gun, and ordered him out. Hank went to the passenger's side. "All clear!" he called.

I opened the driver's side door and stood back. "Out of the vehicle. Hands where I can see them."

Len's dark fingers flexed around the leather steering wheel, and his violet irises burned with rage. He wasn't moving. Apprehending an irate jinn was like trying to put a collar on a rabid hyena. No one ever came out unscathed.

Hank came around the SUV, his weapon trained on Len. His steps were careful as he scanned the area under the overpass. "I thought you guys traveled in packs," he said, coming to stand at my side.

Len's answer was to spit at our feet. I cocked an eyebrow at his show of contempt. Like I hadn't seen that one before. "Whatever." I grabbed a handful of his hoodie and jerked him from the vehicle, holding the Nitro-gun at his back as I shoved him against the

SUV's hood and kicked out his feet with my borrowed pumps.

I pulled two knives, a set of brass knuckles, and two spell vials from his person. Hank took each one from me, examined it, and then pocketed the items. "So how much am I worth to the one who brings me in?" I asked as I patted down the insides of his thighs. "Must be a lot if you came alone." Len must have seen an opportunity and taken it. Too bad for him.

"I don't need help with one little female."

Hank's mouth dropped a fraction, obviously offended at being left out of the danger factor. "Uh, hello? Siren here . . . She does have a partner."

I straightened and exchanged a wry smile with Hank, ignoring his remark. "It's got to be the outfit." I had to admit I did look all soft and girly in this getup. "Need I remind you," I said to Len, "who's got who pinned against the side of the car?"

It was never a good idea in any situation to goad a jinn, but I couldn't help it. I had a reputation to uphold.

His muscles tensed right before he twisted around and grabbed my wrist, jerking it aside just as I squeezed the trigger. The blast skipped across the hood of the vehicle. He grappled with my arm, trying to use his force to spin me around and hold my back against his front. His beefy arm encircled my waist as his other hand still worked on trying to relieve me of my gun. I nailed him in the nose with my elbow, using every ounce of strength I had, and heard a sickening crunch for my effort.

"Any time now!" I barked at my partner, jamming the heel of my pump into Len's shin and then dragging it down. He growled, grabbed my hair, and then jerked my head up. Pain flashed across my entire scalp, making my eyes water.

"These are second-rate, man," Hank said to Len, examining one of the spell vials.

"Hank!" It was one thing to know your partner had complete confidence in your fighting abilities . . . But after I got through with Len, I was going to beat Hank senseless with one of my sister's black pumps.

He shook one of the vials and then said, "Duck."

The small glass tube came hurtling toward us. I barely had time to relax my body and drop through Len's arms, despite the fact that he still had a nice chunk of my hair clenched in his fist. As I dropped, I grabbed the chunk to alleviate some of the pain even as hair began to pull from my scalp.

He let go as the vial broke against the side of his smooth, gray head, engulfing us in a cloud of muddy green stench.

Immediately, I held my breath, glad my arms were over my head, shielding me somewhat from the chain reaction above me. If I didn't breathe it in, I was okay. Len stiffened for a count of three, then tipped over like a dead tree in the forest. Coughing from the thick scent of something acrid and tangy, I crawled out from under the small mushroom cloud. Whatever it was, it burned the insides of my nose and throat raw.

I grabbed on to Hank's leg and pulled up, my

fingers digging as hard as they could into his knee, thigh, and then arm.

He was *laughing*. Not out loud, but with his eyes. And to me, that was the same thing.

When I straightened and regained my balance, I shoved him hard. "What the hell is wrong with you?" I coughed again, hacking loudly and trying to get the taste out of my mouth. "Idiot! You could have shot him!"

"Yeah, I know," Hank sighed, chuckling softly.

"I know you're Mister Invincible and everything, but could you *try* to take things seriously once in a while?" I eyed him with a glare of disbelief. "You're so annoying. Don't even talk to me. You almost hit me with that friggin' vial. You have no idea how lucky you are right now."

Blue eyes glittered back at me. He tried to put on a serious face. What the hell was so damn funny? I turned to study Len, and didn't see anything amusing about his unconscious form. I whirled back to Hank. "What the hell was in that potion?"

"It was an attraction spell. To lure a jinn female." He rubbed his chin, studying Len. "Don't think you're supposed to use the entire bottle though."

"Ya think?"

I massaged my closed eyelids, trying to ease the stinging aftereffects of the spell shower. "Come on, let's get him into the back or else we're gonna have the entire female jinn population sniffing him out in no time."

"That guy's not going anywhere near my car." Hank made an offended face. "Neither one of you."

I bent down and grabbed one of Len's ankles, but not before shooting Hank a dark look. "Payback will come, my friend. When you least expect it."

"Hey, all I did was save your ass."

"Uh-huh. Help me get him into the SUV."

It took Hank and me a good fifteen minutes to drag the two-hundred-fifty-pound jinn to the back of the SUV, pick him up, and deposit him into the back. I'd have to drive with the windows down all the way to Underground.

IO

We drove into one of the delivery lanes near Underground, parked, and then Hank heaved Len over his shoulder. Making a scene hadn't been something we'd planned for. In fact, we really didn't have a plan at all. Unless walking into the Lion's Den and asking the biggest tribe boss this side of the Mason-Dixon to forgive an unforgiveable debt was a plan—well then, we had a doozy.

I followed Hank's large form through Underground, acutely aware of the stares and openmouthed gawks we received. It wasn't every day you saw a siren carrying an unconscious jinn through the streets.

Despite the old-fashioned-style streetlamps that burned twenty-four hours a day, the light on Solomon Street was murky at best, the perfect environment for crooks and convicts. Old Savannah bricks paved the street. Peddlers occupied alleyways. Butcher shops, inns, bars, herberies, magic shops, and strip clubs practically spilled onto the sidewalk. Doors stayed open. Inventory was piled against walls and storefronts. Small carts had permanent spaces on curbs. Open fires burned in barrels, making the air steamier than normal. This was the Charbydon quarter, and while they could tolerate the sunlight, they liked things crowded, hot, and dark.

Despite the atmosphere, there was a modicum of safety here during the day. The true danger lurked in the back rooms, alleys, and late nights. But for me, daytime or not, the danger was very real with a debt hanging over my head.

The farther we went down Solomon Street, the more attention we attracted. Business owners and patrons came out of storefronts to watch our procession. There was no way to hide the artificial pheromones Len cast off. Every jinn female stopped and sniffed the air as we passed by. In the darkness, their rapt violet eyes glowed eerily, lit from within.

No one stopped us. There was no need. From the moment we stepped onto Solomon Street, Grigori Tennin had known. I cast a glance over my shoulder, and wasn't surprised to see the hulking silhouettes of four jinn warriors following behind us, spanning the breadth of the street, their dark forms passing in and out of shadow and the orange glare of open fires. There was no turning back now.

Tennin's home and business encompassed the long stretch of buildings at the dead end of the street. A sleazy strip club, bar, and gambling establishment called the Lion's Den was the tribe's base of operations. The bar and strip club covered the first floor. The upper level housed the gambling parlor. The tribe, however, lived in the earth.

Underneath Solomon Street, the jinn had excavated a vast network of tunnels and chambers.

Bulky ironwork framed the rough-planked front door, the coarse handle warm to my touch as I opened the heavy door. The heat had become oppressive. Sweat beaded my brow and lower back. I stood back, allowing Hank to cross the threshold. He wasn't immune to the heat either, or the strain of carrying two hundred plus pounds of jinn warrior. Sweat dampened his shirt and face and darkened his blond hair.

Once inside, the first thing to hit me was the smell; of earth, wood-smoke, and tar. It was like we had just descended into a deep cave near an active volcano.

The bar was doing steady business. A darkling fae—a sidhé fae would never be caught dead in a place like this—danced onstage to an old seductive jazz tune I couldn't name. She was topless and wore only knee-high red boots and a sequined red thong. While her reed-like luminescent body writhed to the music, her face was passionless and void. She danced on autopilot, her slanted eyes open but glazed over and never really focusing on anyone or anything.

A jinn worked behind the bar. The tables were waited on by two jinn females. They were muscular and just as menacing as the males. Except for their gray skin, they reminded me of Amazon warriors with their long black braids and sinewy forms. The rest of the patrons were jinn, ghouls, imps, goblins, and one or two humans thrown in.

As soon as Hank deposited the spell-drunk Len on the wooden floor, the two jinn females swung their heads in our direction and stilled completely, trays in hand, and eyed us with a hunger that bordered on violence.

A bouncer came forward just as our escorts entered behind us. We were surrounded.

Like a domino effect, each being realized who I was. The fae backed off the stage as tension and the unmistakable scent of bloodlust added its mix to the thick earthy air.

"Tell Grigori Tennin we're here," I said, surprised that my voice came out steady.

The bouncer curled his lip and prepared to either spit at me or curse me, but before he could do either, I grabbed his wrist, whirled behind him, and brought his arm to his back, wrenching it as high and hard as I could and bending three of his fingers back at an unnatural angle. I might have been smaller and lighter, but I could bring any male to his knees. And this one hit the floor hard. I shoved my knee against the back of his neck, holding him down. He growled. Chairs scraped across the floor. Weapons were drawn and my heart pounded with adrenaline.

No one moved.

Hank had moved beside me, Nitro-gun drawn.

A door along the back wall creaked and my eye moved off the bartender with his shotgun propped on the bar, aimed at my chest.

A female walked through, tall and unusual looking with large, slanted eyes, a wide mouth, and high cheekbones. Her skin was the color of muted silver, without the shine, and without a single blemish. A hybrid. A rare and prized commodity in the jinn world—the only place one like her was accepted in society. Aboveground she would have experienced discrimination from almost every off-world quarter imaginable. A sad, but true, fact of life. It wasn't fair, by any means.

She walked with slow, fluid steps, her lithe body accentuated by a dark gray jersey dress that ended at the knee and black knee-high boots that added four inches to an already tall frame. While the dress covered her from neck to wrists to knee, it molded to her body and was more provocative than the naked stripper on stage.

As she drew closer, I saw she had the most incredible eyes: violet and indigo blue, a mix I'd never seen on human or off-worlder. They were framed by thick lashes and long, heavy snow-white hair parted in the middle and swept back into a spiky pile at the base of her neck. She was striking, and I found myself staring despite the things I'd seen in my lifetime. I snuck a quick glance at Hank, hoping it wasn't just me. He had the same fascinated reaction.

In fact, everyone had the same reaction, and I got

the feeling they knew her but didn't get to see her nearly as much as they would've liked.

She didn't seem to care about the weapons or the state of near-war in the bar. Her gaze was fixed on me, and she seemed to find the whole thing rather dull. She halted in front of us, taller than me, but only because of the high-heeled boots. Her eyes flicked to Hank and then back to me as her nostrils flared slightly, sampling the air around me. Her eyelids drifted closed for a second. "Hmm," she barely breathed. A cold hand closed lightly over mine, and I released my hold on the bouncer as though in a trance.

She leaned in closer as though breathing me in. The invasion of my personal space should've alarmed me, but I didn't care. My pulse leapt, and I had to force my eyelids to remain open as she leaned toward the left side of my face and neck. A shiver pricked my skin. The scent of pine and earth and something more feminine surrounded her, a faint aroma of fresh mint mixed with something else. Lavender, perhaps. Her soft chuckle stirred my hair.

"Grigori will see you," she said in a deep, smoky tone, straightening back up and then walking back to the side door.

Hank shot me a quick questioning look as we moved forward. I shrugged, not understanding what had just happened any more than he did. The hybrid didn't bother waiting for us to catch up.

I resisted the urge to fix my hair and smooth the skirt and torn sweater set. Instead of looking like a tough-as-nails officer, I was going into Grigori Tennin's lair looking like some deranged secretary. Figured. I was going to make an impression, all right, just not the one I would have liked.

The hybrid led us down a long flight of creaking wooden stairs. The air became wetter and substantially thicker with the smell of warm dirt and stone. The walls had been left bare. Massive wooden beams held up doorways and supported the ceiling in places. Ditches lined either side of the walkway to hold water and condensation that collected on the walls. We passed rooms open to view, fire pits dug into the centers and the ceilings outfitted with a fan-driven ventilation system to draw out the smoke.

I'd heard about this place for years, but this was a moment I never thought I'd see. *It may be the last thing you see*, I thought.

"Hey." Hank's hand nudged my shoulder. "On the left."

I followed his gaze and saw a room occupied by male and female jinn. A few were seated at a large table with piles of flower blossoms spread across the surface. The flowers were easily the size of a man's hand with snow-white petals and the most riveting center I'd ever seen; each one glowed like moonlight and was ringed by a jagged ribbon of red that leaked down the center of each petal like bloody spikes. Jinn females were removing the petals and tossing the centers into a large pot placed over the fire.

The corridor was filled with the scent of honeysuckle.

Ash. It had to be.

The hybrid led us into a vast chamber with torches burning along the walls and a great fire pit in the center. Jinn lurked together in dark corners, sitting around the fire and at tables. All eyes lifted at our procession. This was the largest gathering of females I'd ever seen, and they were all fixated on me. At first I thought it was Hank, but after meeting a few of those disturbing stares, I knew it was me they'd latched on to, and the realization was unsettling.

At the end of the chamber sat an enormous wooden table. Grigori Tennin occupied one long side, facing us.

He was bigger, darker, and meaner-looking than any other jinn around. Colossal shoulders filled the back of an ornately carved chair. He wore a black T-shirt, which had to be XXXL, but it was pulled taut over beefy muscles. He had the thickest neck I'd ever seen. His back was to the wall and on either side of him, standing like sentinels ready to defend, were two jinn females decked in war regalia. Their arms were folded across their chests and their intense regard missed nothing. Their nostrils flared ever so slightly as I approached.

We stopped, as the hybrid walked to the short side of the table and slid into the only empty chair. Grigori didn't look up; too busy cutting a plate-sized steak with a serrated dagger. A goblet of red wine sat next to the pewter plate. He stuck a piece of meat into his mouth and then grabbed the goblet, the rings on his large fingers flashing in the firelight.

His wide jaw flexed like a pit bull's as he chewed. After he swallowed and drank deeply from the goblet, he relaxed against the back of the chair and wiped his mouth. I hadn't come all this way to watch the man eat his dinner and made a move to say so, but Hank's hand on my arm stopped me.

Finally, Grigori turned his attention to us, a faint violet gleam lighting the depths of sharp, calculating eyes.

"I ask myself," he began in a deep, accented baritone, which seemed to have an echo all its own, "how is this . . . Detective Madigan, a female who killed two of *my* warriors, going to come out of this visit with her head still attached to her scrawny human body?"

The hybrid's mouth quirked. "You can give her to the females. She reeks of sex. Even I can smell it on her."

My head whipped to Hank as heat shot to my face. Seriously. I was going to murder him. Apparently the spell worked on other species as well. Len wasn't the only one capable of attracting the entire female jinn population. No wonder they were following my every move with such intensity. It was lust. And it was all over me.

Grigori leaned to the side and smoothed a dark thumb down the hybrid's cheek, but his attention remained fixated on me. "Sian is my daughter. My only heir. She is unique, you see, prized, for human and jinn blood rarely mix. But look at the beauty it creates, beauty the rest of the world shuns." Suddenly his hand went to her throat, and he squeezed hard, practically pulling her onto the table. Her eyes bulged and began to water. Grigori's gaze burned into mine and took on a fervent glow. "But even she is subject to the laws of the tribe. Don't think I wouldn't strike her down."

He shoved her back into the chair. My heart raced as she coughed and quietly tried to overcome near strangulation by her own father. I'd gotten what I came for—evidence that the jinn were manufacturing *ash*. Now I just needed to figure out the connection to the CPP, and get the jinn off my back long enough to get out of here alive and then gather the troops to put a stop to their entire operation.

"This isn't Charbydon," Hank spoke up, his voice coated with steel. "Here you're subject to human law."

The jinn in the chamber nervously mimicked their leader's rumbling chuckle. Grigori eyed Hank beneath hooded lids. Hank's air of confidence never wavered. Grigori leaned forward and plucked his wine goblet off the table, swirling the liquid inside. "Why come here, Detectives?"

"*Ash.*" I figured I might as well push this as far as I could. "You're manufacturing it for the CPP."

He slapped one beefy hand on the table and threw back his head. The deep laughter sent chills down my spine. No one else dared laugh with him. When he was done, he leaned forward and grinned like Satan himself. "So?"

"You're not above the law."

He sat back and threw his arms wide. "Look around

you. I *am* the law. My *word* is law." He paused. "You coming here . . . It amuses me. I assume you want to make payment or bargain?"

"That depends."

"On what?"

Blood pounded through my temples. I swallowed. "Do you take Visa?"

The entire room froze. Even Grigori.

My blood pressure soared. With one bad move I'd be history, and I prayed to God I was reading him right.

Another eruption of laughter boomed through the room, startling me and everyone else. Grigori's chair shook with the sound. As it receded, he wiped the corners of his eyes with his napkin. "Charlie Madigan. You make me laugh. You're not the brightest female in the world coming here like this, but you have *grômms*, I'll give you that. You and me, we will bargain."

A female jinn shot up from a table at the far end of the chamber. "She cannot bargain; she has nothing! Her blood, her blood for my Neruk!"

Jaws dropped. It was obvious she'd made a terrible, fatal mistake.

Grigori pushed back from the table and stood, both hands coming to rest flat on either side of his plate as he focused on her. Her dark gray skin turned to light ash. She fell to her knees and tripped over desperate-sounding words in the jinn tongue.

A vein thickened in Grigori's temple and ran back along his bare head. His eyes glowed brighter and brighter. His breathing became shallow, taxed, but also in a way that suggested he relished this part of his job. He shouted something short and brusque, causing the female's head to jerk up. Their eyes connected. Power leaked into the chamber. The hairs on my arms rose as the female's eyes began to glow so bright, they burned. No one moved to help her. A primal scream tore from her throat as violet-orange flame shot from her eye sockets and open mouth.

Appalled silence descended on the chamber as she fell over dead, black blood and brain matter leaking from her ears, eye sockets, and open mouth.

I gulped down the repulsion that rose in my throat, stunned by her death. I knew the jinn had power, and I also knew the tribe boss possessed the power of life and death over his tribe. I just never realized how literal that statement really was until now.

Hank emanated such intense fury that I closed my hand over his wrist and squeezed.

Grigori scanned the room, daring anyone else to object. Satisfied, he sat down and resumed eating. After he stuffed another huge piece of steak in his mouth, he said, "What can you give me? Why do you come here instead of awaiting my summons?"

Good question. "I came to ask for time, and for information."

"You are confused." He waved his fork as he spoke. "You, Detective, owe *me*. Not the other way around."

"I don't have the monetary value of your two warriors," I said carefully. "And I probably never will. But I do have access to the ITF, to things you might find useful." Hank went rigid beside me. I was treading a very thin line between good cop and bad cop, but I had to find something that would satisfy Grigori for the time being. And then I'd arrest his ass for drug trafficking and murder. I'd say whatever I had to in order to walk out of there in one piece.

He thought as he chewed, eyeing me like a cat deciding how to first play with its mouse before devouring it. "I will consider debt paid for one of my warriors," he began slowly, "if you arrange visitation for one of my jinn to see Lamek Kraw in cold cell"—he spat on the floor at those two words—"and you put my daughter on your payroll at ITF."

Sian sucked in a horrified gasp, just as pleased as I was at the prospect of her working for the ITF.

Sure, getting her a position at ITF could be arranged if it came to that, but getting the folks at Deer Isle Federal Prison in Maine to pull Lamek Kraw out of cold cell confinement for a visit was going to be highly unlikely. But, with luck, I'd have Grigori Tennin joining his jinn brethren in the north as soon as I made it out of this cave.

"And for the second?" I asked.

"The second . . . I will think on it and let you know."

"Done," I said. "I'll need time to make arrangements."

Grigori shrugged as though he couldn't care less, but I saw through the game. He had something brewing inside that huge skull of his and there was only one thing better to a jinn boss than extracting revenge in blood—putting the law in their pockets. Of course, I was lying my ass off and playing a dangerous game with a dangerous criminal, but I didn't have any other options at the moment. I couldn't hide from the jinn and the debt unless I wanted to leave town and disappear. And I wasn't going to turn tail and run, not from my city.

"Jazel Tel is the name of my jinn who will go north. You have two days."

My face was on fire, but I nodded, knowing full well he could see right through my lies, and that made me more concerned than anything else. With a dim glow in his cunning violet eyes, he leaned close and held out his massive hand.

The last thing I wanted was to make contact, but I wasn't about to back down now. Gritting my teeth, I placed my hand in his, ready to shake on it, but he jerked me forward. My ribs crashed into the table as one of the female guards whipped out a wicked-looking blade, stepped to the table, and, in one swift movement, pressed the sharp tip against Hank's Adam's apple, blocking him from making a move.

Grigori slammed my hand down on the table and used his dagger to slice my palm clean open, the sting of cut flesh robbing me of breath. His hand held my wrist firmly, squeezing so hard I was sure the bones would crack. His wide nose nearly touched mine.

Indignation and rage fired my blood, surging through me with that familiar hum of power and clouding my vision so badly it was like wearing prescription eyewear that wasn't yours. Nausea rolled through my stomach. I closed my eyes, using every ounce of strength to bank the power and stay in control.

"Swear it. Swear your oath now, Detective," he demanded in a hiss of words, his eyes bright and fervent and his breath reeking of wine and steak. "In blood. At my table. Do it."

My teeth ground together, as I wanted nothing more than to slam my fist into his overbearing face. "I swear."

Grigori Tennin gave me one last hard look and then released me. "She is bound!" he shouted to the tribe, his words echoing deeply through the chamber.

I slumped against the table for a second to catch my breath and then pushed back, cradling my bloody hand and wondering if being "bound" was really as bad as it sounded. The guard sheathed her dagger and returned to her station behind Grigori.

Grigori's mouth widened in a slow Cheshire grin. "Watch out for the rogues and sympathizers, though, Detective. There are many, I think, who would like to see your blood soak the ground." He chuckled as though he'd made some intensely witty joke and then returned to his meal.

Without a parting look, I pivoted and limped out of the chamber, my ankle still sore. Asshole. The initial pain of the cut had subsided, leaving my palm with a strong, pulsating ache. "We need a sample of that drug," I said to Hank as we passed through the stone archway.

"Not now."

He grabbed my arm as I stumbled on the uneven ground, my chest burning with sour rage. His fingers squeezed my bicep, and he leaned slightly so our words wouldn't carry down the corridor. "You're bleeding, and unless you want to deal with the advances of a bunch of sex-crazed jinn, save it for another time."

Our passing, well, *my* passing drew every jinn female to the archways to watch. "They wouldn't care if it hadn't been for you," I whispered sharply.

We had to press our backs flat against the wall as a group of females carried Len like a trophy down the corridor. I suppressed a shiver at the bright gleam in their eyes. Poor guy had gotten *way* more than he'd bargained for when he bought that spell.

Once we were through the bar and out onto Solomon Street, I had to pause to catch my breath. Every muscle ached and the damn heels were getting on my last nerve. I wanted to hit something or scream at the top of my lungs. Instead I jerked off one of the pumps and flung it with a low screech at the brick wall. It bounced back and nearly hit Hank.

I stood there for a long moment, my good hand on my hip, in utter disbelief at how wrong everything was going. Hank picked up the pump and handed it to me. I glared at him for a long moment before taking the damn thing and putting it back on.

The streetlamp gave me just enough light to inspect my wounded palm. It was angry red and still bleeding. He'd cut me with his nasty steak knife, which meant I needed to disinfect ASAP. I marched down Solomon Street and didn't stop until I came to the plaza where Solomon converged with Mercy and Helios.

Hank was right behind me and grabbed my hand when I stopped. "Here. Let me see." The grave sigh that followed and the grim set of his jaw made me snatch my hand away.

"What? It can't be infected already." I looked down. My heart skipped a beat. It was far from infected. It had partially healed. Already.

"You've started seeing auras. You went ballistic with those jinn in Underground. And you're healing yourself." He pulled me to large water fountain in the center of the plaza and held my hand underneath.

Cold water sent a welcome chill up my arm, and I gave up my anger and resistance, sitting tiredly on the fountain ledge as he rubbed the grime from my palm.

"There's no doubt you have power," he began, quiet and thoughtful. He didn't have to tend to my wound, but I sensed he needed something to do. And for some reason, I let him. "It's wild, sporadic, whatever it is . . ." A lock of sweat-dampened hair fell over his forehead and touched the bridge of his nose. He blew it out of the way, and it made me smile. "Your death could've unlocked dormant abilities, or maybe you're just a late bloomer. We know it runs in the family because of your grandmother and Bryn . . ."

I didn't enlighten him about the special relationship I'd had with my twin brother.

For so long I'd denied having or wanting any extra abilities beyond my own God-given human talents. But now, I couldn't hide it. It was coming out of me whether I liked it or not. The lack of control freaked me out *more* than a little. I didn't know when or where I'd lose it, and the last thing I wanted right now was to be hauled into ITF Headquarters for evaluation and specialized training.

"I know that look," Hank interrupted my thoughts.

"What look?"

"The Queen of Denial look. It's a little too late for that."

"I wasn't going to deny it," I muttered. "I just don't *want* it, whatever it is."

"What're you so afraid of? The average population would kill for any kind of psychic gift, much less the power to heal themselves."

The rhythmic fall of water into the basin *should* have been calming. The cool spray of water *should* have doused the heat in my face. But it didn't. What did he know anyway? "I'm not afraid."

Since it was a lame denial, he didn't bother with a reply, just dropped my hand, sat down on the ledge, rested his elbows on his knees, and pressed both palms against his tired eyes. "The chief might be able to get Sian some sort of dummy job and even pull strings at Deer Isle, but he isn't going to authorize a raid on the Lion's Den."

"Tennin practically admitted it. Besides, you saw them making it."

"You're always so gung-ho, Charlie," he said, flicking a glance my way. "We saw them making *something*. That's not enough to go up against an entire tribe."

"And you're always so damn cavalier. If I wasn't a walking sex pheromone, I probably could've snagged one of those flowers. Then the lab could've analyzed it, connected it to *ash*, and maybe we would've had something solid to take to the chief. And if I don't arrest Tennin's ass in two days, he's going to come after mine."

His shoulder slumped, and his hands grabbed both sides of his head. A short laugh, devoid of humor, escaped him. Then he straightened and looked at me with a wry smile. "Guess lobbing that spell vial wasn't the best idea in the world."

Yeah.

He stood up and shoved his hands into his pockets. "I'll see what the chief can do about Lamek Kraw and Sian. It might be better coming from me." I rolled my eyes, but Hank had a point. He was way better at defusing the chief's temper than me. I always seemed to make things worse. "You want me to walk you to Bryn's, protect you from all your hard-up jinn fans?"

"Ha, ha." It was only a few yards from the plaza. I could make it on my own. I shook my head. "No, go home and get some rest. We'll meet with Mott later. I'm gonna wash this spell off of me, and see if Bryn knows anything about that flower we saw. I'll call you later."

★   ★   ★

People passed by in a blur as I stared at the healing wound on my palm. Hank was right—most people would kill to have this ability, and I wasn't knocking it, but the weight of the unknown, of what this might mean, turned my stomach. I'd faced down ghouls and hellhounds without blinking an eye. I *wasn't* afraid. My throat closed as the truth danced in front of my face. I hated Hank in that moment, hated to admit that he'd nailed it.

Big deal. So I was a little hesitant to admit there was something massively wrong inside me. *Not hesitant, you idiot. You're scared shitless and you know it.*

My shoulders slumped.

I didn't want to be reminded. Feeling the strength and power inside of me was too familiar. It reminded me too much of Connor, of how it felt when he spoke to me in his mind, of all the times from our toddler years to our teens. *Until you cut him off.* The zing, the tiny hum of energy was him all over again. And honestly, it hurt too damn much to tolerate. The fact that part of it was a darkness that seemed to gain ground inside of me every day made it even harder to accept. I was supposed to be the good guy.

With a defeated sigh, I rearranged my hair and straightened the sweater set as best I could, but there was no hiding or fixing the tears in Bryn's clothes. My ankle still hurt, though not as badly as before, and the pumps made an uneven clicking sound on the pavement as I limped toward Mercy Street.

Hodgepodge was busy as usual.

Through the window I caught a glimpse of Emma behind the counter, helping to wrap an item for a customer. The undercover officer, a rookie I'd seen at the station numerous times though never actually met, sat on a stool near the pub next door. He was inconspicuous enough—looked like a bouncer. When he gave me the once-over and recognized me, he nodded. I did the same back and then entered the shop.

Making a beeline to the counter was a little difficult in the maze of shelves, boxes, statues, and customers. Emma and Bryn were too exposed here. After making an enemy of the CPP today and the threat of rogues and vigilantes, I had to get them out of harm's way. And there was still the issue of Grigori Tennin and the second debt hanging over my head.

My fingers drummed against my thigh as I waited for the Wiccan in front of me to pay for her sage bundle. It gave me time to scan the store, looking for anything or anyone suspicious. Gizmo was on guard near the door, and I found myself warming up to the idea of Bryn's security system. At least it was *something*. The Wiccan brushed by me. Emma turned away from the back counter just as I stepped forward. Her face brightened.

Immediately, I put my finger to my lips and hushed the outburst I saw coming. The last thing I wanted was for everyone in the store to know she was my kid.

Bryn came over, her anklets tinkling with each step. "What's wrong?" Then she noticed the ruined outfit. "What the hell happened to my clothes?" She took one step back and waved the air. "It smells like you went for a swim in an algae pond."

"It's nothing," I said, not wanting to alarm Emma. "I was just thinking you could close the store early today."

"But—"

I turned my back toward the counter so Em couldn't see my face and gave my sister a look that spoke volumes. "Please, Bryn, for once just listen and don't argue." I didn't want to frighten Emma, but the urgency to get them both safe ticked against my nerves like a time bomb. There were customers at my back, and any one of them could be a threat.

"Is this about Amanda?" Emma leaned over the counter. "And those jinn?" My head whipped around, and she held up her hands in an innocent gesture. "What? It's all over the Internet and the TV. And stop looking at me like that. I'm not a baby. I'm almost twelve, and that's almost a teenager." Her voice dropped to a whisper. "And I know you didn't shoot those guys because you wanted to. It's your job, Mom. I get it."

I blinked, feeling as though I'd just been whacked over the head with a cast-iron frying pan. Emma was at the age where acting smart, cool, and nonchalant was priority number one. Teen prep, I called it. I shook my head, knowing she had to be concerned, scared, worried . . . And it'd take some coaxing to get her to admit it.

"God," Bryn said, "she sounds just like you, Charlie." She whistled to Gizmo. "Come on, I guess we're closing up shop."

"Good, then Mom can take a shower," Emma muttered under her breath as she put the wrapping paper under the counter.

Gizmo flew toward us, skimming the shelves and skid-landing on the back counter right next to a cat carrier, which, I realized, held Spooky.

"Hank dropped her off earlier," Bryn said, watching Gizmo approach the cat crate, his pug-like face outstretched and sniffing. Suddenly, a black paw shot through the bars and smacked his nose. He squeaked and scrambled back, his claws scratching the counter.

As Bryn steadied Gizmo, I turned to face the patrons, studying each one.

Once the gargoyle had settled into a prone position on the counter, away from the cat, Bryn personally went around to each shopper letting them know the store was closing early and to bring any purchases to the counter. Of course, as a few stood in line to check out, others used the opportunity to keep shopping. I leaned against the counter, my fingers gripping the edge and itching to escort them out Atlanta PD style.

By the time everyone left, my patience had evaporated.

And then Will showed up.

Bryn was in the process of locking the door when he appeared on the other side. Emma raced to let him in, chatting away about school being cancelled.

I pulled Bryn aside, shoving my loose bangs behind my ear. The damn twist wasn't holding. "What is he doing here?"

"I called him."

"You *what*?"

She shrugged. "He needs to know what's going on, Charlie. He's seen the news. Can you blame him for being worried about you and Em? He is her father. He's called three times trying to get in touch with you. It's a legitimate concern."

I rolled my eyes to the ceiling and drew in air, wondering if having this much patience would qualify me for sainthood. *Deep breath, Charlie.* Trying to erase the last embarrassing scene with Will from my mind, being rejected after pleading with him to screw me against the wall, I went to tuck my thumbs into the waistband of what should have been jeans or sensible slacks, but I was still wearing the damned skirt.

Will noticed and his smile amplified to a thousand watts. "Funeral?"

I gave up and threw my hands in the air. "Why does everyone think *just* because I'm in a skirt that I've been to a funeral? I wear skirts . . ."

He and Bryn exchanged looks over the counter as she locked the register.

"Mom. You never wear skirts."

"You're *supposed* to be on my side," I said through gritted teeth as Emma leaned into Will and smiled. "You've been spending too much time with your Aunt Bryn. Go, get Spooky and we'll take her upstairs."

"I boarded your window," Will said once Emma was out of range. "Cleaned up the glass, made sure all the locks were in good shape." He didn't mention the smell, but his gaze swept over the damaged outfit. "How are you holding up?"

My tension deflated a little. "Fine. Thanks for doing that. You didn't have to."

"I wanted to."

Accepting help from him, if it didn't have to do with Emma, remained a hard pill to swallow. Even if he was just being nice. I'd made it a rule not to rely on him for things.

"All right, kids, let's go," I said, ushering them to the door. I'd feel much better when they were all safely inside the brick walls of Bryn's apartment.

As Will followed Emma around to the apartment entrance, I waited for Bryn to lock the store as Gizmo flew to the second-story window and perched on the ledge where she'd let him in once we got inside.

She turned to me. "Ready?"

I fell in step beside her. "Thanks for closing the store." She responded with a shrug. "I wanted to get your take on something I saw earlier in the Lion's Den."

She stopped, mouth open. "You went to the Lion's Den?" I gave her the same simple shrug she'd just given me. "Oh, my God, Charlie." Her hands went to her hips. "You made a bargain with him, didn't you?"

"It's not the end of the world," I said defensively.

"I have a plan . . . sort of . . ." Her eyes fluttered closed, and she mouthed a count of three, before I pulled her along to the door. "A flower," I said, ignoring her lecture about making deals with devils, "as big as a man's hand. White petals with, I swear to God, a white center that *glowed*." She went quiet. "Like those plankton that glow in the ocean—"

"Bioluminescent," she said softly.

"Exactly. The center was ringed with red and red streaks ran down the middle of each petal, but didn't reach the end." I held the apartment door open. "You're the horticultural expert. What is it? And where is it from?"

We stepped inside, trailing Emma and Will. "Are you sure it was glowing and not just the light?"

"One hundred percent sure."

"Seriously?"

We stopped on the third step. "Yeah, why, what is it?"

"And the red, it was bloodred, right?"

I frowned. "Bryn."

Disbelief swam in her eyes and she let out a deep breath as though she didn't quite believe what she was hearing. "*Sangurne N'ashu*. A Bleeding Soul. It's not supposed to exist. It's just a legend."

"Well, not anymore."

11

"Come on, you guys!" Emma called from the landing.

"We'll finish this inside," I told Bryn. "I want to know more about this *legend*."

As we climbed the stairs, I looked up at my waiting family and was immediately struck by flashes of old memories, the times when we'd all come over to Bryn's for dinner. And sometimes she'd come to our house, so Will could cook on the grill. I loved helping him, loved being outside, eating good food, drinking an ice-cold beer, playing in the yard with Em . . . just being happy.

An ache spread across my chest as I trailed Bryn up the stairs.

At the landing, Will turned to Emma. "Go inside with Aunt Bryn. I want to talk to Mom for a minute."

"Okay," she responded with a careless shrug, toting Spooky, and followed Bryn inside.

With Will and me on the landing, the small space quickly became claustrophobic. All six foot three rugged inches of him sucked the air out of the space around us. His scent wrapped around me—this morning's cologne mixed with the smell of his skin.

He scrubbed a calloused hand over his stubbly jaw, sighing heavily. Wary, I leaned against the wall. He caught my gaze and held it with his. My stomach flipped. So much history with him. All the goofy names we'd said, the plans for our future, the way we so innocently believed nothing would ever come between a love so strong.

Yeah, right.

"So, you're a wanted woman," he said, not sounding surprised that I was in serious trouble. "Let me take Emma until this blows over. I can take some time off. We'll go down to Disney World. I've been promising her we'd go."

Actually, that didn't sound like a bad idea. "She'd love that."

He managed a tight smile that didn't reach his eyes. "If it wasn't for her, I'd stay and help you nail the assholes setting you up."

"I know. But you'd be doing the right thing. Em comes first."

"Em comes first," he echoed.

In the break of uncomfortable silence, we heard Spooky screech and Gizmo let out a cry that resembled a chicken squawk. Things fell. Something broke. Bryn and Emma yelled.

"Sounds like Spooky just met Gizmo," Will said, staring the door and wincing as a thud hit the wood.

"I should go help them."

"Charlie," he began before I could make a move to the door. I paused at the brief flash of desolation in his eyes. Then, they clouded over to firm conviction. "I can't stop thinking about the other day. Me and you. We've got to deal with this, work things out." He stilled completely, as though bracing himself. "Do you still love me?"

My nostrils flared. Blooms of heat stung my cheeks. *Damn him!* A riotous mix of anger and heartache flowed through me. He'd always been direct. It was one of the things I liked about him. But why did he have to bring this up now? And why did my body go all haywire lately when he was around?

He kept his features blank, but the muscles in his jaw worked overtime. A storm brewed in his blue eyes, but behind the turmoil there was caution and vulnerability. I hated seeing him like this, like some wounded animal clinging to his last bit of dignity and strength. The last thing I wanted was to hurt him, but I didn't want to *be* hurt either.

My voice croaked when I tried to speak. I cleared my throat and tried again. "Will . . ." After that, I didn't know what to say.

A dark scowl twisted his mouth. It took two steps for him to reach me. I tried to move back, but the damn wall was already flat against my spine. He crowded me, conquering my space with the force of his body and will. The sexual tug of awareness that erupted between us was undeniable. I couldn't tell if he wanted to slam his fist into the drywall or kiss me. Probably both.

"*Do you?*" he ground out, his voice trying to hide the raw hurt.

I swallowed and lifted my gaze to his. "Yes." I drew in another breath and rushed out, "But it doesn't change anything." *You don't stop loving someone overnight*, I wanted to say.

His face was level with mine as he braced his hand on the wall behind me and leaned closer. "It changes *everything*. Why give up on us if we both feel the same?"

"It's not about love. Love isn't the only thing that makes a relationship work." My voice rose as I placed both palms on his chest to keep him back. "It's about trust. Hell, I knew you loved me even when you did what you did." He'd never been able to see my point. "But the crafting, Will . . . that was even worse than what happened with that woman. You knew how I felt about it. You knew Connor . . ."

Some of the urgency in his expression softened. "I know, Charlie, I know." He stepped back and stared at the wreath on Bryn's door before turning back to me. "I thought I could use the crafting to help get the business off the ground, that I could control how much I did and stay away from the really bad stuff. I guess . . . I don't know . . . You trust me with Emma and you wouldn't if you thought for one second I was crafting again. This isn't about trust anymore, Charlie. This is about forgiveness, getting over the betrayal and the pain . . ."

The truth was like a knife to the softest part of the belly.

Fine. So what? I was hurt, and I wasn't ready to let go and forgive him. Maybe he did see now the magnitude of what he'd done. But what did he expect; me to go running back because now he got it? Now *he* was ready?

He made a move closer, went to reach out, but changed his mind. Instead, he shoved his hands into his pockets. "We'd have to work at it, rebuild things together."

Yeah, and hindsight is a bitch.

"Charlie," he breathed on a heavy sigh.

Part of me didn't want to disappoint him. Part of me wanted to make things work. His eyes held so much suffering and loneliness. And hope. How could I keep him apart from the family he wanted so badly? My chest ached, but I drew on every ounce of strength and conviction I had. My voice wavered. "I'm not ready. And I don't know if I'll ever be."

A rigid curtain fell over his features. He nodded and squared his shoulders. "I can wait." He pierced me with one last, hard look to tell me he meant it. Then, he opened Bryn's door and went inside.

I slumped against the wall. Why now? I wanted to scream. *Why the hell now?* Why did he wait until *after* he ripped out my heart and destroyed everything before finally coming clean? Why wasn't I worth it to never take the risk in the first place? Why wasn't our marriage and our family worth it? Yeah, I knew all about the addiction side of things, but this was a question that never stopped cycling through my head in the last eight months. And I knew it was a question I'd never get a satisfactory answer to, no matter how many therapists said Will's addiction had nothing to do with me.

A tornado of emotions whirled inside of me. It was too much, and I didn't have the luxury of time to deal with it right now. With a deep breath and practiced ease, I centered myself and then shoved any thoughts of Will and my feelings aside, but the ache was still there like a thorn stuck under my rib cage.

Just add it to all the other aches and regrets.

Quickly, I wiped at my eyes, took a few more seconds to fan my face, and then I went inside to eat, shower, and change. Bryn wanted to do a little research on the Bleeding Soul legend and disappeared into her bedroom with her laptop. Once I was cleaned up, I told Emma and Will that I'd be back after dinner.

I had a meeting to attend.

After a quick call to Hank to coordinate the meeting at Mott Tech, I declined Will's offer to drive me back to the Mustang, which was still parked near Centennial Park. I wanted some time to myself, so I borrowed two bucks from my daughter for the dollar-seventy-five fare to use the MARTA. I could have driven with Hank, but I'd had enough of emotional men for one day.

Bryn had lent me a black T-shirt, which was rather tight across the chest, but soft and stretchy. Her jeans fit me pretty well, hanging a little lower on the hips than I was used to, but, all in all, I felt normal again. She'd also lent me a jacket to wear to hide my shoulder holsters and sidearm. As an added precaution, I'd taken a glamour spell to change my hair color and eyes, but it'd wear off by the time I got to the security gate at Mott Tech.

My ankle had healed, just a few achy twinges here and there as I exited the MARTA station and walked the short distance to the Green Lot on Marietta Street where I'd parked the car.

The chief deserved a big old kiss for setting me up with his nephew's car. It sat exactly where I'd parked it, shiny and red and totally badass. A smile spread across my face as I strolled to the car, my spirits lifting.

The engine rumbled to life like a growling beast ready to hunt. I shoved it in first and then released the clutch until it caught, giving it gas and surging into traffic. I loved stick shifts, especially the control I had over this V-8, three-hundred-horsepower monster.

Once on I-85, I cranked the stereo. Soul Asylum's "Runaway Train" blared from the speakers. I sang along in my head, humored by the irony of those lyrics, since they were pretty much how I felt these days, and remembering when Connor and I would blast this song in his room and sing at the top of our lungs until Mom came upstairs and blessed us out. That seemed like a lifetime ago.

With the windows rolled down, the radio blaring, I finally felt some peace and quiet in my soul. *Time to open up this baby and see what she can do*, I thought, swinging into the fast lane and gunning it.

Once I'd exited the highway and turned onto the road leading to Mott Tech, I rolled up the windows and turned on the air conditioning. It wasn't helping.

Anticipation bubbled through me, making my skin clammy and hot. I tapped my fingers on the steering wheel and glanced in the rearview mirror constantly. Warnings fired through my brain like fireworks.

Whether it was a setup or not, Mott was going to tell me what really happened to me the night I died. Don't ask me how I knew. I just knew. That night had released or given me surprising and strange abilities. Mott realized it. Now I realized it, too.

Finally, I turned down the winding road, which led to the main facility. Once the guards saw my face, they let me right through. I didn't even have to brake the car to a full stop. The hairs on my arms stood up straight. I used the time it took to drive down the road to calm my nerves using deep, even breaths.

The sun was setting over the rooftop of the one-story building, stinging my eyes for a moment as I drove into the parking lot and found a space in the shadow of the building.

My cell rang. It was Hank.

"I got caught up with the chief," he said straight-away. "I'm leaving the station now. Wait for me."

I was already out of the car. "I'm already here."

"Shit." The stress in his voice stopped me cold. "The CPP has gone over the chief's head. You're to stop the investigation and come into the station to turn in your badge and weapons. You're officially on leave, Charlie. I'm not so sure we'd have backup if we needed it. Just wait for me in the parking lot."

I wasn't surprised the CPP had gotten me recalled. It was only a matter of time. "Okay. Just hurry up."

He hung up. I went back to the car and leaned against the door, wondering what the hell I'd do for the next thirty minutes. If it was a setup, they already knew I was here. We still weren't sure if Titus was involved, or who was the mastermind behind the *ash*. And if Titus did have more info on the night I died, I'd rather hear it alone, without Hank as a witness. This was personal.

I blew a strand of loose hair from my face, chewing over the idea of going in anyway and scanning the parking lot for any recognizable vehicles. No limos, black SUVs, or suspicious sedans. The only thing left to do was wait, so I sat on the hood of the car and watched the orange ball of fire settle into the hazy horizon. Bored, I slid the rubber band off my ponytail, finger-combed my hair, which looked almost red in the glow of the setting sun, and then used the band to secure my tresses in a messy knot. It'd be another cool evening. Maybe, after this was over, Hank and I could walk down to the pavilion by the lake.

Ten minutes later, my cell phone rang again. "Madigan."

"Would you rather talk in the parking lot, Detective?" came Titus's questioning voice.

I glanced at the security camera. The underground lab gave me a trapped feeling, so I took him up on the offer. "Do you mind?"

"Not at all; just give me a few minutes to lock up down here, and I'll come up."

"Great." I flipped my cell closed, feeling a wash of relief. Maybe it wasn't a setup after all.

The sound of tire treads on asphalt edged in on my thoughts. A line of black vehicles blinked through the open spaces of the trees. There wasn't a doubt in my mind who was in the limo.

Damn it!

I jumped into the car, revved the engine, and peeled out of the parking lot, fishtailing. There was only one way in and that was blocked, so I drove onto the grass, gaining speed to bypass the vehicles and come out behind the line of cars. At that moment, I wished the fire-engine-red Mustang was a nice camouflage green.

They noticed me almost immediately, but I'd acted quickly enough to dodge behind them. My teeth clattered as the car bumped wildly over the ground. Coming upon the road, I knew I was going too fast to make the turn, so I shoved the gear into neutral, hit the emergency brake, and spun the wheel, making a one-eighty right onto the blacktop road. *Thank you, Connor!* All those nights doing doughnuts in his old beat-up Camaro had paid off. I shoved the car in gear and took off toward the gatehouse. In the rearview mirror, black SUVs turned around and followed.

As I rounded the corner, the guards were down on their knees in front of the gate, their semis pointed straight at my windshield. Adrenaline surging, I hit the brakes, sliding to a screeching stop.

Nothing sounded but the purring engine and my thundering pulse.

The gatehouse was flanked by stone walls and then woods. There was no way around. And this wasn't an ITF vehicle with bulletproof glass. My hands flexed on the leather steering wheel. Glancing in the rearview mirror showed the SUVs flanking out behind me. I swallowed. Terrific.

Talk about bad timing.

Inhale. Exhale. I pulled the keys out of the ignition and then ducked slowly out of the car, my hands held high, as the limo stopped behind the Mustang.

The driver emerged and opened the back door. Mynogan stepped out, tugged his suit jacket down, and adjusted his cuffs. He looked impeccable, his olive skin glowing against the crisp white of his shirt, nearly as white as his hair. "You have excellent timing, Charlene."

I smirked, my ire bringing out the smart-ass in me. "I could say the same for you, *Mynie*."

Carreg was next to duck out of the limo, straightening to his full height and looking just as sharp as Mynogan. Although, with this Charbydon noble I didn't get the nauseous willies. I couldn't deny he looked damn good in his suit; the jacket open, no tie, and the collar of his light blue dress shirt open. He shoved his hands into his pants pockets, drawing back the flaps to his jacket. He was posing for a magazine spread and didn't even know it.

"Shall we take this back to the lab?" Mynogan snapped his fingers at the jinn nearest to him and then ducked back into the limo. Pompous ass.

I handed my weapons over and got into the back of one of the SUVs, trying like hell to remain calm and not lose control like I had in Underground.

Back at the facility, Andy met us as we proceeded from the parking lot to the glass doors. The uneasy, apologetic expression scrunching his face told me all I needed to know. I'd expected to be hunted down by the jinn and Mynogan, not betrayed by some kid I hardly knew. For some reason that made me more pissed off than being relieved of my weapons.

As we filed into the lobby, Andy made the mistake of getting too close. I grabbed his lab coat and shoved him against the wall.

"I'm sorry!"

Sweat beaded his brow and I could smell his fear. Impossible, but I even heard his heart hammering. "Not as sorry as you're gonna be, you little weasel."

A jinn hand landed hard on my shoulder. I released Andy with a shove.

"Oh, God," he choked, dashing by me to unlock the elevator. He dropped the key card twice before sliding it properly into the reader.

Play it cool, I told myself, banking the anger and hum of power that came with it. There *was* something inside me. Too bad for them, because I was going to let it out after I got the answers I sought. They could take away my weapons, but they couldn't take this. Guess power did have its advantages after all.

After a tight, uncomfortable squeeze into the elevator, sandwiched between two jinn, Mynogan and Carreg behind me, the doors slid open. Thank God. I was about to suffocate from the corrupt auras of malevolence and misplaced ego.

I was forced to step aside and allow Mynogan and Carreg to lead the party down the hallway, which gave me a chance to shoot daggers at Mynogan's stiff back. The only thing that made me feel any better about the situation was knowing Hank would be here soon. He'd find a way around the guards. I just hoped it wouldn't be too late.

Andy opened the door to Mott's lab, pulling it back and mouthing the word *sorry* as I stepped by him. I shot daggers at him, too. Like he'd get any forgiveness from me.

The door shut behind us, and I suppressed a shiver of anxiety.

Squaring my shoulders and settling into work mode, I focused on my years of training. I followed the jinn farther into the room, surveying every crevice and corner, ready for anything. My heart pumped and my palms itched. If it wasn't for needing information, I would've started the fight just to get it over with.

In the corner setup with Mott's couch, chairs, and coffee table, Titus stood to greet Carreg and Mynogan. The doc was scared shitless. His hands trembled, and he reeked of fear, far worse than Andy. His hair was in more disarray than ever and sweat dampened his hairline. I glanced over to the medical lab and saw that Llyran, the Adonai serial killer, was no longer on the hospital bed.

Two jinn left me to go take up wall space behind Mynogan. The other two remained behind me.

I shook my head at Mott. "Why am I not surprised?"

A sincere apology passed through his eyes. To hide his shaking, he shoved his hands into the front pockets of his lab coat. I cocked my head slightly and tuned in to his aura. It was green and slightly dim. Nothing bad there. Interesting. "So what do these two idiots have on you, huh, Mott?"

The jinn behind me sucked in a breath at my name-calling. I didn't have time to brace against the punch to my kidney, which sent me staggering forward and howling in pain. His fingers slid around my neck, and he jerked me back, squeezing hard. "Apologize to the Lords of Charbydon," he hissed in my ear. His breath smelled like rancid meat, nearly taking me to the floor.

In one smooth motion, I yanked my arm away, braced my fist into the palm of my other hand for added force, and then sent my elbow flying back into his nose. "Fuck you." The sickening crack of bone filled me with satisfaction. They fell for that move every time.

Foul, thick fury erupted fast behind me. I spun and braced for his attack, but the jinn froze, his irises burning violet-red hatred. A quick glance over my shoulder showed Mynogan with his hand up. I cocked a triumphant eyebrow at the jinn despite the danger and the retribution he promised me as he backed away.

"Detective," Mynogan began in a smooth voice so evil it crawled up my skin like a handful of scattering roaches. "I suggest you cooperate with us. Certain loved ones' lives may be at risk."

Time stopped as my heart dropped to the floor.

A blink later, white flame erupted inside of me, searing every nerve and cell, every pore and fingertip, clouding my vision and vibrating through my eardrums.

Then, my world came abruptly back into focus. How dare he threaten them! The heat burned. I was on fire, like in my nightmare. Didn't matter. I had control of this power, whatever it was. And damned if he'd harm my loved ones. Instinctively I gathered it, amassing it until I was about to burst with it, then I sent it out like a whip straight for Mynogan.

A gale force wave lit by blue flame arced across the room, leaving a bitter cold void in its place. I shuddered as the power surged into him.

The only assault on his person was the wind moving his white hair. My mouth dropped open. He had absorbed my blow. His pupils glowed red and his aura grew in blackness.

Figures.

I braced, no time for anything else, as he returned the favor without blinking an eye or moving a muscle in his fancy suit. The power hit me so hard it sent me flying through the plate-glass viewing mirror and into the hard, tiled floor. I slid across tile and broken glass, slamming into the far wall.

Wracking pain flared through my skull and back. Gasping for breath and fighting a blackout, I tried to push myself up, to ready myself for the next attack. The iron-rich scent of my own blood mixed with the sudden aroma of Bryn's flowery herbal conditioner as my hair fell loose around my face and shoulders. I'd hit the wall so hard, the rubber band in my hair had snapped. I was cut everywhere. My hands, arms, even through the jeans. Warm trails of liquid red ran down my face and neck. It hurt so badly, I couldn't move.

You should've absorbed your own power back instead of letting it hit you, a voice echoed in my mind.

I shook my head and blinked hard a few times, unsure of whether I was imagining things or that voice was somehow real. The only thing I was certain of was that I had to get up. Now. Holding my breath, I pushed my weight off the floor using the wall at my back. Glass cut into my palms. I let out a groan and slid back down the wall. The room spun around me. My stomach clenched. *Don't throw up. Please, don't throw up.*

Footsteps raced around the corner, shoes crunching on glass. Mott slid down beside me. "Charlie, Charlie, can you hear me?" He patted my face as I tried to focus on him. His touch hurt.

"Get away from me," I managed to slur.

"I'm not a traitor," he whispered quickly. "I didn't know this was what he wanted. I was only trying—"

"To what? Get people, our people, hooked on *ash*?"

Mott frowned as one of the jinn pulled him to his feet. "What?"

"Amanda," I forced out, panting through the pain, "giving drugs to children. No wonder you're in with these guys. You fit right in."

"I have no idea what you're talking about." He struggled against the jinn holding him.

"Go ask your brother. He's been using Mott Tech to manufacture *ash*. That's why your niece is in the hospital right now. She took drugs made from your lab." It was conjecture, but I didn't care.

Titus's face paled, and his eyes held the realization that I was probably telling the truth. That his brother was a drug-addicted loser who had crossed the line into being an enabler to the entire city. His Adam's apple slid up and down slowly. And the only thing he could do was nod.

Through the opening where the glass had once been, I could see Carreg arguing furiously with Mynogan. He wasn't happy. Neither of them. Power stirred in the room, and I knew then that my power was nothing compared to these two ancient beings.

I let my head slump against the wall. Carreg turned to me for a brief second, his inky blue eyes seeming to burn brighter. *Stupid human, heal yourself!*

What the hell? I swallowed the dry lump in my throat. His voice was imperious and impatient in my head. Just as quickly as he glanced at me, he was back arguing with Mynogan. Either I'd hit my head too hard or he was communicating with me telepathically.

Why would he help me? *Who cares! Just do it!* This time, the voice was my own. I closed my eyes and searched inside for power. There was none. I was empty and cold.

Try again, Carreg commanded. *Find goodness, not anger.*

Again, I squeezed my eyelids shut and concentrated, eventually grabbing on to the image of my family, of the good things in my life. Of Emma. Sweet Emma. Her face swam in my mind. Her goofy laugh. Her tough façade. Her hugs and kisses. The overwhelming love I had for her. It stirred in me like a real entity, just like the power I had drawn upon in my anger. But this didn't hurt, didn't blind me. This was comforting and cool.

Granted, I didn't know what to do with it, but what the hell. I was out of options. I drew in a deep breath and then imagined sending the power to every part of my body, urging it, asking it to heal, to energize, to work on my bones and cuts and bruises. Almost immediately, a peaceful glow lit me on the inside as wonderful energy sang through me. It swelled my chest. I gasped and opened my eyes, tingling everywhere. I flexed my bloody fingers, the deep cuts and scratches not stinging and burning as badly as before.

Slowly, I shoved the loose hair from my vision and pushed to my feet, still feeling a hum at work, feeling like I was floating. Amazing. I glanced at my feet to make sure they were still on the ground. They were. I shifted my gaze to my hands and arms. The cuts were healing, though I still felt like roadkill. I caught Mott's astonished gape and asked, "What did you do to me?"

His shoulders slumped suddenly and regret covered his face. "I saved your life."

12

Footsteps ground glass into tile. Mynogan and Carreg came around the corner. "We both did," Mynogan said, flicking a piece of glass off his lapel. The guy had a serious case of OCD when it came to his clothes.

The pain in my body was fading fast, my senses and strength returning. "You both did," I echoed in disbelief, trying to stall another round of punishment as long as I could.

"Oh, surely, some part of you remembers that night. Dying. Your soul leaving. The good doctor, here, coming in. Me, stroking your hair, comforting you." No. "The needle in your vein. Any of it, perhaps, ring a bell, Detective?"

He was trying to psych me out and enjoying every malicious minute of it. I shook my head violently, my gaze desperately searching for the truth and landing on Mott, who studied the floor in front of him. "What was in it?" I cringed at the desperation in my voice. "What was in the needle?"

No one spoke.

"WHAT WAS IN THE FUCKING NEEDLE?!" My scream bounced off the walls.

"Go ahead, tell her, Titus," Mynogan prompted, humor lighting the black of his eyes like fire on obsidian.

"I was *trying* to help," he shot back at Mynogan and then faced me. "Trying to find a way to help humans, the police department, be able to defend themselves, to have a fighting chance. Mynogan was our benefactor, said he wanted to remain anonymous, and that was the only reason I lied to you, Charlie. The chief knew. And we agreed only to try it on someone who wouldn't live otherwise."

The shock of what he was saying hit me full force. I hadn't expected *this*. Bewildered, I shook my head, trying to shake the fuzz of astonishment away. My body was almost healed. Already I was learning about my power and how to use it. I could be calm about this. I *had* to be calm if I was to live through this. "So you injected me with something."

"Gene therapy," Mott said.

"More precisely, DNA from both worlds," Mynogan cut in. "Charbydon and Elysia. My DNA. And a sample stolen from an Adonai priestess."

A laugh blurted from my lips, sounding demented and lost. This kept getter better and better. I was probably unconscious from the hit against the wall. All this was just a dream, a really twisted fucking dream. I wanted to sit down.

Mott hurried to explain. "You were dying, Charlie. I had the knowledge to save you. Well, I didn't know if their DNA would bond with yours, but it did. It failed on the others we tried."

"It worked with you because you have the old blood—diluted, but it's there," Carreg explained. "All humans of limited power have it. It's where their power comes from. Sometime, long ago in your lineage, a Charbydon mated with one of your human ancestors. As did an Elysian. It had to have happened thousands of years ago and spaced widely apart for your family to survive and evolve normally with the infusion of both races' genes. By now the blood is so weak that many in your family tree have no powers at all."

"Then why didn't you just give the injection to any human with power?"

"We tried. Seems it only works with a very select few. And usually they die within a few months. We still don't know why," Mott answered, ashamed.

As their words sunk in, my skin crawled. Mynogan's DNA was in my body. Bile rose to my throat and the urge to retch spasmed through my gut. I nearly did and had to hold my stomach to stop it. Spilled alcohol from broken bottles on the floor stung the insides of my nose and throat.

I had the power of good and evil in me. Now it all made sense. The nightmare. The war inside of me.

Mott had saved me, but inside they'd nearly torn me apart. I knew suddenly, with sickening realization, it was that internal war that had killed the others. They'd been ripped apart. From the inside out.

You're now one of the most powerful humans in the world, Detective. More powerful than most Elysians and Charbydons.

I stared hard at Carreg, but saw nothing in his aura but a swirling midnight blue and his usual marble expression. Why was he helping me?

"You have a choice," Mynogan offered, drawing my attention. "Use what we gave you to help or die along with your family." He said it so simply and matter-of-factly.

"What do you want me to do?"

"We created you so you could create a world for us to live in. Here, on Earth. You simply need to come when we call on you."

"Go to hell."

Mynogan shook his head and laughed, perfect white teeth flashing, as though I was an unruly child. But this was no father gazing lovingly on his child; this was a being whose very air held the assurance of brutality and follow-through. There were no lines this male would not cross. No guilt or hesitation in bringing death.

"Laugh at this, you bastard!" Hank's voice sounded behind Mynogan right before he blasted the Abaddon lord with nitro.

The astonishment that crossed Mynogan's impeccable features was so worth any payback. The jinn surged over glass and furniture to get to Hank. "Charlie!" A Nitro-gun sailed through the air. I leapt up to catch it and immediately began firing at the jinn.

"Get down!" I yelled to Titus, firing as he dove under a table. The jinn knocked over a metal lab cabinet, shielding Mynogan and Carreg, firing bullets over the top as Hank took position across from me behind the corner wall. There was too much debris and distance to get to him, so I ducked behind a wide medical refrigerator.

"It's about time you got here!" I shouted above the gunfire.

"You might want to run, Charlie," he yelled back. "Unless you want to hear my voice!"

He was taking off the voice modifier. Relief flowed over me. About time.

A loud boom and a crack of white blinded me. I screamed and fell to my rear, seeing black spots float behind my eyelids. My eardrums rang.

It felt like minutes had passed.

Using the side of the fridge, I pulled myself to my knees, blinking away the spots and trying to focus.

The lab warbled into view. The entire corner where Hank had taken cover was gone. A sinking panic gripped my throat. *Oh, God.* "Hank!"

I started across the room, but was pulled down by Carreg, who had somehow made it across the floor. He was on his stomach, one hand wrapped around my ankle. "Stay down," he hissed, his face cast in shadows and light from the swinging bulb overhead. My struggles only produced an impatient frown. "I'll take care of your partner. You need to get out of here."

"What?" Bullets dinged the refrigerator once more, sending metal sparks shooting through the smoke-filled air like fireworks. I fired back and then ducked down again. "I'm not leaving him!"

Carreg yanked me close, his nose nearly touching mine. Strong fingers dug into my arms. Stark intensity flashed like lightning in his glower and made me pause. "I said I'd watch out for him. This is nothing compared to the fight you're going to face. You stay and there'll be no one to hide your family. And get some goddamn training. You're gonna need it." He shoved me hard toward the door.

I fell on my hip. My hair spilled over my face as I turned back to Carreg.

How could I leave my partner? It went against everything I believed, everything I was. Carreg rolled his eyes to the ceiling, his mouth set in a strained pose of displeasure. "Give me your hand." He waited, challenging. If I didn't do something soon, the jinn were going to be on top of us. Rising up, I fired a few more rounds to keep them at bay and then I slapped my palm into Carreg's, returning his displeased expression.

"You can trust me," I heard him say as images flooded my mind. His grip held me still and tight, squeezing the hand bones and tendons together. It was like fast-forwarding a movie. Images of him and Mynogan. Meetings and conversations. Thoughts and emotions. So quickly they flashed, I had a difficult time putting them into my short-term memory.

The one thing I did realize—he wasn't involved with *ash* or my DNA manipulation. He'd been just as shocked as I had, but he'd hidden it well. Carreg had been working with Mott to find a way to revive the Charbydon moon, not create a permanent home here on Earth. His political agenda was simply to live and work alongside the rest of us. And it was sincere. He'd been as betrayed by Mynogan as Mott had. He was telling me the truth. He'd protect Hank. He also sent me images of exactly what Mynogan was capable of doing if I didn't get my ass out of there and back to Emma, Bryn, and Will.

He released my hand, and it burned. "Go."

After one hesitant look, when it briefly occurred to me that Carreg could be feeding me false images, I bolted for the door, my family in the forefront of my mind. I would have beaten Hank senseless if our roles were reversed and he hadn't gone to save them.

I had to fight my way to the elevator, blasting two more jinn who guarded the hallway, and clocking Andy in the jaw as he stood, terrified, by the elevator. Payback for leading me into this mess. The kid dropped like a rock.

It was dark by the time I got out of Mott Tech. Once I was topside, nothing stood in my way. Apparently Mynogan and his goons thought so well of themselves, they didn't have a backup plan in case I escaped. Dumbasses. The only one in my way was the limo driver, and he watched me dart by his windshield without so much as a blink. And lucky for me, someone had driven the Mustang back to the parking lot.

My emotions ruled as I drove like a madwoman toward the gatehouse. The guards were just about to run from the structure with guns drawn, but I was too close and going way too fast. They ducked back in as the car blurred by them, splintering the barrier. I hit the brakes, turned the wheel, and swerved onto the side road that led to the Interstate.

I took the exit onto I-85 and headed back to Underground. Mynogan's threat to my family burned in my mind and my heart. If anything happened to them he'd suffer in the worst way possible. And Hank. How could I have left him? I slammed my palms against the steering wheel and let out a frustrated groan. What if Carreg failed to help him? What if Mynogan figured out Carreg was working against him? If Hank got hurt . . . But there was no one, *no one*, more important than my kid, and getting back to her was first priority.

I dialed Bryn's and Will's cell phones. No answer.

It was the longest thirty-minute ride of my life.

Underground was bustling with activity. The bars, eateries, and pubs had thrown open their doors. Techno music wafted toward me as I bolted down the street to Bryn's door. Dried blood clung to crevices between my fingers and to my neck and collarbone. The black V-neck was slashed diagonally across the abdomen, and healed bloody cuts and scratches peeked from rips in the jeans. The sound of my pulse, driven by panic and dread, drowned out most of the sound. I nodded to the undercover cop nearby and then pressed Bryn's buzzer. When she answered, I said between pants, "It's me, let me in."

I took the stairs two at a time. At the landing, I drew my gun and held it down behind my thigh as the door opened to reveal my sister looking none the worse for wear in jeans and an oversize Braves T-shirt.

Relief burst inside me, and I threw my arms around her, hugging her astonished form. "Thank God. Why the hell didn't you answer your phone?" I marched into the apartment for Emma, not waiting for an answer.

She wasn't in the living room or kitchen. Trying not to panic, I threw the bedroom door open. Empty. I returned to the living room.

"Where's Em?"

"At Will's. I just talked to him. They're going to get online and figure out where to stay at Disney. They're planning to leave tonight." Her face had turned pale. "What the hell happened, Charlie? Put the gun down."

I lowered the gun. "It's Mynogan."

"The noble?"

"Yeah. He's . . ." How did I explain? "I think he's

behind the *ash*, and for making me the Jinn's Most Wanted." I didn't even want to mention the gene manipulation.

Spurred by adrenaline, I holstered my gun, hurried to Bryn's bedroom, and rooted around her jewelry box for another hair band. She watched me from the door as I tied my hair back and then jerked the shirt over my head. Her gasp informed me that the slash across the shirt had cut my torso as well. But it was healing slowly. I didn't care.

A cat hissed from under her bed. I glanced over to see Gizmo down on his front legs, his butt and forked tail in the air, antagonizing poor Spooky. A faded rose-colored cotton T hit me in the face. As it slid down into my hands, I saw Bryn closing her dresser drawer. "Sorry, I know you hate pink, but it's the only clean one I have left."

It really didn't matter. Quickly, I pulled on the tee, leaving the jeans.

"You want a towel," she asked quietly, motioning to the blood, "to clean up?"

She was scared. And I would have like nothing better than to reassure her, but there wasn't time. "Yeah, thanks." I swept by her and into the living room, where I pulled out the extra ammo I kept stashed in the back of Bryn's coat closet. After reloading and tucking some extra clips in the waistband of the jeans and inside each boot, I straightened to take a wet towel from Bryn.

I nodded my thanks, holding it in one hand while dialing Will's cell phone number. Voice mail. Again.

"Damn it!" I threw the phone onto the couch and stomped into the bathroom.

I stared at my reflection, wondering how my life could have done a one-eighty so quickly. *Always looking for trouble*, Connor would say. *Why isn't a normal life good enough for you?* both Mom and Dad had repeatedly asked after I'd joined the ITF. *Why risk your life?*

Only Bryn had remained silent and unjudging.

My parents didn't understand, even after I explained my need to protect them and myself after Connor's murder. I'd vowed to *never* be in a situation where I couldn't defend myself. And once I had Emma, the desire to protect and defend became even stronger. It seemed the only other women I knew who completely understood my motivation were others in law enforcement or the military, or those who'd been victims of trauma. My parents' friends and extended family certainly couldn't understand it. And it always made me feel like the renegade/loser of the family. At least in their eyes.

I removed my charm and washed the bloodstained crystal disk and chain, then splashed cold water on my face, using a clean towel to wipe off the excess and dry the necklace, realizing that my sister understood me more than anyone. And I hadn't even given her credit for that, along with everything else.

Finished with the towel, I inspected the scratches and a few deep cuts from my trip through the lab mirror. My bottom lip was still swollen from the deep slice down the middle. Lacerations were healing on my chin and left temple.

Bryn was banging around in the kitchen when I exited the bathroom. "I'm going to make sure Emma and Will get off okay and then I'll be back."

"One sec," she said, her head popping over the cabinet door and then disappearing again. A second later, she came to the counter and handed me a bag of Doritos and a can of Diet Pepsi. "Here, it's all I've got at the moment. Not only do I need to do laundry, but I've got to grocery shop, too."

I hardly ever cried in front of my family. But seeing her standing there, eyes wide and supportive, made my throat close. I couldn't speak, so I nodded my thanks. A small smile tugged on her pale lips.

"Oh, and take this. It's a cloaking charm." She placed a small rectangular silver piece in my hand. It was hammered and irregular. "This took me five months to make. Read the inscription clockwise and you'll go completely unnoticed by those who wish you harm. Say the last word three times to deactivate it once you get to the car." I turned it over and saw inscriptions written around the edge. None of the words made sense, just a jumble of consonants and vowels.

"I don't know how . . . Here, you keep it." I shoved it at her, uncomfortable with magic as I'd always been.

She shoved it back to me. "Trust me, you need it.

There are two black mages across the street. I saw them from the bedroom window, and they're not here to window-shop. They had to have seen you come in, so they'll be waiting. Sound out the words exactly as they're written. It's easy. Just say the words and then get the hell out of Underground."

"What about you?"

"Please. I can take care of myself. Why do you think they're waiting *outside*?"

Her bravado made us both laugh, but I came to another understanding. My sister was a force to be reckoned with. She hadn't earned her spot at the League of Mages by being a weakling. I hugged her one more time over the counter, taking a deep breath of her herby scent. "I love you, Bryn," I mumbled against her hair.

"Love you, too, Charlie." She eyed the charm in my hand. "It's got enough magic in it to use twice, but it'll wear off fast. Should be just enough to get you to the car and back."

A new appreciation blossomed for my little sister. "Thanks."

She walked me to the door. "I'd wait until just before you open the downstairs door before invoking the charm."

"Got it."

I was an emotional wreck walking down the stairs. Thankfully Bryn had closed her door behind me and locked it. The last thing I wanted was an audience when I invoked the charm. Magic made me extremely uneasy. It was a practice that I avoided at all costs.

And now here I was about to invoke my first spell. *Bryn's probably jumping up and down with glee behind the door*, I thought.

At the exit, I drew in a deep breath, reminding myself that I'd faced harder things than this. Invoking a charm should be a breeze. There was nothing to be afraid of, except maybe turning myself into a donkey. *Way to be positive, Charlie.*

Okay, I could do this. I didn't have time to deal with two black mages right now, and getting to the car and then to Will's was priority number one.

With the soda can in one hand, the edge of the Doritos bag held between two fingers, I opened my free hand and read the inscription exactly as it was written. *"Brac sabacus romulatus abento inveridon."* I read the clockwise spiral, repeating the chant the four times it was written before the spiral ended in the center.

Nothing happened on the inside, but the air around me condensed to a palpable energetic force. The hairs on my arms stood straight. *Holy Mary, Mother of God.* I'd done it! Well, at least, I thought so. A feeling of accomplishment went through me. I turned, wanting to race up the steps and tell Bryn.

But it would have to wait.

Here goes nothing. I gripped the knob, creaked the door open, and slipped through the small opening. Hopefully they hadn't seen the movement of the door. I stepped onto the sidewalk and into the hustle and bustle of Mercy Street at night. The exhausts on every pub and restaurant were working overtime, sending the aroma of food into the air. It all smelled like French fries. I scanned the crowd. Shoppers. Pub crawlers. Couples. And then I spied *them* standing in the shadow of a large potted palm tree, which held open the door to Abracas Bar & Grill. A long line of patrons waited for tables in the popular eatery, giving the black mages even more cover.

The undercover cop didn't even see them. I probably wouldn't have either if it wasn't for Bryn. Or maybe I would have if I had remembered to tap into my newly discovered gene pool—hard thing to do if you spent your life relying on your human traits and training.

Their once-green aura was tainted with the smut of darkness. It surrounded them like a dirty cirrus cloud. I and other law enforcement called them Pig-Pens. I didn't make it up, but it sure as hell fit. That was the price they paid for sacrificing their Elysian power for the dark power that fed Charbydon. One male. One female. Both tall and thin with their shoulder-length hair tied back from stoic faces. Their pearly dark eyes scanned the crowd, and they stood so still I wondered if they could be seen by your average Joe.

With a deep breath, I stepped off the sidewalk and into the street at a fast clip. They didn't follow. *Thank you, Bryn!* I thought, breaking into a run.

Twenty minutes later, I pounded on Will's front door in the newly developed and swanky town home community of Weston Heights. He wasn't answering and my concern spiked. "Will?" I called loudly. "Will, open up!" I pounded harder and rang the bell several times.

Please don't tell me I'm too late. I hurried around the landscaped walk and knocked on the neighbor's door. The porch light was off and there were no lights in the windows, unlike Will's brightly lit end unit. My heart thudded hard. Panic surged through me. My hands trembled as I pulled my weapon, moved to his front door, gathered my energy, and kicked the door directly above the knob. It splintered open with a loud crack.

Carefully, I edged inside the hardwood foyer, staying against the wall and praying they were okay.

Down the hall, the living room opened into a vaulted space. Furniture was upended. Pictures askew on the walls. Fear stole my breath. I was too late.

I found Will's body facedown on the floor.

"Will!"

Quickly, I scrambled over the chaos and knelt by his side. His pulse was faint, but still there. Thank God it was there. With shaking hands, I called 911 and then continued through the house, yelling for Emma.

Somehow I knew she wasn't there, but I checked anyway, checked every goddamn room, closet, and corner. In the bathroom, I slumped against the wall, holding my Nitro-gun to my chest, the pain washing over me in enormous waves. The sour burn of raw anguish built in my torso and throat. I couldn't remember how to breathe. It felt as though everything—soul, heart, lungs, skin, and blood—was being sucked away, leaving behind a hollow shell.

She was gone. Em was gone.

Find Em . . . have to find Em. Have to breathe.

My lungs deflated.

Pressure built in my chest and face.

Numbness stole through my oxygen-deprived limbs, but slowly a vibrating, demanding force, my will, shoved me out of my immobile panic. *Breathe, Charlie!* I gasped for air, heart straining and tired lungs filling. Finally.

I pushed away from the wall, my senses returning, and then I sprang into action, flying down the stairs to Will, heart and lungs trying to keep up and recoup.

"Will! Will, wake up!" I turned him over, tears choking my words. My shaking hands roamed over his head, neck, and torso, but there were no outward signs of trauma. Fueled by desperation and adrenaline, I slapped him across the face, screaming his name and shaking him by the shoulders.

His eyes blinked open with a start. *Oh, thank you, God.* "Will, where's Emma?"

He didn't answer, but his gaze darted around the room as though seeing it for the first time.

"Where did they take her? Did they say anything?" My heart was pistoning so fast, tears flowing, throat closing. "Come on, Will, please stay with me."

Will's arms moved slowly over his head, and then he gave a lazy, thorough stretch. I released his shoulders and sat back, dumbfounded, as he yawned, pushed up on his hands, and graced me with a blinding grin.

The aura around him went from his usual cloudy blue to gray with black swirls. Dread sucked the air from my lungs once again. I floundered around for the Nitro-gun, which I'd set on the floor before checking him for injuries, and then scrambled back on my rear, pointing it at him. It clattered in my hand, I shook so badly.

"You must be Charlie." He sat up all the way and inspected his hands.

"Who the hell are you? And where's my kid?"

He stopped examining his hands to study me for a moment. One corner of his mouth twisted into a half smile. A shiver crept along my spine. "I'm the guy your hubby sold his soul to."

Shock siphoned the blood from my face. "I don't believe you. Will would never do that."

His head cocked slowly. It was Will, but it seemed like a puppet worked the strings, a puppet still not used to its body. "I have the paperwork, signature and all."

"Soul bartering is illegal. Restore him to his body now." I stood. Tremors weakened my limbs. I never thought I'd find the sight of Will Garrity eerie and repugnant. I never thought he'd go this far. The reality of what he'd done began to sink in and made my eyes sting.

Will pushed to his feet, unfolding himself slowly,

testing out his new body, stretching his legs and arms, and wiggling his fingers. He tipped his neck both ways until it cracked and then rolled his shoulders. "Soul bartering is not illegal in Canada," he said with a vacant look as he accessed Will's recent memories; the only ones available to him.

"You're not in Canada anymore. Will is a United States citizen. Give him back."

"No."

My fingers gripped the gun harder. *Goddammit, Will!* He'd sold his body and soul to a Revenant—a spirit entity that granted one's greatest desire in exchange for a body to inhabit when it was that body's time to die. Revenants were good at making deals with those whose lives would be cut short. Some said they could see a person's death and, therefore, only made contracts with those who'd die at a young age.

I wanted to hurt this *thing* inside of my husband's body, but I couldn't bring myself to do it. Still in disbelief and my head spinning, I whispered, "Why?" How could he do this?

"Because he loved you," Will's voice echoed in the quiet. "I was going to give him the means to win your heart back, but . . . timing is everything, I guess. The guy sold his afterlife to live out his life with you. Too bad he kicked the bucket before that could happen." He shrugged. "Not my problem, though."

"And you knew," I muttered, my legs giving out. I sank into the chair behind me, the gun hanging limp in my hand. "You knew he was going to die." My stomach clenched hard against the queasiness burgeoning in my gut.

"Not like this. When I met him, the guy had a good ten years at least. He thought it was worth it. But then love makes people do desperate, stupid things. I've seen far worse, believe me." *Will* lifted his arm and delicately sniffed the skin and then brushed his lips against the hairs on his arms. "I didn't swindle him if that's what you're thinking. Look, your ex wasn't an idiot. He knew when I agreed to contract with him that he'd die in the prime of his life. Living out whatever time he had left with you, with all the things he'd ever wanted, was worth it to him. If you're going to go anyway, why not, right?"

I tried not to shout, but it didn't work. "Why not?!" I should just shoot him now. "Why not is because you're giving up any chance of an afterlife, that's why not. His soul is stuck inside a body he no longer controls!" I wanted to kill Will for this! Anger was much easier than guilt. Realizing Will had given up his afterlife just to be with me and Em again was too much to swallow.

He ignored my outburst. "Took quite a beating from the jinn who were here earlier," the Revenant said, delicately straightening Will's bloodied shirt with his fingertips.

I went completely still. "The jinn."

"Yeah. They gave me a message for you: 'The boss says to tell you the second debt is paid.'"

Oh God. Tennin. He had taken payment for the

debt. He had taken Will. I doubled over and grabbed my stomach, rage blinding my vision.

"Have to give him props," the Revenant went on. "Your guy took a hell of a lot more than I expected. His heart was on its last few beats by the time I got here. Good thing, too, or he would've gone straight into the afterlife."

Something I didn't know. I raised my head. "If you're not here to collect at their last breath then they go to the afterlife?"

"Soul and all. Contract null and void. We can't inhabit a dead body without its soul. Just the way it is." He sniffed. "If you wanna reanimate a corpse, go talk to a necromancer."

I forced down the desperation rising in my throat. "Does that mean he's still aware, alive?"

"Eh, sort of like in limbo."

It was a tiny bit of hope, but I grabbed on to it for dear life. If there was a way to save Will and eject this creature, I'd find it. But right now, Emma was out there somewhere. And there were sirens in the distance. We needed to go before getting held up by the police and medics.

I stood, spurred into action, already halfway to the foyer. "C'mon. We need to find my daughter."

"Not my problem."

Oh, no he didn't.

Fuck it. I swung around and shot him with my Nitro-gun.

13

The Revenant flew back against the wall, denting the drywall and sliding down in a heap. He was a supernatural; he'd heal himself just like he'd healed Will's body from the fight. I walked over, knelt down, and tapped his cheek with the barrel of the gun. His eyes popped open. "I need to find my daughter, and you're going to help me, got it?"

He rubbed the back of his head as he straightened. "You didn't have to shoot me. Look, I'm a decent spirit. Did everything legal-like. No need to go all ballistic on me."

"You haven't seen anything yet. Get up. You take Will's body, then you take his responsibilities."

"Says who?"

"Says this." I waved the gun. "And the little part of the soul-bartering contract where it says you must complete any unfinished business of the mortal's life before going about your own."

"You read that part?"

I walked to the front door. "Standard operating procedure. Let's go."

I slid into the driver's seat of the Mustang as the Revenant fumbled with the passenger door handle. Grief swelled my chest. I slid the gear into reverse as *Will* got in, just catching the flash of blue and white as a patrol car turned down the street.

"What's your name?" I asked, glancing in the rearview mirror as I drove off in the opposite direction. Better to separate this being as far from the real Will as I could. As it was, it was near impossible to look at him without wanting to weep.

"Rex."

"Rex?"

He straightened Will's shirt. "It's short for something you could never pronounce."

"Right. Did you or Will hear where they were taking Emma?" I knew he still held enough of Will's last memories to answer for both of them.

"No, they didn't say. Pretty much just beat the piss out of him while a female came in and took out your daughter."

Swift rage flared up again, but this time I absorbed it, biting my cheek hard, and forced it into something I could handle: cold, calculating vengeance. This bitch, whoever she was, would pay for touching my kid. "Did you know her?"

"No. She was Abaddon, though." He snorted. "No mistaking their cold, bitchy demeanor."

The rhythmic sound of the engine became loud in the ensuing silence. I operated the Mustang on autopilot, not really seeing the cars passing by or the traffic lights, just driving with my fingers in a death grip on the steering wheel, and my heart shriveling beneath my ribs.

Rex chuckled softly, the sound so much like Will that I could almost pretend it was him sitting beside me and not this parasitic spirit.

"What?"

"That kid of yours is as tough as nails," he said, staring out the window. "She bit the bitch and drew blood, said her mom was going to kick her ass."

The thought of Emma having to fight made me sick inside and more fearful than I'd ever been in my life, but that she'd stood up for herself—I was proud of her. Cursing, not so much. Tears sprung to the surface. I didn't know whether to be proud or horrified.

"They weren't going to hurt her, if that's what you're worried about." He lifted the shirt and smelled a spot that was free of blood. "I like this cologne."

I ignored that last comment. "How would you know?"

"Abaddon bitches are brutal. If she didn't rip your kid's head off for biting her, that means she was ordered not to. Simple deduction."

A tiny kernel of hope sprouted in my heart. I nodded without looking at Rex, and we drove for several minutes in silence.

Will had sold his soul because he thought he didn't have a chance with me. I wanted to scream. Same old Will. There might have been a chance for us in the future, but it had been too soon. He was always so impatient, always so ready to turn to otherworldly means. The betrayal and guilt nestled deep in my gut like burning sulfur.

"I know what you're thinking," Rex said suddenly. "You can't bring him back."

"Oh, Rex." I shot him a candid look. "There are always loopholes. You more than anyone should know that."

I'd dealt with a few spirits from the demon family tree before: Revenants, and their evil cousins, Wraiths. But I was far from an expert. The one thing I did know: nothing was permanent except death, and even that could be overcome. I was a perfect example of that.

"Yeah," he said, sounding unconvinced. "Good luck with that."

I shot him a cynical smile and then focused on the road.

"Where are we going?"

"You know how to use a gun?"

"No."

I tossed him my Nitro-gun. I had a backup in the waistband of the jeans. "Well, you better figure it out because we're going to Abaddon headquarters."

★   ★   ★

I dialed Hank's number repeatedly and still got no answer while Rex studied every inch of Will's face in the visor mirror, making muttered comments here and there, but overall pleased with his new appearance. When he lifted the waistbands of Will's khakis and boxers and took a look at the equipment, I'd had enough and swatted him hard on the arm.

"Ow!" He rubbed the spot. "You didn't have to hit me."

"Just shut up and sit still."

My thumbs tapped on the steering wheel, my whole body revved and ready to blow. CPP headquarters was housed in a mid-sized glass office building in Five Points, not far from the deli where Hank had picked me up earlier.

When this was all over I was going to sleep for at least a week. In the last two days I'd been beaten, shot at, possibly seen enough naked men to last a lifetime, been beaten again, and torn two of Bryn's outfits. And now my worst fears had come to pass. My family was in jeopardy. My insane ex-husband had sold his body and soul. And my little girl was gone.

As I drove the car into the underground parking deck below the office building, my heart rate kicked into overdrive. The guard at the gate stopped us, but flashing my badge was all it took to get us in.

Once parked, Rex and I headed to the elevator. Our steps echoed loudly in the vast concrete emptiness.

The extra ammo rubbed against my ankle bone, but it only fueled my focus and rage, which I considered good things at the moment.

In the elevator, we were treated to an orchestral version of Lionel Richie's "All Night Long." *Yeah*, I thought, *it's going to be another long-ass night, indeed.*

"She's going to be fine, you know," Rex assured me, his shoulder brushing against mine.

"Shut up and don't talk about her." I stepped forward as the elevator dinged and the doors slid open.

Gun drawn, I marched straight down the hallway, passing large glass-fronted rooms on either side where day workers folded flyers and answered phones. Farther down, the glass ended and a few office doors lined the hallway. At the end, a light spilled underneath one of the doors. Someone was working after hours.

Who needed to use the knob when kicking the damn door felt so much better?

Releasing my frustration, and without halting my stride, I kicked out. The door flew back on its hinges and knocked a hole in the drywall behind it. My gun pointed chest level, straight ahead, I continued into the room without missing a beat.

Otorius jumped up from his leather chair, pants down and penis bouncing. The horror on his face deepened to a scarlet red as he fumbled to cover himself. A human female's head appeared, turning to look curiously over the top of the polished desk as Otorius cursed in Charbydon and grabbed the waistband of his boxers and pants.

"Put your hands up," I commanded. God, I was going to be evil, but I couldn't help myself. Much like the jinn, when I saw an opportunity, I took it.

His hands stilled.

"Put your hands up . . . *now*."

My innuendo was clear. Promising revenge in his coal-black eyes, he dropped his boxers and pants and then lifted his arms. I slid my gaze to the package dangling semi-limp and pink between his legs, and let out a disappointed sigh. "Not very impressive." I'd always wondered about the sex of off-worlders. But his was pretty much the same as an average human male's, except Otorius wasn't circumcised, which made sense.

The female, an intern by the look and age of her, slowly slid her purse off the desk and held it to her chest like a shield. She wore a preppy pink button-down shirt, tight jeans, and her brown hair pulled back with a barrette. "Um, I guess I should be going now." She edged around the desk; face pale, eyes wide, and so freaking young it made me wince.

"Sorry, sweetheart, you're not going anywhere. Rex?"

"Yeah," he said from just beyond my right shoulder.

"Find something to tie her with and then put her in a closet in one of the main rooms. Don't worry," I told her, "someone will find you in the morning."

Her lips trembled, and she started to cry as Rex took her arm. I didn't feel bad at all. In fact, I was helping her to figure out the important things in life, and sucking Abaddon dick wasn't one of them. She could thank me later.

Once we were alone, Otorius spat out, "I can't wait to watch you die, *brougá*."

"Oh, enough with the *brougá* already. Move around the desk."

I stepped back. Had I not been pissed beyond belief, seeing him shuffling around the desk with his pants around his ankles, his hairy white legs a stark contrast to his black slacks and shiny dress shoes, would've been laughable. But as it was, I was ready to kill him.

Leaning my hip on a nearby accent table, I held his fuming stare for a moment. "I'm going to be very clear on what I'm about to say." I spoke slowly and with enough conviction that he nodded. "Tell me where my daughter is, and your penis stays intact."

Simple and effective.

Pale dots appeared on his face, slowly replacing the red until he was covered in an ashen pallor. "I don't know where she is."

"Do you know what this is, Otorius?" I asked, motioning toward the gun. "It's a Nitro-gun. It *freezes* things. Freezes them so badly, they can shatter into a million . . . little . . . pieces."

Rex groaned behind me, and I glanced over to see him moving his hand protectively in front of his— Will's—crotch. "Damn, that's brutal. God," he groaned again, "it hurts just thinking about it. And I thought Abaddon bitches were cruel."

I gave him a droll look and then turned my attention back to Otorius. "Well?"

"Goddammit, Madigan, I don't know where your fucking daughter is!" he barked, panic making his voice tremble. His hands dropped a fraction. He wanted nothing more than to cover himself, to protect himself. In an act of defiance and desperate instinct, he did it anyway.

And I fired.

Rex and Otorius screamed at the same time. The beam shot out and froze both of Otorius's hands. He leapt around the room, screaming in pain, unable to separate one hand from the other and nearly tripping over his trapped ankles.

Adrenaline pumping through me, I moved forward and grabbed him, shoving him face-first onto the desk, his arms over his head, hands still linked, and his bald ass pointing skyward. I stood at his hip and grabbed his neck, holding him down as hard as I could and fighting myself to remain in control. "Tell me!" I shouted. "Tell me where she is right now, or I finish the job!"

"I don't know!" He sobbed and blubbered against the desk. "I don't know! I don't know!"

"Charlie, I think he's telling the truth," Will's voice reached beyond the firestorm in my head. No. That wasn't Will. It was the swindling, hustler body thief. Rex.

"Shut up," I snarled, blinking tears back because I knew he was right. Otorius didn't know where my daughter was.

"Where's the *ash* lab?" I asked instead.

"I don't know, I swear. I only know that the *Sangurne N'ashu* needs heat and moisture to grow. A hothouse maybe. It takes seven years for one flower to bloom, so it'd have to be an established place. That's all I know." I eased my grip on his neck. "You can't stop him, Charlie. You're in way over your head, and he's waited too long for this."

"For what?" I squeezed harder and he laughed.

"He'd hurt me far worse than you ever could."

Otorius's hands finally unlocked, but one was so burnt with frostbite, it had turned completely black. The other hand, which had been under the first, came out in much better shape.

He'd lose the hand.

But it was no more than he deserved. I hauled him off the desk and shoved him at Rex, whose look of horror at seeing a semi-naked male bearing down upon him was actually pretty damn amusing. He caught Otorius, holding the Abaddon representative at arm's length and shooting me an incredulous scowl. "What the hell do you want me to do with him?"

I sat on the edge of the desk, tired. "I don't care. Tie him up and put him in the closet with what's-her-face."

"Her *name* is Darlene, and she's from Michigan," Rex said frankly. "What about his pants? I'm not pulling them up and he can't do it with his hands."

"Then leave them," I shot back. "Just get him out of my sight."

Rex rolled his eyes at me and then slowly led Otorius from the room. I'd just made one hell of an enemy, I thought, looking after them.

Emma. Where are you?

The fist squeezing my heart was so great, I set the gun on the desk and then sank down to the floor, hugging my knees and gasping for breath at the same moment tears flooded down my face. I couldn't control it any longer.

I'd lost her. My little girl.

My hands delved into my hair and I squeezed hard, pulling on the roots as I rocked back and forth. Pressure and heat built in my face and chest. I screamed, a frustrated sound torn from my very soul. My body shuddered as my wail turned to racking sobs.

A body sat down beside me and pulled me into his arms. I knew it wasn't Will, but it smelled like him and felt like him and spoke soothing words like him. I held on tight, releasing the tears into his shirt, my head tucked under his chin as his hand rubbed my back. "We lost our girl," I sobbed against him. "We lost our baby."

"Shhh." He soothed my hair in long strokes. After a long moment, he said, "I've never met a more determined mother than you, Charlie. You'll find a way. Don't lose faith now."

His softly spoken words broke through the grief.

Drawing in a deep breath, I raised my head and looked into the eyes of the man I'd loved for so long, wishing he was there. "I thought you guys were all . . . bad."

Rex's smile was awkward, but flattered. "Common misconception. Not all demon spirits are bad. The Wraiths, running around and possessing humans against their will, making their heads spin around and launch nuclear barf from twelve feet out, kind of gave us all a bad name." I laughed. "Mostly, we just want to experience life, physical life, that's all. The last body I was in was an old fart who'd had a heart attack in his forties. I made him the sensation of The Wolf's Lair Dinner Theater. Starring role six seasons straight. You might have heard of me. James Eblehard."

I shook my head.

"Yeah, well, I could have made him the greatest actor the world has ever seen, but all he wanted was dinner theater stardom." He sighed deeply. "It was an utter waste of my talent. Anyway, he told his wife I'd take over when his time came. She asked me to stay and I did. We Revenants care, no matter what you might have heard otherwise." And then he fixed me with a glare. "But if you tell anybody about this, I'll have to cut out your tongue."

I sniffed and eased back. "And if you tell anybody I lost it, I'll cut off your—"

His hand shot up. "No need to paint a picture! I get it."

Surprised I was able to smile and actually mean it, I stood, grabbing my gun from the desk and sliding it into the holster.

Rex and I left the second floor to the sounds of banging and muffled shouts for help. "God help the poor soul who finds Otorius," Rex muttered.

★   ★   ★

"So where to now?" Rex asked when we got into the car.

"You're cooperating pretty well." I glanced over, finding it odd, despite what he'd told me in Otorius's office.

"I told you, I'm a decent guy. I do every possession by the book. Contract says I got to tie up loose ends, then that's what I'll do. Besides, I haven't had this much excitement in eons. Except"—a pointed finger shot up—"when I met Shakespeare in Bankside." He sighed. "The Globe . . . now *that* was theater."

I started the car and slipped it in first. "We're going to my sister's."

Rex pulled down the visor mirror and inspected his face. "How do I look?" He adjusted the blood-stained shirt, frowning at the big splotches of dark red and the huge area of wetness from my tears. Talk about self-involved. I didn't need to look in a mirror to know my face was still puffy and splotchy from crying and my hair was sticking out at all angles.

"My sister doesn't go for your type, trust me."

He huffed at me. "No need to crush a man's ego."

"You're not a man," I reminded him. "You're a parasite who swindled my husband."

"Oh, look at you now, calling him your *husband*. He wouldn't have needed me if you had been open to calling him that before."

Ouch. "Shut the hell up."

My cell rang. It was Bryn. "Yeah," I answered, giving an evil look to Rex.

"Charlie," she said breathlessly. I stiffened; the panic in her voice was all too clear. "Hank is here." Her voice choked on tears. "You need to come back."

"Already on my way." Hanging up, I cursed under my breath. "Fuck." What else could go wrong? I tapped the steering wheel, thinking, as I dropped the gear in third and passed a dump truck. "Can you heal others?" I asked Rex.

"Just my host body."

"Figures."

Once we parked, I fished in my pocket for Bryn's cloaking charm, intending to use it at the entrance to Mercy Street. The last thing I needed was to deal with the black mages or any other renegade waiting to ambush me.

Underground was still lit up. People milled about, watching workers set up for a block concert. I pulled Rex closer to the storefronts and rounded the corner to Mercy Street.

"Hold it right there."

We stopped dead in our tracks, running straight into the barrel of a 9mm as a figure in a black cloak and hood stepped from behind a large potted fern.

Violet and indigo eyes glowed from the darkness inside of the hood. Sian.

Without thinking, I twisted the gun from her hand. "You fucking bitch!" A stunned expression paled her smooth gray skin as I shoved her back into the alley and slammed her against the rough brick wall with one hand braced flat against the middle of her chest and the other holding her own gun to her throat. "Maybe I should just kill you and see how Daddy likes the feeling."

Confusion creased her brow. "What?"

"The second debt. He tried to kill my husband and my daughter is missing." I pressed the nozzle deep into her neck. "She's *eleven years old*."

A profound weight settled on my shoulders. I couldn't keep the tears from rising to my eyes, but I did keep them from spilling over. Music drifted into the alley. The band, tuning their instruments in spurts of funky guitar strokes and sudden drumbeats, accentuated the fact that this entire day had been an insane combination of disbelief, heartbreak, discovery, and loss on a monumental scale. I just wanted to wake up from this nightmare. Sian's hand came up slowly and pulled the hood off her head.

"I'm sorry. I didn't know," she said in a tone saturated with horror and condolence.

"Right." I waved the gun in front of her nose. "So, what, you just decided to come topside to show me your new toy?"

She swallowed and averted her gaze. "Well, no, I didn't know what exactly I was going to do, but . . . despite what my father wants, I can't work topside. And the only way I could think was to get rid of you or make you bargain with me," she said lamely.

"Holy shit. You're a hybrid," Rex said in awe as it dawned on him.

She blinked back instant tears. "You see? You see why I can't go out in public? I can't do it." Her anxiety and vulnerable state emanated blackness into her purple-and-blue aura.

Her entire demeanor was so different than when I'd first seen her, and she must have seen the thought pass across my face because she said, "I try to be strong in the den, to show my father I am like a jinn . . . But even there they hate me. So I have to be like stone, like nothing matters."

"Did you know your father is working with Mynogan?"

"Yes. My father struck a bargain to make the *ash*. They bring us the Bleeding Souls and we extract the milk and then send it to a lab where it's made into powder. Father calls their bargain Step Two."

"Any idea where the flowers are grown or where this lab is? Or where they'd take a child?"

"None. I'm sorry. The lab is run by Cassius Mott, though, if that helps. I don't know where it is except that it's in or around Atlanta somewhere."

Three steps. Mynogan grew the flowers, Grigori extracted them, and Cass turned them street-friendly. But what the hell Mynogan needed me for was still a mystery.

"Next time you decide to go confront somebody," I said, lifting the gun in front of her face, "you might want to turn off the safety." I shoved her gun into the back of my jeans and turned to leave.

"But what about the job? I just told you things my

father would kill me for! You're supposed to help me now! I can't—"

I paused and looked over my shoulder. "Yeah, well, you won't have to worry about it much longer because Daddy will be dead or in jail." I resumed walking. "Preferably dead."

As I passed Rex, I grabbed his bicep to usher him out of the alley. He walked backwards three steps, lifted one hand to his ear, and mouthed the words *call me* to Sian.

Completely ignoring him, I scanned the open area at the head of the alley. The charm wouldn't cover Rex, but I was hoping the black mages wouldn't be on the lookout for Will. The undercover officer had seen Will now a few times, so he shouldn't give him any trouble at Bryn's door.

I had to grab Rex's hand and drag him behind me. He was like a child and easily distracted by the sights and sounds of Underground. It made me wonder how long it had been since he'd found himself in a young body.

Bryn let us in on the first press of the buzzer.

My pulse pounded hard, but not from my run up the stairs. Hank was back, and I prayed it wasn't as bad as it had sounded over the phone. Rex followed at a leisurely pace, trailing his hand along the wall as he progressed.

Inside, my heart nearly dropped to the floor when I saw Hank lying on the couch, and a tearstained Bryn kneeling at the coffee table, hands shaking as she lit incense and mixed a healing drink of herbs, blessing it under her breath.

I went down on my knees, afraid to touch him. His big body spilled over the cushions, one hand dangling to the floor. Dried blood matted his blond hair. Bruises covered his knuckles and face. My lion had fallen. I bit my lip hard, until the skin popped and a warm drop of blood hit my tongue.

Bryn gasped suddenly and bumped into me in her haste to scramble away, her back hitting the love seat. Over my shoulder I saw Will's rugged form filling the doorway. Bryn's wide brown eyes were fixed on him. Then she glanced at me, the gold and copper flecks bright with fear. She swallowed. "That's not Will."

"I know. That's Rex. He stole Will's body."

Rex slung me an exasperated glower. "Not *stole*." He stepped into the room, scanning every detail. I knew he was experiencing Will's memories of this place, but as Rex, he was seeing it for the first time. As if on an afterthought, he turned back to Bryn, studying her just as intently as he had the surroundings. "William bargained to win back Little Miss Sunshine here. Don't ask me why."

"Go to hell," I responded with the most withering glare I could muster.

Bryn's face paled. Her hand fluttered to her neck as tears filled her eyes and fell over the rims. Her voice was barely a whisper as the cruel understanding dawned on her. "Emma."

I didn't have to answer. She understood. The tears

trailed silently down her cheeks. Her chest rose and fell as though she had trouble breathing. She put her head in her hands and doubled over, rocking and mumbling the words, "Oh, God, oh, God, oh, God . . ."

Watching her fall apart was cracking my own self-control, and I couldn't lose it, not now, not when Emma needed me the most. I went to reach for Bryn to shake her out of her shock and grief, but right before I touched her, she lifted her head, sat straighter, and sniffed. The grim copper gleam that came into her eyes startled even me. "I need to make a call." She staggered to her feet and went into the kitchen.

Gently, I touched Hank's shoulder. "Hank? Can you hear me?" He shrank away. Swollen eyelids slit open. He turned away from me. "Hank?"

"Leave me alone, Charlie," he rasped out, his voice barely a whisper, but loud enough for me to hear true pain, and what sounded like blame.

"Hank. I didn't leave you alone. Carreg was there to help. I had to get back to Em. You heard what Mynogan said."

"Yeah, Carreg the Almighty wasn't quick enough to stop this." He lifted his neck. Both ends of his voice modifier had been fused together. Despair lodged in his throat. "It won't come off." And I knew what that meant. His greatest asset, his greatest power, was gone.

Stunned, I dropped back, my rear end landing on the carpet and my stomach folding into tight knots. The utter desolation in Hank's eyes left me cold and despondent. And when he turned his back on me, I felt a keen sense of loss. I went to pull him over, to try and explain, but his eyes were closed and his breathing slower. He'd passed out.

Bryn came back into the room. Determination seeped from every pore. Still in shock, I stood, not knowing what to do next.

A knock sounded at the door, but the buzzer hadn't gone off. I grabbed my gun, flicked the safety, and trained it on the door, but Bryn came up beside me, one hand on my shoulder and the other stilling my hand. "Reinforcements," she said. "He won't appear inside, but the landing I've allowed."

With a deep, fortifying breath, she walked to the door and opened it. A tall male dressed in black leather pants and a dark green silk tunic that fell to mid-thigh stepped inside at her invitation.

A gorgeous, creative green aura swirled around him. The fact that I was now identifying auras before the actual person should have come as a surprise. But the figure in the doorway pretty much trumped that.

The reinforcement grinned at me. "Detective."

14

"Aaron."

The memory of our meeting in The Bath House came rushing back. His wild black hair, tattoos, easy grin, and all that exposed skin . . . My face grew hot. Somewhere behind me, Rex grumbled as he realized there was male competition in the room. Aaron turned to him, lifting a thoughtful black eyebrow. He said something, a somber greeting perhaps, in Charbydon and Rex nodded.

I shot a questioning glance Bryn's way. She leaned in, bumping my shoulder with her own. "You can trust him. I wouldn't have called him otherwise. I might not like him, but I'd trust him with my life."

Aaron turned to me, ignoring Bryn's remark. "I hear you've made an enemy of an Abaddon elder, among others."

"Yeah," Rex cut in, "she's pretty good at that. You should've seen what she did to—"

"Rex!"

"What?" he asked innocently, plopping down into Bryn's love seat.

Aaron chuckled. "Somehow that doesn't surprise me."

"Does Mynogan have any weaknesses?" I asked. "Anything you can tell me will help."

Before Aaron could reply, the buzzer rang again.

Zara's voice came through the speaker. "Hank asked me to call her," Bryn told me as she went to the intercom. The fact that he'd called on Zara the Crush and not me burned on so many levels.

"It's like a tri-world convention," Rex muttered, fiddling with a glass orb on the side table near the chair.

Irritated more than I'd ever seen her, Bryn darted over and grabbed the red orb from him. "Don't touch my stuff."

I let Zara in. She gave me a quick nod before hurrying to Hank, kneeling down, and gently pulling him over. It took several seconds of soft coaxing for her to wake him. They mumbled together, foreheads touching. The pang of jealousy that went through me made me turn away. And then she gasped when she saw his modifier. Aaron leaned over to see.

"How do we get this off, Aaron?" Zara asked over her shoulder, her hand stroking Hank's arm.

Aaron peered closer. "The metal is a fusion of

Charbydon typanum and steel. You can't cut it or weaken it by heat."

"What about cold?" I asked.

"Possibly."

"But how would you do it without hurting him? It's so close to the skin." This from Bryn.

"Maybe Carreg will know," I said to myself.

Aaron's head whipped around. "You know Carreg? The Astarot noble?"

I shrugged. Slowly, thoughtfully, Aaron nodded. "If he's on your side, it won't hurt. If he's not, you're up against two of the most powerful beings from Charbydon."

"He's on our side." Unsure of it myself, I had to believe in some kind of an edge right now.

"Yeah, well, they're not the only powerful beings around," Hank rasped out, his feverish eyes burning into mine over Zara's shoulder.

Suddenly I was front and center. All eyes turned to me in question. Only I understood Hank's meaning. Carreg had said because of my DNA manipulation, I was now one of the most powerful humans on Earth. Either Hank had overheard, or Mynogan had filled him in after I'd abandoned him.

My gaze traveled over them. Hank. Zara. Rex. Aaron. And Bryn. Bryn, who wanted so badly for me to open up, to be like we used to be before Connor died. She gave me an encouraging nod, an outpouring of support and love, and something broke in me. I dipped my head, wanting to hug her, but now was not the time. I had a waiting audience. And a child waiting for her mother. Everything I did or said from here on out would bring me one step closer to her. So I told them everything I knew.

"When I died in the hospital eight months ago, Titus Mott saved me. But he did so with the help of Mynogan." I drew in a deep breath, feeling violated by what they'd done and hating say the words out loud. "They injected me with his genes and genes from an Adonai priestess. Somehow, they mingled with mine. And . . . well . . . here I am, screwed up in the head when I close my eyes, but otherwise the same old Charlie." I had to believe that. I *was* the same old Charlie.

Mouths dropped open. Even Bryn hadn't expected this. Rex laughed. Zara let out a low whistle.

"DNA manipulation . . ." Aaron linked his hands behind his back, his sharp features becoming philosophical. "I suppose it's possible. But *both* Charbydon and Elysian powers? There's no way they can co-exist."

I opened my arms and then let them fall against my thighs. "Yeah, that's me," I muttered. "Charlie the Freak." Annoyance rippled through me. Not only did I hate talking about myself, but the betrayal at being an unwitting lab rat really pissed me off. But then, I wouldn't be here, living, if not for them. "It works on some of those who already have the genes of both worlds in the family tree." I glanced at Bryn. "Which would explain how some members of our family are gifted."

"Could be," Aaron began, rubbing his chin and pacing slowly across the room. "There was a period long ago in Earth's early history when cohabitation between races took place. You humans refer to it in your Bible. The fall of the angels and the birth of the Nephilim. But even then the number of normal offspring living to adulthood was extremely low. The Nephilim were usually stillborn, severely abnormal, or they went mad from so much power in their blood."

"It's where many believe the psychic humans got their abilities," Zara offered, tucking her perfect honey-red locks behind her ear, her hand possessively on Hank's.

Aaron turned and stared at me. "You're our secret weapon."

"Okay, number one, there is no *our* except for me and Rex over there, and two, this power comes and goes. It wars with the other. I have no clue how to use it. Look," I said, grabbing my jacket, tired of being the anomaly on display, "the only thing that matters is getting Emma back. They won't hurt her until they have what they want, which is me. And don't ask me why. But I'm not going to sit around and wait. The longer she's with them, the more memories she'll have of this, memories she doesn't need."

Hank struggled to sit up. "They have Em? I thought she was with Will—" Then he saw Rex. Understanding paled his tanned skin to white. He lost his strength and fell back into the cushions with a string of mumbled curses. *Now* he understood what we were up against.

I knew he felt as angry and vengeful as I did, and

now that the voice-mod was stuck on his neck—well, I've known my fair share of men—if I had to guess, he was feeling pretty useless right now. He sat up with Zara's help, his body healing courtesy of his Elysian blood. Bryn handed her the herbal tea and Zara helped him to drink.

"I've a fully loaded Nitro-gun," he said after a sip, "and more where that one came from."

"And I can get into Veritas," Zara piped up. "Find out where Mynogan lives, the businesses and real estate he owns. They have to be holding your daughter somewhere, right?"

Bryn stepped next to the couch. "I can fight."

Aaron fell in beside her. "So can I. And I can train you in the meantime, Charlie; help you to control your power. They won't be expecting that."

Rex sighed heavily and didn't bother rising from the love seat. "And I suppose I can take a beating as good as anyone else."

My chest constricted.

"Charlie," Bryn prompted with a hopeful look in her brown eyes.

I could only nod, humbled by the people in this room who would fight for Emma, some who didn't even know her. And those who did; I knew they'd give up their lives for her.

"I don't mean to interrupt this Hallmark moment, people," Rex said, "but has anyone wondered why?"

"Why what?" Zara asked.

"Why Charlie? They turned her into Wonder

Woman, took her kid, and for what? Guys like Mynogan, they're like Scooby-Doo villains; they always
have a master plan."

I leaned against the foyer table. Guess Will could've
done worse. Instead of contracting with an evil son-
of-a-bitch, he got a smart-ass comedian with a love of
theater. Joy. But Rex was right. There was a bigger
picture here, one we weren't seeing. Otorius had all
but said the same.

Aaron cleared his throat. "I might be able to help
with the *why*, but first I need to be sure. The library at
the mages' league should shed some light on things."

I itched to do something, anything other than sitting here and talking about how to get my daughter
back. "Fine. I'll go with you," I told Aaron. "Zara, you
and Hank get into Veritas. Bryn and Rex, pool your
powers. You can divine, right?" I asked her, remembering her mentioning it before. She nodded. "Good, use
a map, see if you can figure out where they're keeping
Emma. If you find the area, Zara and Hank's real estate
info should be able to pinpoint a location."

Heads nodded.

"Good." I turned to Aaron. "Let's go."

When we reached the landing outside of Bryn's
door, he grabbed my hand before I could protest and
said, "Relax, we're taking a shortcut."

The floor dropped out from under me; at the same
moment my body changed from the physical to pure
energy. *What the hell?*

I couldn't gasp or feel my heart racing, though

it felt like those things were happening. I tried to squeeze Aaron's hand, to hold on, suddenly terrified I'd be swept away and dispersed into the air. But no sooner than I decided to panic, I became whole again, Aaron's hand still in mine.

"It's simply an issue of manipulating matter and energy," he said.

I doubted it was as *simple* as that. I dropped his hand, feeling the weight of my body more heavily than before. And then I slugged him in the shoulder. "Next time, try giving me a little warning, k?"

His emerald eyes crinkled at the corners, his lips twisting into an amused smile as he rubbed the spot.

"So, what are you then, a Master?" I asked, knowing not every warlock or mage could do what he just did.

He laughed. "I was. That was two hundred years ago. I'm a Magnus now."

Holy cow. *Thank you, Bryn.* Having a Magnus on our side was a huge bonus. I gave him an impressed nod, then looked around the room.

We stood in the center of a large pentagram, the outline set into a hardwood floor with a deep brown wooden inlay. Two tall windows shrouded by gold brocade curtains and the expensive wallpaper made me feel small and out of place. An altar with ritual paraphernalia sat against the left wall, and shelves full of books, herb pots, and specimen jars lined the right wall. *Yeah. Totally out of place.*

We were definitely in the headquarters of the Atlanta League of Mages. "Nice place," I said, looking up at the ceiling as Aaron guided me to the door. The entire room was framed with thick, ornate crown molding. A vaulted ceiling supported a massive wrought-iron chandelier, and the entire room smelled of sage.

"When we bought the mansion, it was about two hundred years in need of repair—just a skeleton, but with good bones. Now," he glanced around the room, "it has been brought back to its former glory."

The revival of the old Mordecai House had been headline news when the League bought it a few years back. In its heyday it was the biggest antebellum mansion in Atlanta. Now it was home to the mages. And the décor fit. High and lofty, with a scholarly touch.

I kept pace next to Aaron as we headed down a wide hallway planked with old restored hardwoods. Voices drifted from closed doors, but otherwise the atmosphere was respectful and hushed. "You know why Mynogan wants me, why he's done this to me," I stated as we descended a grand old curving staircase to the first floor.

"I have some idea, but I want to check the scrolls to make certain. It all fits, though. The timing. Your body's ability to incorporate the genes . . ."

With a whisper, two massive double doors opened, inviting us into the most beautiful library I'd ever seen. Floor-to-ceiling bookcases. Two levels with an ornate wooden spiral staircase leading to the second level, where a small walkway framed by an iron railing went all the way around the room. Supple leather couches sat opposite each other, and there were several matching chairs tucked into corners. On one side of the room, there were study tables and a large map table, and, on the other side, an enormous stone fireplace held court.

Loving the smell of books and leather, I inhaled deeply as Aaron walked to a section protected by leaded glass. His body blocked the case from my view. All I could see were his wide shoulders encased in the green silk and his dark head, which bowed in concentration. He spoke a series of incantations in a low hum of a voice. A thrill went through me as I responded to the energy, the magic in the room. I was waking up to a whole other world that existed in tandem with the one I knew so well. I had so much to learn, and the realization left me a little overwhelmed and highly impatient.

Two clicks sounded as the latches to the case released. Aaron turned his body slightly, and I watched him carefully remove a burnished, ancient-looking scroll tied with leather strings. He took it to the map table and unrolled it with surgical precision, and then I helped to weigh the corners down with cold brass paperweights forged to look like dragons.

A musty scent mushroomed into the air, but it wasn't like the smell of old paper or books. "Ugh. What *is* that?" I fanned the air over the scroll.

"Skin."

"Skin!"

If it bothered him, he didn't let on. Instead, he peered at the ancient wedge-shaped lines pressed into the skin with black ink, which looked very similar to the cuneiform writing of the ancient Sumerians.

He didn't elaborate. And I didn't ask. In fact, I didn't breathe for the next twenty seconds, giving the scent of ancient *skin* time to disperse. The thought of drawing that into my lungs made my stomach turn. I stepped back. "What does it say?"

"It's in Charbydon. From the House of Astarot. About ten thousand years ago, it was stolen by the House of Abaddon, and then, much later, stolen by another."

The smug tone in his voice drew my attention, and I saw his mouth give one faint twitch. "You?"

He didn't return my look, just shrugged and surveyed the library. "We have a nice collection."

Interesting. Aaron was much more than a Magnus. He was an art thief.

"The scroll details the calling of darkness," he said, "which can only be done in a place other than Charbydon."

While I didn't know exactly what the *calling of darkness* entailed, its purpose made sense. Charbydon existed in darkness, so they wouldn't need to call it there. "So what does this have to do with me?"

"Charbydon is dying, Charlie. In order to be free of sunlight and live as they are accustomed, they must have a new home. They must call the darkness to cover another place."

Goose bumps sprouted on my arms. "Atlanta."

"Yes, I believe so. Eventually, the darkness will

spread, very slowly, and in, oh, I don't know, a hundred years or two, it will cover the planet."

The weight of his words sent me plopping into the nearest chair. Air hissed from the leather cushion as it molded around my body. "So Mynogan's talk about saving their world . . ."

"There's no way to save a dying moon. At least not that I know of."

But Carreg believed. He was trying to find a way. Wasn't he?

I drew my legs in and propped my elbow on the arm of the chair. "And me?" I couldn't wait for this part. It was sure to be a doozy.

"The only being capable of calling the darkness is one who possesses the power of all three worlds in their blood. This scroll is a myth that goes back as far as anyone can remember. No one, no Elysian or Charbydon, has been able to do this. At first, around the time of cohabitation in your world, the House of Abaddon thought they could breed the perfect being, a Nephilim, to call the darkness over the Earth, to create their own realm and be free of joint rule with the House of Astarot. They've wanted this for millennia. Now, instead of looking for a way to live with what they've wrought in Charbydon, they'll steal this land."

I rested my chin on the teepee of my fingers. "That's all well and good *if* I could call the darkness. As it stands, Mynogan will fail simply because I have no clue how to call anything."

Aaron's entire being stilled. The emerald-green of

his eyes dimmed just a little, and his lips drew into a grim line. The hairs on the back of my neck started to rise. "You don't have to *do* anything, Charlie, except spill your blood on unconsecrated ground. Every last drop. Once this blood of three worlds seeps into the soil, darkness will rise, clouding out the sun and overtaking everything." He cleared his throat and straightened. "According to the scroll."

Right. Of course. *Just a typical day in the life of Charlie Madigan*, I thought sourly. "It doesn't explain why he didn't just kill me after injecting me with the DNA. Why wait until now?"

"Perhaps the timing wasn't yet right." He scanned the scroll again, but shook his head when he didn't find the answer he was looking for. "There is nothing here about when to begin the ritual. But timing and astrological alignments are everything in crafting. Mynogan must have had a good reason for waiting until now. Whether the myth is true or not, he believes in it. So, we must be prepared." He turned his back on the scroll, leaning his hip on the table and fixing me with a frank look. "You, my dear, need to learn how to fight fire with fire."

My cell rang. With some effort, I removed myself from the plush leather chair and then pulled my cell from the clip. It was Bryn. "Did you find her?"

"All we can get is a general area. It's somewhere around Morningside and Ansley Park."

Quickly, I turned away from Aaron, not wanting him to see my emotions and wishing I'd left my hair down to cover my face instead of up in the ponytail. My throat closed before I could ask the question that haunted my mind. But Bryn knew me, and she answered the silence over the phone. "I felt her. I didn't sense any pain"— I swallowed a sob; tears clouded my vision—"or true fright. Just a lot of worry, irritation, and anger."

I nodded. It was the only thing I could do without crying. My face was going to be the last fucking thing Mynogan ever saw. I managed to say okay and then close the cell, drawing in a deep breath before having to face Aaron. When I did, compassion shone in his gaze. "Don't look at me like that," I snapped. "Once we get a location, can you flash yourself in, grab her, and get out?"

"Mynogan isn't a fool. He'll have put a ward around her."

"You have a mansion full of mages, powerful ones."

"Not as powerful as an Abaddon elder. We don't exactly have the upper hand here."

"But you'll try." It was a command more than a request. If I had to ask, to beg or plead, I wouldn't be able to keep my despair in check and the tears at bay.

His dark head dipped. "I will. If not, then we'll find another way in. Chances are Mynogan will let you walk right through the door. You're what he wants, after all."

Every part of me wanted to start walking and not stop until I was in front of that bastard. But I knew I had to have a plan if I wanted to save Em first. I had a feeling if I just turned myself over, Emma would not be set free after my blood soaked the ground. No, she had to be free *first*. And I wasn't about to trust Mynogan to simply trade her for me.

I sat on the edge of the seat and put my head in my hands, feeling utterly defeated, feeling the sting rise behind my eyelids as I pressed them with my palms. "I can't do this. I need Emma." Her name repeated in my mind, echoing and bouncing around, tearing my heart in two. This wasn't right. I couldn't just wait. It wasn't in my nature. I wanted to scream, to fight and at the same time to curl into a fetal position on the floor. I'd lost my child. I should have been with her, should have known . . .

Emotions spun inside me, growing bigger and stronger and louder, gathering all that I had, all my fears and hurts and hopes, and turning them into a bloated monster that was bursting at the seams.

A strong hand landed on my shoulder. Spices filled the air. Aaron squeezed gently, the pressure as soft and sure as his voice. "First lesson. Learn how to control your emotions. You won't get anywhere with Mynogan if you're at war inside. You can't fight yourself and him."

No shit, I wanted to shout, but I stayed silent, trying to calm the storm, knowing that everything would depend on my ability to overcome the powers and control them. I needed to be like Aaron. Calm. Confident. Insightful. After a few deep breaths, I narrowed my eyes on him. "You know, you don't look like a wise man." But he sure as hell sounded like one.

"An apprentice could see your turmoil right now.

Auras reflect emotion and balance." He stepped back, crossing his arms over his chest. "What does mine tell you?"

He knew that focusing on something would pull me out of my tailspin. Aaron was astute whether he joked about it or not. I straightened, placed both hands on my knees, and stared hard at him. When I saw his aura earlier at Bryn's, it had been spontaneous, but trying to do it on purpose was another matter.

"Not so hard," he said. "Just relax and let it come naturally."

I drew in a deep breath and tried again. *Relax. See him as he is.* Slowly, the library faded, everything around Aaron dropping away until it was just his form filling my view. A hazy cloud began to take shape around his head and shoulders. But it wasn't enough. I concentrated harder. Something clicked inside, and I knew then that I was the problem. I was holding back, afraid to open myself up and accept the power. To be in control, I had to lose control of my inhibitions and fears.

My fists unclenched. My muscles relaxed and my arms hung loose at my sides. I was open, accepting.

Vibrant shades of green, emerald, fern, jade, and moss, all blossomed through the haze, overtaking it and becoming a living extension of the being in front of me. Power and emotion tickled my senses and in those colors, Aaron was revealed. Intelligence. Creativity. Valor. Anger on behalf of Emma and me. Worry for

Bryn. Determination to succeed. And something else, too, a desire to thwart Mynogan, or perhaps it was the entire House of Abaddon. I sensed a history here. One I couldn't quite see in an aura alone. I probed deeper, and suddenly hit an invisible brick wall.

"Second lesson," Aaron said, "learn how to block those that can see inside of you." Amusement and a splash of ego flickered in his eyes. "Nice try, though."

Now that I understood I had to let go in order to use what was inside of me, I was surprised at how easy it was to tap into the power. Of course, it was simple doing it here in this peaceful library with a teacher who knew what he was doing. If he hadn't been blocked, I could have seen into his heart. But outside, in the real world, where emotions ruled me and my daughter was at risk . . .

"You'll have plenty of raw power to draw upon. For you, the challenge will be identifying which one to use. You have Adonai power, and with it the common power all Elysians are naturally born with. Same for the Charbydon side of you. You also have your human strengths and the gifts that have been passed down through the blood of your family."

"Okay, so how do I know which ones to use?" I was well enough versed in Elysian and Charbydon to know what kind of powers were probably passed along to me, but I wasn't sure how to pick and choose them at will.

"It's simple, really. They don't blend well, obviously,

or else Mynogan would have been successful at this a long time ago. They clash, correct?" I nodded and he continued. "Makes them easy to identify. The darkness and the light. Elysia and Charbydon. Neither one is essentially good or bad—they are just types of energy, power—it's how they are manipulated that turns them into good and evil. Does that make sense?"

"Yeah, it's like wealth. The actual money isn't good or evil—it doesn't care either way—it's what you *do* with it."

"Exactly," he said, impressed. "So, just like you decide which weapon to use, you decide which power will deliver the most . . . *bang* for your effort. The powers will never blend, Charlie. They'll always be at odds."

"Great, so, I'm cursed."

"In a manner, yes. Honestly, you're lucky you're not dead yet."

I was about to throw out some general retort when I paused. "What do you mean, yet?"

It didn't take a genius to see he hadn't meant to spill that little kernel of information. "It means that you can't live forever with opposing powers. One day, it will kill you."

Just like the others before me.

But one day wasn't now, and that was all I needed to know. After Emma was safe, I'd figure it out. "So, how do I fight?"

"With your mind. Someone like Mynogan manipulates. He will use whatever fears you have to win. He took Emma from you, took Hank's power away. He fights dirty. Whatever you send at him, he sends back double."

I remembered back in the lab when I sent out a bolt of power; Mynogan had absorbed it and then sent it flying back to me. "He takes the energy I send, adds his own, and sends it back."

"And you can do that, too. You have all his power; his entire genetic code is now in you, Charlie. Abaddons are masters at coercion, mind control, and calling on dark forces to work for them. They can steal your breath with an invisible hand. But, so can you. The trick is to be calm in the heat of battle, to control the power and be the master. You don't need to learn chants or spells—for specific things, yes, but not for fighting. Fighting comes from within, and you own that."

His words stirred my confidence. Mynogan thought he could control me. But he was forgetting one important thing. I was as powerful as he was. He was just banking on the fact that I didn't know how to use it. "What about the Adonai priestess? Her DNA is in me, too."

"This is where it gets good," he said. "Besides all the auras, heightened intuition, and being able to heal and manipulate matter and energy, Adonai can control the elements. They could sink an island, bring fire to the land by lightning, destroy or create. Theoretically, you should be able to strangle Mynogan from ten yards, manifest his greatest fear, and zap his ass with a lightning bolt."

Despite the dire situation, a laugh escaped me. A

disbelieving laugh. I stood, stretching my legs and arms. He made it sound so easy, and maybe one day it would be. Unless it killed me first.

"It's all theory, of course. You're an anomaly, a lone wolf, Charlie. It has taken thousands of years in the evolution of your family and what Mynogan has done to make you what you are now. I can't say for certain what powers you hold or what you will become. I'm guessing here." Aaron rolled up the scroll. A shiver of revulsion went through me to see him touch what was once a person's or being's skin. After he secured it in the case, whispering his enchantment over the lock, we exited the library.

"So what does *ash* have to do with all this?"

"What do you mean?"

"It's all connected somehow. *Ash* is made from a Charbydon flower called a Bleeding Soul."

"*Sangurne N'ashu*. It's a—"

"A myth, I know. But it is real and the extract is being used to make the drug."

He paused at the bottom of the staircase, and I realized I'd actually stumped him. "They're two separate myths, calling the darkness and the myth of the Bleeding Souls." He shoved his hands in his pocket and let out a quizzical huff. "I don't know."

"Yeah, that makes two of us."

We went silently up the stairs, back to the room we had appeared in earlier.

"So how much, exactly, do you like my sister?" I asked as we stepped inside the pentagram.

A curtain fell over his features. His green eyes became hooded and unreadable, and his mouth stretched into a grim line. Sore subject obviously, but what I'd seen earlier in his aura didn't lie. "Enough," he finally said in a flat, even voice, giving nothing away.

I frowned. "Does that mean *enough* you don't want to talk about it, or *enough* as in you like her *enough*, as in you *like* her, like her?"

Apparently, I wasn't getting anything out of him because he chose that moment to grab my hand. "Wait!" I needed a second to prepare, just to take a deep breath. Then a thought occurred to me. "Can I do this, too?"

"You want to try?"

"Hell, no," I blurted. He broke into a wide grin, something that would have devastated a weaker woman, and I laughed. "I'd end up in the middle of the Atlantic or the top of Mount Everest. I'll leave the traveling up to you."

"For now," he said, closing his eyes, and then *whoosh*.

We were dispersed into thin air, reappearing on the landing at Bryn's flat.

15

I despised the way blinking in and out of reality made me feel, as though my body weighed significantly more than it did. It was like that moment when a downward elevator stops and your body feels like it keeps going for a second or two. Yeah. This was a hundred times worse than that. But, on the brighter side, the sensation went away after ten seconds or so.

Aaron adjusted his silk shirt, swiped his long fingers through his ebony hair, and then rang the doorbell.

The door opened and there was Will, standing there looking down at me. Same handsome face, same stormy blue eyes, same sun-kissed brown hair . . . Except, I realized, as my eyes soaked him in, that Will's crooked smile always came out of affection and happiness, not the crooked smile of the eternally sarcastic.

Rex.

Disappointment blew through me like a desert wind.

"Lesson one," Aaron softly reminded me from behind.

Control your emotions. I squared my shoulders and walked by Rex, my heart firmly back in check.

Bryn sat at the kitchen table, one foot tucked under her rear, leaning over a map and biting her lip in concentration. Her hair was pulled back into a messy twist, and the long bangs were tucked behind her ear. She glanced over and gave me a hopeful smile that laid me wide open. Her aura sprang forth, so beautiful it stole my breath. Lush, vibrant green shot with ribbons of Caribbean blue.

Then I noticed the gray; a thin blanket, stifling all that was good. She loved Emma so much. She loved me. Her worry was suffocating her spirit, yet she was feeding it, allowing it to grow into anger and vengeance.

Aaron tensed beside me, and one look told me he saw the same thing. But he didn't approach her, and I knew whatever was going on or had gone on with them stretched like a canyon between them.

"We keep coming back to the same place." She tapped her pen on the map. I went closer to see she had circled it many times. Her scrying crystal lay on a green velvet pouch next to the map.

Rex grabbed a can of ginger ale from the fridge and then slid into the chair opposite Bryn as though he owned the place. "Like I said for the millionth time, it's the right place. With my power and yours, and that pink chicken, there's no way we could be wrong."

My breath caught, his words like a sucker punch to the belly.

I spun around to find Emma's pink chicken sitting on the counter. *Chickie.* I'd always loved the fluffy stuffed chick with its pastel plaid ribbon and wide, innocent eyes. It chirped when you squeezed it. I swiped it off the counter, hugging it hard against my chest. It chirped. And I ran into the spare bedroom.

It smells like her.

I fell onto the bed, my face squished into her pillow, releasing her Cherry Blast shampoo and baby powder scent. She felt so close, and yet a million miles away. Tears wet the pillow, and I didn't care anymore. I let them come. My nose grew stuffy and my head hot from the pressure. I pulled her pillow closer and curled into a ball, hugging Chickie and tuning out the rest of the world, feeling my heart breaking and not knowing how to stop it.

I woke with a hot, puffy face and dry eyes, which cracked open to see Bryn standing by the bed. I sat up in a panic, the fog of sleep cluttering my mind and speech. "What? Why did you let me fall asleep?"

How could I have fallen asleep at a time like this! I flung my legs over the side of the mattress, cursing my own stupidity. My daughter was out there, needing me, and here I was sleeping like a baby. I was sick, a horrible, horrible mother.

"Charlie." Bryn stepped in front of me, preventing me from standing. "It's okay. You'll do her more good by clearing your head and having had a chance to rest. You were only sleeping for an hour."

An hour. I rubbed my eyes. It felt like days.

My shoulders slumped, and I knew she was right. There wasn't anything I could do until Hank and Zara came through, hopefully with a location that fit within Bryn and Rex's scrying area.

Bryn must've sensed the direction of my thoughts. "Hank and Zara are on their way back now." Then she moved aside and motioned over her shoulder. "This one showed up about twenty minutes ago."

Filling the open doorway, Carreg gazed down at me, his dark features unmoving and blank. The soft light of the bedside lamp caught a glint in his unfathomable eyes.

A thought raced across my mind, shoving aside any lingering traces of sleep. If I wanted, I could see his aura. And I wanted. My strong, inquisitive nature needed to crack the mystery of this quiet Charbydon noble. So I remembered the same cleansing openness I had discovered in the League's library and used it to see Carreg's true self. Auras couldn't lie.

Mesmerizing midnight blue shot with silver threads. Just like the color of his eyes. It was like staring up at a clear, starry sky on a cold winter's night. It took my breath away.

"Charlie." My name came through his lips like the purr of a giant cat. His intensity, an air of strength and power and magnetism, reminded me of those beautiful predators of our world; the wolves and big cats, those that could transfix another by the beauty of their stare and the stillness of their being.

"Carreg," I greeted him neutrally as Bryn gave me a quick nod before leaving us alone. "A little risky to be here. Aren't you afraid Mynogan will find out?"

That made him stiffen a fraction. "Mynogan does not inspire fear in me." He moved to the window and pushed the curtain aside with the back of his hand, glancing out calmly. His suit jacket was gone, and he wore a clean white dress shirt, untucked, with the sleeves rolled to his elbows. The white made his olive skin glow and his hair look like black satin. He turned back to me, tucking both hands into the front pockets of his black slacks, and leaned against the dresser. Such a casual, easy gesture, one that seemed at odds with the powerful being in front of me. "He is, however, a cause for concern."

I braced both hands on either side of my thighs and gripped the edge of the mattress tightly, remembering the images that filled my head when he'd grabbed my hand at the lab. He'd saved Hank, like he said, but was it a ruse? Something to gain my trust, perhaps? "Do you know where my daughter is?"

"No. I didn't realize he'd taken her until I arrived here. Your sister told me." A rueful smile tugged on his mouth. "She also had me sit down and write out every address known to Mynogan and the CPP."

"That proves nothing." I stood, preferring to be on even ground with him as I attempted to gather my power and search beneath the beauty of his aura. What I found was a massive roadblock. "What are you hiding?"

A raven black eyebrow lifted. "I am a private person. I have much to hide." He pushed away from the dresser and took two steps closer. "How are you feeling, Charlie? Any sudden urges for blood?"

What? God, I'd never understand off-worlders. "Only Mynogan's and those who aid him."

A silky chuckle escaped him. "I'm going to let you in on a little-known fact, Detective Madigan. After all, you're now one of us. The noble Houses are cursed. Abaddon must take blood to survive. It stands to reason; the curse also extends to you."

"Blood," I repeated bluntly. "Are you trying to tell me Abaddons are vampires?"

"Not in your sense of the word, no. They abhor Elysian blood, and while humans are a step up, most nobles wouldn't stoop so low unless starved to the brink of death. No, they take it mostly from Charbydons."

Was this what Mynogan had referred to in the limo? The powers he spoke of. The threat to take my blood there and then if he wanted.

I cocked my head, refusing to be daunted by Carreg's words. It might be true, but I had no desire whatsoever for anyone's blood, so he could shove his words up his ass for all I cared. "And you? You said *our* Houses, so what is your House cursed with?"

"Life," he joked softly, dipping his head closer so that the warmth of his breath brushed my ear and neck. Shivers danced along my spine as subtle notes of sage and cedar enveloped me. I couldn't move. "That spark inside every spirit, that light that feeds and energizes, makes a being *want* to live. A fulfilled spirit, an excited spirit"—he drew in my scent and then lifted his head to pierce me with a challenging gaze—"has enough life force in it to share with those of us unfortunate enough not to have any at all. And, unlike Abaddon, we have no problem with humans."

Breathe, Charlie.

Whatever the hell he was doing to me, he needed to stop. Now.

Refusing to step back, I ducked around him, dragging in a deep breath of air and composing myself before facing him again. Damned if I'd be drawn into his innuendo and talk of blood and excited spirits. I'd kill myself before taking another's blood to feed some curse.

"Mynogan has defied the agreement made between my House and his," Carreg said easily, as though he hadn't just come on to me. "For the first time in ages, we stopped bickering and made a pact to work together to save Charbydon. What he has planned now will leave our world to ruin and cause greater destruction here in yours."

"And why do you care?"

"Because I know our moon can be saved. Charbydon is my home. It has been home to my family for untold millennia. To give up our history, to let the blackness consume all of it without trying is the highest grievance there is." He took another step closer, staring down at me with hard, penetrating eyes. "Would you let your world go? Walk away from it without trying? Would you take another that is not yours to take?"

"Of course not." Perhaps we weren't so different after all.

"You are right to be wary of me, Detective." His voice dropped an octave to an intimate tone usually reserved for conspirators or lovers. My mouth went bone dry. Swallowing the lump in my throat, I forced myself to keep his gaze and not back down. "But in this, your war against Mynogan, I am on your side. I take great risk in aiding you. He must believe I'm with him in his endeavor. Make no mistake. I'm not doing it for you. I help you to help myself, nothing more."

I cocked my head. "We'll see." He wanted me to trust him, yet he was warning me not to misinterpret his motives. Fine, then I'd warn him right back. "Turn against me and it'll be the last thing you do in this world or the next." I gave him a pointed stare and then walked away, just catching the hint of approval in his expression before I opened the door and stepped into the cool air of the living room.

Being close to Carreg was like standing in front of my Uncle Walter's pizza oven during Friday night rush. I headed for the fridge for cold water.

A few seconds later, Carreg entered the living room.

"How long until Hank and Zara get back?" I asked Bryn, sliding onto an empty counter stool as she set down a mug of coffee for Aaron at the kitchen table. She offered me one, but I shook my head, lifting the water.

"Not long. Twenty minutes maybe."

I downed several refreshing gulps of my water, noticing Rex and Aaron eyeballing me from the kitchen table. Something was up. "What?"

Carreg stood at the end of the counter. It was as though they were all waiting for something.

Bryn drew in a breath. "We were talking while you were asleep. And, we thought it might be good for you and Emma if we tried."

Instantly, I tensed. My grip on the water bottle tightened until the plastic dented with a loud crack. "Tried what?"

"Come sit down at the table," she said, coming around to grab the empty counter chair. I followed, pulling my chair along so we'd all have a place to sit. I shoved it under the table, holding on to the back of it as Bryn took her place beside me, leaving the empty chair she'd brought over for Carreg on my other side.

"We're gonna call your kid," Rex said, wiggling his eyebrows at me.

"It's a bridge, from us to your daughter," Aaron explained as Carreg sat down beside me. "It won't help us locate her, unless, of course, she can tell us herself, but with all our powers pooled and concentrating on her, we should be able to connect mind to mind. That might be a ward Mynogan hadn't considered placing on her. And we all agree you need it."

"Sit down," Bryn said with all the kindness and gentleness of a mother deer nudging her fawn out into the snow for the first time. "We'll join hands and combine our power." I sat down. Bryn squeezed my hand and smiled. "Carreg says that with enough people it could work."

Not hiding my surprise, I turned and met Carreg's stony gaze. "You?" He inclined his head lightly and then leaned back in the chair, completely enigmatic.

"All right, kids," Rex said impatiently. "Let's get this party started."

The reality of what we were about to try hit me, and a wave of apprehension swept away my confidence and hope. Emma. What would I say to her? If she heard me, it could make her upset, or worse, totally freak her out. She'd want to be out of there so badly and hearing me might make it even more difficult for her. Was it selfish of me to contact her just for my own peace of mind? Would it do more harm than good?

Carreg slid his hand on the table in front of me and turned it palm up.

His calm voice swept into my mind. *A child always needs its mother no matter what, Charlie. Or are you just afraid to touch me now that you know what I am? Afraid I might take a nibble of your life force?*

Honestly, I didn't know what to make of the

Astarot noble. His motives were his own; he'd made that clear, so why did he comfort me? Why even suggest what we were about to do? I stared at his hand, deciding not to look a gift horse in the mouth, and then slid mine into his. It was just a hand. No biggie.

Warmth enveloped me. He gave a subtle squeeze. I refused to look at him and instead drew in an audible breath and said, "Okay, I'm ready."

Under Carreg's direction, we focused our minds and then linked our power through our hands. Energy sizzled into my fingertips and zinged all the way to my toes and the top of my head.

"Envision yourself a circuit, a conduit," he instructed. "Don't hold it in. Just let it flow through you to me. We are all of one mind and one purpose . . ."

The hum of everyone's personal power slowly built and presented itself as music, blending and strengthening, merging together in a symphony of notes and undertones.

Soon, I could pick out each individual by their power. Bryn's was like springtime; open, adventurous, prideful, and determined. It played like a melody that revealed each emotion. Aaron's was deep and steadfast, quick and tumultuous, but tempered by iron will and intelligence. Rex's was as I'd expect; wild and free, a no-holds-barred joy of living and fun, now that he had a body to live in. For a moment, I could actually sympathize and see why he dealt in life and death. To be simply an entity, one who couldn't feel, touch, or taste, was a hell I'd never want to know. And then there was Carreg, a potent, dark song full of turbulence and heat and passion, of steely control and a force of will that pounded relentlessly throughout.

My own power came back into me, completing the circle. It was an unharmonious clash of two warring powers, a sharp, thunderous song that spoke of uncontained strength and chaos. But amid the frenzy there was a faint soulful melody of my human powers, the grief I held on to, the mistrust and fear, the anger and injustice, all blended with the love and loyalty I had for my family, and a singular note so beautiful that it could only be my bond with Emma.

A twinge of embarrassment went through me. The others were so in control of their powers, each one balanced in their own way. A part of me wanted to apologize for the clang and screeching of my own hectic tune. Bryn squeezed my hand, the same moment Carreg did. Acceptance swept into the circle, flowing through me and making my chest burn.

"Focus now on Emma." Carreg's voice sounded deep and harmonious over the circuit of power. "Her name, her face, her scent . . . Imagine sending the circuit out into the world to connect with her, imagine the circle is not complete without her."

A tear slid down my cheek. Bryn sniffed beside me.

More than anything in the world, I wanted to find my child, to connect with her in this moment, so I poured all of myself into the effort, opening my mind to her infectious laughter, the way she breathed when she slept, and the way her hugs imbued peace and joy inside of me.

It felt like hours had passed.

The circuit suddenly shimmered. Bryn gasped.

Emma. I knew her immediately. Her spirit flowed into me like a clear lake in a pristine alpine forest. Refreshing. Innocent. Wonderful. My chest swelled.

Doodlebug. I said her toddler nickname on instinct in my mind. From the time she'd been able to hold things, there was always a crayon, marker, or some other writing instrument in her hand.

Momma?

Relief surged out of me on a choked cry.

Emma. It's me, Mommy's here.

Am I dreaming?

I laughed. Tears streamed down my face. *No, baby, I'm here. Don't ask me how, but I'm here. Are you all right?*

Yeah. I don't like them. And the smell is making me sick. Would you come and get me already?

Soon. What kind of smell? Can you describe where you are?

Um . . . just a room with a cot. I sensed she was walking around. *It feels underground. No windows. It's stuffy and hot, and there's a sound like air conditioning always going. And the smell is, like, gaggingly sweet.*

That's good. You're doing good. The next question I didn't want to ask, but I had to. *Did they hurt you?*

No. Pride came into her voice. *I kind of freaked out*

on them a little. They won't even come in now. They open the door and slide my food in. She paused for a second and the weight of her worry and fear swept through the circuit. *Is Daddy okay?*

My heart stopped. She'd witnessed the fight between Will and the jinn. He was dying when she'd last seen him. My concentration wavered.

I'm right here, Emma. Will's voice came strong and sure. *Everything's going to be okay.*

My eyes flew open, and I was met with Rex's glassy, sad stare. He shrugged as though he didn't feel a thing, but I could tell he did. I dipped my head in a gesture that seemed far too lame for the circumstances. Her relief swept through me so quickly that I knew she'd been holding in tears and a mountain of stress and worry. She sighed audibly. *All they're feeding me is stupid soup. I hate soup.*

I know you do. All I wanted was to hold her, to stroke her hair and give her comfort. *But you need to eat it, all of it, you hear? It'll help you stay strong.*

The circuit faded and then came back. Keeping this up was taking its toll on everyone at the table, even the strongest of us.

Emma?

Yeah?

I am coming for you, okay? I will get you out of there.

I know.

She said it so matter-of-factly. She believed one hundred and ten percent in me. She wasn't scared, she was just waiting. Waiting for me to come. I didn't want this to end, but thankfully I didn't have to say the hard goodbye that was looming.

Just hurry, Momma. I have to go, it's soup time again. Joy.

I chuckled. *I love you, Emma. You hear me? I love you. I will see you very soon.*

'K. Bye.

And the link to her was broken. The circuit seemed bereft and dull, the songs not as intriguing as before. Just a blank empty hole. Nothing.

Bryn pulled at my hand. "Charlie, you can let go now."

My stiff fingers uncurled painfully. When I glanced around the table, it was to watery eyes and grim faces. I knew, truly knew, then that I was not alone. If I failed. If Bryn failed. They would continue on to save my daughter. Even Rex; as much as he seemed to deny any responsibility or care in the world.

For a long moment no one spoke. Rex got up and walked into the living room, plopping down into the love seat with a loud exhale. Bryn wiped at the corners of her eyes. Aaron and Carreg exchanged determined looks, the anger coming off them making the air thick. I scrubbed my hands down my wet cheeks and chin and then went to use the guest bathroom, where I splashed cold water on my face.

I looked like shit. Eyes red, face puffy, cheeks mottled. I splashed again until the heat left my skin, then I redid my hair, twisting it into a knot with Bryn's rubber band. The woman looking back at me appeared lost and confused. Everything I shouldn't be.

I drew in a long breath and let it out slowly, letting out the fear and uncertainty along with it. My shoulders straightened. A few copper sparks glinted in my irises. What was it Carreg had said about me? I was one of the most powerful humans in the world. Well, I'd have to be in order to save my child. I cocked an eyebrow at my pale reflection, seeing parts of the old Charlie emerge. The tough detective who didn't take an ounce of crap from anyone, and a royally pissed off, all-powerful mother who was about to kick some serious Abaddon ass.

On my way out of the bathroom, I came face-to-face with Carreg. "Thank you," I forced out, "for . . ." I didn't know how to say it, so I nodded toward the kitchen table and what had just transpired there.

He regarded me for a long second. "It was a good way to see how far Mynogan went to guard her." Then he walked out of the apartment.

Bryn came up beside me and put her arm around my shoulders. "He's going back to CPP headquarters to try and contact Mynogan. You okay?"

I let my head fall against hers. "Actually, all things considered, I'm hanging in there. I'm getting Em back. There's no question." The words were enforced by a sweeping sense of positive belief.

Bryn stared hard at the door. "We won't stop until we do."

"She's definitely being held wherever the Bleeding Souls are grown. Underground. The humidity, the heat, the smell . . . It all fits."

"Prime growing conditions," Bryn said thoughtfully. "I still can't believe it exists. You know why it's called a Bleeding Soul? It's part of the Charbydon creation myth. It was used in the Great War when the nobles first appeared in Charbydon and fought with the jinn for control. The nobles used it as a weapon, the biological warfare of their time. It forced the soul to separate from the body. Myth says that's where the Revenants and Wraiths came from, that they're really the souls of jinn warriors who have wandered so long that they've forgotten who and what they once were."

I glanced over at Rex.

"Yeah, I know." Bryn said, an octave lower. "Makes you wonder, if the flower exists, what else is true."

16

Hank and Zara arrived a few minutes later to give us the list of real estate holdings they'd stolen from Veritas's files. Once again, we gathered around the kitchen table. Mynogan had holdings in everything from downtown condos and office buildings to single-family rental homes and country clubs. We concentrated our efforts in the area Bryn and Rex had zoned in on during the scrying, and found a matching address. Mynogan owned a small, but very exclusive, bath house and spa sandwiched between Morningside and Ansley Park, two large neighborhoods north-northeast of downtown. It bordered part of Oglethorpe Park. Pricey area.

"The guy's gotta be loaded," Rex muttered, scanning the list.

Over the map, I studied Hank. He'd yet to look

at me. His face had healed somewhat, but there were still a lot of bruises and cuts. He must've fought like a maniac. And he would have died if Carreg hadn't kept his word. Despite the fact that I didn't regret going after my family and leaving him there, the guilt lay heavy in my gut. He must have felt my gaze, because he pushed away from the table and left.

Great.

He came back with a black ITF duffel bag, plopping it onto the table and unzipping. "I got everything I could fit in the bag. Hefties, Nitro-guns, human firearms. A few tear gas grenades and additional ammo."

"And they just let you walk out of the weapons depot?" I asked.

"No," he answered, his voice tight. "Zara helped."

Oh, way to go, Charlie. Why don't you just make him admit to everyone that he needed help from a girl? I couldn't win.

Zara fiddled with her voice modifier. Anyone who had potentially come into their path, she'd taken care of with her voice. "No one will even remember we were there," she said.

"Impressive." She'd broken the law to help my kid, and she deserved way more than what I'd given her, but my heart was still smarting over Hank. And as much as I wanted to like Zara, I wanted my friend back more. I hated that he'd turned to her instead of me.

"So, what now?" Bryn asked, her expression eager to begin, to win back one of our own.

I hesitated. Proud as I was, I couldn't lose another sibling. She was all I had left. But I was also turning over a new leaf. Bryn was capable and talented. She loved Emma and had every right to fight for her, too.

"First we need to scope the location, identify how many are guarding the place. Priority number one is finding Em and getting her to safety. Then, we destroy the Bleeding Souls." I should be having this conversation with a team of ITF agents and full agency support, not friends, strangers, and family.

"Take out those damn flowers and we cut off the *ash* supply," Hank said.

"Sounds like a plan to me," Bryn said. "So who's going to scout the location?"

Aaron draped an arm over the back of the chair, meeting my gaze. "I believe I can help with that."

I nodded in agreement. He was the only one among us who could blink in and out. They'd never even know he was there. He started for the door. "Be back in a few." His form disappeared into a cloud of mist as he literally disintegrated into the closed door.

"Neat trick," Hank said.

Rex pushed away from the table. "Who wants to order pizza?" At our look, he said, "What? We gotta eat, don't we?"

"He's right. DeLarano's stays open 'til one, I'll order something." Bryn went to the phone.

Keeping her head low, Zara glanced from me to

Hank, an apprehensive frown marring her perfect face. "I'll just go and wash up."

Her departure was obvious. She was leaving us alone to talk. Once it was just Hank and me, I regarded him for a long moment as he zipped the weapons bag. I had no idea what to say or how to say it, so I just went with my gut. "How are you doing?"

The muscle in his jaw jumped. "Been better. You?"

"Could say the same." Well, at least he'd asked. That was a small step in the right direction. "Look, Hank, I'm sorry you got hurt," I began as sincerely as I felt. "But I'm not sorry for leaving. I didn't really have a choice, and I'd do the same damn thing again if my daughter was threatened."

Still, he didn't look at me. A lock of blond hair fell into his eye. He shoved it aside with a quick drag of his fingers. With only his profile to go on, I had little in the way of judging his emotions.

"Don't worry about it." He lifted the bag off the table.

Feeling as though I was losing him, I grabbed his arm. Hard, sapphire-blue orbs gazed down at me. His look was so guarded, angry, and betrayed. "Hank." Why couldn't he understand? "Why are you doing this? You would've done the same exact thing, and I would've been pissed if you hadn't."

He pulled his arm away. "No kidding. Just let me be for a little while, Charlie." With that he walked away.

I sighed and braced my palm on the kitchen table,

the other hand on my hip, debating whether to confront him now rather than let this divide grow any bigger.

Zara exited the bathroom as Hank sat down, his back to me. She came over, looking like she should be in a *Sports Illustrated* swimsuit issue rather than here in Underground helping a group of misfits go up against a Charbydon Elder. "He's having a hard time."

"Really." She didn't deserve the sarcasm, but Hank and I had been together for so long. It was always us against the world, two people who had grown to love and respect one another, willing to give our lives to protect the other. I didn't understand. And I didn't like being left out.

"Sirens are different," she started, ignoring my rudeness. "He's angry, but it's more to do with losing his powers than anything. He knows you did the only thing you could at the time. I would have gone after my daughter, too, if someone had threatened her."

Her words deflated my ire somewhat. "It's just . . . he's Hank. My partner." I shook my head, unable to explain further.

"And he just lost everything that makes him who he is. It's like you losing your ability to walk or hear. Now, to him, he is weak and of no good to anyone. At least that's how he's feeling. Just give him a chance to work through it. He'll come around."

Maybe she was right. I studied her for a long second. "I never really thanked you for helping out."

She shrugged, tucking her sunset locks behind her ear with a small smile. "It's nothing."

"Breaking into Veritas wasn't nothing. You could lose your job and be forced to return home with a criminal record."

"*If* they find out. They won't." A spark lit her crystal-blue eyes. Sirens, especially the females, had always seemed the same to me. Haughty, full of themselves because of their beauty, and demeaning to anyone else they viewed as below them in status, birth, or looks. Maybe I'd been wrong about them, too. Like so many other things. Zara was indeed beautiful, there was no denying that, but she was giving, adventurous, and willing to sacrifice her time and safety for a cause that had nothing to do with her.

"No wonder Hank likes you," I finally said.

She blushed. "It took him long enough. I was starting to think I'd have to wear a sign on my forehead before he'd get that I was interested."

I laughed. "Yeah, that's Hank for you." Laughing felt good. But the feeling was all too brief. "You don't have to do this, you know. It's gonna be one hell of a fight."

"I know." A wide smile split her face. "Haven't had one of those in decades. Besides, I like my home and this city. The last thing I want is for Mynogan to mess it up."

I nodded and then sat down at the table as Zara went to join Hank on the couch.

Pizza arrived just after midnight. Anxiety curbed my appetite, but I ate a piece anyway, knowing it was better to keep up my strength. Rex acted like he was having an orgasm every time he took a bite. I wanted to tell him to give it a rest, but the guy obviously hadn't enjoyed real food in a while. Watching him eat made my thoughts turn to Will.

Slowly, I chewed a bite of pepperoni and cheese, completely stunned that Will had turned to such a desperate outlet. He had seemed to be doing so well. But maybe I just hadn't seen how serious his despair had become, his hopelessness at being able to make things right with me. He had destroyed our marriage, something he never really wanted to do, but had done anyway. And no amount of therapy, addiction counseling, twelve-step programs, or love could erase the past. Something I was sure he must have realized, and probably the thing that made him turn to a proverbial genie in a bottle.

I tore off a piece of crust, feeling downright pissed off. If he had just stuck with it . . . been patient. Who knew what might have happened.

A knock interrupted my thoughts. Bryn answered the door. Aaron had returned. I wiped my hands on a napkin and stood as he slid into the chair and rested his elbows on the table.

"Well?" Bryn was the first to prompt him.

I grabbed him a water from the fridge.

"Thanks," he said, throwing a look at Bryn. Hank and Zara leaned over the back of the couch, waiting as Aaron drank deeply. Finally, he said, "Sign says closed for renovations. No patrons to worry about, so that's good. Bad news is it's heavily warded."

"How heavily?"

"More than a Magnus can break. There are only two others like me in the city, and even if we pooled our power, it'd take at least two days to break it. This ward was made by an Elder. Most likely Mynogan. Everyone who comes and goes from the building must possess a complex key, an amulet, which allows them passage. No amulet, no passage. But, if we can get in, the odds move in our favor. I only detected two Abaddon nobles, six jinn warriors, a black mage, and a hellhound."

"I thought hellhounds were illegal," Zara said.

"They are. But every once in a while one gets smuggled in," I told her, returning my attention to Aaron. "How would you break the ward, if you had to?" He'd gotten the ancient skin scroll from the House of Abaddon. Surely he knew of a way to break into Mynogan's bath house.

A smile split his face. He knew exactly what I was thinking. "Actually, I have a plan. Simple, really. All we have to do is lure the guards through the ward and take their keys."

Disbelieving expressions passed across everyone's face except Aaron's.

"Am I the only one who thinks that sounds way too easy?" Hank asked.

"There is one other thing. We must have their

blood on our hands. Each amulet is made with a drop of the person's blood. You can't borrow someone else's key and expect to walk through the ward. But, if you have enough of their blood on you when you make the attempt, it usually works."

"Okay," Rex said, "I'm not bathing in anyone's blood. There are health risks, you know . . ."

"You won't have to bathe in it," Aaron told him. "Just enough to cover your hands should do the trick."

Suspicion narrowed Bryn's eyes. "How the hell do you know this stuff?"

Aaron shrugged. "It's in my interest to know details such as these. I'd be an unworthy Magnus otherwise."

"How do we lure them through the ward?" I asked.

"They'll know if someone is trying to break it," Hank said.

"Right. So Bryn and I attempt to break it, the guards will come out. Even if enough of them don't come through the ward, one of us goes through, throws the amulet back out to the next person, they cover their hands, and so on . . ."

"That'll also draw them out of the building and away from Emma. Once we're all inside, we get rid of anyone else, find Em, and destroy the crop." All eyes were on me, and I made sure to look at each person in the room. They all nodded. "We'll hit them in an hour."

★   ★   ★

We left Bryn's apartment in two groups. Aaron transported me and Bryn to the parking deck in case Mynogan still had the black mages watching the apartment, and the others would meet us at the car.

When my weight returned to normal, I helped Bryn adjust the spare shoulder holster I'd hooked around her back earlier. I made sure to equip her with a fully charged Nitro-gun and a Hefty. Gone were the floaty skirts and the charm anklets, and in their place was a grim, near mirror image of me. In fact, she looked downright kick-ass. I couldn't help but smile.

"What?"

"Nothing," I replied as pride blossomed through me. "It's just . . . this is a new side of you."

"Yeah, well, you're not the only Madigan who can do damage." She fixed me with a stern expression and even sterner voice. "I know you think I'm weak and flighty, Charlie, but I've got strengths you don't even know about."

I blinked. "I never said—"

"You don't need to say it. I see it in your eyes all the time. Every time you come into my shop."

"No, I've never thought you weak, Bryn. Ever." How could she think that? "Sure, maybe a tad 'out there,' but weak?" Before she could sidestep me, I grabbed both of her shoulders and pulled her away from Aaron and the car. "Listen to me," I said, angry that she'd even accuse me of what she had. "You're not weak. You never have been. You know how much courage it takes to be your own person, to embrace your gifts and move forward? If anyone's weak, it's me. I've been too afraid to even explore what's inside me. And the only reason I'm doing it now is because I have to." I released her shoulders, shaking my head and wondering how I'd given her this impression. God. I'd screwed up with so many people in my life.

Bryn stared at me openmouthed for a split second and then composed herself. The striking woman in front of me suddenly became the small kid who used to follow me and Connor around, begging to join in and threatening us if we didn't let her.

I shrugged. "I love you, Bryn. You're my baby sister." What else could I say?

Before I could react, she threw her arms around my neck, sending me back several feet before I regained my balance. "I love you, too, Charlie." She leaned back and her smile blinded me. "Now, let's go kick some alien butt."

I laughed. That was the first time she'd ever called them aliens, an echo of the many times I'd used that term despite the fact she didn't like it.

"Aliens, huh?" Hank said, walking up behind us with Zara and Rex. A faint smile lingered at one corner of his mouth. "I thought you were more PC than that, Bryn."

"Well, by definition, you fit," she muttered uncomfortably, red creeping into her cheeks. "Beings from another world, and all . . ."

"I think Charlie's starting to rub off on you."

"Eh, not such a bad thing in my book," she said with a wink thrown my way, "See you guys there." She went to stand next to Aaron. He grabbed her hand and they blinked out of sight.

Rex and Zara piled into the backseat of the car as Hank put the duffel bag into the trunk.

I went to stand next to him, needing this moment alone. "You know once we do this, there's no turning back." I was pretty sure my fiasco with the jinn in Underground had already sealed my fate as an ex-ITF agent, but Hank . . . If he joined me on this, he'd lose his job and be brought up on charges right along with me, and the list was going to be a mile long by the time we were through.

"I know," he said. "I'm not about to leave you now." He shut the trunk and the fixed me with a determined look. "Ready, kiddo?"

A relieved breath flowed from my lips and my shoulders relaxed. I would have done this on my own, but having Hank and the others with me gave me a much-needed boost of strength and confidence.

We rode in silence to Oglethorpe Park. No one had to speak. We all knew what was at stake.

We parked in the public lot on the opposite side of the bath complex and then blended into the darkness of the woods, at first following the park's paved walking trail until it wrapped around to the back side of the complex.

The air had a slight chill, the temperature and the cleansing scent of leaves and bark adding a boost of energy to our steps. A near-full moon shed light into the blackness of the woods. And through the trees, the long, rectangular bath complex came into view amid the soft orangey glow of widely spaced street-lamps. We walked single file in complete silence, viewing the back of the building. All the windows were dark, the blinds drawn down.

Finally we came to the center of the building where a large patio spread out into the lawn complete with vine-covered pergola, columns with gauzy curtains, outdoor furniture, and large fire basins. The curtains swayed ever so slightly and seemed to catch the moonlight. Clouds of steam rose from vents evenly spaced along the base of the building.

Bryn and Aaron were already in place at the edge of a small patch of trees that backed up to the walking path. We stopped, and I motioned for Aaron and Bryn to begin.

They walked to the edge of the tree line, linked hands, and closed their eyes. Slowly the air around them coalesced into a soft green mist. The hairs on my arms and legs rose as energy hummed around them. While their hands were linked in the center, their free hands began moving as though part of one being, unraveling the ward.

A low growl split the silence. Hank, Zara, Rex, and

I immediately dropped to our haunches. Hank's hand shot out to keep us still as he moved forward, getting a better view between the tall pines. Seconds later, he moved back and whispered, "Hellhound."

I looked at Rex. "You're up."

"I should be on Broadway right now," he muttered. "Instead I'm here in the Blair Witch forest, about to get eaten by a hairless fucking dog on gigantic fucking steroids. Why can't Zara do it?"

"Because my voice only works on the animals of this world and Elysia, not Charbydon."

His eyes rolled as though he figured that was what she'd say, and then he let out a resigned sigh. "For the record, let it be noted that I hate you all."

I shoved him toward the trees. He swatted at me, but crawled slowly and halfheartedly into the darkness, hesitating for a moment to shoot a dark glower back at us before blending into the trees. I didn't like the fact that a Revenant was living in Will's body, but, in that moment, I formed a soft spot for Rex. He wasn't just doing this to fulfill a contractual obligation. I'd seen his face after we contacted Emma. He was doing this for her.

"Here, doggie, doggie . . ." a faint whisper came back to us.

Another growl sounded, followed by a soft whistle from Rex and then silence.

Chain links echoed fast over the stone patio. I was about to curse our luck that the hound was chained, but then there was a loud snap.

Rex darted through the trees at full speed, arms pumping. "I hate you guys!" He leapt over the azaleas by the path and disappeared into the woods on the other side just as the hellhound bounded across the pavement hot on his heels. We ducked, but the tiger-sized, hairless beast didn't even notice. Its red eyes and slobbering jaws were fixed solely on Rex.

Floodlights lit the patio.

We took up positions on either side of our mages, hiding in the darkness and waiting to pounce.

Through the trees, three jinn warriors in parkas and a black mage appeared, filing through the massive French doors and onto the stone patio. Even from this distance I could see their eyes glowing violet. They didn't need sunglasses at night, but they did need the coats. And hopefully the chill would slow them down. One of them leaned down and grabbed the broken chain.

"Brimstone is loose again."

"Fucking great. That means another body to dispose of."

As if on cue, a far-off high-pitched scream echoed through the night.

"I'll go check the disturbance on the ward," the black mage said. "If it's those damn amateur kids again thinking they can break the ward, I'm going to kill them."

As the mage stomped across the lawn, the jinn argued over who would go after the hellhound. I glanced over at Hank. We waited, knowing once they separated, taking them down would be easier.

Hank and Zara moved further down the path to intercept the jinn recruited to go after the hound. They could use his amulet to get through, while I stayed put to take down the mage.

He never knew what hit him.

His focus was solely on Aaron and Bryn as he stepped through the ward's boundary. Just before he called upon his power to knock them out of their trance, I zapped him with my Hefty.

That left two on the patio. After nudging Bryn to bring her and Aaron back to reality, I stood over the mage's body, reluctant to cut him open. But, all I had to do was think of Emma and I was down on my knees, pulling his sleeve up and slicing his arm with my boot knife. His blood oozed warm from his body, creating a puff of steam in the chilly air. I placed my hands in the trail, wetting them on both sides and scooping some up to rub between my fingers, around my wrists, and up my forearms. *Probably should have removed the amulet first*, I thought as I dripped blood all over his face trying to remove it from his neck.

When I stood, Bryn and Aaron approached. "Well, here goes nothing," I said, holding up the amulet in my slick red hand.

They dragged the mage closer to the perimeter of the ward as I hesitated at the edge of the lawn. I turned to them, squeezing the carved amulet in my hand. "As soon as I enter, I'll toss this back to you and then take out those two." I motioned toward the remaining two guards standing on the patio. "Make sure you get enough blood on your hands."

Bryn took a deep breath and nodded.

Maybe I should have smeared more blood on me, I thought, right before I drew in a deep breath and stepped onto the bright lawn. A painful tingle of energy passed over me, and then I was through. Quickly, I tossed the amulet back through the ward and pulled my Nitro-gun, only having a few seconds before the two guards noticed me.

I focused, straightened, then marched purposefully over the grass, the gun held behind my thigh.

The move startled the jinn into what I knew would only be a small window of surprise. But that was all I needed. As I walked toward them, I said, "Your hound is loose," and then I whipped my gun in front of me and shot twice, once to the left and once to the right. The gun went off silently, the setting on lethal. They dropped with the confused expressions still on their faces.

My pulse pounded, adrenaline rushing through my system and putting me back into my element, doing what I did best. All my years of training had prepared me for this.

Aaron and Bryn ran across the sod and joined me, their hands as bloody as mine.

"Jesus, Charlie," Bryn breathed, eyeing the dead jinn. "I can't believe you just walked right up to them like that."

We all took a moment to wipe the blood from our

hands. "Yeah, well," I echoed her words from earlier, "I have strengths you don't even know about, too."

"The jinn would call those *grômms*," Aaron said frankly.

True.

I moved toward the French doors and peered around the frame. "It's the main bath. There are three jinn inside, to your left."

I turned to Aaron. "Detect any sign of the two nobles?"

"Underground. That's all I'm getting."

Hank and Zara ran onto the patio and took cover against the wall. I motioned about the three inside. "Zara and I can handle the three," Hank said. "The rest of you go underground. Those two nobles should be close to Emma. Once you take them out, she's ours."

"Bryn, Aaron, once that happens, get her out of here. The rest of us will destroy the Bleeding Souls." I took a deep breath. "Everyone ready?"

We ducked inside, Hank and Zara going left and the rest of us heading right around the thick palms and heavy curtains. If we stayed low we should be able to make it down the length of the large pool and to the main entrance.

"What's the stupid hound done this time?" a jinn voice called from the other side of the pool, thinking the footsteps he was hearing were his brethren returning.

We were almost to the main entrance when chairs scraped over tile. Shots rang out, the guards equipped with human firearms. A piece of the stone wall erupted a few feet behind us and rained pieces down on the tile. I heard the whine of a Nitro-gun. And then a voice, splitting my eardrums, a singular tone, like the blare of a trumpet that shook anything that wasn't bolted down.

Once we made it into the lobby, we straightened and split up, me going down the left hall and Aaron and Bryn taking the right. Every room was empty and dark. I ran back as Bryn met me in the lobby, out of breath. "It's this way," she said.

We raced to a door marked *boiler room*. I took lead, easing down the steel stairwell, feeling as though each step brought me closer to hell; the heat was intense. One flight down, the stairs ended at another door.

Locked.

Aaron stepped forward, weaved his hands over the lock, and it released. Neat trick. Carefully, we entered a short hallway that opened up into a vast area of large boilers that supplied endless hot water to the baths above. Steam shot out of release valves, adding intense humidity to the air.

We weaved our way through the labyrinth of pipes, boilers, and controls.

I held up my hand as the area opened up into a control center. An Abaddon female sat behind the counter with her feet propped up, reading a magazine. Behind the control station was a pass-through with a downward ramp.

Aaron motioned toward the ramp. I would go on

ahead. He and Zara would take care of the female. I nodded and leaned back to let them pass. They had to completely engage her before I ran for the ramp. The last thing I wanted was for her to call for help.

Both mages dipped their chins. The air stirred around them. A fierce emerald glow lit Aaron's eyes. The gold flecks in Bryn's irises turned to fire. It was a beautiful, yet scary, sight to see the power gathering within them. I eased backward, taking another direction to the ramp.

The Abaddon shot to her feet, sensing our presence. I hesitated, worried about my sister. No. Bryn could take care of herself. I had to move.

As I positioned myself at the end of a massive pipe, I checked the all clear, just catching a glimpse of Aaron appearing behind the Abaddon as Bryn lifted her hands straight over her head and then brought them down with a circle motion. A shimmering green circle shot toward the Abaddon.

I darted across the empty space, through the pass-through, and then slammed my back against the earthen wall. A door slammed from somewhere below. I couldn't see what lay below me, so I stuck to the wall and inched my way down the ramp and soon found myself staring at a long chamber, two stories high, with beam-supported earthen walls and a floor of soil and large rocks. Condensation dripped from the ceiling of the cavern. Patches of Bleeding Souls grew from the spaces where the rocks met the soil. There was no artificial light here. None was needed.

A soft moonlit glow from the flowers lit the cavernous chamber, and the area was saturated with the scent of honeysuckle and dirt. I swallowed hard, trying not to gag.

Tools lined a portion of one wall, and carts had been placed neatly in a line along one edge of the field.

With a deep breath, I hurried down the chamber, my footsteps completely muted by the dirt. Further in now, the far wall came into view. It rose high enough so that there were open rooms on the ground level, probably for the harvesters, and then a line of rooms over those, with windows that overlooked the field.

A light appeared in the second-story window. I heard footsteps above as I quickly found the stairs leading to the second floor.

The landing was empty. I moved down the hall to check the first closed door. No sooner had I reached for the doorknob than I was thrown forward into the door. Pain flowed through my face as it smacked the wall. The Nitro-gun dropped from my hand.

Before I could recover, I was moved again by an invisible force, this time flying backward and straight through the drywall, between the studs, scraping bloody trails down my arms and shoulders and seriously bruising my hips, and then through another wall.

The breath got knocked out of me again when I landed in a cloudy heap of dust and debris inside a room.

Something had pulled me through.

Correction. Two somethings. So much for there only being one Abaddon down here. As the dust settled, my vision cleared. Two Abaddon females stood in front of me, one with long, straight black hair, thigh-high leather boots, and a tight black mini dress, and the other whose black hair was pulled into a bun so tight it pulled on the corners of her eyes. But her taste in clothes, black slacks and a white T-shirt, was far more subdued.

I pushed to my feet, using my hands to brush off my jeans. "So which one of you bitches grabbed my kid?"

Bunhead smirked. "That would be me," she said in a thick accent that reminded me of Romanian or Russian.

"Good to know," I said, right before punching the other one in the jaw, catching her off guard. She went down hard as I went to draw the second Nitro-gun from the back of my jeans.

Bunhead smirked again and raised her hands, shoving me back into the wall without even touching me, without giving me a chance to grab my gun. An invisible hand closed around my throat. I couldn't even gasp for air. Pressure built in my head and face. Legs and arms flailing, I fumbled for my human firearm on my hip, relief washing over me as my hand slid around the cool metal handle.

My finger flipped the safety on my gun. I let off four rounds into her stomach. She flew back, but I knew it would be temporary. Bullets did not kill beings from Charbydon. Released from her vicious hold, I dragged in large drafts of precious air, my lungs burning.

I was hit from behind by Mini. She flipped me over with a thought and then blasted my mind with horrors.

A scream tore from my bruised throat. Searing heat engulfed my brain as I grabbed my head with both hands. Nightmares ripped through my mind and stole my breath. Flashes of death, torture, blood. Me. Emma. The fear on her face. The hurt. *No! No! No!* My mind was being torn apart by them. Tears closed my throat. So real. It felt so real.

But the shock wore off and the sickening images began to bring out my sense of justice.

God, this was low, even for an Abaddon bitch.

She was trying to incapacitate me with horrors of my daughter. Big-ass mistake.

The anger of it allowed me to fight back. I remembered my power. I was Abaddon, too. What she could do, theoretically I could do.

I sat up, eye to eye with her, and grabbed her face, sending my anger, and with it my power, through my arm and into my hand. I gave her a nightmare all Charbydons feared. Cold. Snow. She was trapped in it. Ice crept up her legs, freezing and cracking flesh, so cold it burned her. I poured it into her. All that I had. And up it went until it covered her face and chilled my own hand.

I let go.

Jesus.

I scrambled back. My back hit the wall, and my breathing was labored and loud in the sudden quiet.

She was frozen solid.

Abaddons could give nightmares that left the mind wounded beyond repair, but as far as I knew they couldn't make them *real*. I blinked and glanced down at the hand that had caused such unbelievable damage, *my* hand, right before Bunhead lifted me off the floor and sent me flying into the window.

Shit.

Two seconds later, the flesh peeled from the bone of my elbow as glass met skin. Then I was falling, a brief feeling of weightlessness before I slammed into the soft dirt below.

17

The landing knocked the breath from my lungs. Pain shot through my back as the second Nitro-gun in my waistband shoved deep into my kidney. White dots danced in my vision. I moaned, forcing down a queasy swallow. Minuscule particles of glass, wood, and dirt floated from the second floor. I coughed and a sharp sting of pain burned through my side. Lifting my head, I saw a sliver of glass pierced through my left side. My head was too heavy to hold. I let it fall back into the dirt. I fumbled around with my hand, trying to find the sliver. Thank God it wasn't near my organs. But it was enough to stop me cold.

Bunhead would be coming down the steps. I had to get this out and move.

Shouts and gunfire echoed from somewhere far off. Gasping and trying to stay lucid, I wrapped my hand around the sliver and pulled, screaming. The glass digging into my palm was nothing compared to the excruciating pain that seared my flesh and turned my stomach. The end of the sliver came out with a sucking sound, the faint slurp of flesh and blood making bile rise to my throat. I couldn't hold it in any longer. I turned and vomited, letting the sliver fall into the dirt as a warm rush of blood oozed from the entry and exit wounds.

Charlie? Carreg's voice swept through my mind all harsh and commanding. *You need to get—*

I'm a little busy right now, I said in my mind, rolling back to stare at the ceiling. The sound of the shouts and fighting suddenly seemed so far away.

Listen to me.

I didn't. Instead, I rolled to my uninjured side, onto my stomach, and then pushed up using my hands and knees. Fuck. I hurt.

Where are you? I asked him. *You should be here. Oh no, wait. Let me guess. It wasn't to your benefit to be here.*

I felt his huff and frustration more than heard it. *I met with Mynogan. Get everyone out of there now, Charlie. You don't have much time.*

I pulled one foot from underneath me and used my hands braced on my knee to stand. *Not without Emma.*

Emma is already gone.

Glass crunched under feet. I lifted my head to see Bunhead sauntering toward me, victory gleaming in her black eyes. Carreg's words settled in my empty stomach.

Emma was gone. I was too late.

My nostrils flared. Failure and rage stung my eyes and sent a new batch of adrenaline surging through my system. With an angry scream I rushed her, tackled her, and we both went flying to the ground. I recovered before she did, sitting on top of her stomach and wrapping both hands around her throat.

"Where is she?!" I shouted, the pain forgotten in favor of desperate frustration and wrath. "Where is my daughter?!"

Amusement made her dark eyes glitter. I eased my hold on her throat so she could speak. Her lips curled. "Get off me, you stinking human."

I pulled the gun from the back of my waistband and rested the nozzle between her startled eyes. The familiar zing of the building nitro charge sounded in dead silence. I cocked an eyebrow. "Where is she?"

"Fuck you."

Coldness settled over me. I shoved the gun into her mouth. "I'm going to ask one more time. Where's Emma?"

She flipped me the bird, waving it in front of my face.

I pulled the trigger.

Her face froze in a mask of hard, horrified ice.

I rolled off of her and stumbled to my feet, eyes going in and out of focus. Everything inside of me was racing too fast—blood, heart, lungs, thoughts, emotions . . . I had to slow down, had to concentrate. I rested my palms on my knees and let my head fall, eyes closed and counting until some semblance of calm entered me.

We weren't quick enough. Someone had called for help, and Emma was gone.

But the Bleeding Souls were still here.

I was without the help of Aaron and Bryn's magic to destroy them, so I looked around the ground level until I found a water valve. There were two large ones on either side of the back wall. Glass and dirt ground into my palms as I turned the heavy wheels to release the water and flood the chamber. Then I made my way down the cavern and up the ramp to the boiler room. It was empty and quiet. My apprehension heightened. My legs trembled badly, and dirt scratched my eyes as they moved.

I had to pull myself up the steel steps, my hands a mess now. My hips ached and began to stiffen. My shoulders, elbow, and arms were drenched in blood. And my side, oh God, my side . . . I held my hand over the wound, but it didn't help to stop the flow of blood. Weakness stole over me as I opened the door to the main floor and then rested against the wall, using it to help me stay on my feet as I went toward the lobby.

Heal. I commanded over and over again, knowing I had done it once. Knowing I had it in me. But I was so weak and dizzy. Depleted. There was nothing left. I wondered what Aaron would say. Probably something like *You fucked up big time, Charlie.* No, that would be more like Rex.

I made it to the lobby, falling to my knees at the unbelievable scene before me. "No," the word whispered out of my cracked lips. I squeezed my eyes closed, hoping it was all a hallucination, but when I opened them again, nothing had changed.

They were all there. Rex. Hank. Zara. Aaron and Bryn. On the floor, lying entangled. "No, no, no . . ." I crawled to Bryn and pulled her onto her back. Her eyes were wide open. And opaque.

Ash.

"Bryn." My voice broke as I shook her gently. "Wake up." I knew I shouldn't have let her come! What was I thinking? My throat closed. I rested my head against her shoulder for a long moment. "Please, wake up . . ."

No one was waking. No groaning or moving.

I tipped back onto my ass, too weak to move, too shocked to cry. Somehow they'd been exposed to *ash.* Confusion and exhaustion made my eyelids heavy. How could this have happened?

I pressed my bloody palm over my nose. It had to be airborne. I glanced down and my hand trailed a line in a faint shimmering powder. It dusted everything. Oh, God. I crawled, holding my breath until I was in the foyer and couldn't hold it any longer.

Carreg! You have to come. They. . . I need your help.

No answer. I'd probably pissed him off with my comment earlier. I had to get the car, get them to the hospital. Grabbing the front doorknob, I pulled myself up and then stepped out into the night.

Bright, white light flared. I shielded my eyes.

"Put your hands behind your head and get on the ground!" a voice called through a bullhorn.

What the—

My arms were too heavy to lift behind my head, but I raised my hands and saw through squinted eyelids the flashing red and blue. It looked like the entire precinct had mobilized. Thank God. I stumbled down the two front steps. "I'm Detective Charlie Madigan," I shouted, my voice slurring from pain, exhaustion, shock . . . "We need medics and—"

Guns clicked. A red dot caught my vision and splayed over my heart.

"Don't move. Get on the ground now!"

"But I'm an officer, I—"

"Ma'am, you're under arrest for three known counts of murder. Now get down on the ground or we *will* use force."

I blinked in slow motion. The red and blue lights blended together. Murder? Ah, yes. The jinn who'd attacked Auggie. A sharp, ironic laugh spurted through my lips. I swayed on my feet. Guess Otorius had gotten out of the closet and gone over the chief's head to have me arrested. No surprise after what I'd done to him.

Just wait until they saw the damage inside. I laughed again and then my knees gave out . . .

I hit the ground as blissful darkness surrounded me.

I was lost.

Dreams and images and bursts of semiconsciousness ricocheted through my fuzzy mind. Mynogan and Mott stood before me under the full moon picking pieces of my flesh like children doling out marbles. I couldn't move. My knees sank into the soft earth and my hands lay limp at my sides. I burned everywhere as they pulled me apart.

One piece for me. One piece for you.

Then, images of the fight flashed through my mind. My friends and my sister on the floor. Falling from the window. The glass in my side, a side that ached relentlessly.

The *ash*.

Voices drifted like echoes, bounding off walls and hovering above me just out of range. I tried to listen, but as my consciousness finally returned, I prayed to fall back into sleep. The pain had a stranglehold over every inch of my body.

The voices became clearer. I cracked my eyes open. I was in a white room, lying on a bed and covered with a white blanket. An IV dripped steadily into a line attached to my vein. Whatever pain medicine I'd been given was wearing off at a startling rate.

A massive form in blue regalia began to take shape. "Chief?" I moaned. Speaking even hurt.

The form turned to me and leaned down. It was the chief, and the anger and concern on his face had caused a deep red blush to appear under his dark skin. "Charlie."

"Where am I?"

He glanced over his shoulder, his look fierce, like a grizzly giving a big-ass warning. "You're in the med hold."

The med hold was a cell in our precinct reserved for wounded criminals. It was outfitted with everything needed to see to the survival of a felon until they could be extradited or transferred to the hospital, depending on their condition.

I didn't understand. I frowned. Pain shot through my head. I tried to sit up, but couldn't even make it an inch off the pillow. My wrists were strapped to the bed.

"Relax, Detective."

"What time is it?"

"About ten-thirty."

"Emma." I let my head sink into the pillow. "They have Emma."

The chief frowned and leaned closer. "Who?"

"Mynogan."

A voice erupted into laughter behind the chief. He straightened as Otorius stepped next to the bed. Satisfaction dripped from every pore. "She's obviously delusional," he said, giving me a menacing smirk. His right arm was in a sling, the wrist covered in thick bandages.

I struggled to sit up again. The heart monitor began to beep faster. A nurse on the other side pushed me back to the mattress. "You need to be still, Detective," she said.

She leapt back when I kicked at her. I ignored the pain and pushed my stiff body to a sitting position, braced by my palms on the mattress. The effort made me pant, but Otorius was in my crosshairs, and I wished I'd killed him when I had the chance. "You lying sonofabitch," I ground out and then turned to the chief, wishing my voice would work properly and not come out so slow and slurred. "He's lying. They took her. Mynogan took her."

"Do you have any evidence, Charlie?" the chief asked, ignoring the laugh from Otorius.

But I couldn't ignore it. "How's your hand, Otorius?"

He lunged for the bed, his face blood-red and seething with anger, but the chief held him back. "You bitch!" He lifted his arm. "I lost my hand! You little fucking whore!"

"That's enough!" the chief commanded.

My arms shook, too weak to support my weight. I fell back to the bed. Trying to think clearly amid the heavy clouds in my mind was like trying to run up a cliff backward. "Will," I forced out, "they took her from Will. Killed him. Go to his apartment. You'll see." The chief glanced over his shoulder and nodded to an officer standing guard. "A Revenant took over his body. The others. Bryn, Hank . . . Are they alive?"

"Charlie," the chief asked more gently than before. "What are you talking about?" I could tell by the softening of his hard expression that the more I tried to explain the more ridiculous it all sounded.

"Didn't you find them? In the spa. All of them, drugged."

"We didn't find anyone except for the victims."

I frowned. No, that didn't make sense. They were there. I'd seen them. If only my head would clear! Sluggish, I shook my head and swallowed. "No . . . Where are they?"

"It may be the pain meds talking," Doctor Berk said, coming to stand at the foot of the bed.

"It's not the fucking meds!" Bright rainbow stars of pain flashed behind my eyelids. I jerked against the restraints, grabbing at the chief's wrist. My vision swam so badly, his features blended to a lump of flesh. "Please help me. I'm not lying." The chief was like a father to me. And he'd betrayed me. He'd allowed me to be Titus Mott's lab rat. "How could you, how could you agree to do that to me? You and Titus . . ."

He gave me a gentle pat on my hand and a reassuring squeeze. "We'll talk about that later, Charlie. You need to rest now."

"She will stand trial as soon as we can set a date," Otorius said tightly.

"The only place she's going is to the hospital as soon as I can arrange it. You never should have brought her here like some criminal."

"She *is* a criminal!"

"And I say she's not. Not until my investigation is complete." The chief stepped toward the Abaddon representative, standing toe-to-toe with him. "Let me get one thing straight, this is *my* detective and my precinct. I don't take orders from you. We do this by the book. You get me?"

"If we did this by the book, she would have been brought in days ago, before more of *my* countrymen died, and I lost my hand!"

The chief's voice was low and deadly. "And I didn't have a warrant a few days ago."

The room grew silent, and I imagined the chief was using his infamous stare down. I smiled slightly as I heard a low curse and the door open. "You have no idea who or what you're dealing with," Otorius said in a serious, even tone. "There's more than one monster in this city." The door closed.

"I need a moment alone," the chief said tiredly, his steps growing louder as he approached the bed. A chair scraped across the floor as two sets of footsteps, Doc Berk's and the nurse's, faded away behind the click of the door.

My heavy eyelids opened again as he sat down and regarded me with a mixture of annoyance and caring. He shook his head. "You've got this entire department into one hell of a mess." I opened my mouth, but he cut me off. "I know, I know. It wasn't you, right? Doesn't matter, Charlie. We're under a microscope right now." He sat back, letting out a huge sigh. "Did you have to go and massacre eight Charbydons and an Elysian mage?" He rubbed his face. "This isn't like you."

"He was a black mage," I mumbled and then took a deep breath. "Go to Mynogan's bath house, and you'll see. It's grown there. Then it goes to the Lion's Den. Tennin, he has a bunch of it. You'll see. You'll find the *ash*. We need those flowers for an antidote or all of them . . . they won't wake up."

He pinched the bridge of his nose. "Mynogan is running for city council, Charlie. And Grigori Tennin . . ."

"Is a murderer and a drug dealer," I slurred, growing tired. I closed my eyes. "You scared of him?"

"Hell, no, I ain't scared of him. Goddammit," he sighed. "Look, I'll check into it. And if Hank and the others have gone off the radar like you say . . . well, the fuck if I know, but we'll figure something out."

"Just get me out of here, Chief."

He eyed me for a hard second. "Can't do that. You don't think I'm under the gun? I'm already up shit's creek for pulling strings at Deer Isle because of your asinine bargain with Tennin. If you go free now, it'll be the end of my career, and I sure as shit won't be able to help you then."

"I don't care about your damn job right now," I spat.

The chief walked to the door and stopped. "You're the biggest piece of trouble I've ever known, Madigan."

"Yeah, I know," I whispered on a faint breath.

When he was gone, I relaxed back into the thin mattress, body limp and out of breath. I needed to heal, but my wounds were much worse this time around, and all I wanted was to slip back into unconsciousness. My body and mind begged me to. Maybe just a little nap.

No!

God, no. I couldn't. There wasn't time.

I let my eyelids close and remembered my conversation with Aaron. *Be calm.* Both Charbydons and Elysians had the power to heal. It was inside of me somewhere. The dark power and the light. I realized at that moment, I'd relied mostly on the dark, had used every ounce in me. But the Elysian power, I'd barely tapped. And I knew just how to do it.

Emma.

All I had to do was imagine her in my mind and she was there. Drawing on our bond, I freed my emotions, all the warmth and love. Her smile lit the darkest part of my soul. The sound of her laughter filled me with joy and peace. And her love for me was absolute, and so damn humbling. I'd sacrifice the world and more for her.

And she was my pathway to the light.

Only the good, I commanded as thoughts of her kidnapping came into my mind. My Emma. Strong-willed, passionate, kind. Pride swelled my chest, mingling with all the wonderful emotions she brought out in me.

The goodness unlocked something and behind my closed lids a light grew, and the Elysian power released, flooding into my own light and the light that my child created inside of me. I realized then, as my fingers and toes tingled and my body hummed, that the darkness had nearly overtaken me. I had relied upon it so much in my anger and desperation that it had grown and adapted to me while this power had not been given much of a chance.

Well, now it had. And I held on to it, letting it course through my veins, every sinew and muscle, every cell and bone, welcoming it and fusing it with my human side and the dark side.

It was like a giant helping of morphine. For a moment everything—my side, the bruises, cuts, and stiff muscles—became pain free, but it didn't last long. Once it ebbed, I was left with some serious aches and pains, but not enough to keep me from getting my ass out of there and finding Emma.

"Will you help me sit up?" I asked the nurse sitting by the bed reading a novel. From her tired look, I wondered how long I'd been healing myself. It hadn't seemed that long.

"Sure." She set the book down and raised the bed.

Relieved, I scanned the room, noting the two doors, one to a small bathroom and the other—my path to freedom. As she fluffed the pillow for me, I pulled on the restraints around my wrists. "Is there anything you can do about these?"

She gave me a sad look. "Sorry."

"What if I have to use the bathroom?"

"One of the guards will come in and stand outside the bathroom door while you go."

"Fine by me. I have to go."

"Let me check your side first," she said, coming around the bed to inspect the bandage around my torso. "No bleeding. How do you feel?"

"Trust me, good enough to go to the bathroom."

After patting me on the leg, she went to the door to tell the officer that I had to pee. *Way to put it bluntly.*

Trying to formulate a plan in that short amount of time was impossible. But one, I did have to pee, and two, I desperately wanted out of those restraints. And three, if I was able to stand on my own two feet, then I knew I could make it out of there somehow.

One of the officers came in and unlocked the restraints. He lent the nurse a hand in helping me to my feet. Chills flew up my legs and thighs as my bare feet hit the cold tile, but I didn't mind. It woke my body. Those first few steps were wobbly and painful, but as I shuffled toward the bathroom door, my strength slowly returned. *Some clothes would be nice*, I thought.

"Will you tie me tighter?" I asked the nurse, turning my back to her and away from the guard. I didn't need to flash my ass at him or anyone else during my escape. She tied the four sets of strings into double knots. It would leave gaps between ties, but it was better than nothing.

After doing my business, I washed my hands and face and then gripped the sides of the sink, staring at my reflection in the small mirror and ignoring the cuts and bruises on my face. I was so gaunt, I barely recognized the wild-haired woman staring back at me. *Come on, Charlie. Think!*

I had no weapons, and I sure as hell wasn't strong enough to overpower anyone. I'd have to rely on my powers, which were nearly as weak as my body.

Once I came out of the bathroom, I asked the nurse for something to eat and was rewarded, after being helped back into the bed and waiting a good twenty minutes, with a tray of generic meat loaf, mashed potatoes, and carrots. It looked suspiciously like a Banquet TV dinner. At least I was permitted to eat on my own, further delaying their reattaching the restraints. I ate slowly, all the while willing myself to continue the healing process and trying to figure out how to escape.

I was on my last bite of processed meat when the door opened and Titus Mott hurried inside, looking almost as bad as I did. I set the tray aside, feeling satisfaction roll through me at his busted lip and black eye. His brown hair was in more disarray than usual and his lab coat was smudged with blood, probably his own. A fine crack split the left lens of his eyeglasses.

"That's the problem with guys like Mynogan," I said, easing back into the pillow. "They always turn around and bite you in the ass." *Translation: it sucks to be betrayed, doesn't it, you asshole?*

"Charlie," he began in a defeated tone. I mean, really, what excuse could he possibly give for what he'd done to me? Yeah, he'd saved my life, but injecting me with off-world DNA? I might be extremely grateful to him for being alive, but I didn't have to *like* him for it. He stayed a few feet away from the bed as though I'd hurt him if he got too close. Smart man.

He went to speak but I cut him off. "Where's Emma?"

"At Mott Tech with the rest of your friends." His gaze dropped to the floor, but he spoke quickly as though he was running out of time. "Charlie, I didn't know. I had no idea Cass was using one of my labs to process *Sangurne N'ashu*. If I had, I would have stopped him immediately. I'll do whatever you need me to, to find him and make him stand charges. And I'll put all my resources to finding a cure for *ash's* effects." The miserable expression on his face didn't elicit a single ounce of sympathy from me.

His hand slipped into his pocket. A tingle wove along my spine, and I tensed. Something was up. "I'm to take you to the lab," he said.

Before the nurse realized what he meant, he pulled a stun gun and fired. The tag hit her in the right shoulder, her mouth open in a scream that never quite made it out. Paralyzed, she hit the ground hard.

My mouth dropped open. "What the hell are you doing?"

"I told you. Taking you to the lab. Your daughter is not the only one threatened, you know." A spark of anger lit his eyes.

Finally, he gets a backbone, I thought. He stepped forward, hands trembling so badly, I was afraid he'd accidentally shoot himself or me. I jerked the gun from his grasp and swung my legs over the bed.

I wasn't about to look a gift horse in the mouth. "Amanda," I surmised, knowing how much Titus cared for his niece. If he had a weak spot, that was it, and Mynogan had used it just as he'd used Emma to get to me. He answered with a slight nod. I checked the chamber of the gun. Three tags left out of six, which meant . . . "*You* took out the guards?"

He slipped around me and opened the door, sticking his head into the hallway. "I have a car parked out back. We should go before someone else comes."

"I need weapons." I peeked out to see the hallway was empty for now.

Titus whirled on me, his face no longer apologetic. "I won't risk it, Charlie. If I don't get you back to the lab in"—he glanced at his watch—"forty minutes, my niece will be dead."

I was so mad, I wanted to pound him into the tile floor, but I knew exactly what it was like to have a loved one's life at risk. And the last thing I wanted for Amanda was to be late.

I led the way into the hallway. I knew Station One inside and out. We were on the basement level, which meant it stayed relatively quiet. There were extra holding cells, file rooms, the weapons depot, and supply closets. We should be able to make it to the back stairs and then out into the parking deck at the back of the building.

But just as we began our journey up the back stairs, a door opened and footsteps sounded above us.

18

It was too late to hide. I stepped in front of Titus and aimed.

The chief came down the back steps with a tray of Styrofoam iced teas and a Bojangles bag.

"Charlie," he blubbered in surprise. His big body froze on the landing. "What the hell are you doing now?" But understanding had already dawned on him.

I inched up the steps, keeping the gun trained. "Sorry, Chief." There was no other choice but to shoot him. He knew it, too. If they found him shot on the steps, he'd be free of suspicion. "It should wear off in a few hours."

He drew in a deep breath, totally irate. "You can forget about being invited to the company picnic. That goes for you, too," he said, eyeing Titus. "In fact, you're both fired. *Fired*. You hear me?"

"Titus, take the tea." If the chief was going to drop, I'd rather save the tea because I was dying of thirst.

Titus took the tray and the bag as the chief sat down on the dirty floor of the landing. "Anne-Marie will kill me if I fall and break something," he said with a growl. "Well, what the hell are you waiting for? Just do it already. And don't hit the leather jacket."

He deserved it, and he knew it. The chief would always hold a soft spot in my heart and one day I'd forgive him for his part in the gene therapy. But not today. I aimed and fired, jumping with a start as the stun tag sank into his beefy thigh. He let out one curse before listing to the side and then slumping over.

"Come on," I muttered to Titus, running by the chief and to the back door.

Outside, I stumbled to a stop. I'd been prepared for daylight, but it was dark. I'd missed an entire day. Titus pointed over my shoulder. "Over there."

Spurred on, we raced down the steel steps and across the parking lot. The chill of the October night flew through the thin hospital gown and my bare feet dug into the minuscule asphalt pebbles that littered the lot.

I took the driver's side, sliding into the seat in a rush of adrenaline. The key had been left in the ignition. Once Titus was in, I started the car and drove out of the parking lot with the headlights off. I didn't turn them on until we were halfway down the block.

It took another five minutes to access the interstate. *Thank God*, I thought as we joined the flow of traffic. *We made it*. I glanced at the clock. And we had just enough time to make it to Mott Tech before Amanda's time ran out.

"He has people at the hospital," Titus said quietly, gazing out the window for a silent moment. "I'm sorry about my brother. It's time he took responsibility for what he's been doing . . ."

"I'll hold you to that," I said. I took one of the teas, pierced it with a straw, and took a long, loud drink. Then I voiced an idea that had been forming in the back of my mind. "The weapon you're working on with that Adonai, Llyran, the one that can neutralize power," I said. "I want you to use it on me."

Taken aback, he blinked. "It's nowhere near to being ready. And why would you want to use it on yourself?"

"Because eventually, these two powers will kill me, and I'm rather fond of my life. One of them has to go. Preferably both."

He dug into the Bojangles bag and handed me a wrapped chicken sandwich. I shook my head. "You can have it."

"I'll tell you what," Titus said, putting the sandwich back into the bag. "If we make it out of this, I'll make it my number-one priority."

"After the *ash*," I said.

He nodded. "Of course."

There was no one else on this planet who could accomplish the things Titus Mott had. And despite how I felt about him, he was the only one who might be able to help me and most everyone I loved.

We arrived at Mott Tech right on schedule, the guards waving us through.

I parked the sedan at the front of the building, my headlights beaming two jinn as they waited in front of the glass doors. One of them used the radio while the other motioned for me to turn off the high beams. I waited a good five seconds before complying.

"Any ideas?" Titus asked, popping the door handle.

"Yeah. Kill Mynogan."

I stepped out of the car, practically naked in my bare feet and napkin-thin hospital gown. As the jinn came forward, they leered at me. I leered back. Assholes. One of them grabbed my arm, but I jerked away, falling in behind the other jinn as he led the way around the side of the building.

We followed a flagstone path away from the building and into the landscaped gardens. The cold brush of wind that came off the lake and through the woods stirred my loose hair and covered me in chills. I crossed my arms over my chest as I stepped carefully over the cold stones.

Titus walked behind me, the other jinn bringing up the rear. At least I had Titus at my back rather than the jinn.

The songs of crickets and katydids echoed all around us. Moonlight bathed the area in a soft glow, lighting our way as we wound through the trees. The scent of the lake grew stronger, and the long, drawn-out croaks of frogs became louder. Soon, we were on a path, which skirted the lake.

Ahead was the pavilion. Hank told me once he'd attended a wedding out here. I could see the attraction. It was a romantic setting, with an arched bridge spanning a creek that fed the lake, and the pavilion, which had been built to resemble an old Victorian gazebo.

Figures in shadows waited, lining the path to the pavilion. Three on each side. All dressed in black. How clichéd. Surprisingly, we skirted the pavilion and came to a large meadow at the back of the building where a wide, circular area of soft grass had been cut. Surrounding it was a garden straight out of a Monet painting. My heart began to pound, steady and stronger and faster.

Mynogan stood in the center of the lawn.

Alone.

I marched around the jinn in front of me, the words snarling out of me as his hot hands clamped over my upper arms to hold me back. "Where's my daughter, you sick sonofabitch?"

"Ah, Charlene. Always a class act." He folded his hands behind his back, the moonlight glinting off his white hair and skin, making his black eyes even more menacing, like two black holes lost in the shadows. "Your daughter is there in the pavilion."

I whirled, but then was dragged back around to face Mynogan. "Let me go!" I threw back my head and busted the jinn in the jaw. He stepped back, doubling over. I spun and roundhouse-kicked him in the same spot. Pain shattered through my bare foot as it connected with thick bone.

And then I was running.

Almost there, the back steps of the pavilion just within reach, my heart in my throat, my arms pumping. A hand delved into my flying hair, pulling me up short and so hard that I was lifted off my feet. The breath left me as my back hit the ground. My vision wavered, making the moon bounce back and forth in the sky.

The first tug on my hair made me reach and grab the hand, trying to pry the fingers off as I was dragged across the lawn flat on my back, kicking and screaming. Sharp, stinging pain seared my scalp. I twisted my body but couldn't get traction to push or pull myself to my feet.

The jinn stopped in front of Mynogan and forced me onto my knees. I lashed out again, my arms flailing as he released my hair and then pinned my wrists behind my back.

Pants came out of me in ragged succession. I glanced up. Mynogan stood before me, smiling.

And then it hit me. My heart stopped.

Oh, God.

This was my nightmare all over again. In the grass. On my knees. Mynogan and Titus both there. Mynogan in black and Titus in his white lab coat. But this time Titus was watching pale-faced and scared shitless.

"What do you want from me?!" My voice cracked, thick with desperation.

"You may release her," Mynogan said to the jinn. As soon as his hands were off me, I leapt to my feet and moved to counterattack, but an invisible hand had me by the throat. My chest burned with hatred. Power swirled around Mynogan like a vicious wind. *Big fucking deal*, I thought, refusing to be scared. He was a bully hiding behind power, the same kind of power flowing through my veins. Everything in his makeup was in me, too. I had to remember that, to distance my emotions and remain calm.

"You have a choice, Charlene. I'll make it simple so you can understand. Your lifeblood, for your daughter's." A brutal eyebrow cocked, and I wanted to wipe the slimy smirk right off his face. "All of it."

"Why not just kill me now?" He had me. He had Emma. Why make a deal?

"You must do it yourself. A *willing* gift to the primordial darkness of Charbydon."

I blinked. "Suicide?" Aaron's words came back to me. The ritual. Mynogan's belief that only a person with the blood of all three worlds in their veins could raise the darkness. Funny. Aaron never mentioned the suicide part. An unbelievable laugh swelled up, but lodged in my throat. "And I suppose we just happen to be standing on unconsecrated ground."

Triumph swelled his chest. "Civil War burial ground for criminals and traitors."

Weigh your choices, Charlie. Carreg's deep voice glided through my mind. *There'll be no light. No food will grow. Unlike our world, yours cannot be sustained by darkness. If it comes, it'll spread over time.*

"I want to see my daughter first," I told Mynogan, and then to Carreg, *If you're so worried about it, get your ass out of hiding and fight with me.*

Fighting Mynogan now will start a war between the Houses of Abaddon and Astarot. I cannot help you openly. She is one child. His honey-slick voice was nonchalant, almost goading me. *What is one child compared to thousands, millions? You can have others.*

His words lit a raging fire in the center of my chest, burning a path through every neuron and cell until it engulfed me. I had to clench my fists tightly, nails digging painfully into my palms, to keep from cursing him out loud. He knew nothing! Emma *was* my world. How could I look in her eyes and sacrifice her? How? Carreg was dumber than a doorknob if he thought for one second I'd make that choice. I'd find another way because I wasn't giving up my kid. I'd die before that happened.

So, you'll just stand by and let the darkness come? I shot back at Carreg.

I will not try to stop him, no. There are things, reasons, you don't understand.

Agreeing to my demand to see Emma, Mynogan motioned to a dark figure standing next to the pavilion.

My mind racing, I thought, *I'll make a deal with you.* Carreg didn't give a shit about me or Emma, and he certainly didn't know what it meant to be a parent. He obviously didn't care too much for my city or the planet, either. He wasn't about to put his plans on the line to help. But I knew the one thing he'd find beneficial. Mynogan dead. *When the time comes, you keep my family safe.*

And in return?

I'll kill Mynogan.

Carreg's laughter filled my head. *You're going to try to do that anyway.*

Not if you don't promise me. His DNA is inside of me, Carreg. I have the same powers, the same strength. Who do you think has more to fight for? Who do you think won't quit until he's dead? I can do this. And if you don't keep Emma and the others safe, I'll let him live within an inch of his life and turn him over to ITF. How long before you think his lawyers get him out? How long until he's back in control of the Council of Elders and realizes you helped me? You want him gone? You want control? Then you place your bet with me. You have nothing to lose. Just free the others from the lab and get Em out of here when I spill my blood. That's all I'm asking.

Desperation nearly overwhelmed me, and I wasn't even sure I was making sense, but he was the only one I knew who could do it. There was no one else. I'd run out of options. And I needed insurance. There wasn't a doubt in my mind that whatever happened, the jinn would kill Titus and Emma if Carreg didn't act.

Get her to my sister, I said softly. *Please.*

"Momma?"

That one small, terrified word burst through the night like the brightest shooting star. The hold on my throat vanished, and I spun to see Emma being led from the pavilion by a dark-figured Abaddon.

It wasn't an Abaddon. It was Carreg.

"Emma!"

"Mom!"

Carreg released her and she ran to me, launching herself into my arms. I caught her and held on for dear life. My chest swelled with her presence. I breathed her in. My hand cupped her head, the other on her back. I squeezed her hard, nearly bursting with love. It sang through me with such wonderful relief, tears spilled down my cold cheeks. She was all that mattered.

Finally, I lessened my hold and held her back from me, cupping her face and staring into her eyes. So happy she was all right, yet heart-stricken to be here, like this, with her. "Are you okay?"

She nodded, her bottom lip quivering, tears trailing lines down her cheeks. "Are you?"

I grinned, denying my tears, refusing to show her the fear coursing through my system. "I'm much better now. I told you I'd come."

The urge in me to become hysterical was overwhelming. I hugged her again and kissed her cheek. "Listen to me. You trust me, right?" She nodded. "You see that man over there?" I glanced at Titus.

"Amanda's uncle."

"Right. He's gonna take you somewhere safe while I finish up here."

She glanced around the field, her face so pale and full of fear. "Hey," I said, drawing her attention back to me. "I know what I'm doing. This is what I do, remember? The superhero of Atlanta and all that." I squeezed her arms and smiled, remembering her words only a few days ago when I'd wanted to transfer to a desk job. A half-hearted laugh escaped her. *That's my girl.*

I gazed over her shoulder to Carreg's stony face. His head dipped in a faint nod. Deal on. Relief washed over me. I winked at her. "Chin up. I'll see you in a bit, okay?"

She lifted her chin and swallowed hard. "Okay. But hurry up."

My heart constricted, but I forced a light voice. "You got it, kiddo."

I hugged her tight one last time and drew on the emotions coursing and building, hoping that it would be enough. Opening my mind, I tapped into the same emotions as I had earlier to heal myself. Our bond. Mother and daughter. I imagined a path to her mind, a link open and accepting. Once the familiar hum of energy pushed against every cavity and crevice of my body, I poured it into her. "Sleep," I whispered to my daughter. "Sleep, baby." *Please work.* Profound gratefulness went through me as she went slack in my arms. I braced for the full force of her weight.

Whether using my power weakened me or not, I didn't care. I was determined to keep Em from witnessing what was about to follow.

I faced Mynogan. Emma was not going back into that pavilion. "Once this is done, she goes with Titus. They walk out of here alone and unharmed."

"Agreed."

I kissed the top of her head, letting my lips linger as I carried her over to Titus. Gently, he took her in his arms, but his gaze was fixed on me. "Charlie. You can't do this," he whispered, glancing at Emma. "I understand, but the city . . ."

"Just . . . don't say it. I know what I'm doing. And if you don't keep her safe, I'll be coming after you next."

Two jinn fell in behind Titus as he sat in the grass with my daughter. My only option was to continue with the ceremony and hope to hell Carreg would come through if I couldn't find a way to thwart Mynogan's plan and get to my kid.

My legs felt wooden as I proceeded voluntarily toward the center of the circle. From the corner of my eye, I saw Carreg edge back into the shadows of the pavilion. Weariness swamped me. I was so tired. And I really didn't think I could handle any more emotion.

That's good, I convinced myself, *just center yourself and focus*. Bryn's crystal charm warmed my chest and gave me the calming comfort of her presence. When she'd given it to me after my death experience, I'd never really asked about its properties. And the only thing she'd told me was that it would help protect me. Fat chance of that now. But if it eased some anxiety, that was good enough for me.

The soft ground dipped beneath my feet, the cool dewiness against my bare skin sending chills up my arms and releasing the scent of tangy grass into the clean air. *It's too beautiful a night for blood and death.*

The six figures, Abaddons no doubt, surrounded us, widely spaced around the large circle of grass. My blood pressure rose. How did one kill an Abaddon noble? I drew in a resigned breath. I guessed I was about to find out. Strategies darted through my mind, elusive and insubstantial as I came to a halt in front of Mynogan. I'd become brain-dead. Great.

A victorious gleam came into Mynogan's eyes as he pulled a dagger from his coat and held it to the moon. It was iron. Black. And so sharp the moonlight glinted off the blade. There was no decoration of any kind on the weapon, giving it an even more sinister appearance.

If there was ever a death blade, this was it.

He chanted in Charbydon, which sounded similar to ancient Hebrew or Aramaic. His confident, rhythmic words stirred power into the night air. Energy gathered and coalesced within the circle. Every hair on my body lifted. Even the ends of my hair curled up as though acknowledging a change in the atmosphere around us. I thought I heard the faint echo of drumbeats, the sound vibrating through me like a second pulse. But there were no drums here.

I swayed as memories darted just out of reach, evading me like teasing fireflies. Not my own, but familiar. Primeval. Basic. Like the drums. On an elemental level, I recognized the power growing within the circle. It was earth. It was matter. Water. Life. Creation. My eyelids grew heavy, my thoughts hazy. Somehow I knew I was connected to this in a way no one else could claim. I was part of three worlds. The individual energy that ran through them all, and made up them all, ran through me.

The cold, rough iron hilt of the dagger pressed into my palm. I glanced down, seeing my hand, a pale contrast to the coal-black dagger. Shivers snaked through me, and it took all my effort just to stay lucid and focused, the chanting having some kind of hypnotic effect.

With a slow glance over my shoulder to Emma, sleeping in Titus's arms, his face stricken and white as a ghost, and Carreg edging ever closer to them, I drew in my courage, squeezed the blade tightly, and held out my left arm. This was going to hurt like hell.

My pulse beat hard and fast like the drums inside of my head. Tensing, I pressed the blade into my flesh until vivid red blood blossomed over the pale skin. Then, I drew a burning, stinging line from the middle of my forearm down to my wrist, cleanly slicing the artery. I'd seen enough successful suicides to know how to do it right.

Mynogan's breath hissed from his thin lips, his eyes drawn to the gush of red spreading out in a warm thick line against my skin. I swayed again, but kept my arm out where he could see it, his reaction stirring something in me and triggering a sudden hunger. To kill. To take.

My grip flexed on the dagger. My blood pounded in my ears, blending with an ancient memory of frenzied, writhing bodies dancing around fire as the chanting grew louder. The power in the circle fed me, making these images in my mind, images as old as time. My vision warbled and tilted. I tried to swallow, but my throat and mouth had gone hot and dry.

I blinked slowly. Once. Twice. Then, Mynogan's fuzzy form came snapping back into view. He remained transfixed and distracted by the blood. And I knew then. I knew what I had to do. It all made perfect sense.

Gathering my waning strength and knowing I had to be fast, I pulled back my right hand and plunged the dagger into Mynogan's neck.

Startled, he stumbled back.

I was on him like some crazed lunatic in her hospital gown before he could draw on his power, arms and legs wrapping around him and sending him to the ground. Instinct took over. Thighs clamped firmly around his torso, I held his head down with my hand on his forehead and locked my mouth over the wound, pushing the horror of what I was doing from my mind.

The first taste of blood on my tongue threw me into another time and place. The time of Charbydon curses and rituals. The warm, sticky liquid slid down my parched throat, easing the hunger. I bled my blood into the aromatic grass and replaced it with pure evil.

The House of Abaddon had been cursed by blood. Blood to sustain them. And without blood, it would kill them.

Mynogan cursed loudly and struggled beneath me, trying to draw upon his power, but the source of it was his blood, the raw essence of life. And I was taking it for my own. His hand beat frantically at my back, but I ignored it. His power tried to shove me off, but I ignored that, too, taking it from him in long, thirsty gulps. His panic was raw and fierce, but he was weakening under the loss of blood.

No blood. No life. No Mynogan.

Desperate screams tore from his throat. Like a worm, he writhed in my grasp, his movements violent and fast. His voice broke. His nails dug into my back, carving deep, bloody ditches. I felt the skin open, but didn't feel the sting.

I kept him pinned, sensing that all around me the circle of dark figures was frozen, taken aback by what they were witnessing. The power swirling within the circle threatened anyone stupid enough to enter.

Carreg, I forced out of my chaotic mind, *get them away from here now.*

He didn't answer, but I sensed an agreement muted by shock.

Time slowed.

It felt like ages had passed, but, little by little, Mynogan's body went limp. I relaxed my thighs and hands. The scent of blood hung heavy and sweet in the sticky air. My lips were numb, and my throat and cheek muscles sore from drawing and drinking.

I sucked hard at the last drop of blood from his being and, feeling full and disgustingly sick, I rolled off the body onto my back, my gaze connecting with moonlight and stars. My breath came heavy and fast. The blood that flowed from my arm slowed to a trickle.

My eyelids drooped, my heartbeat slowed.

The ground beneath me shuddered, rousing my waning attention. The moonlight and stars slowly disappeared as a cloudy haze filled the sky. Darkness shot up through the earth like smoke through a screen, swirling in the circle, the force of its wind making my hospital gown wave across my knees and stomach.

A deranged chuckle bubbled from my throat.

There was no way Mynogan's blood could sustain me. I was human, not Charbydon, and I was dying here in a circle of smut. Smut that grew and burgeoned and would soon cover the city.

Way to go, Madigan. Way to fucking go.

My laughter mixed with hot tears. I should have taken a desk job. I rolled to my stomach and crawled from the circle on my elbows and the insides of my knees, trying not to focus on my left arm flayed open like a butterfly shrimp.

Damned if I'd die in this crap.

Using the last of my will, for it was all I had left, I made it outside the circle and into cleaner air, the creek somewhere close by. I lay down, one side of my face cushioned by the soft grass.

I'd chosen to save my child and to try to save the city, too, and I knew in my heart that I'd done the *only* thing I could. If I made it out of this, I'd figure out a way to fix things. There was always a way to fix things.

A small one-syllable chuckle eased through my lips, my breath stirring the grass and tickling my nose. Stupid thought. Stupid, unhinged Charlie. I wasn't making it out of here.

No regrets, I thought on a sigh that ended in blackness. *No regrets*—

19

"Pick her up. Easy, you fool."

"Call me a fool again, Rex, and you'll be—"

"Guys, guys, c'mon. Help a siren out here. Carreg, grab her arm, make sure it doesn't dangle." Hands dug under me and lifted. My head thudded against a hard chest as another hand placed my wounded arm gently over my stomach.

The bounce of footsteps jarred me somewhat, but otherwise I was protected in a cradle of warmth. This must be some kind of residual memory. I'd died. Hank, Rex, and Carreg had come back to rescue me, but they were too late and now they were carrying my dead body home.

Suddenly, a burst of understanding jolted me. Carreg had made it. Rex and Hank were free from the lab. That meant . . . Emma was safe. A flood of relief soothed my thoughts. Emma was safe. Now I could rest in peace. Peace out. Laughter bubbled out of me.

"She's laughing," Rex's voice sounded from somewhere behind me. "What the hell is she laughing about? Dude, maybe she's brain damaged or something."

Poor Rex. He was once just a spirit. Like me. He must be hearing my incorporeal self.

I was floating, floating over the grass and woods, and the crickets and katydids, through the crisp nighttime air. And into blackness.

"Uh, Charlie?" Fingers tapped my cheek. It was Will's voice. "Hello? Can you hear me?" More annoying taps.

"Stop tapping her cheeks like that. She doesn't like it." This from Emma.

She was right—I didn't like it. *You tell him, baby.*

"Momma," she said, so close to me, I could feel the soft brush of her breath on my other cheek. It smelled like bubble gum. "Can you wake up now, please?"

Instinct lifted my hand, wanting nothing more than to run my fingers through her hair. A gasp reached my ear as my hand landed on a real head of soft hair. Stunned, my eyes cracked open.

What the—

I blinked rapidly until my sight adjusted to the overhead light and the grinning face hovering above me. "Emma?" I croaked out through papery lips.

I'd never seen her smile so big. She turned away from me for a second and said, "See, I told you I could do it. You owe me twenty bucks."

"Yeah, whatever," Rex muttered. "Here, you little thief."

She grabbed the twenty and then turned back to me. "I love you, Mommy." Then she hugged me tightly.

There was nothing like it in the world. I breathed her in, amazed and humbled that I was here. Apparently alive by some insane miracle. It all dawned on me at once. I swallowed the lump rising in my throat, my eyes too dry for tears. God, she smelled so good.

Emma drew back, and I scrutinized every inch of her. She looked perfect and unharmed. Her brown eyes were bright, her auburn-brown hair in the usual ponytail, and those few freckles splattered across her little upturned nose. Over her shoulder, Rex was staring down at me with a happy, slightly goofy, smile.

I was in a hospital room, lying in an elevated position. To my left, Hank's big sleeping body was sprawled over a worn out recliner. To my right, the curtain was drawn back to reveal my sister lying in a similar bed, her head turned and staring, teary-eyed, at me.

"Bryn?"

A smile came slowly to her face, and though it was a happy one, there was an air of sadness about her, a flat, haunted look that hovered behind her eyes and dimmed the light that was usually there. My lips parted, about to ask her what was wrong when Aaron came through the door with two vases of Gerbera daisies. I bit my tongue. Immediately, he headed toward Bryn's bed, but when he saw where her attention was fixed, his gaze shifted to my bed. "Well, it's about time."

"Hello to you, too." I coughed, my throat dry and sore, as he set one of the vases by my bed and the other by Bryn's. When that was done he glanced from sister to sister, shook his head, and grinned, taking a seat in the empty chair next to Bryn's bedside.

"Would someone mind telling how I got here, and why Bryn is in that bed?"

Emma scooted more fully onto my bed as Rex sat at the foot, making me move my feet over.

"*Ash*," Aaron explained. "It doesn't have the same effect on us as it does on humans. Bryn was in a coma for five days. But with Titus Mott's help, she and the others are now on the road to recovery."

"And outside, what's been happening on the streets?"

"It's quiet. A few more overdoses trickled in, but, so far, it appears that field you flooded halted the supply. And no other cities have reported any cases, so looks like we got to it before it went wide."

For now. It was only a matter of time before someone else picked it back up again, or introduced something entirely new into society.

"And you should know," Aaron continued, "it's dark outside. Charbydon dark."

My eyelids fluttered closed for a few seconds as I composed myself. I knew it. I'd felt it in the circle, had seen it shooting up from the ground, and I felt it now, in my bones, in the faint thrum of my Charbydon side. I accepted the news with a nod, not ready to deal with those repercussions right now. "How long have I been out?"

"Seven days."

"Seven days!" I tried to sit straighter, but gave up as weakness stole over me. I hadn't used my muscles in a week. My gaze drifted to Emma. "Where were you this whole time?"

She shrugged and popped a bubble with her chewing gum. "I stayed at Aunt Bryn's with Daddy."

Okay, so maybe I hadn't woken up all the way. Surely I hadn't heard that correctly. "Come again?"

Rex gave me a pointed look. "Em and I took care of the shop, and looked after Gizmo and Spooky. Disney World will just have to wait."

My pulse surged. I'd dreaded the moment when Emma would discover that the man she knew as her father was gone. I never had the time to sit down and really think about how I would tell her or what I would tell her. Panic shot through me. I wasn't prepared.

Rex stopped making eyeballs at me since obviously I wasn't getting his meaning. He let out an impatient huff, and leaned in for a hug. His mouth pressed against my ear as he whispered. "I know, not many actors can pull off a role like this," he said, clearly amazed by himself. "Good thing for you I just happen to be an exceptional artist. You can thank me later. And just remember to call me Will." Emma grinned at his display of affection, and I felt the most horrible sensation in my gut as I realized he was playing the part of Will. Lying to my kid was not something I was comfortable doing.

I put an arm around him and made like I was kissing his cheek. "We'll talk about this later . . ."

A low chuckle bathed my cheek in warm breath. "Oh, Charlie," he said loudly. "I'm glad to see you, too, baby." He straightened and let out a happy sigh. *Yeah. Exceptional, my ass.*

Emma beamed at the man she thought was her father.

"You sure you're okay?" I asked her.

"Uh, yeah. Everyone can stop babying me now." She rolled her eyes. "Although, I'm cool with the extra junk food and later bedtime."

Rex shushed her with a hand over her mouth, but she just giggled and shoved him away. "C'mon, kid." he said "Let's go tell the doctor she's awake before you rat me out some more."

She gave me a happy eye roll that said, *Daddy has lost his mind, but I like it,* and then hopped off the bed.

As they left, I sat there stunned for a long moment, unsure how I felt about him taking care of my kid for the last week, or the fact that he, *we*, were lying to her. I'd have to tell her. Sooner rather than later.

"She's been well looked after, Charlie," Aaron said.

"Hank's been sleeping over at Bryn's, too. Rex seems to have taken on the role of father like he was born to it."

The doctor came in, so we shelved the conversation as he listened to my heart, checked my blood pressure and the bandages on my arm and back. He gave me another day in the hospital before I could leave, which I immediately objected to. I wanted to go home. My bed. My clothes. My life to get back to normal as soon as possible. We finally settled on me leaving mid-morning tomorrow if everything still looked good.

Hank woke during the exam, shell-shocked to see me sitting up and speaking. Watching him try to wake up and digest it all was an amusing distraction. His hair was ruffled and one side of his face held the pattern of the checkered pillow he'd been sleeping on. The voice-mod was still stuck on his neck, but I tried not to let my gaze or thoughts dwell on it and ruin the moment.

After visiting for a little while and keeping things light, Aaron and Hank left, followed a few minutes later by Rex and Emma. She had school in the morning and homework to finish.

"Amanda came by a few times to visit you," Bryn told me once we were alone. "They let her go home yesterday. Cass fled the country. He left the lab and everything in it, so Titus had all the samples he needed to study the drug."

I turned more to face her. "Are you sure you're okay?"

"I'm awake," she said as though it was one step above a *No, I'm not okay.* "I don't like the fact that every other day I have to take a small, regulated amount of *ash* to keep my system from shutting down. And if you want to know the truth, I feel like a fucking drug addict."

I winced. Bryn never cussed like that. "I'm sorry."

"Don't be." She shrugged. "I'd do it again in a heartbeat." An air of depression settled around her, and for a long moment she didn't speak. "Rex is good with Em," she finally said, changing the subject. "I don't think you need to worry about him. But there is one other thing . . . He, um, sort of rescued a pet. It's living in your backyard."

"Why do I have a feeling this is not going to be good?"

"It's the hellhound. Brimstone. Once he found out Animal Control was going to euthanize it, he had a fit. He and Aaron broke into the pound and stole him."

I closed my eyes and breathed deeply.

"He bought him a reinforced kennel and is working with him, training him."

I nodded. Great. Just great. Now I had an illegal hellhound living in my backyard. "That hound gets anywhere near my kid and I'll shoot it."

"Yeah, I told him. So did Hank. But you should see it, Charlie. Anytime Emma goes out to visit him in the kennel, he becomes completely docile. I've never seen anything like it."

This was the first time since I woke that she

sounded like the old Bryn. "Thank you," I said, knowing our fight had cost her far more than she'd ever admit. "For what you did. Do you want to talk about it?"

"Not really."

An ache blossomed in my chest. Bryn always wanted to talk about things. That was—had been—part of her personality. Now she was different. Changed. Like me. Like Hank. Like Will. Tears stung my eyes, but I blinked them back before Bryn could see. But it didn't really matter. When I looked over, she had fallen asleep.

Waking up to two giant forms hovering over me wasn't exactly the best way to start the morning. I gasped and sat up as one of the forms reached over and hit the lamp switch.

The chief and Hank stood on either side of the bed. Hank with his hands shoved deeply into his front pockets, in dire need of a shave and haircut, and the chief, folding his big, leather-clad arms over his chest. I suddenly felt very small and very under-dressed.

"What is this? ITF's version of a wake-up call?" I asked, voice groggy and scooting up. I went to adjust the bed's angle with the control, but the loud burst of sound made me stop; I didn't want to wake Bryn.

But then I noticed she wasn't exactly in the room.

Her bed was made. Her table cleared off. I continued to raise the bed.

"Where is Bryn?" I asked.

"She was released about three hours ago," Hank said. "Aaron picked her up. She didn't wake you?"

What the hell? She left without saying good-bye, just snuck out without a word? Granted, I knew she was seriously troubled and still physically suffering from her ordeal, but to just leave like that . . . "Guess not," I said, feeling confused and hurt and a whole lot concerned. Maybe she was worse off than I thought.

The chief cleared his throat, obviously seeing my mind wandering. I focused on him. The last time I'd seen the chief, I'd shot him with a stun gun, and I still didn't feel bad about it. "How's your leg?"

"It hurt like hell, Madigan," he barked and then shook his head. "But it worked. No one blamed your little escape on me, except Otorius, but that was no surprise. Listen," he began more quietly and a hell of a lot more uncomfortably, "about that . . . I just want to say . . . well, I'm sorry for keeping that whole DNA thing a secret. Titus had a chance to save you, and I don't regret giving him the go-ahead."

I absorbed his words, knowing that, in a round-about way, I owed him my life. But I still wasn't ready to let him off the hook for keeping the details from me. I dipped my head slightly and changed the subject. "So, one of you going to tell me where we stand?"

"We've got Interpol looking into Cass's whereabouts. We've been cleaning and processing the lab. Your friend Carreg has dropped out of sight. And if there was a connection between Mynogan bringing *ash* to the city and his plan to call the darkness, hell if we can figure it out."

"And Tennin?"

The chief's dark face went blustery. "Well, let's see," he said growing more perturbed by the minute. "That string I pulled at Deer Isle for you ended up getting Lamek Kraw killed by his visitor. Murdersuicide. Yeah. It was a hit. Feeling a little used yet?"

My lungs deflated. Shit. "What else?" I knew there was more.

"Oh, it gets better, Madigan. I went and raided the Lion's Den. And you know what? Didn't find a goddamn thing! Held that bastard in cold cell for three days while we searched! And you know what all it's gotten me?"

I was afraid to ask. But I didn't have to.

"Fired! That's what it got me!"

Hank and I winced at the same time.

"So what about us? The department knows now that I was attacked, that Mynogan was behind the kidnapping."

A sharp laugh jiggled the chief's angry cheeks. "You're not off the hook! Neither one of you is. You can't just go renegade and run around the city killing off-worlders, even if they are bad. What you both did should land you in jail."

"Should?"

The chief's indignation diffused somewhat, and he relaxed into the chair by the bed. "I've been offered a new job."

"What?" Hank and I said in unison.

"Yeah, and you two nutcases are coming with me."

A quick glance at Hank told me he was as stunned as I was. And we were both hesitant to ask where.

"All right, I'll ask," Hank finally said. "Going where?"

"The fifth floor." At our confused faces, he laughed. "Yeah, I know. There is no name for where we're going. Just a floor. The fifth in ITF Building One."

"But the fifth floor is the clerical floor. There's nothing up there but accountants, bookkeepers, and records clerks." What the hell was the chief talking about?

"Have you ever been up there, either of you?" We both shook our heads. "Well, there you go. Look, we've been given a chance by the higher-ups to keep our heads above water after this fiasco. We answer to no one but them, and as far as the ITF is concerned, they're on a need-to-know basis."

"So, what, we're classified now?" A laugh escaped me.

"To the rest of the world, pretty much. To the assholes and criminals on the street, we're gonna be their worst nightmare."

A slow grin split Hank's face. "I'm liking the sound of this."

I liked it, too, but then my sane voice interrupted.

I couldn't do this anymore. I'd almost died twice in one year. There was my daughter to consider here. I shook my head and let out a deep sigh. "I can't do it, Chief. I can't."

The chief's pupils dilated to hard points. "You don't have a choice, Madigan. It's either prison or this. You tell me which one is better for your kid." I felt as if the breath had been kicked out of me. "Look, I know how you're feeling right now. I know why you don't want to do this anymore. But damn it, Charlie, the higher-ups aren't doing this to be nice. They want you and Hank, and they'll use any leverage they've got. Look at it this way," he said, sitting back. "You can heal yourself now. You got more protection than any off-worlder I know. You bled out almost entirely. Hell, you didn't even need a transfusion when you got to the hospital."

That shocked me. "I didn't?" A creepy sensation crawled up my spine, and all I could see was blood in my vision and the taste of it in my mouth.

I'd kept Mynogan's blood. Oh, God, I was going to be sick.

Hank was beside me, hand on my back. "Breathe through it," he said gently. "Deep breaths."

I put my head toward my knees as waves of nausea rolled through me.

"He's not *in* you, Charlie. Your body used what it could to keep you alive, but you had enough of your own blood in you to recoup it as you healed."

It sounded like a theory to me, not fact, but I had

to give props to Hank for trying. "So what kind of job are we talking?" I asked, easing back onto the pillows and not wanting to think about blood.

"Well, let's just say the ITF has cases that need to be handled outside the normal confines of the law. That's where we come in. You answer to me. I answer to a contact in Washington. And you two have already proven you'll go above and beyond. The head honchos have been looking for a new team to work Atlanta for months. I know it's not fair, Charlie, but it's all we got, and I wouldn't look a gift horse in the mouth."

The chief stood, signaling the end of this little meeting. "As soon as you're recovered, we'll get to work. The CPP may be disbanded, but Mynogan had a loyal following. And we still have a lot of unanswered questions when it comes to *ash* and Tennin's involvement. It's not over." He opened the door and sighed. "And apparently we have an escaped Adonai serial killer on the loose."

For some reason that didn't surprise me. Just add it to the other things on the list: nailing Grigori Tennin, getting Will's soul back, fixing Hank's voice-mod problem, ridding myself of this power inside of me, having a heart-to-heart with my daughter because there was no way I could keep lying to her . . . And now Llyran had escaped.

Just a day in the life, I thought ruefully.

After the chief left, Hank sat on the edge of the hospital bed and, like me, took a long moment to ponder the chief's words. Finally he straightened his back, dragged his fingers through his hair, and turned his gaze to me. "So, are we doing this, then?"

What choice did we have?

Going off the grid, having no one to answer to but the chief, being the worst nightmare to criminals who deserved it . . . I gave him a shrug, feeling a small smile tug the corners of my mouth. "What the hell."

It was fitting that my first view of the darkness I'd brought to Atlanta would be seen with Hank at my side. I'd kept the hospital curtains drawn, hadn't asked about it, and had basically avoided the issue until the last possible minute. And now it couldn't be avoided; I had to leave the hospital. Of course, leaving in a wheelchair wasn't exactly my style, but I co-operated because, quite frankly, I wasn't sure I'd be able to stand once I saw the damage I'd done.

Maybe sitting down was the best thing for everybody.

"Aaron said it won't last," Hank said quietly as he pushed me through the elevator door and into the hallway that led to the main lobby. "You made it out of the circle before your last drop was spilled and your life force gone. He's not sure how long, but the League seems to think the darkness shouldn't spread too far or last forever." He paused, and I heard a small sigh. "I won't lie to you, Charlie, it's been hell trying to calm the fear and panic once it reached the city. The ITF has managed to keep your name out of the media so far, but you should know . . . some people in the department blame you. Others think you're a hero."

Joy. "And you?"

"I think you're out of your mind, as usual."

I laughed even though my hands clenched and unclenched the armrests. "Thanks." And then he turned the corner.

My heart hammered quick and hard against my rib cage.

I could see it through the main lobby's wall of glass. My mouth went dry, too dry even to swallow. The front doors slid open, and we glided past a florist, through another set of glass doors, and then we were out.

Outside. In the dark. At 11 A.M.

The blue sky and sunlight had been replaced by an undulating, churning mass of gray. It was not the complete darkness of night, more like the darkness of a total eclipse or a very nasty thunderstorm with the darkest damn thunderclouds you ever saw. Occasionally a bright flash, similar to heat lightning, would illuminate the darkness, but it was the only light from above. It moved and seethed like a living entity, an entity built on my blood. My gut twisted.

"Excuse me," a voice interrupted my horror. I glanced over my shoulder as the florist we'd passed approached. "The lady at the front pointed you out," he said to both of us and then switched his gaze to me. "You're Charlie Madigan, right?"

"Yeah?"

"These are for you."

He stuck them out, but Hank snagged the flowers with an unamused glare that made the guy dip his head and then hurry to his van.

Once he was driving away, Hank handed me the flowers. They were lilies. Bloodred. I secured the vase between my thighs and picked out the note card, feeling a sudden pang of apprehension.

> *Charlie,*
> *I like what you've done with the place.*

My vision distorted. Hank's voice drifted away as he asked me who the flowers were from, but I couldn't answer because I couldn't breathe.

Panic blasted through me like an arctic wind, then doubled back to blanket me. It was the panic of the trapped, of that precise moment when you realize that you can't move, can't breathe, can't do anything physical at all. You can only think and feel the drumming of your heart and the intense surge of adrenaline as it races through your system.

Then, just as suddenly as the feeling came, it was gone.

The world blinked back into focus—sharp, gray, slithering focus that lay like a living shroud over the city. A dark city. Electric goose bumps snaked down my arms and thighs. A Charbydon paradise. Hell on Earth.

There's more than one monster in this city. The last words Otorius had spoken to me echoed through my mind.

I knew who had engineered me and made me call the darkness, and that monster was dead. But why the hell did I get the feeling this was only the beginning, like I'd just been played big time, like I'd fallen into something way bigger and far more complex than darkness and *ash*?

As I sat there in the wheelchair, hospital traffic going by, people walking in and out, the earthy scent of lilies invading the air, I knew one thing. Grigori Tennin might *like what I've done with the place*, but I had created the darkness. It was my blood that had called it, and it was my blood that would fix things. I was the lone wolf, the only one of my kind in existence, and I had the power inside me to change everything.

Grigori Tennin was about to learn a valuable lesson: there was one thing more dangerous than making a deal with the devil, and that thing was *me*.

Acknowledgments

Immense and heartfelt thanks to FinePrint Literary and my superb agent, Colleen Lindsay, for believing this book had merit, and for always being the calm voice of knowledge and reason. And to the folks at Pocket Books and my equally superb editor, Ed Schlesinger, for giving me a job and whose brilliant insight and brainstorming genius has made this book "glow" (you know I had to use that word somewhere!).

A huge debt of gratitude goes to Jenna Black for her friendship, kindness, and critiques (and those three-hour lunches). Her enthusiasm for this book, from its earliest incarnations, gave me the encouragement I needed to keep trying.

To my sister, Kameryn Long, who reads everything I write, good or bad, and who always asks for more, regardless. Thanks for always being there and for being my best friend. You rock.

To my parents, Cheryl and Allen Hogan, who have always believed in me and my dream of becoming a writer even as a teen (thanks for that word processor!), and whose unwavering support is one of the reasons I am still writing today.

To all my family, friends in real life, and those in the WWW (you all know who you are); I'm so grateful for your support. I wish I had room to list you all, but in this round, I'd like to mention: Chester Groves, the Pixie Chicks, the Wildcards, and HCRW. And my girlfriends who continue to be my friends even though I'm in hermit/writer mode 95 percent of the time: Jaime Foutty, Sheri Widmann, and Coleen Heathcock (and a shout-out to the hubs, Joe and Kevin).

And, finally, I am deeply and happily indebted to one Jonathan Gay who makes my writing day possible in more ways than one; to Audrey for being patient, helpful, and an all-around cool kid; and to Jamie— well, just because. Without you guys this book never would have been written.

About the Author

KELLY GAY is a multiple award–winning writer who lives in North Carolina. This is her first published novel. Visit her online at www.kellygay.net.

Coming soon from Pocket Books

The Darkest Edge of Dawn

by
Kelly Gay

Turn the page for an exciting preview!

"So how did you like my show today, Charlie? Darkness on Ice. What a performance."

I stilled, the razor on my calf, the ball of my foot resting against the corner of the tub and hot water beating down on my back. Jesus Christ. I knew that voice. My heart gave a hard thump.

A serial killer was in my bathroom. In my heavily warded house. This was *so* not good.

"I thought it quite spectacular. It's all over the news."

My nostrils flared as goose bumps erupted on my arms and legs. Slowly, I straightened. I was completely bare. No weapons. No way out. My grip on the razor tightened. His outline moved beyond the white shower curtain, pacing from one end of the floor to the other. "What do you want, Llyran?"

He ignored the question as though I hadn't uttered a word. "I suppose you're wondering what I'm doing here in your bathroom."

"Um, yeah, and how the hell you got into my house," I said evenly as my mind scrambled for a plan—any plan—but I didn't have much to work with, unless stabbing him with the blunt edge of a Wonder Smooth Vibrating Razor was a plan.

"Oh, that part was easy, Charlie. I can mask myself . . . make myself a wisp of air. You can't see me, smell me, sense me until it's too late." His outline stopped at the sink, his height, slumping somewhat, giving me the impression that he was leaning against the countertop. "You can do that, too, you know. All that and more. You have great power in you. Great . . . potential."

"So you broke into my house just to tell me that?" I reached for the bar of soap with my other hand. If he came for me, it was going right into his eye. Might give me a chance to make it to the bedroom and the night-table drawer where I kept an extra set of weapons.

Small clinks and movement echoed above the shower spray. The faint scent of my perfume reached my nose, and I knew the creepy bastard was examining my toiletries, picking things up, setting them back down. "Nice," he muttered. "You see, the thing is, Charlie, you and I are a lot alike. Unique. Determined. Powerful."

"I'm not a murdering sonofabitch."

"Necessary evils," he said simply. Another glass bottle clinked onto the marble countertop. "I came to make you an offer, Detective."

My fists tightened around my "weapons." The soap shot from my grip and hit the shower wall with a loud bang. Great.

Okay, calm down.

He was here. The shock was over. My weapons were stupid, and I had to concentrate. I closed my eyes and began to focus, to seek out the Elysian part of me that I was just learning how to use.

"Come with me, Charlie, and I'll stop playing badly with others."

I blinked. "Stop killing? Just like that?"

The shower had turned lukewarm, but I shivered as though it were freezing, taking a small step back so the spray hit below my thighs, totally baffled that Llyran had invaded my home just to make me a deal. A freaking deal. I almost laughed. History proved I sucked at making deals.

I rubbed a hand down my face and tried to focus again.

"I want to open your eyes," he said. "Show you the future."

Focus, Charlie. Focus on the light. You know it's there. It's there in your blood, in every part of you, just waiting for you to say the word.

The small drops of water that bounced off my

skin began to hover. I no longer felt chilled because the warm vibration of power began to hum through me, growing, becoming attuned to my thoughts and my wishes. My prey had come to me, and if I could keep him here long enough to gather my strength, I had a good shot at ending his playtime for good.

"Well?" he asked.

"You know what I think, Llyran? I think you're a schizophrenic sicko with a massive ego problem. I'm surprised you even got into my house with a head as big as yours."

I let my hands fall to my sides, still gripping the razor, and closed my eyes, completely immersed in the thrumming line of power that ran through me, like a live wire just waiting for a switch to be hit.

Visualize your thoughts. Give direction to your power.

And . . . now!

I hit the switch.

The bathroom door slammed shut as the spray of the shower amplified, directing outward and blowing out the shower curtain. It flew straight for Llyran's shadowy form, covering him. He cursed, struggling to remove it and slipping on the wet floor as the water swirled around the room.

His surprise would only last a second. I stepped onto the ledge of the tub and then dove at his curtain-covered form. We both went down to the wet floor, sliding to the wall. Elbows, legs, and shower curtain flailed. I absorbed the pain of random jabs and punches, trying my damnedest to wrap him tighter in the curtain. He growled, shoving me off. I spun across the tile and slammed into the wall.

Shit.

Llyran tore the curtain away and sat up, furious. And there I was, on the floor, naked, both hands flat on the tile, sitting on my hip, facing him, my breath coming hard and fast. My eyes bored into his as I tried to gather my power again.

His red hair was in disarray, but the sight of him awed me just the same, despite the fact that I knew what he was, what he was capable of doing to another living being. He was a mass murderer masquerading in the gorgeous body of a Viking angel, his heart as black as iron.

He blinked, obviously shocked by the sight of me. But his aura practically glowed; he could unleash his own gifts anytime he wanted.

"You are remarkable, Charlie."

I sat back, and angled slightly, so he only had a side view as his gaze flicked to my breasts. Asshole.

"Why are you killing?"

"Because it is necessary to my cause."

I cocked my head. "And that would be?" My hip was starting to hurt. I'd have to move soon.

He pushed to his feet, his black tunic and jeans soaked, shaking the water from his red hair. His blue eyes were so light they appeared almost white. He smiled again as I copied his movement, pushing to my feet—hell if I was going to sit on the floor while he stood over me.

Being bare like this and having to endure his blatant ogling brought the dark power of Charbydon coursing through my veins. So easy and swift to rise, this dark energy of mine.

A ruddy eyebrow cocked and he grinned. "I have to admit I didn't think I'd be seeing this much of you . . . so soon anyway."

"What is it with you Adonai? Not every female is going to fall down at your feet."

A perverse smile tugged his generous mouth. "They all bend in the end, Charlie. And we hardly have to lift a finger. That's why, when someone like you comes along, it makes the chase thrilling."

A disgusted shiver shot up my spine, but I kept from flinching. "Is that what this is, a chase? Let me tell you something, you fucking scumbag, not a *single* thing about you appeals to me on any level. I hunt and destroy degenerates like you on a regular basis, and I *love* my job."

A deep, disappointed sigh whispered through his lips. "I know."

Let's see how he liked a little Charbydon justice.

I drew the power from every part of my body, sucking it into a tight ball in the center of my chest and then sending the dark energy surging down my arms. I clapped my hands together, forcing the power into a single bolt aimed straight toward Llyran's chest. Rex taught me that one.

The Adonai tensed, his eyes narrowing. Just before it hit him, his big hand whipped out and snagged the bolt. He flicked his wrist, slinging the energy backward like a whip. The bolt wrapped around me, and then Llyran yanked.

I screamed, slamming into him, the breath knocked from my lungs, blinking in shock at how he'd grabbed my power. *Grabbed* it. I still had so much to learn. He tried to seize my wrists, but I slapped and kicked, able to evade a firm hold because of my slippery skin.

For whatever reason, he wasn't using his powers and I wasn't complaining.

His curses filled the air as he lost his balance and landed on his ass, his back against the tub. Finally he got hold of both my wrists, my stomach pressed flat against his chest and kept there by the fact that he held my wrists wide, arms straight out on either side of me. My nose was inches from his face and I was panting hard.

"You'll change your mind, princess. In the end, we'll see exactly what you're made of." His eyes took on a fanatical glow. "In the meantime, I'm going to cut a path across your dark city until the streets bleed red. My next one will be just for you."

"No," I said, "there won't be a next one, you bastard."

I reared back, gritted my teeth, and slammed my forehead into his face.

Pain shot through my skull as Llyran let go of my wrists, cursing. I slumped against him and then rolled off, sliding back on my bare bottom as Llyran covered his nose with one hand. Then he closed his eyes and began chanting.

Every wet hair on my body rose. The bathroom window smashed in . . . I covered my head as glass rained down . . . and then my attention was snagged by the wind. The lamppost outside the window illuminated the darkness whirling overhead.

A small tendril of darkness snaked downward, enchanted by Llyran's summoning.

My eyes widened in total disbelief at the realization of what I was seeing, what it meant. Llyran could manipulate the darkness. Fuck.

Don't miss
The Darkest Edge of Dawn
by Kelly Gay

Coming soon from Pocket Books!

TAKE A WALK ON THE DARK SIDE...

Pick up an urban fantasy from Pocket Books!

Maria Lima
MATTERS OF THE BLOOD
Book One of the *Blood Lines* series

M.L.N. Hanover
UNCLEAN SPIRITS
Book One of *The Black Sun's Daughter*

Stacia Kane
DEMON INSIDE

J.F. Lewis
STAKED

Linda Robertson
VICIOUS CIRCLE

Adrian Phoenix
IN THE BLOOD
Book Two of *The Maker's Song*

Available wherever
books are sold or at
www.simonandschuster.com

**Explore
the darker side
of the afterlife with
URBAN FANTASY
from Pocket Books.**

A RUSH OF WINGS
Adrian Phoenix
His name is Dante.
His past is a mystery.
His future is chaos.

STAKED
J. F. Lewis
Being undead isn't easy—
but it sure beats the alternative...

WICKED GAME
Jeri Smith-Ready
Set your dial to WVMP for the biggest hits
from yesterday, today, and beyond the grave.

UNCLEAN SPIRITS
M.L.N. Hanover
In a world where magic walks and demons
ride, you can't always play by the rules.

**Available wherever
books are sold.**